MARION HARLAND'S WORKS.

ALONE	1 vol. 12mo	$1 50
HIDDEN PATH.	"	1 50
MOSS SIDE.	"	1 50
NEMESIS.	"	1 50
MIRIAM.	"	1 50
HUSKS.	"	1 50

HUSKS.

COLONEL FLOYD'S WARDS.

BY

MARION HARLAND.

"He would fain have filled himself with the husks that the swine did eat; and no man gave unto him."

NEW YORK:
SHELDON & COMPANY, 335 BROADWAY.
1863.

HUSKS.

CHAPTER I.

It was a decided uncompromising rainy day. There were no showers, coquetted with by veering winds or dubious mists, that at times grew brighter, as if the sun were burning away their lining; but a uniform expanse of iron-gray clouds—kept in close, grim column by a steady, although not violent east wind—sent straight lines of heavy rain upon the earth. The naked trees, that, during the earlier hours of the deluge had seemed to shiver for the immature leaf-buds, so unfit to endure the rough handling of the storm, now held out still, patient arms, the rising sap curdled within their hearts. The gutters were brimming streams, and the sidewalks were glazed with thin sheets of water.

The block of buildings before which our story pauses, was, as a glance would have showed the initiated in the grades of Gotham life, highly respectable, even in the rain. On a clear day when the half-folded blinds revealed the lace, silken, and damask draperies within; when young misses and masters—galvanized show-blocks of purple and fine linen, that would have passed muster behind the plate-glass of Genin or Madame Demorest—tripped after hoops, or promenaded the smooth pavement; when pretty, jaunty one-horse carriages, and more pretentious equipages, each with a pair of prancing steeds, and two "outside passengers" in broadcloth and tinsel hat-bands, received and discharged their loads before the brown-stone fronts—had the afore-mentioned spectator chanced to perambulate this not spacious street, he would have conceded to it some degree of the fashion claimed for it by its inhabitants. There were larger houses and wider pavements to be had for the same price a few blocks further on, in more than one direction, but these were unanimously voted "less eligible" and "deficient in style," in spite of the fact that as good and better materials were employed in their construction, and they were in all respects equal in external show and inside finish to those in this model quarter. "But our block has a certain air—well—I don't know what; but it is just the thing, you know, and so convenient! So near the Avenue!" would be the concluding argument.

The nameless, indescribable charm of the locality lay in the last clause. "Just step around the corner and you are in the Avenue," said the favored dwellers in this vicinity, as the climax in the description of their abode, and "that way *fashion* lies" to every right-minded New Yorker of the feminine gender.

But the aristocratic quiet of the neighborhood, rendered oppressive and depressing by the gloom of the day, was disturbed by a discordant sound—a child's cry; and what was especially martyrizing to refined auriculars, the lament had the unmistakable plebeian accent. The passionate scream with which the pampered darling of the nursery resents interference with his rights and liberty of tyranny, or the angry remonstrance of his injured playmates, would have been quite another species of natural eloquence, as regards both quality and force, from the weak, broken wail that sobbed along the wet streets. Moreover, what respectable child could be abroad on foot in this weather? So, the disrespectable juvenile pursued her melancholy way unnoticed and unquestioned until she reached the middle of the square. There a face appeared at a window in the second story of a house—which only differed from those to its right, left and opposite in the number upon the door—vanished, and in half a minute more a young lady appeared in the sheltered vestibule.

"What is the matter, little girl?"

The tone was not winning, yet the sobs ceased, and the child looked up, as to a friendly questioner. She was about eleven years of age, if one had judged from her size and form; but her features were pinched into unnatural maturity. Her attire was wretched, at its best estate; now, soaked by the rain, the dingy hood drooped over her eyes; the dark cotton shawl retained not one of its original colors, and the muddy dress flapped and dripped about her ankles. Upon one foot she wore an old cloth gaiter, probably picked up from an ash-heap; the remains of a more sorry slipper were tied around the other.

"I am so cold and wet, and my matches is all sp'ilt!" she answered in a dolorous tone, lifting the corner of a scrap of oil-cloth, which covered a basket, tucked for further security, under her shawl.

"No wonder! What else could you expect, if you would go out to sell them on a day like this? Go down into the area, there, and wait until I let you in."

The precaution was a wise one. No servant in that well-regulated household would have admitted so questionable a figure as that which crept after their young mistress into the comfortable kitchen. The cook paused in the act of dissecting a chicken; the butler—on carriage days, the footman—checked his flirtation with the plump and laughing chambermaid, to stare at the wretched apparition. The scrutiny of the first named functionary was speedily diverted to the dirty trail left by the intruder upon the carpet. A scowl puckered her red face, and her wrathful glance included both of the visitants as alike guilty of this desecration of her premises. The housemaid rolled up her eyes and clasped her hands in dumb show of horror and contempt, to her gallant, who replied with a shrug and a grin. But not a word of remonstrance or inquiry was spoken. It was rather a habit of this young lady's to have her own way whenever she could, and that she was bent upon doing this now was clear.

"Sit down!" she said, bringing up a chair to the fire.

The storm-beaten wanderer obeyed, and eagerly held up her sodden feet to the red grate.

"Have you no better shoes than those?"

"No, ma'am."

"Humph! Nor dress—nor shawl?"

"No, ma'am."

"Are you hungry?"

A ray shot from the swollen eyes. "Yes, ma'am!"

The lady disappeared in the pantry and presently returned with five or six slices of bread and butter hastily cut and thickly spread, with cheese and cold meat between them.

"Eat!" She thrust them into the match-girl's fingers. "Wait here, while I go and look for some clothes for you."

As may be supposed, the insulted oracle of kitchen mysteries improved the time of the benefactress's absence by a very plain expression of her sentiments towards beggars in general, and this one in particular; which harangue was received with applause by her fellow-servants, and perfect equanimity by its object. She munched her sandwiches with greedy satisfaction, watching, the while, the little clouds of steam that ascended from her heated toes. She was, to all appearance, neither a sensitive nor intelligent child, and had known too much of animal want and suffering to allow trifles to spoil her enjoyment of whatever physical comfort fell to her lot. Her mother at home could scold quite as virulently as the cook was now doing, and she was more afraid of her anger, because she beat while she berated her. She was convinced that she stood in no such peril here, for her protectress was one in power.

"Have you eaten enough?" said the clear, abrupt voice behind her, as she held two sandwiches in her fingers, without offering to put them to her lips.

"Yes, ma'am. May I take 'em home?"

"Certainly, if you like. Stand up, and take off your shawl."

She put around the forlorn figure a thick cloak, rusty and obsolete in fashion, but which was a warm and ample covering for the child, extending to the hem of her dress. The damp elf-locks were hidden by a knitted hood; and, for the feet, there were stockings and shoes, and a pair of India-rubbers to protect these last from the water.

"Now," said the Humane Society of One, when the refitting was at an end, "where do you live? Never mind! I don't care to know that yet! Here is a small umbrella—a good one—which belongs to me. I have no other for myself when I go out in bad weather. I mean to lend it to you, to-day, upon the condition that you will bring it back to-morrow, or the first clear day. Will you do it?"

The promise was readily given.

"Here's an old thing, Miss Sarah!" ventured the butler, respectfully; producing a bulky, ragged cotton umbrella from a corner of the kitchen closet. "It's risky—trusting such as *that* with your nice silk one."

"That will let in the rain, and is entirely too large for her to carry. You understand, child? You are to bring this safely back to me, the first time the sun shines. Can you find your way to this house again?"

"Oh yes, ma'am, easy! Thank you, ma'am!"

She dropped an awkward courtesy, as Miss Sarah held open the door for her to pass, and went out into the rain—warm, dry, and shielded against further damage from the storm.

Unheeding the significant looks of the culinary cabinet, Sarah Hunt turned away and ascended the stairs. She was a striking-looking girl, although her features, when in repose, could claim neither beauty of form nor expression. Her complexion was dark and pale, with a slight tinge of olive, and her hair a deep brown, lips whose compression was habitual, an aquiline nose, and eyes that changed from dreamy hazel to midnight blackness at the call of mind or feeling, gave marked character to her countenance. Her sententious style of address to the child she had just dismissed was natural, and usual to her in ordinary conversation, as was also the gravity, verging upon sombreness, which had not once during the interview relaxed into a smile.

The family sitting-room, her destination at present, and to which we will take the liberty of preceding her, was furnished elegantly and substantially; and there, leaning back in lounging-chairs, were Miss Lucy Hunt, the eldest daughter of the household, and her bosom friend, Miss Victoria West. Each held and wielded a crochet-needle, and had upon her lap a basket of many-hued balls of double or single zephyr worsted, or Shetland or Saxony wool, or whatever was the fashionable article for such pretty trifling at that date. Miss West had completed one-quarter of a shawl for herself, white and scarlet; and her friend had made precisely the same progress in the arduous manufacture of one whose centre was white and its border blue.

"Yours will be the prettiest," remarked Lucy regretfully. "Blue never looks well in worsteds. Why, I can't say, I'm sure. It is too bad that I can wear so few other colors! But I am such a fright in pink, or scarlet, or any shade of red!"

"As if *you* could be a fright in any thing!" returned her companion, with seeming indignation.

Lucy smiled, showing a set of faultless teeth that, to a stranger's first glance, would have appeared by far the most attractive point in her physiognomy. If closer examination discovered that her skin was pearly in whiteness and transparency, that her form was exquisite, with a sort of voluptuous grace; her hands worthy, in shape and hue, to become a sculptor's model; still, in the cold, unflattering light of this rainy afternoon, her want of color, her light gray eyes, her yellow hair, drawn straight back from the broad, low brow, precluded the idea that she could ever, with all the accessories of artificial glare, dress, and animation, be more than a merely pretty girl. Miss West knew better, and Lucy realized the power of her own charms with full and complete complacency. Secure in this pleasant self-appreciation, she could afford to be careless as to her everyday looks and home-people. She saw and enjoyed the manifest surprise of those who, having seen her once in morning déshabille, beheld her afterwards in elaborate evening toilet. Then the abundant hair, waved in golden ripples about the classic head, the most artfully simple of tasteful ornaments—a camellia, a rosebud, or a pearl hairpin, its sole adornment; her eyes, large, full, and soft, were blue instead of gray, while the heat of the assembly-room, the excitement of the crowd, or the exultation of gratified vanity supplied the rounded cheek with rich bloom, and dewy vermillion to the lips. But nature's rarest gift to her was her voice, a mellow contralto, whose skilful modulations stole refreshingly to the senses amid the sharp clash of strained and higher tones, the castanet-like jingle which most American belles ring unmercifully into the ears of their auditors. Lucy Hunt was not "a great talker," still less was she profound or brilliant when she did speak; yet she invariably conveyed the impression to the mind of a new acquaintance of a thoroughly cultivated woman, one whose acquirements were far beyond her modest exhibition of thought and sentiment. The most commonplace phrase came smoothly and roundly from her tongue, and he was censorious indeed who was willing to lose the pleasure afforded by its musical utterance in weighing its meaning. At school she had never been diligent, except in the study of music, and her pains-taking in this respect was rewarded by the reputation, justly earned, of being the finest vocalist in her circle of associates. In society she shone as a rising star of the first magnitude; at home she was happy, cheerful, and indolently amiable. Why should she be otherwise? From her babyhood she had been petted and admired by her family, and the world—*her* world—was as ready with its meed of the adulation which was her element.

There were, besides the two sisters already introduced to the reader, three other children in the Hunt household—a couple of sturdy lads, twelve and fourteen years of age, and little Jeannie, a delicate child of six, whom Lucy caressed with pet titles and sugar-plumbs of flattery, and Sarah served in secret and idolatrous fondness. This family it was Mrs. Hunt's care and pride to rear and maintain, not only in comfort, but apparent luxury, upon the salary which her husband received as cashier of a prominent city bank, an income sufficient to support them in modest elegance, but which few besides Mrs. Hunt could have stretched to cover the expenses of their ostensible style of living. But this notable manager had learned economy in excellent schools; primarily as a country girl, whose holiday finery was purchased with the proceeds of her own butter-making and poultry-yard; then as the brisk, lively wife of the young clerk, whose slender salary had, up to the time of his marriage, barely sufficed to pay for his own board and clothes, and whose only vested capital was his pen, his good character, and perfect knowledge of book-keeping. But if his help-meet were a clever housewife, she was likewise ambitious. With the exception of the sum requisite for the yearly payment of the premium upon Mr. Hunt's life-insurance policy, their annual expenses devoured every cent of their receipts. Indeed, it was currently believed among outsiders that they had other resources than the cashier's wages, and Mrs. Hunt indirectly encouraged the report that she held property in her own right. They lived "as their neighbors did," as "everybody in their position in society was bound to do," and "everybody" else was too intent upon his personal affairs, too busy with his private train of plans and operations to examine closely the cogs, and levers, and boilers of the locomotive Hunt. If it went ahead, and kept upon the track assigned it, was always "up to time," and avoided unpleasant collisions, it was nobody's business how the steam was gotten up.

Every human plant of note has its parasite, and Miss Lucy Hunt was not without hers. There existed no reason in the outward circumstances of the two girls why Miss Hunt should not court Miss West, rather than Miss West toady Miss Hunt. In a business—that is, a pecuniary—point of view, the former appeared the more likely state of the case, inasmuch as Victoria's father was a stock-broker of reputed wealth, and with a probable millionaireship in prospective, if his future good fortune equalled his past, while Mr. Hunt, as has been stated, depended entirely upon a certain and not an extravagant stipend. But the girls became intimate at school, "came out" the same winter at the same party, where Lucy created a "sensation," and Victoria would have been overlooked but for the sentimental connection between the *débutantes*. Since then, although the confidante would have scouted the imputation of interested motives with virtuous indignation of wounded affection, she had nevertheless "made a good thing of it," as her respected father would have phrased it, by playing hanger-on, second fiddle, and trumpeter-general to the belle.

"As if *you* could be a fright in any thing!" she had said naturally, and perhaps sincerely.

Lucy's smile was succeeded by a serious look. "I am sadly tempted sometimes! Those lovely peach-blossom hats that you and Sarah wore this past winter were absolute trials to my sense of right! And no longer ago than Mrs. Crossman's party I was guilty of the sin of coveting the complexion that enabled Maria Johnston to wear that sweet rose-colored silk, with the lace skirt looped with rosebuds."

"*You* envy Maria Johnston's complexion? Why don't you go further, and fall in love with her small eyes and pug nose?" inquired Victoria, severely ironical. "I have heard that people were never contented with their own gifts, but such a case of blindness as this has never before come under my observation."

"No, no! I am not quite so humble with regard to my personal appearance as you would make out. Yet"—and the plaintive voice might have been the murmur of a grieving angel—"I think that there are compensations in the lot of plain people that we know nothing about. They escape the censure and unkind remarks that uncharitable and envious women heap upon those who happen to be attractive. Now, there is Sarah, who never cares a button about her looks, so long as her hair is smooth and her dress clean and whole. She hates parties, and is glad of any excuse to stay out of the parlor when gentlemen call. Give her her books and that 'snuggery,' as she calls it, of a room up-stairs, and she is happier than if she were in the gayest company in the world. Who criticises *her?* Nobody is jealous of her face, or manners, or conversation. And she would not mind it if they were."

"She has a more independent nature than yours, my dear. I, for one, am rejoiced that you two are unlike. I could not endure to lose my darling friend, and somehow I never could understand Sarah; never could get near to her, you know."

"I do not wonder at that. It is just so with me, sisters though we are. However, Sarah means well, if her manner *is* blunt and sometimes cold."

The entrance of the person under discussion checked the conversation at this point, and both young ladies began to count their stitches aloud, to avoid the appearance of the foolish embarrassment that ever overtakes a brace of gossips at being thus interrupted.

Sarah's work lay on her stand near the window, where she had thrown it when the crying child attracted her notice, and she resumed it now. It was a dress for Jeannie. It was a rare occurrence for the second sister to fashion any thing so pretty and gay for her own wear.

"Have you taken to fancy-work at last?" asked Victoria, seeing that the unmade skirt was stamped with a rich, heavy pattern for embroidery.

"No!" Sarah did not affect her sister's friend, and did not trouble herself to disguise her feelings towards her.

Lucy explained: "she is making it for Jeannie. She does every thing for that child."

"You are very sisterly and kind, I am sure," Victoria continued, patronizingly. "You must quite despise Lucy and myself for thinking of and doing so much for ourselves, while you are such a pattern of self-denial."

A blaze shot up in Sarah's eye; then she said, coldly: "I am not self-denying. Have I ever found fault with you or Lucy for doing as you like?"

"Oh no, my dear! But you take no interest in what we enjoy. I dare say, now, you would think it a dull business to work day after day for three or four weeks together, crocheting a shawl which may go out of fashion before one has a chance to sport it at a watering-place."

"I certainly should!" The curl of the thin upper lip would have answered for her had she not spoken.

"And you hate the very sight of shell-work, and cone-frames, and Grecian painting, and all such vanities?"

"If I must speak the truth, I do—most heartily!"

Victoria was not easily turned from her purpose.

"Come, Sarah! Tell us what you would have us, poor trifling, silly things, do to kill the time."

"If you must be a murderer, do it in your own way. I have nothing to say in the matter."

"Do you mean that time never hangs upon your hands? that you are never *ennuyée—blasée?*"

"Speak English, and I will answer you!"

"I want to know," said the persevering tormentor, "if the hum-drum books up-stairs, your paint box, and your easel are such good company that you are contented and happy always when you are with them? if you never get cross with yourself and everybody else, and wonder what you were put into the world for, and why the world itself was made, and wish that you could sleep until doomsday. Do you ever feel like this?"

Sarah lifted her eyes with a wondering, incredulous stare at the flippant inquisitor.

"I *have* felt thus, but I did not suppose that you had!"

"Oh! I have a 'blue' turn now and then, but the disease is always more dangerous with girls of your sort—the reading, thinking, strong-minded kind. And the older you grow, the worse you will get. I haven't as much book knowledge as you have, but I know more of the world we we live in. Take my advice and settle down to woman's right sphere. Drive away the vapors with beaux and fancy-work now. By and by, a husband and an establishment will give you something else to think about."

Sarah would have replied, but Lucy broke in with a laugh, light and sweet.

"You two are always at cross-questions! Why can't you be satisfied to let one another alone? Sarah and I never quarrel, Vic. We agree to disagree. She gives me my way and I don't meddle with her. If she likes the blues (they say some people enjoy them), where's the harm of her having them? They never come near me. If I get stupid, I go to bed and sleep it off. Don't you think I have done ten rows, since breakfast? What a godsend a rainy day is, when one has a fascinating piece of work on hand!"

Too proud to seem to abandon the field, Sarah sat for half an hour longer, stitching steadily away at the complicated tracery upon the ground to be worked; then, as the dimmer daylight caused the others to draw near to the windows, she pushed aside her table and put by her sewing.

"Don't let us drive you away!" said Victoria's mock-polite tones; and Lucy added, kindly, "We do not mean to disturb you, Sarah, dear!"

"You do not disturb me!" was the reply to the latter. The other had neither glance nor word.

Up another flight she mounted to a room, much smaller than that she had left and far plainer in its appointments. The higher one went in Mrs. Hunt's house, the less splendid every thing became. In the state spare chamber—a story below—nothing of comfort and luxury was wanting, from the carved rose-wood bedstead, with the regal-looking canopy overshadowing its pillows, down to the Bohemian and cut-glass scent bottles upon the marble of the dressing-cabinet. Sarah's carpet was common ingrain, neither pretty nor new; a cottage bedstead of painted wood; bureau and wash-stand of the same material; two chairs, and a small table were all the furniture her mother adjudged needful. To these the girl had added, from her pittance of pocket-money, a set of hanging bookshelves; a portable desk, an easel, and two or three good engravings that adorned the walls.

She locked the door after her, with a kind of angry satisfaction in her face, and going straight to the window, leaned upon the sash, and looked down into the flooded street. Her eyes were dry, but there was a heaving in her throat; a tightening of the muscles about the mouth that would have made most women weep for very relief. Sarah Hunt would have scorned the ease purchased by such weakness. She did not despise the sad loneliness that girt her around, any more than the captive warrior does his cell of iron or stone, but she held that it would be a cowardly succumbing to Fate, to wound herself by dashing against the grim walls, or bring out their sleeping echoes by womanish wailings. So, presently, her throat ached and throbbed no longer; the rigid muscles compressed the lips no more than was their wont; the hands loosened their vise-like grasp of one another—the brain was free to think.

The rain fell still with a solemn stateliness that befitted the coming twilight. It was a silent storm for one so heavy. The faint hum of the city; the tinkle of the car-bell, three blocks off, arose to her window above its plashing fall upon the pavement, and the trickle of the drops from sash to sill. A stream of light from the lamp-post at the corner flashed athwart the sidewalk, glittered upon the swollen gutter, made gold and silver blocks of the paving-stones. As if they had waited for this signal, other lights now shone out from the windows across the way, and from time to time a broad, transient gleam from opening doors, told of the return of fathers, brothers, husbands from their day's employment.

"In happy homes he sees the light."

What was there in the line that should make the watcher catch her breath in sudden pain, and lay her hand, with stifled moan, over her heart, as she repeated it aloud?

Witness with me, ye maternal Hunts, who read this page —you, the careful and solicitous about many things—in nothing more ambitious than for the advancement and success in life of your offspring—add your testimony to mine that this girl had all that was desirable for one of her age and in her circumstances. A house as handsome as her neighbors, an education unsurpassed by any of her late school-fellows, a "position in society;" a reasonable share of good looks, which only required care and cultivation on her part, to become really *distingué*; indulgent parents and peaceably inclined brothers and sisters; read the list, and solve me, if you can, the enigma of this perturbed spirit—this hungering and thirsting after contraband or unattainable pleasures.

"Some girls will do so!" Mrs. Hunt assured her husband when he "thought that Sarah did not seem so happy as Lucy. He hoped nothing ailed the child. Perhaps the doctor had better drop in to see her. Could she be fretting for any thing? or had her feelings been hurt?"

"Bless your soul, Mr. H.! there's nothing the matter with her. She always was kind o' queer!" (Mrs. Hunt did not use her company grammar every day), and she's jest eighteen year old. That's the whole of it! She'll come 'round in good time, 'specially if Lucy should marry off pretty soon. When Sarah is 'Miss Hunt,' she'll be as crazy for beaux and company, and as ready to jump at a prime offer as any of 'em. I know girls' ways!"

Nor am I prepared to say that Sarah, as she quitted her look-out at the high window, at the sound of the dinner-bell, could have given a more satisfactory reason for her discontent and want of spirits.

CHAPTER II.

MRS. HUNT'S china, like her grammar, was of two sorts. When her duty to "society" or the necessity of circumstances forced her to be hospitable, she "did the thing" well. At a notice of moderate length, she could get up a handsome, if not a bountiful entertainment, to which no man need have been ashamed to seat his friends, and when the occasion warranted the display, she grudged not the "other" china, the other silver, nor the other table-linen.

She did, however, set her face, like a broad flint, against the irregularity of inviting chance visitors to partake of the family bread and salt. Intimate as Victoria West was with Lucy, she met only a civil show of regretful acquiescence in her proposal to go home, as the dinner hour approached; and Robbie or Richard Hunt was promptly offered to escort her to her abode upon the next block. If she remained to luncheon, as she *would* do occasionally, Lucy, in her hearing, begged her mother to excuse them from going down, and to send up two cups of tea, and a few sandwiches to the sitting-room. This slight repast was served by the butler upon a neat little tray, in a *tête-à-tête* service—a Christmas gift to Lucy, "from her ever-loving Victoria," and sentimentally dedicated to the use of the pair of adopted sisters.

Therefore, Sarah was not surprised to find Victoria gone, despite the storm, when she entered the dining-room. An immense crumb-cloth covered the carpet; a row of shrouded chairs, packed elbow to elbow, stood against the further end of the apartment, and a set of very ordinary ones were around the table. The cloth was of whity-brown material, and the dishes a motley collection of halt and maimed—for all Mrs. Hunt's vigilance could not make servants miraculously careful. There was no propriety, however, according to her system of economy, in condemning a plate or cup as past service, because it had come off second best, to the extent of a crack, or nick, or an amputated handle in an encounter with some other member of the crockery tribe. "While there is life there is hope," was, in these cases, paraphrased by her to the effect that while a utensil would hold water, it was too good to be thrown away.

It was not a sumptuous repast to which Sarah sat down after she had placed Jeannie in her high chair and tied the great gingham bib around her neck. On the contrary, it came near being a scant provision for the healthy appetites of seven people. Before Mr. Hunt, a mild, quiet little man, was a dish of stew, which was, in its peculiar line, a thing—not of beauty—but wonder.

Only a few days since, as I stood near the stall of a poultry vender in market, a lady inquired for chickens.

"Yes, ma'am. Roasting size, ma'am?"

"No; I want them for a fricassee."

"Ah"—with a look of shrewd intelligence. "*Then*, ma'am, I take it, you don't care to have 'em overly tender. Most ladies prefers the old ones for fricassee; they come cheaper, and very often bile tender."

"Thank you," was the amused rejoinder. "The difference in the price is no consideration where the safety of our teeth is concerned."

Mrs. Hunt suffered not these scruples to hinder her negotiations with knowing poultry merchants. A cent less per pound would be three cents saved upon the chicken, and three cents would buy enough turnips for dinner. It is an ignorant housekeeper who needs to be informed that stewed chicken "goes further" than the same fowl made into any other savory combination. Mrs. Hunt's stews were concocted after a receipt of her own invention. Imprimis, one chicken, weight varying from two and a half to three pounds; salt pork, a quarter of a pound; gravy abundant; dumplings innumerable. It was all "stew;" and if Jeannie's share was but a bare drumstick, swimming in gravy and buried in boiled dough, there was the chicken flavor through the portion.

For classic antecedent the reader is referred to the fable of the rose-scented clay.

To leave the principal dish, which justice to Mrs. Hunt's genius would not permit me to pass with briefer mention, there were, besides, potatoes, served whole (mashed ones required butter and cream), turnips, and bread, and Mrs. Hunt presided over a shallow platter of pork and beans. What was left of that dish would be warmed over to piece out breakfast next morning. The children behaved well, and the most minute by-law of table etiquette was observed with a strictness that imparted an air of ceremonious restraint to the meal. If Mrs. Hunt's young people were not in time finished ladies and gentlemen, it was not her fault, nor was it for the lack of drilling.

"Do as I tell you, not as I do," were her orders in these matters. Since Lucy had completed her education, the mother added: "Look at your sister; *she* is never awkward!" This was true: Lucy was born the fine lady. Refinement of manner and grace of movement, an instinctive avoidance of whatever looked common or underbred were a part of her nature. Only the usage of years had accustomed her to her mother's somewhat "fussy" ways. Had she met her in company as Mrs. Anybody else, she would have yielded her the right of way with a feeling of amazement and amiable pity that one who meant so well should so often overdo the thing she aimed to accomplish easily and gracefully. Following out her excellent system of training, the worthy dame demanded as diligent and alert waiting from her butler as if she were having a dinner party. The eggless rice pudding was brought on with a state that was absolutely ludicrous; but the family were used to the unsubstantial show, and took it as a matter of course.

After the meal was over Mrs. Hunt withdrew to the kitchen for a short conference with the cook and a sharp glance through the closets. It was impossible that the abstraction of six slices of bread from the baking of the preceding day, three thick pieces of cheese, and more than half of the cold meat she had decided would, in the form of hash, supply the other piece of the breakfast at which the beans were to assist, should escape her notice.

Mr. Hunt was reading the evening paper by the drop-light in the sitting room, Lucy was busy with her shawl, and Sarah told a simple tale in a low voice to Jeannie, as she leaned upon her lap, when the wife and mother entered, with something like a bluster. All present looked up, and each one remarked the cloud upon her brow.

"What is the matter, mother?" said Mr. Hunt, in a tone not free from alarm.

"I am worried! That's the whole of it! I am downright vexed with you, Sarah, and surprised, too! What upon earth possessed you, child, to take that beggar into my kitchen to-day? After all I have told you and tried to learn you about these shameful impostors! I declare I was beat out when I heard it. And to throw away provisions and clothes upon such a brat!"

Lucy opened her great eyes at her sister, and Mr. Hunt

looked perplexedly towards his favorite, for at heart he was partial to his second child.

"I took the poor creature to the fire, mother, because she was wet and cold; I fed her because she was hungry; I gave her some old, warm clothes of mine because hers were thin and soaked with rain."

"Poor little girl!" murmured Jeannie, compassionately.

Sarah's hand closed instantly over the little fingers. The simple-hearted babe understood and sympathized with her motive and act better than did her wiser elders.

"Oh, I have no doubt she told a pitiful story, and shed enough tears to wet her through, if the rain had not done it already. If you listen to what these wretches say, and undertake to relieve their wants, you will soon have not a dress to your back nor a house over your head. Why didn't you send her to some society for the relief of the poor?"

"I did not know where to find one, ma'am."

This plain truth, respectfully uttered, confounded Mrs. Hunt for a second.

"Mrs. James is one of the managers in a Benevolent Association," she said, recovering herself. "You had ought to have given your beggar her address."

"Even if I had known that fact, mother, the girl would have been obliged to walk half a mile in the storm to find this one manager. What do you suppose Mrs. James would have done for her that was not in my power to perform?"

"She would have asked the child whereabouts she lived, and to-morrow she would have gone to hunt her up. If she found all as she had been told, which is not likely—these creatures don't give a right direction once in ten times—why, she would have brought the case before the board at their next meeting, and they would help them, if neither of her parents was a drinking character."

"God help the poor!" ejaculated Sarah, energetically. "God help the poor, if this is man's style of relieving his starving brother! Mother, do you think that hunger pinches any the less when the famished being is told that next week or next month may bring him one good meal? Will the promise of a bushel of coal or a blanket, to be given ten days hence, warm the limbs that are freezing to-night? Is present help for present need, then, always unsafe, imprudent, insane?"

"That all sounds very fine, my dear." Mrs. Hunt grew cool as her daughter waxed warm. "But when you have seen as much of the world as I have, you will understand how necessary it is to be careful about believing all that we hear. Another thing you must not forget, and that is that we are not able to give freely, no matter how much disposed we may be to do so. Its pretty hard for a generous person to say 'No,' but it can't be helped. People in our circumstances must learn this lesson." Mrs. Hunt sighed at thought of the curb put upon her benevolent desires by bitter necessity. "And after all, very few—you've no idea how few—of these pretended sufferers are really in want."

This preluded a recital of sundry barefaced impositions and successful swindles practised upon herself and acquaintances, to which Mr. Hunt subjoined certain of his personal experiences, all tending to establish the principle that in a vast majority of cases of seeming destitution the supplicant was an accomplished rogue, and the giver of alms the victim of his own soft heart and a villain's wiles. Jeannie drank in every syllable, until her ideal beggar quite equalled the ogre who would have made a light supper off of Hop-o'-my-Thumb and brothers.

"You gave this match-girl no money, I hope?" said Mrs. Hunt, at length.

"I did not, madam. I had none to give her." Impelled

by her straightforward sense of honesty that would not allow her to receive commendation for prudence she had not shown, she said, bravely: "but I lent her my umbrella upon her promise to return it to-morrow."

"WELL!"

Mrs. Hunt dropped her hands in her lap, and stared in speechless dismay at her daughter. Even her husband felt it his duty to express his disapprobation.

"That was very unwise, my daughter. You will never see it again."

"I think differently, father."

"You are too easily imposed upon, Sarah. There is not the least probability that your property will be returned. Was it a good umbrella?"

"It was the one I always use."

"Black silk, the best make, with a carved ivory handle—cost six dollars a month ago!" gasped Mrs. Hunt. "I never heard of such a piece of shameful imprudence in all my born days! and I shouldn't wonder if you never once thought to ask her where she lived, that you might send a police officer after it, if the little thief didn't bring it back to you?"

"I did think of it." Sarah paused, then forced out the confession she foresaw would subject her to the charge of yet more ridiculous folly. "I did think of it, but concluded to throw the girl upon her honor, not to suggest the theft to her by insinuating a doubt of her integrity."

Mr. Hunt was annoyed with and sorry for the culprit, yet he could not help smiling at this high-flown generosity of confidence. "You are certainly the most unsophisticated girl of your age I ever met with, my daughter. I shall not mind the loss of the umbrella if it prove to be the means of giving you a lesson in human nature. In this world, dear, it will not do to wear your heart upon your sleeve.

Never believe a pretty story until you have had the opportunity to ascertain for yourself whether it is true or false." And with these titbits of worldly wisdom, the cashier picked up his paper.

"Six dollars! I declare I don't know what to say to you, Sarah!" persisted the ruffled mother. "You cannot expect me to buy you another umbrella this season. You must give up your walks in damp weather after this. I can't say that I'm very sorry for that, though. I never did fancy your traipsing off two or three miles, rain or shine, like a sewing girl."

"Very well, madam!"

But, steadied by pride as was her voice, her heart sank at the possibility of resigning the exercise upon which she deemed that so much of her health, physical and mental, depended. These long, solitary walks were one of the un-American habits that earned for Sarah Hunt the reputation of eccentricity. They were usually taken immediately after breakfast, and few in the neighborhood who were abroad or happened to look out at that hour, were not familiar with the straight, proud figure, habited in its walking dress of gray and black, stout boots, and gray hat with black plume. It was a uniform selected by herself, and which her mother permitted her to assume, because it "looked genteel," and became the wearer. Especially did she enjoy these tramps when the threatening storm, in its early stages, kept others of her class and sex at home. The untamed spirit found a fierce pleasure in wrestling with the wind; the hail that ushered in the snow-storm, as it beat in her face, called up lustre to the eye and warm color to the cheek. To a soul sickening of the glare and perfume of the artificial life to which she was confined, the roughest and wildest aspects of nature were a welcome change.

I remember laughing heartily, as I doubt not you did

also, dear reader, if you saw it, at a cut which appeared several years ago in the Punch department of *Harper's Magazine.* A "wee toddler," perhaps four years old, with a most lack-a-daisical expression upon her chubby visage, accosts her grandmother after this fashion: "I am tired of life, grandmamma! The world is hollow, and my doll is stuffed with sawdust, and, if you please, ma'am, I should like to go to a nunnery!"

Yet, that there are natures upon which the feeling of emptiness and longing herein burlesqued seizes in mere babyhood is sadly true. And what wonder? From their cradles, hundreds of children, in our so-called better classes, are fed upon husks. A superficial education, in which all that is not showy accomplishment is so dry and uninviting that the student has little disposition to seek further for the rich kernel, the strong meat of knowledge, is the preparatory course to a premature introduction into the world, to many the only phase of life they are permitted to see, a scene where all is flash and froth, empty bubbles of prizes, chased by men and women with empty heads, and oh, how often empty, aching hearts! Outside principles, outside affections, outside smiles, and most pitable of all, outside piety! Penury of heart and stomach at home; abroad a parade of reckless extravagance and ostentatious profession of fine feeling and liberal sentiments!

"Woe," cried the Preacher, "to them that make haste to be rich!" If he had lived in our day, in what biting terms of reprobation and contempt would he have declaimed against the insane ambition of those who forego the solid comforts of judicious expenditure of a moderate income would afford; spurn the holy quiet of domestic joys—neglect soul with heart culture—in their haste to *seem* rich, when Providence has seen that wealth is not to be desired for them! Out upon the disgusting, indecent race and scramble! The worship of the golden calf is bad enough, but when this bestial idolatry rises to such a pitch of fanaticism, that in thousands of households, copies in pinchbeck and plated-ware are set up and served, the spectacle is too monstrous in its abomination! This it is, that crowds our counting-rooms with bankrupts and our state-prisons with defaulters; that is fast turning our ball-rooms and other places of fashionable rendezvous, into vile caricatures of foreign courts, foreign manners, and foreign vices; while the people we ape—our chosen models and exemplars—hold their sides in inextinguishable laughter at the grave absurdity of our laborious imitation. It is no cause for marvel, that, in just retribution, there should be sent a panic-earthquake, every three years, to shake men to their senses.

Such was the atmosphere in which Sarah Hunt had always lived. In the code subscribed to by her mother, and the many who lived and felt and panted and pushed as she did for social distinction, nothing was of real, absolute value except the hard cash. Gold and silver were *facts.* All things else were comparative in use and worth. The garment which, last winter, no lady felt dressed without, was an obsolete horror this season. The pattern of curtains and furniture that nearly drove the fortunate purchaser wild with delight, three years back, was now only fit for the auction room. In vain might the poor depleted husband plead for and extol their beauties. The fiat of fashion had gone forth, and his better half seasoned his food with lamentations, and moistened her pillow with tears until she carried her point. We have intimated that Sarah was a peculiar girl. Whence she derived her vigorous intellect; her strong, original turn of thought; her deep heart, was a puzzle to those who knew her parents. The mother was energetic, the father sensible, but both were commonplace, and followed, like industrious puppets, in the wake of others. They were pleased that Sarah brought home all the prizes offered at school, and both considered that she gained a right, by these victories, to pursue her studies at home, provided she did not obtrude her singular views and tastes upon other people. Mrs. Hunt sighed, frequently and loudly, in her presence, that her genius had not been for shell, or bead, or worsted work, instead of for reading volumes, that did not even decorate the show book-case in the library.

"If you must have so many books, why don't you pick out them with the tasty bindings?" she had asked her daughter more than once. "And I wish you would paint some bright, lively pictures, that would look handsome on the walls, instead of those queer men and women and cloudy things you have got up-stairs. I'd have 'em framed right away, and be real proud to tell who done them."

Sarah remained proof against such hints and temptations, and, shrinking more and more from the uncongenial whirl around her, she turned her eager, restless spirit into her secret, inner life, where, at times, it was flattered into content by the idealities upon which it was fed; at others, ramped and raved, like any other chained wild thing. The sweetest drop of pleasure she had tasted for many a day was the thrill she experienced when the forlorn object she had rescued from the power of the storm stood before her, decently and comfortably clad. The rash confidence she had reposed in so suspicious a stranger was the outgoing of a heart too noble and true in every impulse to pause, for a moment, to speculate upon the chances of another's good or bad faith. The great world of the confessedly poor was an unknown field to her—one she longed to explore. Her footsteps loitered more often near the entrance of some narrow, reeking street or alley, down which she had promised her mother not to go, than on the spacious *pavé*, where over-dressed women and foppish men halted at, and hung around bewitching shop-windows. She wondered how such throngs of breathing beings contrived to exist in those fetid, cramped quarters; how they lived, spoke, acted, *felt*. The great tie of human brotherhood became daily more tense, as she pondered these things in her heart.

On this particular day, as she sat, silent and thoughtful, at her needle, the chit-chat of her companions less heeded than the continual dropping of the rain without, the wail of the shivering wanderer caused a painful vibration through every nerve. The deed was done! the experiment was tried. She was ashamed that an event so trivial held her eyes waking, far into the night. At least, she said to herself, she would not be without a lesson of some kind; would learn whether deceit and falsehood prevailed in the lowest, as well as the higher ranks of society. If, as she still strove to believe would be the case, the child returned the borrowed property, she would make use of her, as the means of entering upon a new sphere of research and action. After so complete a refutation of her theories respecting the utter corruption of all people, who had not enough to eat and to wear, her mother could not withhold her consent to her petition that she might become a lay-missionary—a present relief committee to a small portion of the suffering, toiling, ill-paid masses. She would then have a work to do—something to call out energy and engage feeling in healthy exercise—and soothed by the romantic vision, she fell asleep with a smile upon her lips.

The morning dawned between breaking clouds, that soon left the sky clear and bright. All through the day Sarah watched for her visitor of the preceding day—watched with nervousness she could not wholly conceal, from morn to night, for two, three days—for a week. Then she looked no longer while at home; her question, at entering the house, after a drive or walk, ceased to be, "Has any thing been left for me?" So palpable was her disappointment that her father forbore to make any allusion to her loss, and Lucy, albeit she was somewhat obtuse to the finer points of her sister's character, good-naturedly interposed to change the subject, when her mother sought to improve the incident to her daughter's edification and future profit. Mr. Hunt was right in supposing that the "unsophisticated girl" had learned something. Whether she were happier or better for the lesson thus acquired was another thing.

Once again Sarah had an opportunity for speech with her delinquent *protégé*. Two months later she was passing through a by-street in a mean neighborhood, very far up town, in her morning ramble, when her progress was arrested, for an instant, by two boys, who ran out of an alley across the walk. One overtook the other just in front of the lady, and catching him by his ragged collar, threw him down.

"That's right! beat him well! I'll help!" screeched a girl, rushing out of the court whence they had come.

Grinning with delight, she flung herself upon the prostrate form and commenced a vigorous assault, accompanied by language alike foul and profane.

Sarah recognized her instantly, and while she paused in mingled amazement and anger, the child looked up and saw her. In a twinkling she relinquished her grip of the boy's hair—jumped up and sped back into the dirty alley, with the blind haste of guilty fear.

Yes! Mr. Hunt was a wise man, who knew the world, and trebly sage in her generation, was his spouse. If their daughter had never acknowledged this before, she did now, in her disgust and dismay at this utter overthrow of her dreams of the virtuous simplicity to be found in lowly homes, where riches and fashions were things unknown.

CHAPTER III.

SUMMER had come to the country with its bloom and its beauty, its harvests and its holidays. In town, its fever heat drew noisome smells from overcharged sewers, and the black, oily paste to which the shower that should have been refreshing had changed the dust of crowded thoroughfares. Cleaner pavements, in the higher portions of the city, burned through shoe-soles; glass radiated heat to polished stone, and stone radiated, in its turn, to brick, that waited until the evening to throw off its surplus caloric in hot, suffocating waves that made yet more oppressive the close nights. The gay procession of fashionable humming-birds had commenced their migrations, steamboats and excursion-craft multiplied at the wharves, and the iron steed put forth all his tremendous might to bear onward the long train of self-exiled travellers.

The Hunts, too, must leave town; Lucy must, at all events, have a full season, and a brilliant one, if possible, for it was her second summer, and much might depend upon it. Her mother would accompany her, of course; and equally of course her father could not; that is, he must return after escorting them to Saratoga, and spend the remainder of the warm months at home. His business would not allow him to take an extended vacation. The boys were easily disposed of, being boarded every summer at the farm-house of an early friend of Mr. Hunt's, where they were acceptable inmates, their clothes as well cared for as they were at home, and their morals more diligently cultivated. The younger girls caused that excellent manager, their mother, more perplexity. This was not the first time she had repented her indiscretion in allowing Sarah to "come out" before her elder sister had "gone off." But "Sarah was so tall and so womanly in her appearance that it looked queer, and would set people to talking if I kept her back," she was accustomed to excuse her impolitic move to her friends. This summer she realized, as she had not done before, the inconvenience of having two full-fledged young ladies upon the carpet at once. Lucy's elegant and varied wardrobe, and the certain expenses in prospect for her and her chaperon at Spa, seaside, and *en route*, left a balance in hand of the sum allotted for the season's expenditure that was startling in its meagreness. Mrs. Hunt was a capital financier, a peerless economist, but the exigency taxed her resources to the utmost.

One morning she arose with a lightened heart and a smoother brow. "I've settled it!" she exclaimed to her husband, shaking him from his matutinal doze.

The "Eureka!" of the Syracusan mathematician was not more lofty in its exultation. Forthwith she unfolded to him her scheme. She was a native of New Jersey, "the Jarseys" she had heard it called in her father's house—had probably thus denominated the gallant little State herself in her girlhood. In and around the pretty, quiet village of Shrewsbury there were still resident scores of her relatives whose very names she had sedulously forgotten. One alone she could not, in conscience or in nature, dismiss to such oblivion. This was her elder and only sister, long married to a respectable and worthy farmer, and living within a mile of "the old place," where both sisters had drawn the first breath of life. Twice since Mrs. Hunt had lived in the city had this kind friend been summoned on account of the dangerous illness of the former, and her presence and nursing had restored peace, order, and health to the household. The earlier of these occasions was that of the second child's birth, and in the softened mood of her convalescence Mrs. Hunt had bestowed upon the babe her sister's name—Sarah Benson—a homely appellative she had ofttimes regretted since. At distant and irregular intervals, one, two, three years, Mr. or Mrs. Benson visited their connections in "York;" but the intercourse grew more difficult and broken as time rolled on and the distance widened between the plain country folk and their rising relations. Then, again, death had been busy in the farmhouse; coffin after coffin, of varying lengths, but all short, was lifted over the threshold and laid away in the village graveyard, until but one was left to the parents of the seven little ones that had been given to them, and to that one nature had denied the gifts of speech and hearing. Grief and the infirmities of approaching old age disinclined the worthy pair to stir from home, and their ambitious sister was too busy in building up a "set" of her own, and paving the way for her daughters' distinction, to hide her light for ever so short a period in so obscure a corner as her former home.

Aunt Sarah, however, could not forget her nurseling. Every few months there arrived some simple token of affectionate remembrance to "the child" she had not seen since she wore short frocks and pinafores. The reception of a basket of fruit, thus despatched, was the suggestive power to Mrs. Hunt's present plan. She had made up her mind, so she informed her husband straightway, to write that very day—yes! that very forenoon, to "Sister Benson," and inquire whether she would board Sarah and Jeannie for a couple of months.

"I don't s'pose she will let me pay board for them, but she will be pleased to have 'em as long as they like to stay.

It's never been exactly convenient for me to let any of the children go there for so many years, and it's so fur off. But dear me! sometimes I feel real bad about seeing so little of my only sister!"—a heavy sigh. "And there'll be the expenses of two saved, out and out, for they won't need a great variety of clothes in that out-of-the-way place."

"But how will the girls, Sarah and Jeannie, fancy being sent off so?" inquired Mr. Hunt.

"Oh, as to that, it is late in the day for *my* children to dispute what *I* say shall be done; and Sarah's jest that odd that she'll like this notion twenty times better than going to Newport or Saratoga. I know her! As to Jeannie, she is satisfied to be with her sister anywhere. She is getting thin, too; she looks real peakèd, and there's nothing in creation so good for ailing children as the salt-water bath. They have first-rate still-water bathing not a quarter of a mile from sister's. It's jest the thing, I tell you! The wonder is it never came into my head before."

Mr. Hunt had his sigh now. "Somehow or other he was always down in the mouth when the family broke up for the summer," his wife frequently complained, and his lack of sympathy now excited her just ire.

"Upon my word, Mr. H.! anybody would think that I was the poorest wife in the world to you to see and hear you whenever I talk to you of my plans and household affairs. You look as if you was about to be hanged, instead of feeling obliged to me for turning, and twisting, and contriving, and studying, day and night, how to save your money, and spend what we must lay out to the best advantage. I can tell you what—there's few women would make your income go as far as I do."

"I know that, my dear. The question is"—. Mr. Hunt paused, cleared his throat, and strained his nerves for a mighty effort, an unprecedented exercise of moral courage

—"the question is, Betsy, whether our income is stretched in the right direction!" Mistaking the stare of petrified incredulity he received for fixed attention, the infatuated man went on; "This doubt is always forced upon me when we separate in July, some to go to one place, some to another, a broken, wandering family for months together. I am growing old, and I love to have my children about me; I begin to feel the want of a home. There is Johnson, in the —— Bank, gets five hundred less per annum than I do; yet, after living quietly here a few years, he bought himself a snug cottage up the river, and has his family there in their own house, every thing handsome and comfortable about them. I have been in the harness for a long while; I expect to die in it. I don't mind work—hard work! but it seems to me sometimes that we would all be better satisfied if we had more to show, or rather to hold, for our money; if there were less of this straining after appearances, this constant study to make both ends meet."

"And it has come to this!"—Mrs. Hunt sank into a chair and began to cry. "This is my thanks for slaving and toiling for better than twenty years to get you and your children a stand in the world! It isn't for myself that I care. I can work my fingers to the bone, and live upon a crust! I can scrape and save five dollars or so a month! I can bury myself in the country! But your children! those dear, sweet girls, that have had the best education money can buy, and that to-day visit such people as the Murrays, and Sandersons, and Hoopers, and Baylors, and meet the Castors and Crinnalls at parties—millionaires, all of 'em, the cream of the upper crust! I don't deny that I *have* been ambitious for them, and I did hope that you had something of the same spirit; and now to think of your complaining, and moping, and groaning over the money you say I've been and wasted; Oh! oh! oh!"

"You misunderstood me, my dear; I merely questioned whether we were acting wisely in making so much display upon so little substance. *We* are not millionaires, whatever may be said of the girls' visiting acquaintances, and I tremble sometimes to think how all this false show may end."

Mr. Hunt's borrowed courage had not evaporated entirely.

"That's distrusting Providence, Mr. H.! It's downright sinful, and what I shouldn't have looked for from you. I can tell you how it will end. If both of us live ten years longer, you will see your daughters riding in their own carriages, and leaders of the *tong*, and your sons among the first gentlemen of the city. If this does not turn out true, you needn't ever trust my word again. I've set my head upon getting Lucy off my hands this summer, and well off; and mark my words, Mr. H., it *shall be done*."

One part of her mother's prophecy was fulfilled in Sarah's manner of receiving the proposition so nearly affecting her comfort during the summer. Lucy wondered at the cheerful alacrity with which she consented to be "hidden away in that horrid bore of a farmhouse," and Jeannie cried as her elder sister "supposed that they would eat in Aunt Sarah's kitchen, along with the servant-men."

"Lucy, be quiet!" interposed her mother. "Your aunt is not a common poor person. Mr. Benson is a man of independent means, quite rich for the country. They live very nicely, and I have no doubt but that your sisters will be happy there."

Sarah had drawn Jeannie to her, and was telling her of the rides and walks they would take together, the ducks and chickens they would feed, and the merry plunges in the salt water that were to be daily luxuries. Ere the recital was concluded, the child was impatient for the hour of departure, and indignant when she heard that Aunt Sarah must be heard from before they could venture to present themselves, bag and baggage, at her door. There was nothing feigned in Sarah's satisfaction; her preparations were made with far more pleasure than if she were to accompany Lucy. The seclusion that would have been slow death to the latter was full of charms for the book-loving sister. Aunt Sarah would be kind; the novel phases of human nature she would meet would amuse and interest her; and, besides these, there was Jeannie to love and pet, and river, field, and grove for studies and society. She panted for the country and liberty from the tyrannous shackles of city customs.

Aunt Sarah wrote promptly and cordially, rejecting the offered compensation, and begging for her nieces' company as long as they could content themselves in so retired a place. Simple-minded as she was, she knew enough to be sure that the belles and beaux of the neighborhood would be very unsuitable mates for her expected visitors. If her own girls had lived, she would have asked nothing higher for them in this world than to have them grow up respected, beloved, and happy, among the acquaintances and friends of their parents; but "Sister Betsy's children had been raised so differently!" she said to her husband. "I don't know what we will do to amuse them."

"They will find amusement—never fear," was the farmer's response. "Let city folks alone for seeing wonders where those that have lived among them all their lives never found any thing uncommon. They are welcome to the pony whenever they've a mind to ride, and Jim or I will find time to drive them around a'most every day; and what with riding, and boating, and bathing, I guess they can get rid of the time."

Before the day set for the coming of the guests there appeared upon the stage an unexpected and welcome ally to Aunt Sarah's benevolent design of making her nieces' sojourn agreeable. This personage we will let the good woman herself describe.

"You needn't trouble yourself to fix up for tea, dear," she said to Sarah, the afternoon of her arrival, as she prepared to remove her travelling-dress. "There's nobody here besides husband, and me, and Charley, except husband's nephew, Philip Benson, from the South. He comes North 'most every summer, and never goes back without paying us a visit. He's been here three days now. But he is just as easy as an old shoe, and sociable as can be, so you won't mind him."

"Uncle Benson has relatives at the South, then?" said Sarah, seeing herself called upon to say something.

"One brother—James. He went to Georgy when he wasn't more than sixteen years old, and has lived there ever since. He married a rich wife, I believe,"—sinking her voice —"and has made money fast, I've heard. Philip never says a word about their wealth, but his father owns a great plantation, for husband asked him how many acres they worked. Then the children—there are four of them—have had fine educations, and always spend money freely. Philip is not the sort to boast of any thing that belongs to him or his. He is a good-hearted boy. He was here the August my last daughter—my Betsy—died, and I shall never forget how kind and tender he was then. I can't look at him without thinking how my Alick would have been just his age if he had lived. One was born on the fourth and the other the fifth of the same April."

Keeping up a decent show of interest in these family details, Sarah divested Jeannie of her sacque and dress, and substituted a cool blue gingham and a muslin apron. Then, as the child was wild to run out of doors, she suffered her to go, charging her not to pass the boundary of the yard fence. Aunt Sarah was dressed in a second mourning de laine; with a very plain cap, and while the heat obliged Sarah to lay aside the thick and dusty garment she had worn all day, she had too much tact to offer a strong contrast in her own attire to her unpretending surroundings. A neat sprigged lawn, modest and inexpensive, was not out of place among the old-fashioned furniture of her chamber, nor in the "best room," to which they presently descended.

Aunt Sarah ushered her into the apartment with some stiffness of ceremony. In truth, she was not herself there often, or long enough to feel quite at ease, her property though it was. Alleging the necessity of "seeing to the tea," she bade her niece "make herself at home," threw open a blind that she "might see the river," and left her.

First, Sarah looked around the room. It was large and square, and had four windows, two in front and two in the rear. The floor was covered by a well-saved carpet, of a pattern so antique that it was in itself a curiosity; heavy tables of a mahogany dark with age; upright chairs, with slippery leathern seats; a ponderous sofa, covered with hair-cloth; small mirrors, with twisted frames, between the windows; two black profiles, of life-size, over the mantel, and in the fire place a jar of asparagus boughs, were appointments that might have repelled the looker-on, but for the scrupulous, shining cleanliness of every article. It was a scene so strange to Sarah that she could not but smile as she withdrew her eyes and turned to the landscape commanded by her window.

The sight changed the gleam of good-humored amusement to one of more heartfelt pleasure. Beyond the grassy walks and flower-borders of the garden behind the house lay green meadows, sloping down to the river, broad and smooth at this point, so placid now that it mirrored every rope and seam of the sails resting quietly upon its surface, and the white cottages along the banks, while the banks themselves, with their tufts and crowns of foliage, drooping willows and lofty elms, found a faithful yet a beautified counterpart in the stream. The reflected blush of the crimson west upon its bosom was shot with flickers of golden light, and faded in the distance into the blue-gray twilight. The air seemed to grow more deliciously cool as the gazer thought of the hot, pent-up city, and the beds of thyme and lavender added their evening incense.

The hum of cheerful voices joined pleasantly with the soothing influences of the hour, and, changing her position slightly, Sarah beheld the speakers. Upon a turfy mound, at the foot of an apple-tree, sat Jeannie beside a gentleman, whose hands she watched with pleased interest, as did also a boy of fifteen or thereabouts, who knelt on the grass before them. Sarah divined at once that this was her aunt's deaf and dumb son. The gentleman was apparently interpreting to Jeannie all that passed between himself and the lad, and her gleeful laugh showed it to be a lively dialogue. Could this be Mr. Benson's nephew, the beardless youth Sarah had pictured him to herself from Aunt Sarah's description? He could not have been less than six-and-twenty, had dark hair and a close, curling beard, an intelligent, handsome face, and notwithstanding his loose summer sack and lounging attitude, one discerned plainly traces of uncommon grace and strength in his form.

"What is he, I wonder? A gallant professional beau, who will entangle me in my speech, and be an inevitable appendage in the excursions? I flattered myself I would be safe from all such drawbacks," thought Sarah, in genuine vexation, as she obeyed her aunt's summons to tea.

Perhaps Mr. Benson read as much in her countenance, for, beyond a few polite, very unremarkable observations, addressed to her when his hosts made it necessary for him to do so, he paid her no visible attention during the whole evening. The next day he set off, the minute breakfast was over, with his gun and game-bag, and was gone until sunset.

Sarah sat at her chamber window as he came up to the back door; and, screened by the vine trained over the sash, she watched him as he tossed his game-bag to Charley and shook hands with Jeannie, who ran up to him with the familiarity of an old acquaintance.

"What luck?" questioned his uncle.

"Nothing to boast of, sir; yet enough to repay me for my tramp. I have been down to the shore."

"Philip Benson! Well, you beat every thing! I suppose you have walked as much as ten miles in all!" exclaimed Aunt Sarah, with a sort of reproachful admiration.

"I dare say, madam, and am none the worse for it to-night. I am getting used to your sand, uncle; it used to tire me, I confess."

He disappeared into the kitchen, probably to perform the ablutions needful after his day's walk and work, for it was several minutes before he returned. Charley had carried the game-bag to the mound under the tree, and was exhibiting its contents—mostly snipe and red-winged black birds—to his little cousin.

"It is refreshing to see something in the shape of man that is neither an effeminate dandy nor a business machine," soliloquized Sarah. "Ten miles on foot! How I would like to set that task for certain of our Broadway exquisites!"

"She isn't a bit like a city girl!" Aunt Sarah was saying, as she followed Philip into the outer air.

"I am glad to hear that she is likely to be a nice companion for you, madam. I thought, from her appearance, that you would suit each other," was the reply, certainly respectful enough, but whose lurking accent of dry indifference sent the blood to Sarah's face.

Hastily withdrawing from the open window, and beyond

the reach of the voices that discussed her merits, she waited to recover equanimity before going down-stairs. In vain she chided herself for her sudden heat. Mortified she was, and even more ashamed of herself than angry with the cool young man who had pronounced her to be a fitting associate for her excellent but unpolished aunt. While his every look and intonation bespoke the educated gentleman, a being as different in mental as in physical muscle from the fops who formed her sister's train, had he weighed her against the refined woman of his own class and clime, and adjudged her this place? At heart she felt the injustice, and, stimulated by the sting, arose the resolve that he should learn and confess his error. Not tamely or willingly would she accept an ignoble station at the hands of one whom she inwardly recognized as capable of a true valuation of what she esteemed worthy.

She looked haughty, not humbled, when she took her seat opposite her critic at the tea-table. "A nice companion," she was saying over to herself. The very phrase, borrowed, as it was, from Aunt Sarah's vocabulary, seemed to her seasoned with contempt. She kept down fire and scorn, however, when Mr. Benson accosted her with the tritest of remarks upon the probable heat of the day in town as contrasted with the invigorating breeze, with its faint, delicious sea flavor, that rustled the grapevines and fluttered the white curtains at the dining-room door and windows. Her answer was not exactly gracious, but it advanced the one tempting step beyond a mere reply.

Thus was the ice broken, and for the rest of the meal, Aunt Sarah and "Uncle Nathan"—as he requested his nieces to style him—had respite from the duty of active entertainment, so far as conversation went. To Sarah's surprise, Mr. Benson talked to her almost as he would have done to another man. He spoke of notable persons, places, and books—things of which she had heard and read—without affectation of reserve or a shade of pretension; and to her rejoinders—brief and constrained for awhile—then, as she forgot herself in her subject, pertinent, earnest, salient, he gave more than courteous heed. It was the unaffected interest of an inquirer; the entire attention of one who felt that he received more than he gave.

They parted for the night with a bow and a smile that was with each a mute acknowledgment of pleasure derived from the companionship of the other; and if neither looked forward to the meeting of the morrow as a renewal of congenial intercourse, both carried to their rest the effects of an agreeable surprise in the events of the evening.

CHAPTER IV.

A WEEK had passed since the arrival of the city nieces at the farmhouse. An early tea, one of Aunt Sarah's generous and appetizing repasts was over; and through the garden, out at the gate that terminated the middle walk, and across the strip of meadow-land, danced Charley and Jeannie, followed at a more sedate pace by Philip Benson and Sarah. Seven days' rustication had wrought a marked change in the town-bred girl. There was a lighter bound in her step, and in her cheek a clear, pink glow, while her eyes looked softly, yet brightly, from out the shadow of her gypsy hat, a look of half surprise, half confidence in her companion's face.

"One week ago," he was saying, "how firmly I made up my mind that you and I could never be any thing but strangers to each other! How I disliked you for coming down here to interfere with my liberty and leisure!"

"But even then you thought that I would prove a 'nice companion for Aunt Sarah—' perceived my suitableness to her society," was the demure reply.

"Who told you that I said so?"

"Not Aunt Sarah herself, although she considered it honest praise. I overheard it accidentally from my window, and I can assure you properly appreciated the compliment, which, by the way, was more in the tone than the words."

"And you were thereby piqued to a different style of

behavior. Bravo! did ever another seed so worthless bring forth so rich a harvest? I am glad I said it! Here is the boat."

It was a pretty little affair—Charley's property and care, and he was already in his seat at the bow, oar in hand. Philip helped Sarah in, placed Jeannie beside her, and stationing himself upon the middle bench took up a second pair of oars. A noiseless dip of the four, and the craft glided out into the stream, then up against the tide, the water rippling into a foamy wake on either side of the sharp bow. A row was now the regular sequel to the day's enjoyments, and to Jeannie, at least, the climax of its pleasures.

"Pull that way, please, Mr. Benson!" she cried. "There! right through that beautiful red water!"

A skilful sweep brought them to the spot designated, but the crimson deserted the wave as they neared it, and left dull gray in its stead.

"It is too bad!" complained the child, pointing back to the track of their boat, quivering amidst the fickle radiance she had thought to reach by this change of course. "It is behind us and before us—everywhere but where we are!"

"Is there a moral in that?" questioned Philip, smiling at Sarah.

"Perhaps so."

A fortnight before, how assured would have been her reply! How gloomy her recognition of the analogy! Changed as was her mood, a shade fell over her countenance. Was it of apprehension, and did Philip thus interpret it?

"I could not love life and this fair world as I do, if I conceded this to be universally true," he said. "That there comes, sometimes, a glory to the present, beside which the hues of past and future fade and are forgotten, I must and will believe. Such, it seems to me, must be the rapture of reciprocal and acknowledged affection; the joy of reunion after long separation from the beloved one; the bliss of reconciliation after estrangement. Have you ever thought how much happier we would be if we were to live only in the Now we have, and never strain our eyes with searchings for the lights and shades of what may be before us, or with 'mournful looking' after what is gone?"

"Yet is this possible?" asked Sarah, earnestly. "Does not the very constitution of our natures forbid it? To me that would be a miserably tame, dead-level existence over which Hope sheds no enchanting illusions; like this river, as we saw it three days ago, cold and sombre as the rain-clouds that hung above it. Oh, no! give me any thing but the chill, neutral tint of such a life as thousands are content to lead—people who expect nothing, fear nothing—I had almost said, *feel* nothing!"

"That is because every principle of your being is at war with common-places. Tell me frankly, Miss Sarah, did you ever meet another woman who had as much character as yourself?"

"I do not know that I understand the full bearing of your question." She leaned on the side of the boat, her hand playing in the water, her lips working in an irresolute timidity that was oddly at variance with their habitual firmness.

"I am aware," she began, slowly and gravely, "that I express myself too strongly at times; that I am more abrupt in language and action than most other girls. I have always been told so; but it is natural to me. My character has many rough and sharp edges that need softening and rounding—"

"In order to render you one of the pretty automatons, the well-draped, thoroughly-oiled pieces of human clock-work that decorates men's *homes*—falsely so called—in these days of gloss and humbug!" interrupted Philip with energy. "I am sick to death of the dollish 'sweet creatures' every boarding-school turns out by the score. I understand all the wires that work the dear puppets—flatter myself that I can put them through their paces (excuse the slang!) in as short a time as any other man of my age in the country. The delightful divinities! A little music, and a little less French; a skimming of the arts and sciences; and it is a rare thing to meet one who can tell an art from a science ten days after she has graduated—a stock of pet phrases—all hyperbolical, consequently unmeaning—a glib utterance of the same; a steady devotion to balls, beau-catching, gossip, and fancy-work; *voilà* the modern fine lady—the stuff we are expected to make wives of! Wives! save the mark! I never think of the possibility of being thus ensnared without an involuntary repetition of a portion of the Litany—'From all such, etc., etc.!' "

He plied his oars with renewed activity for a moment, then suspended them to continue, in a softer tone: "And this is the representative woman of your Utopia, Miss Sarah?"

"Did I intimate, much less assert, such a heresy?" responded she, laughing. "But there is a golden mean somewhere—a union of gentleness and energy; of domestic and literary taste; of independence and submission. I have seen such in my day dreams. She is my ideal."

"Which you will one day embody. No reproachful looks! This is the sincerity of a friend. I have promised never to flatter you again, and do not violate the pledge in speaking thus. From my boyhood, I have made human nature my study, and it would be hard to convince me that I err in this case."

"You do! indeed you do!" exclaimed Sarah, with a look of real pain. "I lack the first characteristic of the portrait

I have drawn. I am not gentle! I never was. I fear that I never will be!"

"Let us hear a competent witness on that head. Jeannie!" to the child, who was busy spelling on her fingers to Charley; his nods and smiles to her, from the far end of the boat, being more intelligible to her than were her attempts to signal her meaning to him. "Jeannie!" repeated Philip, as he caught her eye. "Come, and whisper in my ear which of your sisters you love the best. Maybe I won't tell tales out of school to the one you care least for."

"I don't care who knows!" said the saucy, but affectionate child. "Sis' Lucy is the prettiest, and she never scolds me either; but she doesn't make my clothes, and tell me nice stories, and help me with my lessons, and all that, you know. She isn't my dear, *best* sister!" And, springing up suddenly, the threw her arms around Sarah's neck, with a kiss that answered the question with emphasis.

Sarah's lip trembled. The share of affection she had hitherto dared to claim as her own had barely sufficed to keep her heart from starving outright. She had often dreamed of fulness of love as a stay and comfort, as solace and nutriment in a world whose wrong side was ever turned to her. Now there dawned upon her the sweetness and beauty of a new revelation, the *bliss* of loving and being beloved. Over life floated a warm, purple tinge, like the sunset light upon the river. For the first time within the reach of her memory her heart *rested!*

In the smile whose overflowing gave a tender loveliness to her features, Philip saw the effect he had wished and anticipated, and, motioning to Charley to let the boat drift with the current, he picked up the guitar, that by Sarah's request was always taken along in these excursions.

"The dew is on the blossom,
And the young moon on the sea;

It is the twilight hour—
  The hour for you and me;
The time when memory lingers
  Across life's dreary track,
When the past floats up before us,
  And the lost comes stealing back."

It was a love song, inimitable in its purity and tenderness, with just the touch of sadness that insured its passage to the heart. Sarah's smile was softer, but it was a smile still, as the melody arose on the quiet air. When the ballad was concluded, she only said; "Another, please!"

Philip sang more than well. Without extraordinary power, his voice had a rich and flexible quality of tone and a delicacy of expression that never failed to fascinate. To the rapt and listening girl it seemed as if time could bring no more delicious fate than thus to glide on ever upon this empurpled, enchanted stream, the summer heavens above her, and, thrilling ear and soul, the witching lullaby that rocked her spirit to dreams of the youth she had never had, the love for which she had longed with all the wild intensity, the fervent yearning, her deep heart could feel.

Still they floated on with the receding tide, its low washing against the sides of their boat filling up the pauses of the music. The burning red and gold of the sky cooled into the mellower tints of twilight, and the pale curve of the young moon shone with increasing lustre. Jeannie fell asleep, her head upon her sister's lap; the dumb boy sat motionless as stone, his dark eyes fixed on the moon; there seemed some spell upon the little party. Boat after boat passed them, almost noiselessly, for far into the clear evening went the tones of the singer's voice, and the dullest hearer could not withhold the tribute of admiring silence until beyond its reach.

And Sarah, happy in the strange, restful languor that locked her senses to all except the blessed present, dreamed on, the music but a part of her ideal world, this new and beautiful life. Into it stole presently a theme of sadness, a strain of grief, a heart-cry, that, ere she was aware, wrung her own heart-strings with anguish.

"The long, long, weary day
Is passed in tears away,
And still at evening I am weeping.
When from my window's height
I look out on the night,
I am still weeping,
My lone watch keeping.

"When I, his truth to prove,
Would trifle with my love,
He'd say, 'For me thou wilt be weeping,
When, at some future day,
I shall be far away;
Thou wilt be weeping,
Thy lone watch keeping.'

"Alas! if land or sea
Had parted him from me,
I would not these sad tears be weeping;
But hope he'd come once more,
And love me as before;
And say, 'Cease weeping,
Thy lone watch keeping.'

"But he is dead and gone,
Whose heart was mine alone,
And now for him I'm sadly weeping.
His face I ne'er shall see,
And naught is left to me
But bitter weeping,
My lone watch keeping."

If ever a pierced and utterly hopeless soul poured forth its plaint in musical measure, it was in the wondrously simple and unspeakably plaintive air to which these words are set. There breathes in it a spirit wail so mournfully sincere that one recognizes its sob in the very chords of the accompaniment. The mere murmur of the melody, were no words uttered, tells the story of grieving desolation.

Sarah did not move or speak, yet upon her enchanted ground a cloud had fallen. She saw the high casement and its tearful gazer into the night, a night not of music, and moonlight, and love, but chill, and wet, and dreary. Rain dripped from eaves and trees; stone steps and pavements caught a ghastly gleam from street lamps; save that sorrowful watcher, there was no living creature abroad or awake. She grew cold and sick with looking into those despairing eyes; the gloom, the loneliness, the woe of that vigil became her own, and her heart sank swooning beneath the burden.

As she ceased the song, Philip looked up for some comment or request. To his surprise, she only clasped her hands in a gesture that might have been either relief from or abandonment to woe, and bowed her head upon them. Puzzled, yet flattered by her emotion, he refrained from interrupting her; and, resuming his oars, lent the impetus of their stroke to that of the tide. Nothing was said until the keel grated upon the shelly beach opposite the farmhouse. Then, as Philip stooped to lift the unconscious Jeannie, he imagined that he discerned the gleam of the sinking moon upon Sarah's dripping eyelashes.

The fancy pursued him after he had gone up to his room. Seated at his window, looking out upon the now starlit sky, he smoked more than one cigar before his musing fit was ended. It was not the love-reverie of a smitten boy. He believed that he had passed that stage of sentimentalism ten years before. That Southerner of the male gender who has not been consumed by the fires and arisen as good as new from the ashes of half a dozen never-dying passions before he is eighteen, who has not offered the heart and hand, which as often as otherwise constitute his chiefest earthly possessions, to some elect fair one by the time he is one-and-twenty, is voted "slow" or invulnerable. If these susceptible sons of a fervid clime did not take to love-making as naturally as does a duckling to the pond by the time the eggshell is fairly off of its head, they would certainly be initiated while in the callow state by the rules and customs of society. Courtship is at first a pastime, then an art, then when the earnestness of a real attachment takes hold of their impassioned natures, it is the one all-absorbing, eager pursuit of existence, until rewarded by the acquisition of its object or thwarted by the decided refusal of the hard-hearted Dulcinea.

This state of things, this code of Cupid, every Southern girl understands, and shapes her conduct accordingly. Sportively, yet warily, she plays around the hook, and he is a very fortunate angler who does not in the moment of fancied success discover that she has carried off the bait as a trophy upon which to feed her vanity, and left him to be the laughing-stock of the curious spectators of this double game. She is imperturbable to meaning *équivoques*, receives pretty speeches and tender glances at their current value, and not until the suit becomes close and ardent, the attachment palpable to every one else, and is confessed in so many words, does she allow herself to be persuaded that her adorer is "in earnest," and really desires to awaken a sympathetic emotion in her bosom.

Philip Benson was no wanton trifler with woman's feelings. On the contrary, he had gained the reputation in his circle of an invincible, indifferent looker-on of the pseudo and real combats, in Love's name, that were continually transpiring around him. Chivalrous in tone, gallant in action, as he was, the girls feared while they liked and admired him. They called him critical, fastidious, cold; and mockingly wondered why he persisted in going into company, that, judging the future by the past, was so unlikely to furnish him with the consort he must be seeking. In reality, he was what he had avowed himself to Sarah—a student of human nature; an amateur in this species of social research—than which no other so frequently results in the complete deception of the inquirer. Certainly no other is so apt to find its culmination of devotion in a cold-blooded dissection of motive, morals, and sentiment; an unprincipled, reckless application of trial and test to the hearts and lives of its victims and final infidelity in all human good, except what is concentrated in the inspector's individual, personal self. Grown dainty amid the abundant supply of ordinary material, he comes at length to disdain common "subjects." Still less would he touch one already loathsome in the popular estimation, through excess of known and actual crime. But a character fresh and noble from the Creator's hand; a soul that dares to think and feel according to its innate sense of right; an intellect unhackneyed, not vitiated by worldly policy or the dogmas of the schools; a heart, tender and delicate—yet passionate in love or abhorrence; what an opportunity is here presented for the scalpel, the detective acid, the crucible, the microscope! It is not in fallible mortality to resist the temptation, and even professors of this ennobling pursuit, whose motto is, "The proper study of mankind is Man," are, as they allow with shame and confusion of face, themselves mortal. Of all the dignified humbugs of the solemn farce of life, deliver me from that creature self-styled "a student and judge of character!"

In Sarah Hunt, Philip discovered, to his surprise, a rare "specimen;" a volume, each leaf of which revealed new matter of interest. The attentions he had considered himself bound to pay her, in order to avoid wounding their kind hosts, were soon rendered from a widely different motive.

It did not occur to him that he was transcending the limits of merely friendly courtesy, as prescribed by the etiquette of the region in which he was now a sojourner. He was by no means deficient in appreciation of his personal gifts; rated his powers of pleasing quite as highly as did his warmest admirers, although he had the common sense and tact to conceal this; but he would have repelled, as an aspersion upon his honor, the charge that he was endeavoring to win this young girl's affections, his heart being as yet untouched.

"Was it then altogether whole?" he asked himself to-night, with a coolness that should have been an immediate reply to the suggestion.

Side by side, he set two mental portraits, and strove deliberately, impartially, to discern any traces of resemblance between the two. The future Mrs. Benson was a personage that engrossed much of his thoughts, and by long practice in the portrayal of her lineaments, he had brought his fancy sketch very nearly to perfection. A tall, Juno-like figure, with raven locks, and large, melting eyes, unfathomable as clear; features of classic mould; an elastic, yet stately form; a disposition in which amiability tempered natural impetuosity, and generous impulse gave direction to gentle word and deed; a mind profoundly imbued with the love of learning, and in cultivation, if not strength, equal to his own; discretion, penetration, and docility combined in such proportions as should render her her husband's safest counsellor, yet willing follower; and controlling and toning the harmonious whole, a devotion to himself only second in degree, not inferior in quality, to worship of her Creator. This was the ideal for whose embodiment our reasonable, modest Cœlebs was patiently waiting. Answer, oh ye expectant, incipient Griseldas! who, from your beauteous ranks, will step into the prepared niche, and make the goddess a reality?

And how appeared the rival picture in comparison?

"No, no!" he ejaculated, tossing the remnant of his third cigar into the garden. "I must seek further for the 'golden mean.' Intellect and heart are here, undoubtedly. I must have beauty and grace as well. Yet," he continued, relentingly, "there are times when she would be quite handsome if she dressed better. It is a pity her love for the beautiful does not enter into her choice of wearing apparel!"

In ten minutes more he was asleep, and dreamed that he stood at the altar with his long sought ideal, when, as the last binding words were spoken, she changed to Sarah Hunt, arrayed in a light blue lawn of last year's fashion, that made her look as sallow as a lemon, and, to his taste, as little to be desired for "human nature's daily food."

Poor Sarah! The visionary robe was a faithful reflection upon the dreamer's mental retina of a certain organdie which had formed a part of Lucy's wardrobe the previous summer, and having become antiquated in six months' time, was altogether inadmissible in the belle's outfit of this season.

"Yet it cost an awful sum when it was new!" reasoned Mrs. Hunt, "and will make you a very useful dress while you are with your Aunt Sarah. It's too good to cut up for Jeannie!"

"But the color, mother?" objected the unwilling recipient.

"Pooh! who will notice that? Besides, if you had a good complexion, you could wear blue as well as anybody."

Sarah's stock of thin dresses was not plentiful, and, recalling this observation, she coupled it with the fact that she was growing rosy, and dared to equip herself in the azure garment, with what effect she did not dream and Mr. Philip Benson *did!*

CHAPTER V.

On a pleasant, although rather cloudy forenoon in July, our young pleasure-seekers carried into execution a long-talked-of expedition to the Deal Beach, distant about ten miles from Shrewsbury.

By Aunt Sarah's arrangement, Charley and Jeannie occupied the back seat of the light wagon, and Sarah was to sit by Philip in front, that she "might see the country." Having accomplished this apparently artless manœuvre, the good woman handed up to them a portly basket of luncheon, and two or three additional shawls, in case of rain or change of weather, and bade the gay party "Good-by" with a satisfied glow in heart and face. To her guileless apprehension there was no question how affairs were progressing between her niece and her nephew-in-law; and in sundry conferences on the subject between "husband" and herself, it had been agreed that a matrimonial alliance would be the best thing that could happen to either of the supposed lovers. In her simple, pious soul, the dear old lady already blessed the Providence that had accomplished the meeting and intercourse under her roof, while she wondered at "the strange things that come about in this world."

Philip had been aware of her innocent attempts to facilitate his suit for several days past, and Sarah's blush, as she hesitated, before accepting the proffered seat by the driver, showed that this move was so transparent as to convey the alarm to her also. For a full half mile Philip did not speak, except a word now and then to the pair of stout grays, who were Uncle Nathan's greatest earthly boast. He appeared thoughtful, perhaps perturbed—so Sarah's single stolen glance at him showed—and in the eyes that looked straight onward to the horizon, there was a hardness she had never seen there before. She was surprised, therefore, when he broke the silence by an unimportant observation, uttered in his usual friendly tone, and for the remainder of the ride was gay and kind, with a show of light-heartedness that was not surpassed by the merry children behind them.

There was hardly enough variety in the unpicturesque country bordering their route to give the shadow of reasonableness to Aunt Sarah's pretext in selecting her namesake's seat, and, despite her escort's considerate attentions, Sarah had an uncomfortable ride; while her manner evinced more of the haughty reserve of their introduction than she had shown at any subsequent stage of their acquaintance. The grays travelled well, and a little after noon they were detached from the carriage, and tied in the grove of scrub-oaks skirting the beach.

While Philip was busied with them, the others continued their course down to the shore; the children, hand-in-hand, skipping over sand-hills, and stopping to pick up stones; Sarah strolling slowly after them. She had seen the ocean-surf before, but never aught like this, with its huge swells of water, a mile in length, gathering blackness and height on their landward career; as they struck the invisible barrier that commanded, "Thus far and no farther!" breaking in white fury, with the leap of a baffled fiend, and a roar like thunder, against their resistless opponent, then recoiling, sullenly, to gather new force for another, and as useless an attack. The beach was wide and uneven, of sand, whose whiteness would have glared intolerably had the day been sunny, drifted into hillocks and undulating ridges, like the waves of the sea. Here and there the hardy heather found a foothold amid the otherwise blank sterility, the green patches adding to, rather than lessening the wild, desolate aspect of the tract. Fragments of timber were strewn in all directions, and Sarah's quick eye perceived that it was not formless, chance driftwood. There were hewn beams and shapely spars, and planks in which great iron bolts were still fast. When Philip overtook her, she was standing by an immense piece of solid wood, lying far beyond the reach of the highest summer tides. One end was buried in the sand; the other, bleached by sun and wind, and seamed with cracks, was curved like the extremity of a bow. Her late embarrassment or hauteur was forgotten in the direct earnestness of her appealing look.

"Am I mistaken?" she said, in a low, awed tone. "Is not this the keel of a ship?"

"It is. There have been many wrecked on this coast."

"Here!" She glanced from the fierce, bellowing breakers to the melancholy testimonial of their destructive might. "I have never heard that this was esteemed a dangerous point."

"You can form but an imperfect idea of what this beach is in winter," remarked Philip, signing to her to seat herself upon the sand, and throwing himself down beside her. "I was here once, late in the autumn, and saw a vessel go to pieces, scarcely a stone's throw from where we are now sitting. The sea was high, the wind blowing a perfect gale, and this schooner, having lost one of her most important sails, was at the mercy of the elements. She was cast upon the shore, and her crew, watching their opportunity, sprang overboard as the waves receded, and reached firm ground in safety. Then came a monster billow, and lifting the vessel farther upon the sand, left her careened towards the land. It was pitiful to see the poor thing! so like life were her shudders and groans, as the cruel surf beat against her, that my heart fairly ached. The spray, at every dash, arose nearly as high as her mast-head, and a cataract of water swept over her deck. Piece by piece she broke up, and we could only stand and look on, while the scattered portions were thrown to our very feet. I shall never forget the sight. It taught me the truth of man's impotence and nature's strength as I had never read it before."

"But there were no lives lost! You were spared the spectacle of that most terrible scene in the tragedy of shipwreck."

"Yes. But the light of many a life has been quenched in that raging caldron. A young man, a resident of Shrewsbury, with whom I hunted last year, described to me a catalogue of horrors which he had beheld here, that has visited me in dreams often since. An emigrant ship was cast away on this coast, in midwinter. High above the roar of the wind and the booming surf, was heard the cry of the doomed wretches, perishing within hail of the crowd of fellow-beings who had collected at news of the catastrophe. The cold was intense; mast, and sail, and rope were coated with ice, and the benumbed, freezing wretches were exposed every instant to the torrents of brine that swept over them like sleet. The agony was horrible beyond description, but it was soon over. Before the vessel parted, the accent of mortal woe was hushed. Not a man survived to tell the tale!"

For an hour, they sat thus and talked. The subject had, for Sarah, a fearful fascination, and, led on by her absorbed attention, Philip rehearsed to her wonders and stories of the mysterious old ocean, that to-day stretched before them, blanched and angry, under the veil of summer cloud, until to his auditor there were bitter wailings blent with the surge's roar; arms, strained and bare, were tossed above the dark, serpent-like swell of water, in unavailing supplication, and livid, dead faces stared upon her from beneath the curling crests of the breakers.

That day on the Deal Beach! How quietly happy was its seeming! how full of event, emotion, fate—was its reality! Charley and Jeannie wandered up and down the coast, filling their baskets with shells and pebbles; chasing the retiring waves as far as they dared, and scampering back, with shrieks of laughter, as the succeeding billow rolled rapidly after them; building sand-houses, and digging wells to be filled by salt-water; exulting greatly when a rough coralline fragment, or a jelly-fish of unusual dimensions was thrown in their way. They all lunched together, seated upon the heather-clumps, around Aunt Sarah's liberal hamper.

"Sister!" said Jeannie, when the edge of her sea-side appetite was somewhat blunted by her repast, "I like living here better than in New York—don't you?"

"It is more pleasant in summer, my dear."

"But I mean that I am happier here! I wish you would write to mother, and ask her to let us live here always."

"But what would she do without her baby?" asked Philip, emphasizing the last word.

The little lady bridled instantly.

"Cousin Phil! I *do* wish you would never call me a 'baby' again! I am seven years and two weeks old. I could get along very well without mother for a while. Of course, I would go over sometimes, and pay her a visit and get new dresses. Shrewsbury is a nice place; I would like to buy that pretty white house next to Uncle Nathan's, and live there—sister, and Charley, and I—and you—if you would promise not to tease me ever!"

"Thank you!" said Philip, with admirable gravity, seeming not to note Sarah's heightened color at this proposal of copartnership. "You are very kind to include me in your household arrangements, and nothing would please me better, if I could stay here. But you know, Jeannie, my dear little cousin, that my home is far away from this quarter of the world. I have remained here too long already." There was a touch of feeling or nervousness in his voice. "I had a letter last night, reminding me that I ought to have left a week ago, to join a party of friends, whom I promised to meet in New York, and travel with them until the time for our return to the South."

He did not look at Sarah, but she felt that the explanation was intended for her—that, whether intentionally or not, he was preparing her for a blow to heart and hope.

"I shall be obliged to leave Shrewsbury and all my friends there, to-morrow morning, Jeannie!"

The child's exclamation of dismay, and Charley's quick, mute remonstrance to his cousin, as his playfellow communicated the news to him, gave Sarah time to rally firmness and words.

"This is unexpected intelligence," she said, calmly. "We shall miss you. Your kindness has, directly and indirectly, been the means of affording us much pleasure during our visit to our good aunt. It will seem dull when you are gone."

There was a flash in Philip's eye that looked like pleasure—a mixture of relief and surprise, as he turned to her.

"I am selfish enough to hope that you *will* miss me for a time, at least. I shall not then be so soon forgotten. We have had some pleasant days and weeks together; have we not?"

"*I* have enjoyed them, assuredly."

She was a little pale, Philip thought, but that might be the effect of fatigue. Her cheek was seldom blooming, unless when flushed in animated speech, or by brisk exercise. She spoke of his going with politeness, that seemed scarce one remove from carelessness; and, man-like, his pleasure at the thought that their association in the country house had not been followed by the results Aunt Sarah wished and predicted, gave way to a feeling of wounded vanity and vexation, that his summer's companion could relinquish him so easily. While he repeated to himself his congratulations that his friendly and gallant attentions had not been misconstrued, had not awakened any inconvenient, because futile "expectations," he wondered if it were a possibility for a girl of so much sense and feeling, such genuine appreciation of his talents and tastes, to know him well—even intimately—without experiencing a warmer sentiment than mere approval of an agreeable associate's mind and manners, and Platonic liking for him on these accounts.

With the respectful familiarity of a privileged acquaintance, he drew her hand within his arm, as they arose at the conclusion of the collation.

"We have yet two hours and more to spend here, before we set out for home. We can have one more walk and talk together."

They took but one turn on the beach, and returning to their morning's seat beside the half-buried keel, tried to talk as they had done then. It was hard work, even to the man of the world, the heart-free student of human nature. Gradually the conversation languished and died away, and, for a while, both sat silent, looking out upon the sea. Then Philip's gaze came back to his companion—stealthily at first, and, as she remained unconscious of his scrutiny, it lingered long and searchingly upon features, form, and attire.

There were white, tight lines about her mouth, and a slight knitting of the brow, that imparted a care-worn look to the young face, it pained him to see. Her hands were clasped upon her knee, and the fingers were bloodless where they interlaced one another. Was she suffering? Was the threatened parting the cause of her disquiet? If this were so, what was his duty as a man of honor—of common humanity? And if he were forced to admit that he held her happiness in his power, and to accept the consequences that must ensue from his idle gallantry and her mistaken reading of the same, was the thought really repulsive? Would it be a total sacrifice of feeling to a sense of right? It was a repetition, grave and careful, of the revery of that July night, two weeks ago.

Sarah's hat—a broad-brimmed "flat" of brown straw—had fallen back upon her shoulders, and the sea-breeze played in her hair, raising the short and loose strands, and giving to the whole a rough, "frowzy" look. Her plain linen collar and undersleeves showed her complexion and hands to the worst possible advantage. Upon her cheeks, this same unfriendly wind had bestowed a coat of tan and a few freckles, that were all the more conspicuous from her pallor, while her fingers were as brown as a gypsy's. Her gray poplin dress had lost most of its original gloss, and being one of Mrs. Hunt's bargains—"a cheap thing, but plenty good for that outlandish Shrewsbury"—already betrayed its cotton warp by creases that would not be smoothed, and an aspect of general limpness—a prophecy of speedy, irremediable shabbiness. Cast loosely about her shoulders was a light shawl, green, with black sprigs—another bargain; and beyond the skirt of her robe appeared the toe and instep of a thick-soled gaiter, very suitable for a tramp through damp sand, yet any thing but becoming to the foot it protected.

With an impatient shake of the head, involuntary and positive, Philip closed his final observation. And cutting off a large splinter from the weather-beaten timber, against which he leaned, set about trimming it, wearing a serious, settled face, that said his mind was fully made up.

What had Sarah seen all this while?

Heavens, over which the films of the forenoon had thickened into dun cloud-curtains, stretching above, and enwrapping the world; a wild, dreary expanse of troubled waters, whose horizon line was lost in the misty blending of sea and sky, ever hurrying and heaving to moan out their unrest upon the barren beach. In the distance was a solitary sail; nearer to the land, a large sea-bird flew heavily against the wind. In such mateless, weary flight, must her life be passed; that lone, frail craft was not so hopelessly forlorn upon a gloomy sea, beneath a sky that gloomed yet more darkly—as was her heart, torn suddenly from its moorings—anchor, and rudder, and compass gone! Yet who could syllable the mighty sorrow of the complaining sea? And were there words in human language, that could tell the anguish of the swelling flood beating within her breast?

"Going away! To-morrow!" For a little space this was all the lament she kept repeating over to herself. Pregnant with woe she knew it to be, yet it was not until she was allowed to meditate in silence upon the meaning of the words that she realized what had truly come upon her. She had thrown away all her hope of earthly happiness—risked it as madly, lost it as surely, as if she had tossed it—a tangible pearl—into the yawning ocean. Her instinct assured her that, were it otherwise, the tidings of Philip's intended departure, his suddenly formed resolution to leave her, would have been conveyed to her in a far different manner. Her keen backward glance penetrated Aunt Sarah's simple wiles; his obvious annoyance thereat; his determination to save himself from suspicion; his honorable fear lest she, too, should imagine him loving, where he was only civil and kind. Yes, it was all over! The best thing she could hope to do, the brightest prospect life had now for her, was that her secret should remain hers alone, until the troubled heart moaned itself into the rest which knows no waking. She was used to concealment. All her existence, excepting the sweet delusive dream of the past three weeks, had been a stern preparation for this trial. But she was already weary, and faint—fit to lie down and die, so intense had been the throe of this one struggle.

"How long is this to last? How long?"

The exclamation actually broke, in an inarticulate murmur, from her lips.

"Did you speak?" inquired Philip.

"I think not. I am not sure. I did not intend to do so!"

"Grant me credit for my forbearance in not obtruding my prosaic talk upon your musings," he went on, playfully. "It was a powerful temptation—for I remember, constantly, that this is our last opportunity for a genuine heart and head confabulation, such as I shall often linger for, after I leave you—and sincerity! You have done me good, Miss Sarah; taught me Faith, Hope, Charity—a blessed sisterhood!"

"May they ever attend you!"

"Amen! and thank you! And what wish shall I make in return for your beautiful benediction?"

"Whatever you like. My desires are not many or extravagant."

"You are wrong. You have a craving heart and a craving mind. May both be fed to the full, with food convenient for them—in measures pressed down, shaken together, and running over."

"Of what? Husks?" was Sarah's unspoken and bitter reply. She could not thank him, as he had done her. She only bowed, and, bending forward, took up a handful of the fine white sand that formed the shore. Slowly sifting it through her fingers, she waited for him to speak again.

Was this careless equanimity real or feigned? The

judge of character, the harpist upon heart-chords, made the next move—not the candid manly friend.

"I am going to ask a favor of you—a bold one."

"Say on."

"By the time I am ready to retrace my steps southward, you will be again settled in New York. Will you think me presumptuous, if I call at your father's house to continue an acquaintance which has been, to me, at once agreeable and profitable?"

The fingers were still, suddenly. A warm glow, like sunrise, swept over cheek and forehead. A smile, slight but sweet, quivered upon her lips. Drowning in the depths, she heard across the billow a hail that spoke of hope, life, happiness.

"We will all be glad to see you," she said, with affected composure.

"Not half so glad as I shall be to come. Will you now, while you think of it, give me your address?"

He handed her a card and a pencil. She wrote the required direction, and received in exchange for it the now smooth bit of wood, which had afforded occupation to Philip for half an hour past. It was tendered in mock ceremony, and accepted smilingly. Upon the gray tablet was inscribed, "Philip Benson, Deal Beach, July 27th, 1856." A playful or thoughtless impulse caused him to extend his hand for it, after she had read it, and to add a motto, stale as innocent in his eyes: *Pensez à moi!*"

"I shall preserve it as a souvenir of the day and place," observed Sarah, slipping it into her pocket.

Twilight overtook them before they reached home, and the night was too cloudy and damp for a promenade, such as they often had in the garden walks and lane, or for the customary family gathering in the long porch. Yet Aunt Sarah was surprised that Philip was apparently content to spend the evening in the sitting-room, with herself and husband by, to spoil the *tête-à-tête* he must be longing for.

Still more confounded was she, when, after her clever strategy of coaxing Uncle Nathan into the kitchen, that the coast might be clear, she heard Philip's step close behind them.

"I must clean my gun to-night, aunt," he said, taking it from the corner; "I shall not have time to do it to-morrow."

With the utmost *nonchalance* he began the operation, whistling softly a lively air over his work. Aunt Sarah gave her partner a look of bewildered despair, which he returned by a confirmatory nod, and a smile, half comic, half regretful.

After breakfast next morning, the nephew-guest said affectionate farewells to his relatives and Jeannie; a grave, gentle adieu to Sarah, accompanied by a momentary pressure of the hand, that may have meant much or little; and upon the snug homestead settled a quiet that was dreariness itself to one of its inmates.

CHAPTER VI.

MEANWHILE, how had the time sped to the nominal head of the Hunt household—the solitary, toiling father and husband? The servants were dismissed when "the family" left town, although Mr. Hunt continued to sleep at home. A peripatetic maid-of-all-work—what the English denominate a char-woman—was engaged to come early every morning to clear up the only room in the establishment that was used, before the cashier went out for his breakfast, which he procured at a restaurant pretty far down town. The same quiet coffee-house furnished him with dinner and an early tea, after which last refreshment he was at liberty to pass the evening in whatever manner he liked best. There was nothing in the city worth seeing at this season, even if he had not lost all taste for shows and gayety. Those of his acquaintances who were not absent with their wives and daughters, were living like himself, furniture in overalls; carpets covered; apartments closed, with the exception, perhaps, of one bedroom; and had no place in which to receive him if he had been in the habit of visiting, which he was not. He was very tired, moreover, by the time night came on, and as the heat increased, and the days grew longer, his strength waned more and more, and his spirits with it. Meekly and uncomplainingly he plodded through his routine of bank duties, so steady and so faithful that his fellow-workers and customers had come to regard him as a reliable fixture; a piece of machinery, whose winding up was self-performed and whose accuracy was infallible.

When, therefore, on a sultry August afternoon, he turned to leave his desk at the close of business hours, grew terribly pale, and dropped upon the floor in a fit of death-like faintness, there was great consternation, and as much wonder as if no human clock-work had ever given out before, under a like process of exhausting demands.

Clumsily, but with the best of intentions, they brought him to his senses, and in half an hour or so he was sufficiently recovered to be taken home. There was a twitching of the lips that might have passed for a sarcastic smile, as he heard the proposal to convey him to his house; but he only gave his street and number, and lay silently back in the carriage, supported by his friends, two of whom insisted upon seeing him safely to his own abode.

"Is this the place? Why, it is all shut up!" exclaimed one of these gentlemen, as the driver drew up before the dusty steps.

Mrs. Hunt's orders were that the entrance to her mansion should present the most desolate air possible during her absence. It had "an aristocratical look in the summer time, when everybody but nobodies was rusticating."

Again that singular contortion of the mouth, and the master (?) of the forlorn-looking habitation prepared to descend, fumbling in his pocket for his pass-key.

"I am obliged to you, gentlemen, for your great kindness, and will—not—trouble—you—longer."

In trying to raise his hand to his hat for a bow, the ghastly hue again overspread his face, and he staggered. Without further parley, his two aids laid hold of him, one on each side, and supported him into the house, up one, two flights of linen-draped stairs, to a back bedroom.

Mrs. Hunt would have let her husband faint on the sidewalk before she would have received company in that chamber in its present condition; for the handsomest articles of furniture stood covered up in another apartment, and their place was supplied by a plain bureau, wash-stand, and bed belonging to the boys' room, a story higher up. The wisdom of this precaution was manifest in the signs of neglect and slovenliness displayed on all sides. One could have written his name in the dust upon the glass; there was dirt in every corner and under each chair and table; the wash-basin was partly full of dirty suds, and the towels and counterpane shockingly dingy.

These things were not remarked by the intruders until they had got their charge to bed, resisted no longer by him, for he began to comprehend his inability to help himself.

"There is no one beside ourselves on the premises, not even a servant," one of them said, apart to his associate, after a brief absence from the room. "If you will stay with him until I come back, I will go for a doctor."

The invalid caught the last word.

"Indeed, Mr. Hammond, there is no need for you to do any thing more—no necessity for calling in a physician. I am quite comfortable now, and shall be well by morning."

Mr. Hammond, who was a director in the bank, and sincerely honored the honest veteran now prostrated by his devoted performance of duty, took the hot, tremulous hand in his.

"I cannot allow you to peril your valuable health, my dear sir. Unless you positively forbid it, I shall not only call your physician, but drop in again myself this evening, and satisfy my mind as to whether you require my presence through the night."

He was as good as his word; but no amount of persuasion could induce Mr. Hunt to accept his offered watch. He would be "uneasy, unhappy, if his young friend sacrificed his own rest so uselessly," and loath as he was to leave him to solitude and suffering, Mr. Hammond had to yield. At his morning visit, he found the patient more tractable. After tedious hours of fevered wakefulness, he had endeavored to rise, only to sink back again upon his pillow—dizzy, sick, and now thoroughly alarmed at the state of his system. He did not combat his friend's proposal to obtain a competent nurse, and to look in on him in person as often as practicable; still, utterly refused to allow his wife to be written to on the subject of his indisposition.

"I shall be better in a day or two, probably before she could reach me. I have never had a spell of illness. It is not likely that this will be any thing of consequence. I greatly prefer that she should not be apprised of this attack."

Mr. Hammond was resolute on his part—the more determined, when the physician had paid another visit, and pronounced the malady a low fever, that would, doubtless, confine the sick man to his bed for several days, if not weeks.

"It is not just to your wife and children, Mr. Hunt, to keep them in ignorance of so important a matter!" he urged. "They will have cause to feel themselves aggrieved by you, and ill-treated by me, if we practise this deception upon them."

Mr. Hunt lay quiet for some minutes.

"Perhaps you are in the right," he said. "Sarah would be wounded, I know. I will send for her!" he concluded, with more animation. "She will come as soon as she receives the letter."

"Of course she will!" rejoined Mr. Hammond, confidently; "you are not able to write. Suffer me to be your amanuensis." He sat down at a stand, and took out his pen. "Where is Mrs. Hunt at present?"

"I am not sure. Either at Saratoga or Newport."

Mr. Hammond looked surprised. "But it is necessary, sir, that we should know with some degree of certainty, or the letter may miscarry. Perhaps it would be well to write to both places."

"The letter! Both places!" repeated Mr. Hunt, with perplexity. "I alluded to my daughter Sarah, sir, my second child, who is spending the summer with her aunt in Shrewsbury, New Jersey. May I take the liberty of asking you to write her a short note, mentioning my sickness in as guarded terms as you can use, and requesting her to come up to the city for a few days? She has my youngest child—a little girl—with her. If she can be contented to remain with her aunt, Sarah had better leave her there. She would be an additional burden to her sister if she were here."

Whatever Mr. Hammond thought of the marked preference shown to the daughter above the wife, he said nothing, but proceeded to indite the desired epistle, adding, in a postscript, on his own account, that he would take pleasure in meeting Miss Hunt at the wharf, on her arrival, and for this purpose would be at the boat each day, until she made her appearance in New York.

He went, accordingly, the next afternoon, although very sure that she could not have received his letter in season to take that boat. Mr. Hunt had proved to him and to himself the utter impossibility of her coming, yet his eyes brightened with expectancy as his friend entered, and faded into sadness as he reported the ill-success of his errand.

"He is evidently extremely partial to this one of his children," thought Mr. Hammond, as he paced the wharf on the second evening, watching, amid noisy hack-drivers and express-men, for the steamer. "I have seen the girls at parties, but do not remember their names. One of them is very pretty. I wonder if she is 'Sarah!'"

It was growing dusk as the boat touched the pier. So dim was the light, that Mr. Hammond was obliged to station himself close beside the gangway, and inspect the features of each lady passenger more narrowly than politeness would, in other circumstances, have warranted. They hurried across, men and women, tall and short, stout and slender, until there tripped towards him the figure of a young girl, attired in a gray dress and mantle, and carrying a small travelling bag in her hand. She would have passed him, had he not stepped forward and spoken.

"Miss Hunt, I believe!"

In the uncertain twilight, he could see that she grew very pale.

"How is my father?"

There was no preamble of civility or diffidence; no reserve in addressing him, a mere stranger; no trembling, preparatory queries; but a point-blank question, in a tone whose impatient anguish moved his kind heart; a piercing look, that would know the truth then and there!

"He is better, to-day"—and he led her out of the press of the onward stream. "He has not been dangerously ill. We hope and believe that he will not be."

"Is that true?" Her fingers tightened upon his arm.

"It is! I would not, for the world, deceive you in such a matter."

"I believe you! Thank Heaven! I feared the worst!" She covered her face with her hands, and burst into tears.

Hammond beckoned to a hackman, close by, and when the short-lived reaction of over-wrought feeling subsided so far as to allow Sarah to notice surrounding objects, she was seated in the carriage, screened from curious or impertinent gazers, and her escort was nowhere to be seen. Several minutes elapsed before he again showed himself at the window.

"I must trouble you for your checks, Miss Hunt, in order to get your baggage."

Already ashamed of her emotion, she obeyed his demand without speaking.

"You have given me but one," he said, turning it over in his hand.

"That is all, sir."

"Indeed! You are a model traveller! I thought no young lady, in these days, ever stirred from home without half a dozen trunks." To himself he added, "A sensible girl! An exception to most of her sex, in one thing, at any rate!"

Sarah sat well back into her corner, as they drove up lighted Broadway, and was almost rudely taciturn, while her companion related the particulars of her father's seizure and subsequent confinement to his room. Yet, that she listened with intense interest, the narrator knew by her irregular breathing and immovable attitude. As they neared their destination, this fixedness of attention and posture was exchanged for an eager restlessness. She leaned forward to look out of the window, and when they turned into the last street, quick as was Mr. Hammond's motion to unfasten the door of the vehicle, her hand was first upon the lock. It was cold as ice, and trembled so much as to be powerless. Gently removing it, he undid the catch, and assisted her to alight.

The hired nurse answered their ring, and while Sarah brushed past her, and flew up the stairway, Mr. Hammond detained the woman to make inquiries and issue directions.

"It is all very dreary-like, sir," she complained. "Every thing is packed away and locked up. There's no getting at a lump of sugar without a hunt for the key, and all he's seemed to care for this blessed day, was that his daughter should be made comfortable. He sent me out this afternoon to buy biscuits, and sardines, and peaches for her tea, and told me where I'd find silver and china. It is not at all the thing for him to be worrying at such a rate. He'll be worse for it to-morrow, and so I've told him, Mr. Hammond."

"Perhaps not, Mrs. Kerr. His daughter's coming will cheer him and quiet him too, I doubt not. I will not go up now. Please present my regards to Mr. Hunt, and say that I will call to-morrow."

He purposely deferred his visit until the afternoon, supposing that Miss Hunt might object to his early and unceremonious appearance in the realms now under her control; nor when he went did he ascend at once to the sick-chamber, as was his custom before the transfer of its superintendence. Sending up his name by the nurse, he awaited a formal invitation, among the shrouded sofas and chairs of the sitting-room.

"You'll please to walk up, sir!" was the message he received; and the woman subjoined, confidentially, "Things is brighter to-day, sir."

They certainly were. With wonderfully little noise and confusion, Sarah, assisted by the nurse, had wrought an utter change in the desolate apartment. With the exception of the bureau, which had been drawn out of sight into the adjoining dressing-room, and the bedstead, the common, defaced furniture had disappeared, and its place was supplied by more comfortable and elegant articles. The windows were shaded, without giving an aspect of gloom to the chamber; the bed-coverings were clean and fresh; and the sick man, supported by larger and plumper pillows than those among which he had tossed for many weary nights, greeted his visitor with a cordial smile and outstretched hand.

"I thank you for your kind care of my daughter last

evening, sir. Sarah, my dear, this is my friend, Mr. Hammond, to whose goodness I am so much indebted."

"The debt is mine no less," was the frank reply, as she shook hands with her new acquaintance. "We can never thank you sufficiently, Mr. Hammond, for all you have done for us, in taking care of him."

"A genuine woman! a dutiful, affectionate daughter!" was now Hammond's comment, as he disclaimed all right to her gratitude. "None of your sentimental, affected absurdities, with nothing in either head or heart!"

This impression was confirmed by daily observation; for politeness first, then inclination, induced him to continue his "professional" calls, as Sarah styled them. He seemed to divide with her the responsibility of her position. Its duties were onerous; but for this she did not care. She was strong and active, and love made labor light—even welcome to her. A competent cook was inducted into office below stairs, and household matters went forward with system and despatch. The eye of the mistress, *pro tem.*, was over all; her hand ever ready to lift her share of the load, yet her attendance at her father's bedside appeared unremitting. His disease, without being violent, was distressing and wearing, destroying sleep and appetite, and preying constantly upon the nerves. To soothe these, Sarah read and talked cheerfully, and often, at his request, sang old-time ballads and childish lullabys to court diversion and slumber.

Occasionally Lewis Hammond paused without the door until the strain was concluded, drinking in the notes with more pleasure than he was wont to feel in listening to the bravuras and startling, astonishing cadenzas that were warbled in his ears by the amateur cantatrices of the "best circles;" then, when the sounds from within ceased, he delayed his entrance some moments longer, lest the songstress should suspect his eaves-dropping. He ceased to speculate upon the reasons of Mrs. Hunt's protracted absence at a time when no true-hearted wife could, from choice, remain away from her rightful post. When, at the expiration of a fortnight from the day of the attack, the physician declared his patient feebly, but surely convalescent, his young friend had decided, to his entire satisfaction, that things were best as they were. Mr. Hunt had made a most judicious selection from the female portion of his family, and what need of more nurses when this one was so efficient and willing? He caught himself hoping that the fussy dame he had met in society would not abridge her summer's recreation on account of an ailing husband. He had designed going to Saratoga himself, for ten days or two weeks; but he was very well. It was difficult to get away from business, and this affair of Mr. Hunt's enlisted his sympathies so deeply, that he could not resolve upon leaving him. If he had never before enjoyed the bliss that flows from a disinterested action, he tasted it now.

Mrs. Hunt was not kept in total ignorance of what was transpiring at home. Sarah had written, cautiously and hopefully, of her father's sickness and her recall; repeating Mr. Hunt's wish that his consort should not hurry back through mistaken solicitude for his health and comfort; and they were taken at their word. A week elapsed before an answer arrived—a lengthy missive, that had cost the writer more pains and time than the preparation for her annual "crush" generally did. She was an indifferent penman, and sadly out of practice; but there was much to be said, and "Lucy, *of course, circumstanced as she was*, could not spare time to be her scribe."

The significant phrase underscored quickened Sarah's curiosity; but there was nothing for the next three pages that fed or quieted it. They were filled with minute directions about housewifery—economical details, that would have served as capital illustrations of "Poor Richard's" maxims; injunctions, warnings, and receipts sufficient in quantity to last a young, frugally-disposed housekeeper for the remainder of her natural existence. It was a trial to this exemplary wife and mother, she confessed, to absent herself so long from her home duties; but circumstances had compelled her stay at Saratoga. Of their nature, Sarah had already been informed in her sister's last letter.

"Which I cannot have received, then—" Sarah interrupted herself to say, as she read to her father: "I have not heard from Lucy in four weeks. I have thought hard of her for not writing."

"But," concluded Mrs. Hunt, "matters looks well just now, and I know your father will aggree, when he heers all about our season's work, that our labor and Money has been a good investment. Take care of the keys yourself, Sarah. Be pruedent, keep a sharp Lookout on the cook, and don't negleck your poor father. Your Affectionate mother, E. HUNT.

"P. S. Your kitchen Girl must have a Great deel of spair Time. Set her to work cleening the House, for you may expeckt us home in two weeks, or maybe Less.

"E. H."

Lucy had slipped a note in the same envelope—a thin, satiny sheet, hardly larger than the little hand that had moved over its perfumed page. Her chirography was very running, very light, very ladylike, and, we need not say, very italical.

"Mamma tells me, Sarah dear, that she has given you a *hint* of how matters are progressing between your humble servant and *our particular friend*, of whom I wrote in my last. The poor, dear woman flatters herself that it is all *her* work; but *somebody else* may have *his* own opinion, and I certainly have *mine.* I have had to caution her repeatedly, to prevent her from showing her delight *too* plainly to my 'Goldfinch,' as Vic. and I have *dubbed* him. Don't be in a hurry with your congratulations, *ma chère.* 'There's many a slip 'twixt the cup and the lip;' and although the season is so near over, I *may* yet see some one whom I like better than *His Highness.* Vic. has a beau, too—a rich widower, less fascinating than *my devoted;* but a very agreeable man, *without encumbrance,* and very much *smitten.* So we pair off nicely in our rides and promenades, and, *entre nous,* are quite the talk. You are a good little thing to nurse papa so sweetly—a great deal better than I am. I told *my knight* of this proof of your excellence the other day, and he said that it was only what might have been expected from *my sister!* Don't you *feel flattered?* Poor fellow! Love is blind, you know.

"Love to papa. I am sorry he has been so unwell. I do not imagine that I shall have time to write again before we leave this *paradise.* We will telegraph you when to expect us. *Perhaps I may have an escort home*—some one who would like to have a private *conference* with my respected father. *Nous verrons!*

"Lovingly, LUCIE."

Mr. Hunt twisted himself uneasily in his arm-chair as his daughter, by his desire, reluctantly read aloud the double letter. A shade of dissatisfaction and shame clouded his countenance when she finished, and he sighed heavily.

"I am glad they are still enjoying themselves," said Sarah, forcing a smile. "Lucy has secured a captive too, it appears—one whom she is likely to bring home at her chariot wheels."

"In *my* day daughters were in the habit of consulting their fathers before giving decided encouragement to any admirers, strangers especially," said Mr. Hunt, with displeasure. "In these times there are no parents! There is the 'old man' and 'the Governor,' who makes the money his children honor him by wasting, and the 'poor, dear woman,' who plays propriety in the belle's flirtations, and helps, or hinders, in snaring some booby 'Goldfinch.' It is a lying, cheating, hollow world! I have been sick of it for twenty years!"

"Father! my dear father," exclaimed Sarah, kneeling beside him, and winding her arm about his neck. "You misjudge your children, and their love for you!"

"I believe in you, child! I cannot understand how you have contrived to grow up so unlike your sister and your—" The recollection of the respect his daughter owed her mother, checked the word.

"You do not deal fairly with Lucy's character, father. She has one of the kindest hearts and most amiable dispositions in the world. I wish I had caused you as little anxiety as she has. Remember her obedience and my wilfulness; her gentleness and my obstinacy, and blush at your verdict, Sir Judge!"

She seated herself upon his foot-cushion and rested her chin upon his knee, looking archly up in his face. She was surprised and troubled at this degree of acrimony in one whose habitual manner was so placid, and his judgment so mild; but, for his sake, she was resolute not to show her feeling. He laid his hand caressingly upon her shoulder, and sank into a revery, profound, and seemingly not pleasant.

Sarah took advantage of his abstraction to remove the wrapper of a newspaper received by the same mail that had brought her letters. The operation was carefully performed, so as not to invite notice, and the envelope laid away in her work-box. She knew well who had traced the clear, bold superscription, and what initials composed the mysterious cipher in one corner of the cover; nor was this the only token of recollection she had from this source. The article marked in the number of the literary journal he had selected as the medium of correspondence, was an exquisite little poem from an author whose works Philip had read to her in the vine-covered porch at Shrewsbury. Slowly, longingly she perused it; gathering sweetness from every word, and fancying how his intonations would bring out beauties she could not of herself discover. Then she took out the wrapper again, and studied the postmark. On the former papers he had sent the stamp was illegible, but this was easily deciphered—"Albany."

"So near! He is returning homewards!" was the glad reflection that flooded her face with joy.

"Sarah!" said her father, abruptly. "Do you ever think of marriage?"

"Sir?" stammered the girl, confused beyond measure.

"I mean, have you imbibed your sister's ideas on this subject? the notions of ninety-nine hundredths of girls in your walk of life. Do you intend to seek a husband, boldly and unblushingly, in all public places? to degrade yourself by practising the arts they understand so well to catch an 'eligible' partner, who may repay your insincerity and mercenary views by insult and infidelity—at best by indifference! Child! you do not know the risk match-making mothers and husband-hunting daughters run; the terrible retribution that may be—that often is in store for such! I had rather see you and your sister dead, than the victims of that most hateful of heartless shows—a fashionable marriage! Poor Lucy! poor Lucy!"

"I hope you are distressing yourself without reason, sir.

Mother is not the person to surrender her child to one whose character and respectability are not indisputable. Nor is Lucy sentimental. I do not fear her suffering very acutely from any cause."

"I grant that. You would be more to be pitied as an unloved or unloving wife, than she. I tremble for you sometimes, when I think of this chance. My daughter, when you marry, look beyond the outside show. Seek for moral worth and a true heart, instead of dollars and cents!"

"I will! I promise!" said Sarah, her amazement at his earnestness and choice of topics combining to shake her voice and constrain her smile. "But there is time enough for that, father dear. When the man of heart and worth sues for my poor hand, I will refer him to you, and abide entirely by your decision."

"Mr. Hammond is down-stairs," said the servant at the door. And Sarah, gathering up her papers, escaped from the room before he entered.

CHAPTER VII.

Mr. Hunt was able to resume his place in the bank several days before his wife returned. Uncle Nathan had brought Jeannie home as soon as her father could leave his room, and the boys had likewise been written for; so that the family reunion was apparently near at hand.

Weak as he was, Mr. Hunt met his spouse and daughter at the dépôt, and the noise of their entrance in the lower hall first apprised Sarah of their arrival. To the bound of pleasurable excitement her heart gave at the certainty that they had come, succeeded a sigh at the termination of the free, yet busy life she had led of late—the probability that she would be compelled to resume her old habits of feeling and action. Driving back the selfish regret, she ran down to welcome the travellers.

"How well you're looking, Sarah!" said Mrs. Hunt, after kissing her. "I declare, if you was to arrange your hair different, and study dress a bit, you would come near being right down handsome."

"'Handsome is as handsome does!'" quoted Mr. Hunt, stoutly. "According to that rule, she is a beauty."

"Thank you, sir!" said Sarah, bowing low. And she tried to forget, in her sister's affectionate greeting, the chill and heart-sickness produced by her mother's business-like manner and compliment.

"Having disposed of one daughter, she means to work the other into merchantable shape!" was her cynical deduction from the dubious praise bestowed upon herself.

Mrs. Hunt pursued her way up the steps, examining and remarking upon every thing she saw.

"Them stair-rods ain't so clean as they had ought to be, Sarah. I'm afraid your girls are careless, or shirks. When did you uncover the carpet?"

"Some time ago, mother, while father was sick. There were gentlemen calling constantly, and the cover looked shabby, I thought."

"It couldn't be helped, I s'pose; but the carpet is more worn than I expected to see it. With the heavy expenses that will be crowding on us this fall and winter, we can't afford to get any new things for the house."

Lucy, who preceded her sister, glanced back and laughed meaningly. And Sarah was very glad that her father had not overheard the observation, which confirmed her belief that the beauty's hand was disposed of without the form of consultation with her natural and legal guardian.

Dinner was announced by the time the travelling habiliments and dust were removed. Sarah had spared no pains to provide a bountiful and tasteful repast, at the risk of incurring her mother's reproof for her extravagant proclivities. But the dame was in high good-humor, and the youthful purveyor received but a single sentence of deprecation.

"I hope you have not been living as high as this all the time, Sarah!"

"No, madam. Father's wants and mine were very few. I foresaw that you would need substantial refreshment after your journey."

"You was very thoughtful. We both have good appetites, I guess. I know that I have."

"Mine will speak for itself," said Lucy.

"You have no idea how that girl has enjoyed every thing since she has been away," observed Mrs. Hunt to her husband. "There was Vic. West, who took it into her head that she ought to look die-away and peaking, and refuse food, when her beau was by; but Lu., she just went right along and behaved natural, and I'm sure that *somebody* thought more of her for it."

Mr. Hunt's face darkened for a moment; but he could not find fault with his eldest child on her first evening at home.

"So you have been quite a belle, Lucy," he said, pleasantly.

"Better than that, Mr. H.!" Mrs. Hunt checked her triumphant announcement as the butler re-entered the room. "I shouldn't wonder," she resumed, mysteriously, "if Lucy was disposed to settle down into a steady, sedate matron after her holiday."

"Don't you deceive yourself with that hope!" laughed Lucy.

She was evidently pleased by these not over-delicate allusions to her love-affairs, and, like her mother, extremely complacent over the result of her recent campaign. Sarah felt that, were she in her place, she would shrink from this open jesting upon a sacred subject; still, she had not expected that her sister would behave differently. Lucy's nature was gentle without being fine; affectionate, but shallow. She would have had no difficulty in attaching herself to any man whom her friends recommended as "a good match," provided he were pleasing in exterior, and her most devoted servitor.

The sisters had no opportunity of private converse until they adjourned to the parlor for the evening. Lucy was very beautiful in a blue silk, whose low corsage and short sleeves revealed her superb shoulders and rounded arms. Her complexion was a rich carmine, deepening or softening with every motion—one would have said, with every breath. Her blue eyes fairly danced in a sort of subdued glee, very charming and very becoming, but altogether unlike the tender, dewy light of "Love's first young dream."

"How lovely you have grown, sister!" said Sarah, earnestly. "Oh, Lucy, I don't believe you rightly value the gift of beauty—as I would do, if it were mine!"

"Nonsense!" The dimples, that made her smile so bewitching, broke her blushes into rosy waves, as the conscious fair one turned her face towards the mirror. "I am pleased to hear that I am passable to-night. We may have visitors. A friend of ours has expressed a great desire to see me in my home—'in the bosom of my family.' Ahem!"

She smoothed out an imaginary wrinkle in her bodice, an excuse for tarrying longer before the glass.

"He came to town with you, then?" ventured Sarah.

Lucy nodded.

"And promised to call this evening?"

"Right again, my dear!"

She was graver now, for she had conceived the happy notion of appropriating to her own use a cluster of white roses and buds she discovered in the vase on the marble slab under the mirror. If any thing could have enhanced the elegance of her figure and toilet, it was the coiffure she immediately set about arranging. The flowers were a present to Sarah from Lewis Hammond; but she thought little of him or of them, as Lucy laid them first on one, then the other side of her head, to try the effect.

"And you really care for him, sister?" came forth in such a timid, anxious tone, that Lucy burst into a fit of laughter.

"You dear little modest piece of romantic simplicity! One would suppose that you were popping the question yourself, from your behavior. Care for him? Why shouldn't I? I need not say 'yes' unless I do, need I?"

"But you take it so coolly! A betrothal is, to me, such a solemn thing."

"And to most other girls, perhaps. (There! if I only had a hair-pin. Don't rob yourself! thank you! Isn't that an improvement?) As I was saying, why should I pretend to be pensive and doleful, when I am as merry as a lark? or lovesick, when I have never lost a meal or an hour's sleep from the commencement of the courtship until now? That is not my style, Sarah. I am very practical in my views and feelings. Not that I don't play talking sentiment in our genuine love-scenes, and I really like unbounded devotion on the other side. It is decidedly pleasant to be adored. I was surprised to find how I enjoyed it."

"Oh, sister! sister!" Sarah leaned her forehead on the mantel, repelled and well-nigh disgusted by this heartless trifling—this avowed counterfeit—so abhorrent to her feelings. But Lucy was as much in earnest as she could be on such a theme. She went on, unheeding her sister's ejaculation.

"You must understand, of course, that we are not positively engaged. I gave him—Goldfinch—a good scolding for violating the rules of etiquette by addressing me while I was away from home; but it was just like him. He is as impulsive as he can live. To punish him I refused to answer him until after our return to New York, and his interview with father. He would have written to him on the spot, had I not forbidden him. He behaved so beautifully, that I consented to his taking charge of us to the city, and I suppose the rest must follow in good time. How melancholy your face is! Are you very much afflicted at the thought of losing me? Why, Sarah! my dear child, are those tears in your eyes? If she isn't crying in good earnest!"

And Lucy's musical laugh rolled through the rooms in her enjoyment of the joke. What else could it be to her, elate with her success in achieving the chief end of woman—the capture of a rich and handsome, in every respect an unexceptionable lover?

"Hist!" she said, raising her finger. "He has come! Your eyes are red! Run, and make yourself presentable!"

The door, opening from the hall into the front parlor, swung on its hinges as Sarah gained the comparative obscurity of the third and rear room. A strong impulse of interest or curiosity there arrested her flight to enable her to get a glimpse of her destined brother-in-law. Lucy had not mentioned his proper name, since her earliest letter from Newport had eulogized a certain George Finch, a Bostonian, wealthy, and attentive to herself. Sarah's backward glance fell upon the visitor as he met his queenly bride elect directly under the blazing chandelier.

It was *Philip Benson!*

Chained to the spot by weakness or horror, the looker-on stood motionless, while the suitor raised the lily fingers he held to his lips, and then led Lucy to a seat. His voice broke the spell. As the familiar cadences smote her ear, the sharp pain that ran through every fibre of her frame awakened Sarah from her stupor.

How she gained her room she never knew; but she had sense enough left to direct her flight to this refuge—and, when within, to lock the door. Then she threw up her arms with a piteous, wailing cry, and fell across the bed, dead for the time to further woe.

Alone and painfully she struggled back to consciousness. Sitting upright, she stared wonderingly around her, unable to recollect what had stricken her down. The chamber was imperfectly lighted by the rays of the street lamp opposite, and with the recognition of objects within its narrow limits there crept back to her all that had preceded her retreat thither. For the next hour she sat still—her head bowed upon her knees, amid the wrecks of her dream world.

Dreary and loveless as had been most of her previous life, she had never endured any thing like this, unless one miserable hour upon the Deal Beach, when Philip broke the tidings of his intended departure, were a slight foretaste of the agony, the utter despair, that claimed her now for its victim. Since then, she had been hopeful. His promise of a visit, the tokens of remembrance he had transmitted to her every week, had kept alive memory and expectation, and this was his coming! this the occasion she had pictured so fondly, painted with the brightest hues Love could borrow from imagination! She had heard again the voice that had haunted her dreams, from their parting until now —heard it in deeper, softer tones than it had ever taken in speech with her; heart-music which told that his seekings and yearnings for the one and only beloved were over. And was not *her* quest of years ended likewise? Truly, there are two senses in which every search, every combat may be said to be closed; one when the victor grasps his prize, or waves aloft his sword in the moment of triumph; the other, when, bleeding, maimed, or dying, the vanquished sinks to the earth without power to rise!

A tap at her door started Sarah. She did not stir until it was repeated, and her father called her name. A stream of light from the hall fell upon her face as she admitted him.

"Daughter, what ails you?" was his exclamation.

"I am not very well, father."

"I should think not, indeed! Come in here and lie down!" He led her to the bed, and, lighting the gas in the chamber, came back to her and felt her pulse.

She knew what was the direction of his fears; but to correct his misapprehension was to subject herself to further questioning. Passively she received the pressure of his hand upon her head, the gentle stroking of the disordered hair; but, when he stooped to kiss her, he felt that she trembled.

"Dear child! I shall never forgive myself if you have taken the fever from me!"

"I do not fear that, father. My head aches, and I am very tired. I have been so busy all day, you know."

"Yes, and for many other days. You are, without doubt, overworked. I hope this may prove to be all the matter with you. A night's rest may quite cure you."

"Yes, sir," she answered, chokingly. "You will excuse me to ——, down-stairs?"

"Certainly. Would you like to have your mother come up to you?"

"Oh, no, sir! Please tell her there is no need of it. I shall be better to-morrow."

"Your sister"—and he looked more serious, instead of smiling—"has a visitor. Her *friend* is an acquaintance of yours, also, it appears—the Mr. Benson whom you met at your aunt's in July."

"Yes, sir. I know it."

"I understood you to say that Lucy had never said positively who her lover was; but this was not the name you told me of, as the person whom you imagined him to be."

"I was misled for a time myself, sir," replied the poor girl, pressing her temples between her palms.

"I see that I am tiring you. Forgive me! but it is so natural to consult you in every thing. I must trouble you with some questions, which it is important should be answered to-night, before this gentleman and myself have any conversation. Is Mr. Benson a man whom you consider worthy of trust? Your mother represents him to be enormously wealthy—a reputation I had concluded he possessed, from Lucy's pet name for him. It is well that your sister has a prospect of marrying advantageously in this respect, for she would never be happy in an humble sphere; but antiquated people like myself regard other things as of greater consequence in concluding a bargain for a lifetime. Is your opinion of Mr. Benson favorable as to disposition, principles, and conduct?"

Sarah's head rested on the foot-board of her couch, in weariness or pain, as she rejoined: "I saw and heard nothing of him, during our intercourse in the country, that was not creditable. His uncle and aunt are very partial to him, and speak of his character in high terms. Their testimony ought to have weight with you, for they have known him from his boyhood up."

"It ought and does! I am relieved to hear all this! very much pleased!" said Mr. Hunt, emphatically. "I have all confidence in Nathan Benson's judgment and integrity. I hope his nephew is as sterling a man. Thus far," he continued, playfully, "I have learned but one thing to his discredit, and that is, that having seen this one of my daughters, he could afterwards fall in love with the other."

"I am not beautiful and good like Lucy, father."

"Very dear and lovely in my eyes, my child! Again forgive me for having worried your poor head with my inquiries. I was unwilling to decide a matter where Lucy's happiness was involved, without obtaining your evidence in the case. A last good-night! and God bless you, my dearest, best daughter!"

Sarah held up her face for his kiss without attempting to speak. This burning ordeal, the harder to endure because unexpected, was over. She was as weak as a child with conflicting passions when she arose and endeavored to undress. After stopping several times to regain breath and strength, she was at last ready to creep into bed, there to lie until morning broke, sleepless and suffering.

Her sharpened senses could discern her father and mother's voices in the sitting-room, in confidential talk—interrupted, by and by, by Lucy's pure mellow tones, apparently conveying some message to the former. Its import was easily surmised, for his step was then heard in the hall and on the stairs, until he reached the parlor where Philip awaited him. Their conference did not occupy more than twenty minutes, which time Lucy spent with her mother—how gayly, Sarah could judge by the laugh that, again and again, reached her room. Mr. Hunt returned, spoke a few sentences in his calm, grave way, and the closing door was followed by a flutter of silk and fall of gliding footsteps, as Lucy went down to her now formally and fully betrothed husband.

"Husband!" Yes! it was even so! Henceforth the lives of the pair were to be as one in interest, in aims, in affection. Erelong, they would have no separate outward existence in the eyes of the world. Was his chosen love, then, in a truer and higher sense, his other self—the being sought so long and carefully? The pretty *fiancée* would have stretched her cerulean orbs in amazed wonder at the ridiculous doubt, and asked, in her matter-of-fact way, how the thing could have happened, if it had not been intended? Philip's indignant affirmative would have gained fervor from his exultant consciousness of possession—so novel and sweet. But one above stairs, taught sagacity by the depth of her grief, looked further into the future than did they, and read there a different reply.

She heard the clang of the front door as it shut after the young lover, and, in the still midnight, the echoes, faint and fainter, of his retreating footsteps—the same free, light tread she used to hearken for in porch and hall of that riverside farm-house; and as the remembrance came over her she turned her face to the wall, murmuring passionately, "Oh! if I could never, never see him again!"

This feeling, whether born of cowardice or desperation,

was the ruling one, when her mother looked in upon her before breakfast, and expressed her concern at finding her still in bed.

"I am not well enough to get up, mother!" Sarah said sincerely, and Mrs. Hunt, reading in the parched lips and blood-shot eyes proof of the justice of the fears her husband had expressed to her the preceding evening, resolved that the doctor should see her "before she was two hours older."

In vain Sarah entreated that this should not be done, and prophesied her recovery without his assistance. For once her parents were a unit in sentiment and action, and the physician was summoned to his second patient.

"All febrile symptoms were to some extent contagious," he affirmed; "and while Mr. Hunt's malady was not generally classed with such, it was very possible that his daughter had contracted an analogous affection, in her constant attendance upon him."

This decision Sarah dared not overthrow, much as she wished to do so, when she saw how it afflicted her father.

Undaunted by any fears of infection, Lucy repaired to her sister's chamber when she had despatched her breakfast.

"Isn't it too provoking that you should be sick just at this time?" she began, perching herself, school-girl fashion, on the foot of the bed. "I really admired your staying up stairs last night; but I did not dream that you really were not well. I promise you that I made capital of your absence. I told Philip (how odd it sounds, doesn't it?) that you ran away when he rang the bell, because you had made a fright of yourself by crying over the prospect of my leaving you, and that I had no doubt that you had grieved yourself into a headache. He wanted to know forthwith if you objected to my marrying him; but I said 'No;' that you were charmed with the match, and preferred him to any other admirer I had ever had; but that we—you and I—were so devoted to one another, that it was acute agony to us to think of parting. About ten o'clock he asked to see father, and they soon settled affairs. When I went down again, he tried a little ring on my finger that he always wears, and it fitted nicely. So I knew what it meant when he put it back upon his own hand, and that with that for a measure he could not go wrong in getting the engagement-ring. I *do* hope it will be a diamond. Vic. West declares that she would not accept any thing else. I considered for a while whether I couldn't give him a delicate hint on the subject, but I did not see how I could manage it. And don't you think, while I was studying about this, he fancied I was sober over 'the irrevocable step I had taken,' and became miserable and eloquent at the suspicion! I wish I could remember all he said! It was more in your line than mine! But he is a good, sensible fellow, with all his romantic notions. He has a handsome fortune, independent of his father, left him by his grandfather, and we are to live in Georgia part of the year only, and travel every summer. Mother says his account of his prospects and so forth to father was very satisfactory, but she has not got at all the particulars yet. Father is so worried about your sickness that he cannot spare a thought for any thing or anybody else. The light from that window hurts your eyes—doesn't it? I will let down the shade."

But Sarah lay with her hand protecting her eyes, when her sister resumed her position and narration.

"We are to be married in December. He begged hard for an earlier day, but I was sure that I could not be ready before then. As it is, we shall have to hurry when it comes to the dresses, for, in order to get the latest fashions, we must wait until the eleventh hour. Won't I 'astonish the natives' down South? I couldn't state this to Philip, you know; so I referred him to mother, who is to say, when he asks her, that her preference would be to keep me just as long as she possibly can. *Entre nous*, my dear, our good mamma has said truer things than this bit of sentiment—but *n'importe!* These embellishments are necessary to such transactions."

Miss West's friendship or curiosity could not endure longer suspense, and the intelligence that she was below checked the monologue.

"I will run up again whenever I can," promised Lucy, by way of compensation for her abrupt departure, "and keep up your spirits by telling you all that I can about our concerns. But Philip is to take me to ride this afternoon. I forbade him to come here before then, but I don't much think that he can stay away. Don't be vexed if you don't see me again in some hours. Vic. and I are about to settle our trousseaux. If you believe me, we have never been able yet to decide upon the wedding-dresses!"

And she vanished, warbling delicious roulades from a duet she had engaged to sing that evening with her betrothed. She showed herself up-stairs again, when she was ready for her ride and the carriage at the door—very fair, very bright, and very happy. She was exquisitely dressed, and called on her sister to admire her toilet and envy her her escort.

Sarah listened to the cheerful exchange of cautions and promises between her mother and Philip, at the door beneath her open window, and to the rolling wheels that bore them away.

Mrs. Hunt received none of her friends that day, being busy "getting things to rights;" and for a like reason she absented herself from her child's sick-room, content with sending up Jeannie, now and then, to inquire how she was getting on. In the abject loneliness that oppressed her, when the first violence of passions had spent itself, Sarah would have been relieved in some measure by the society of this pet sister, the sole object upon earth, besides her father, that had ever repaid her love with any thing like equal attachment. But the child shrank, like most others of her age, from the quiet dark chamber of illness, and longed to follow her mother through the house, in her tour of observation and renovation. Sarah detected her restlessness and ill-concealed dislike of the confinement imposed upon her by compliance with her humble petition,—

"Please, Jeannie, stay a little while with your poor sister!" And her sensitive spirit turned upon itself, as a final stroke of torture, the conviction that *here*, also, love and care had been wasted.

"Go, then!" she said, rather roughly, as Jeannie wavered, "and you need not come up again to-day. I know it is not pleasant for you to be here. Tell mother I want nothing but quiet."

"I have had a splendid drive!" said Lucy, rustling her many flounces into the door at dusk.

The figure upon the bed made no response by motion or word.

"I do believe she is asleep!" added the intruder, lowering her voice. "I suppose she is tired and needs rest." And she went out on tiptoe.

Sarah was awake a minute later, when her father came in to see her. She smiled at him, as he "hoped she was better," and asked whether she might not get up on the morrow. Mr. Hunt thought not. The doctor's opinion was that perfect repose might ward off the worse features of the disease. She had better keep her bed for a couple of days yet, even should she feel well enough to be about. He sent up her dinner to her room with his own hands; and when she learned this, she strove to do some feeble justice to the viands, but without success.

Philip dined with the family that day by special appointment; and, shortly after his arrival, Lucy again presented herself in that small third-story bedroom.

"Choose! which hand will you take?" she cried, hiding both behind her.

Sarah would make no selection; and, after a little more trifling, the elder sister brought into sight two elegant bouquets, and laid them beside the invalid.

"This is Philip's present—'a fraternal remembrance,' he told me to say. Here is his card. Doesn't he write a lovely hand? The other is from your admirer, Mr. Hammond. What a sly puss you were to make such a catch as he is, without dropping us a hint! He is rather too sober for my notions; but he is getting rich fast, they say. He left those flowers at the door himself, and insisted upon seeing father for a moment, to know exactly how you were. Cannot you hurry up somewhat, and let us have a double wedding? I showed the bouquet to Philip, and told him of your conquest, and he was as much pleased at your prospects as I was. Did you ever see such magnificent roses? your beau paid five dollars, at the lowest computation, for these flowers. I congratulate you upon these signs of liberality!"

Sarah had heard only a portion of this speech. Her eyes were fixed upon the card her sister had put into her hand: "Will Miss Sarah accept this trifling token of regard from one who is her stanch friend, and hopes, in time, to have a nearer claim upon her esteem?"

"Very neatly turned, is it not?" said Lucy, satisfiedly. She had read it on her way up-stairs. "What shall I say to him from you?"

"Thank him, and explain that I am not able to write a reply."

This meagre return of compliments assumed a tone both grateful and sisterly as Lucy rehearsed it to the donor of the fragrant offering. The barest phrase of civility came gracefully and meaningly from her tongue. Serene in mind and countenance, she seated herself at the piano, and, as Philip took his stand at her side, he wondered if the world held another couple more entirely adapted each to the peculiar soul-needs of the other, more perfectly happy in the knowledge of mutual affection. Like the generality of theorists, your student of human nature is prone to grievous error when he reduces his flawless system to practice.

In one respect, the two certainly harmonized well. Both loved music; both sang finely, and their voices accorded without a jarring note.

Mr. Hunt read the evening papers in Sarah's room; turning and folding them with great circumspection, lest their rattling might annoy her, and detract from her enjoyment of the music. How could he guess the infatuation that caused her to listen greedily to sounds, under whose potent spell feeling was writhing and brain reeling? In every pause between the songs there arose in her memory two lines of a poem read long ago, when or where she knew not:—

> "Seek not to soothe that proud, forsaken heart
> With strains *whose sweetness maddens as they fall!*"

The performers had just completed a duet, in which each voice supported and developed, while blending with the other, when Lucy took up the prelude to a simpler lay; repeating it twice over with skilful variations, as if she were, meantime, carrying on a colloquy with her companion, that delayed the vocal part. This was ended by Philip's raising alone the burden of the plaintive German air Sarah remembered so truly—"The long, long, weary day."

As his voice, full and strong, with its indescribable and irresistible under-current of pathos—flowing out here into passionate melancholy—swelled and floated through the quiet house, Sarah sat upright.

"Father! father!" she whispered, huskily, "I cannot bear that! Shut the doors!—all of them, or I shall go mad!"

She was obeyed; Mr. Hunt hurrying down to the parlors to silence the lovers, with the representation that Sarah was too nervous to endure the excitement of music. For the remainder of the evening, a profound stillness pervaded the upper part of the mansion—a silence that, to Sarah, throbbed with the melody she had tried to hush; and look where she might, she gazed into that rainy, ghastly night—the pale, comfortless watcher, the shadowy type of *her* deeper, more blighting sorrow.

CHAPTER VIII.

For three days Philip Benson lingered near his beautiful enslaver; on the fourth, he carried a sad, yet trustful heart upon his Southern journey. Sarah had not seen him once since the evening of his coming. Through Lucy, she received his adieux and wishes for her speedy recovery. On the next day but one she left her room, and appeared again in the family circle—now complete in all its parts.

In that short season of bodily prostration, the work of years had been wrought upon her inner life. Outwardly there was little alteration save that effected by physical weakness; but in her views of existence and character, of affections and motives, the doubter had become the skeptic; the dreamer the misanthrope. To the gentler and more womanly aspirations that had for a season supplanted the somewhat masculine tendencies of her mind and tastes had succeeded a stoicism, like the frozen calm of a winter's day, uniform as relentless. This was the surface that locked and concealed the lower depths she had sworn should be forever covered. Others could and did live without hearts. She could thrive as well upon the husks and Sodom apples of this world's goods as did they; holding as Life's chief good, complete and final subjugation of all genuine emotion, which, at the best, was but the rough ore—fit for nothing until purged, refined, and polished in its glitter. She found no other creed that suited her present desperate mood so well as the most heartless code of the thorough worldling—the devotee to show, and fashion, and wealth.

Such was her mother, whose domestic virtues were extolled by all who knew her; such, behind her mask of tender grace and amiability, the sister who had won, by these factitious attractions, the heart for which Sarah would have perilled life, sacrificed ease and inclination, bowed her proud spirit to the estate of bond-servant to his every caprice, become the willing slave to his tyrannical behest. Yet Philip Benson was a professed judge of character; a man of sense, education, and experience, and, knowing both girls as he did, he had made his choice; set the stamp of his approval upon the shining, rather than the solid metal. The world, as its young would-be disciple believed she had at length learned, was made up of two classes: those who floated, and those who sank. To the latter she determined that she would *not* belong.

These and kindred thoughts were rife in her mind, and stirring up many a spring of gall within her bosom, one morning as she lay back in an arm-chair in the sitting-room, listening with secret scorn to the prattle of the pair of betrothed maidens—Lucy and her friend. Lucy's engagement-ring *was* a diamond, or, rather, a modest cluster of these precious stones, whose extreme beauty did not strike the casual eye with the startling effect of Victoria's more showy *gage d'amour*. This apparent difference in the value of the two was the source of many discussions and considerable heart-burning, disguised, of course, and threatened in time to produce a decided coolness between the attached wearers of the articles under debate.

On this particular day, Victoria, after some adroit skirmishing, brought out as a "poser" the fact that, to lay the question to rest without more ado, she had, since their last interview, been to Tiffany's, and had her ring valued. Lucy's face was all aglow as her soul-sister named the price of her treasure. She clapped her hands joyously.

"Isn't that the joke of the season, mother?"—as that personage entered. "Don't you think that Vic. was as cunning as we were? She carried her ring to Tiffany's yesterday, too. Wouldn't it have been *too* funny if we had met there? Mine came from there, they said, and it cost a cool fifty dollars more than yours did, dear!"

Victoria flushed hotly; but further controversy being useless and dangerous to her, she acquiesced with assumed carelessness in Lucy's proposal, that, since both were suited, the rival brilliants should not be again referred to as a disputed matter. They accordingly turned to the safer and endless conferences upon the trousseaux, whose purchase must be commenced immediately.

Their incomplete lists were produced, compared, and lengthened—Mrs. Hunt suggesting and amending; Sarah surveying the busy group with the same intense disdain she had experienced throughout the conversation.

"Oh, I forgot to tell you! Margaret Hauton called on me yesterday!" exclaimed Victoria. "Did she come here, too?"

"Yes; but we were out. What *did* she say?" queried Lucy, breathlessly.

"Why, the stupid creature never alluded to my engagement; and when I mentioned yours, pretended not to have heard of it before. I took care she should not go away as ignorant on the subject as she had come, and—I know it was wicked in me, but she deserved it—all the time I was praising your Goldfinch, and telling how handsome and liberal he was, I sat looking down at my new ring, slipping it up and down my finger, as if I were not thinking of it, but of the giver. She could not help seeing it, and, to save her life, she could not keep from changing countenance."

"Good!" said Lucy. "Do tell me how she is looking now?"

"Common enough! She had on that everlasting lilac silk, with the embroidered flounces, although the style is as old as the hills—and that black lace mantle, which, happening to be real, she never leaves off until near Christmas. But her hat! black and corn-color. Think of it! corn-color against her saffron skin! When *I* pretend to lead society, I hope to dress decently. But I had my revenge for her supercilious airs. Mr. Bond—George—called in the afternoon to take me to ride. I told you of the handsome span of fast horses he has been buying. Well! we concluded to try the Bloomingdale road, and just as we were sailing along, like the wind, whom should we overtake but my Lady Hauton, lounging in her lazy way (she thinks it aristocratic!) on the back seat of her father's heavy, clumsy barouche—not a soul in it but her mother and herself. Didn't I bow graciously to her as we flew by! and again, as we met them creeping along, when we were coming back? I wouldn't have missed the chance of mortifying her for a thousand dollars."

Lucy laughed, with no sign of disapprobation at the coarse, vindictive spirit displayed in this petty triumph of a small soul.

"How many evening-dresses have you put down on your paper, Vic.?"

"Half a dozen only. I will get others as I need them. The styles in these change so often that I do not care to have too many at a time."

"There you will have the advantage of me," said Lucy, ingenuously. "It will not be so easy a matter to replenish my stock of wearable dresses. I wish I had asked Philip about the Savannah stores. I wonder if he knows any thing about them?"

"He ought to—being such a connoisseur in ladies' dress. I declare I have been absolutely afraid of him since

I heard him say that he considered a lady's apparel a criterion of her character."

"He has exquisite taste!" said Lucy, with pardonable pride in her lover. "It is a positive pleasure to dress for him. He sees and appreciates every thing that I could wish to have him notice. He has often described to me what I wore, and how I looked and acted the evening he fell in love. How little we can guess what is before us! I did not care to go to the hop that night, for Mr. Finch was to wait on me, and he was so stupid, you know, after we discovered that it was a mistake about his being rich. I think I see him now, with his red face and short neck! Oh dear! the fun we had over that poor man! I told you—didn't I, Sarah—that we named him Bullfinch, because he looked so much like one? When Phil. came we called him Goldfinch, and the two went by these names among us girls. The Bullfinch heard of it, and he was ridiculously angry! So I put on a white tarlatan, that one with the double jupe, you know, Vic., festooned with white moss rose-buds, and I had nothing but a tea-rose in my hair. I danced once with the Bullfinch—one of those solemn quadrilles that are only fit for grandmothers—and vowed to myself that I would not stand up again, except for a Polka or the Lancers. While I was sitting down by the window, saying 'Yes' and 'No,' when Bullfinch spoke, Mr. Newman introduced 'Mr. Benson' to 'Miss Hunt,' and the work was done!"

"No more waltzing, then!" was Victoria's slyly malicious sequel.

"I did not care so much for that as I thought I should!" replied easy-tempered Lucy. "You cannot find a man who has not some drawback. Before I had a chance for another round, mother there managed to telegraph me that my fresh acquaintance was worth catching. She had gotten his whole story out of Mrs. Newman. He let me know, pretty soon, that he had some queer scruples about fancy dances, and I thought it best to humor him for one evening, or until I should ascertain whether he was really 'taken' or not. I have never repented my self-denial, although I grant that it cost me a struggle to give up 'the German.' "

"George lets me waltz to my heart's content," said Victoria. "He is the very soul of indulgence. As to laces—I have not a thing fit to wear. I must get every thing new. I am glad of it! I enjoy shopping for them. If I have a passion, it is for laces!"

A sneer curled Sarah's lip, and Victoria, happening to glance that way, could not mistake its application, whatever she might surmise as to its origin.

"I suppose you despise us as a couple of love-sick girls, Sarah?" she said, with a simper designed to be sentimental, whereas it was spiteful instead.

"I think love the least dangerous of your complaints," was the rejoinder.

"What do you mean?"

"Just what I said!"

"She means that people do not die of love in these days," exclaimed Lucy, whose pleasure-loving nature always shuddered at the idea of altercation in her presence; her sensations, during the occasional sparrings of her sister and her friend, bearing a strong resemblance to those of an innocent white rabbit, into whose burrow a couple of belligerent hedgehogs have forced their way.

"You will understand us better one day, when your turn comes," said Victoria, with magnanimous condescension. "I shall remind you then of your good opinion of us."

"You may."

"I would give any thing to have you engaged, just to see how you would behave. Would not you, Lucy?"

"Yes; if she were likely to do as well as we are doing. Philip says that you have many fine qualities, Sarah. He quite admires you."

The complacent betrothed had none but the most amiable intentions in making this patronizing speech; therefore, the angry blood that surged over her sister's face at hearing it would have been to her but the blush of gratified vanity, had not the sparkle of her eye and the contemptuous contortion of her mouth undeceived her.

"Indeed he did say so!" she hastened to repeat. "And he was in earnest! He said something else which I don't mind telling, now that he belongs to me fast and sure. He said that he sat up until twelve o'clock one night after you had been out boating, deliberating whether he should be smitten with you or not. There!"

The color retreated as quickly as it had come. But for the consciousness of Victoria's malicious scrutiny, Sarah could not have summoned strength to utter a word.

"An equivocal compliment, I must say!" she retorted, sarcastically. "Your gallant Georgian's confessions must have been ample and minute indeed, if they comprised such distant approaches to love affairs as the one you honor me by mentioning. I do not think that I have ever heard of another case where a gentleman considered it necessary to enumerate to his *fiancée*, not merely the ladies he had loved, but those whom he had not!" She arose and left the room.

Poor Lucy, rebuffed and overwhelmed, caught her astonished breath with a sigh. "Can anybody tell me what I have done *now* to fret Sarah? She is so cross since she was sick!"

"And before, too!" mutely added Victoria's shrug and lifted eyebrows.

"We must bear with her, my dear!" said the prudent mother. "Her nerves are affected, the doctor says."

Victoria made random pencillings upon the important list—her thoughts in fast pursuit of a notion that had just struck her. She was neither witty nor intelligent; but she possessed some natural shrewdness and a great deal more acquired cunning. She detested Sarah Hunt, and the prospect of obtaining an engine that should humble her arrogant spirit was scarcely less tempting than her own chance of effecting an advantageous matrimonial settlement.

While she was engaged in defining her suspicion to herself, and concerting measures for gathering information with regard to it, Mrs. Hunt went out on some household errand, and Lucy was obliged to descend to the parlor to see callers.

"Don't go until I come back, Vic. It is the Dunhams, and they never stay long," she said, at quitting her associate.

"Oh, I always make myself at home here, you know, my dear!" was the reply.

Jeannie was sitting on a cushion near the chair Sarah had occupied, dressing her doll.

"It won't fit!" she cried, fretfully, snatching off a velvet basque she had been endeavoring to adjust to the lay-figure.

"Bring it to me! I can fix it!" offered Victoria, winningly. "It's too tight just here, you see. I will rip open the seam and alter it. Who makes your dolly's clothes?"

She was well aware that but one member of the family ever had leisure to bestow upon such follies; but it suited her plan for Jeannie to introduce her name.

"Sister Sarah."

"This is a pretty basque. When did she make it?"

"Yesterday."

"Oh! I thought perhaps she did it while you were in the country, and that the doll had fattened as much as you did there."

Jeannie laughed heartily.

"You had a nice time there, I suppose?" pursued Victoria.

"I guess we did!" Her eyes danced at the recollection. "A splendid time! I wish we lived at Aunt Sarah's! There isn't room for me to move in this narrow house."

"Mr. Benson was there a day or two, was he not?"

"Yes, ma'am—a great many days! He took us all around the country in Uncle Nathan's carriage. I love him very dearly!"

"Did you ever go sailing with him?"

"Every evening, when it was clear, in a pretty row-boat. He used to take his guitar along, and sing for us. He sings beautifully! Did you ever hear him?"

"Oh, yes! Did your sister always go boating with you?"

The spy, with all her hardihood, lowered her voice, and felt her face warm as she put this leading question.

"Yes, ma'am, always. Mr. Benson would not have gone without her, I guess."

"Why do you guess so?"

The little girl smiled knowingly. "Because—you won't tell, will you?"

"Why no! Of course I will not."

"Charley said it was a secret, and that I mustn't say any thing to sister or Mr. Benson about it, for they would be angry."

"Who is Charley?"

"Don't you know? He is Aunt Sarah's son. He is deaf and dumb; but he showed me how to spell on my fingers. He is a nice boy—"

"Yes; but what was the secret?"

"He said that Mr. Benson—cousin Phil. I call him when I am talking to him—was sister's beau; and he would take me off with him when we went to drive or walk, because, you know, they might not like to have me hear what they were talking about. They used to talk, and talk, and talk! and sister had a great deal more to say, and looked prettier than she does at home. I will tell you something else, if you won't ever let anybody know it. I never told Aunt Sarah even, only Charley. Sister cried ever so long the night after Cousin Phil. went away. She woke me up sobbing; but I made believe that I was asleep; and in the morning her pillow was right wet. Charley said that all ladies that he had read about in his books did so when their beaux left them."

"See here, my little lady!" said the dissembler, with a startling change of tone. "You are altogether mistaken—you and Charley both! Mr. Benson is going to marry your sister Lucy, and never was a beau of Sarah's. Be very careful not to talk about Charley's wicked story to your father, or mother, or sisters, for they would be very much displeased, and maybe punish you for repeating such fibs. Little girls ought never to hear or know any thing about courting or beaux—it's naughty! I won't tell on you, if you will promise never to do so again. I am shocked at you! Now take your dolly and go!"

The frightened child encountered Lucy at the door. Miss West had calculated her time to a minute. Her eyes swimming in tears, her features convulsed with the effort to keep back sob and outcry, Jeannie started up to her attic playroom. Sarah's door was ajar, and engaged as she was with thoughts of her own troubles and insults, she could not but remark the expression of her darling's face, in the momentary glimpse she had as it passed.

"Jeannie! come back!" she called.

The child hesitated, half way up the next flight. Sarah repeated the summons, and seeing that it was not obeyed, went up and took the rebel by the hand.

"What is the matter with you?"

A reddening and distortion of visage, and no reply. Her sister led her back to her chamber, shut the door, and put her arms around her.

"Tell me what ails you, dear!"

Jeannie fell upon her comforter's neck—the repressed torrent breaking through all restraint. "Oh, sister, I can't help crying! Miss Vic. West has been scolding me!"

"Scolding you! She! I will go down and speak to her this instant! How *dared* she?"

"No, no! please don't! She told me not to say any thing to you about it."

"The contemptible coward!" said Sarah, between her teeth. "How came you to have any thing to do with her?"

"Mother and sister Lucy went down-stairs, and she said she would alter my doll's basque, and—and—and" a fresh burst of lamentation.

"There, that will do, pet! I see that she only made it worse!" soothed Sarah, believing that, in the unfinished state of dolly's wardrobe, she had discovered the root of the trouble. "Never mind, dear! I will set all that to rights directly. Now wipe your eyes, and let me tell you something. This afternoon father is to take me to ride, and you shall go, too. As for Miss Victoria, we will let her pass, and keep out of her way, hereafter."

Secretly, she was very angry—far more so than she was willing to have the child suspect. As the patient fingers repaired the effects of the original bad fit, and Miss West's meddling, Jeannie stood by, thankful and interested, yet ashamed to look her wronged sister in the eyes. Not that she had the remotest conception of the mischief that might grow out of her imprudent disclosures; but she had broken faith with Charley, been accused of tattling and indelicacy, and warned too stringently against repeating the offence to suffer her to relieve her conscience by a full confession to the being she most loved and honored.

At four o'clock Sarah and her charge were ready, according to Mr. Hunt's appointment. The carriage was likewise punctual; but from it stepped, not the parent of the expectant girls, but a younger and taller man—in short, Mr. Hunt's particular favorite—Lewis Hammond. Jeannie, who had stationed herself at an upper window to watch for her father's appearance, was still exclaiming over this disappointment, and wondering why "Mr. Hammond must call just now to keep sister at home," when the footman brought up a note to Sarah.

It was from Mr. Hunt, explaining the cause of his unlooked-for detention at the bank, and stating that Mr. Hammond, whom he had met earlier in the day, and acquainted with his design of giving his daughter this ride, happened to drop in, and seeing him engaged with business, had asked leave to officiate as his substitute in the proposed airing. He urged Sarah to take Jeannie along, and not hesitate to accept Mr. Hammond's polite attendance, adding, in phrase brief, but sincere, how lightly he should esteem his hour of extra labor, if he knew that she was not a sufferer by it.

Sarah passed the note to her mother, and drew her shawl about her shoulders.

"Of course you'll go!" said Mrs. Hunt, radiant with gratification. "It is perfectly proper, and Mr. Hammond is very kind, I'm sure."

She was hurrying towards the door to convey in person her thanks for his gallantry, when Sarah spoke firmly and very coolly:

"I will say whatever is necessary to Mr. Hammond, if you please, mother. I shall go because father wishes it, *and for no other reason.* Come, Jeannie!"

"Won't she be in your way?" asked Mrs. Hunt, awed, but not extinguished.

"No, madam."

Sarah suffered Mr. Hammond to place her in the carriage, and himself opposite to her; and keeping before her mind carefully the fact that he was her father's friend, perhaps the savior of his life, she unbent, as much as she could, from her distant, ungracious bearing, to sustain her part of the conversation. She must have been purblind not to see through her mother's wishes, and manœuvres for their accomplishment; but to these views she was persuaded that Mr. Hammond was no party. She saw in him a sedate, rather reserved gentleman of thirty-two or three, who had passed the heyday of youthful loves and joys; sensible and cultivated to an uncommon degree for a man of business—for such he emphatically was.

A poor boy in the beginning, he had fortunately attracted the regard of a thriving New York merchant, and retained that favor through the years that had elevated him from the lowest clerkship to a partnership in the now opulent firm. For probity and punctuality no man in the city had a higher reputation; but his virtues were of that quiet nature which, while they inevitably retain regard once won, are slow to gain admiration. To matrimonial speculators, as in financial circles, he was known as a "safe chance," and many a prudent mamma on his list of acquaintances would have rejoiced had he selected her daughter as mistress of his heart and fortune. Whether he was aware of this or not could not have been determined by his modest, but dignified deportment. He did not avoid company; went whither he was invited, and, when there, comported himself like a conscientious member of society, talking, dancing, or listening, with as due regard to law and order as he manifested in his daily business life. Fast girls called him "awfully matter-of-fact," and "terribly sensible;" fast youths of the other sex put him down among the "old fogies," and wondered what he did with his money. "Could it be possible that he *saved* it!" He was intimate nowhere except in the household of his whilom employer and present partner, whose daughters were all married and settled in houses of their own. If he had ever cared to look twice at the same lady, the watchful world had not yet laid hold of this marvellous departure from his fixed habits.

His intercourse with Mr. Hunt's family was, as we know, purely accidental in its commencement, and in its earlier stages might have been induced by humanity or friendship for the sick father. In Sarah's brain there had never arisen a suspicion of any ulterior motive in the pointed attentions directed of late to herself. Before Lucy's return, the care of her invalid parent and her day-dreams had engrossed heart and thought to an extent that precluded much inquiry into other themes. Since that memorable night, inward torture had abstracted her mind still more from outward impressions.

This afternoon she talked calmly and indifferently to Mr. Hammond, without an idea that he made any greater effort to please her. To Jeannie she was tender beyond her usual showing, in remembrance of the wrong done the sensitive child in the forenoon. Mr. Hammond emulated her in kindness to the third member of their party; and in the course of their ride, raised himself unwittingly to the rank of rivalship with "Cousin Philip," her model gentleman.

Mr. Hunt came out to assist his daughter to alight, upon their return. There was a heartiness in his acknowledgment of his deputy's politeness, and invitation to enter the house and pass the evening with them, which Sarah had seldom heard him employ towards any visitor. Mr. Hammond may have remarked it likewise, for his declinature was evidently against his inclination, and coupled with a promise to call at an early day. His visits were not altogether so agreeable as formerly, for he was received in the spacious parlors on a footing with other callers, and in the presence of several members of the family; still he came repeatedly, with pretext and without, until his sentiments and design were a secret to no one except their object.

Wrapped in the sad thoughts that isolated her from the rest of the world, even while she made a part of its show, Sarah omitted to mark many things that should have been significant signs of under-currents, and tokens of important issues to her and those about her. Lucy had ceased to harp perpetually upon her lover's perfections and idolatrous flattery to herself, and while the wedding arrangements went vigorously forward, the disengaged sister was rarely annoyed by references to her taste and demands for her sympathy. There had never existed much congeniality between the two, and their common ground was now exceedingly narrow. Lucy was gentle and pleasant, peacefully egotistic as ever, and Sarah understood her too well to expect active affection or disinterestedness. The only part of her behavior to herself to which she took mental exception was a certain pitying forbearance, a compassionate leniency with respect to her faults and foibles, that had grown upon her of late. Once or twice the younger sister had become so restive under this gratuitous charity as to reply sharply to the whey-like speeches of the mild elder, and, without any appearance of wounded feeling, yet with not a word of apology or reason for so doing, Lucy had left the apartment, and never hinted at the circumstance afterwards.

Lucy was certainly the soul, the very cream of amiability. It was unaccountable to her admirers—and they included most of her associates—that Lewis Hammond, with his peculiar habits and tastes, should prefer that severe-looking, strong-minded Sarah. But be it remembered that he had learned this love under far different influences; in circumstances wholly unlike those in which he now beheld its object. His respect for unobtrusive intent and feeling; his longing for a home which should be the abode of sacred domestic virtues; and the sweet peace that had fled from the habitations frequented only by the frivolous, heartless, and vain—these found in the sick-room of the father, and the affectionate fidelity of the daughter, something so like the embodiment of his fancy of earthly happiness, that he accepted as a benignant fate the accident which had admitted him to the arcana of their private life. Sarah's temporary illness had taught him the meaning of his dreams, by seeming to peril the chances of their fulfilment; and from that hour he strove patiently and sedulously, as it was his habit, to seek all great ends for the acquisition of the heart whose depth he, perhaps, of all who knew her, best understood.

The most impatient person of those directly or indirectly concerned in the progress of this wooing was Mrs. Hunt. Her husband, with unwonted firmness, had forbidden that any one of the household should speak a word in raillery or otherwise to Sarah touching Mr. Hammond's intentions. "However earnestly I may desire his success," he said to his wife—"and there is no man living whom I would rather call 'son'—I would not influence her by the weight of a single syllable. Hers is the happiness or the misery of a life with her husband—whomsoever she may choose, and hers shall be the entire choice. If she can love and marry Lewis Hammond, I shall be gratified; if not, she shall never guess at my disappointment."

"La, Mr. H.! you are as foolish and sentimental as the girl herself! For my part, I ain't such a saint, and I *do* say, that if Sarah Hunt allows such a catch as this to slip through her fingers, she shall hear a piece of my mind!"

"I insist," said Mr. Hunt, with immovable resolution, "that Sarah shall be allowed to follow the guidance of her own will in this matter. It is not often that I interfere with your plans; but in this one instance I must be obeyed!"

With which astounding declaration of equal rights, if not of sovereignty, he left his consort to her reflections.

Ignorant of the delicate watchfulness maintained over her by this best of friends, Sarah walked on her beclouded way —without hope, without one anticipation of any future dissimilar to her present, until awakened with a shock by a formal declaration of love from Lewis Hammond.

CHAPTER IX.

It was at the close of an evening party which both the Hunts attended, and where Mr. Hammond's devotion was as marked as any thing so modest could be, that Sarah felt him slip an envelope into her hand, as he put her into the carriage. Surprised as she was at the singularity of the occurrence, and disposed to take offence at the familiarity it implied, she had yet the presence of mind to conceal the missive from Lucy, and talk about other things, until they were set down at home. In the privacy of her chamber, she broke the seal and read her first love-letter.

It was a characteristic composition. If the strong hand had trembled above the lines, the clear, clerkly penmanship did not witness to the weakness. Nor was there any thing in the subject-matter that did not appear to Sarah as business-like and unimpassioned. It was a frank and manly avowal of attachment for her; a compliment implied, rather than broadly stated, to her virtues; the traits that had gained his esteem, then his love—a deprecatory sentence as to his ability to deserve the treasure he dared to ask—and then the *question!* in plain black and white, unequivocal to bluntness, simple and direct to curtness.

"As he would ask the price of a bale of goods!" burst forth Sarah, indignant, as she threw the paper on the floor, and buried her burning face in her hands.

"That there comes sometimes a glory to the Present, beside which the hues of Past and Future fade and are forgotten, I must and will believe. Such, it seems to me, must be the rapture of acknowledged and reciprocal affection!" This was the echo memory repeated to her soul. She saw again the gently gliding river, with its waves of crimson and gold; breathed the pure fragrance of the summer evening; floated on, towards the sunset, with the loved voice in her ear; the dawn of a strange and beautiful life, shedding blissful calm throughout her being.

And from this review, dangerous as it was, for one fleeting instant, sweet, she returned to the proposal that had amazed and angered her. Lewis's undemonstrative exterior had misled her, as it did most persons, in the estimate of his inner nature. Kind, she was compelled to confess that he was, in the remembrance of his goodness to her father; his demeanor was always gentlemanly, and she had caught here and there rumors of his generosity to the needy that prevented a suspicion of sordidness. No doubt he was very well in his way; but he wanted to marry *her!* With the intensity of her fiery spirit, her will arose against the presumptuous request. It was the natural recoil of the woman who already loves, at the suggestion of a union with another than the man of her choice; the spontaneous outspeaking of a heart whose allegiance vows have been pledged and cannot be nullified. But she would not see this. Upon the unfortunate letter and its writer descended the storm of passionate repugnance aroused by its contents. With the reaction of excited feeling came tears—a plentiful shower that relaxed the overwrought nerves, until they were ready to receive the benediction of sleep.

Lewis had not asked a written or verbal reply.

"I will call to take you to drive to-morrow afternoon," he wrote. "Should your decision upon the question I have proposed be favorable, your consent to accompany me in my ride will be understood as a signal that you have accepted my graver suit. If your conclusion is adverse to my hopes, you can signify the same to me in a letter, to be handed me when I ask for you. This course will spare us both embarrassment—perhaps pain. In any event, be assured that you will ever have a firm friend in

"Yours truly,

"LEWIS HAMMOND."

Sarah's lip curled as she reperused this clause of the letter on the following morning.

"It is a comfort to know that I have not to answer for the sin of breaking my ardent suitor's heart!" she said, as she drew towards her the sheet upon which she was to indite her refusal. It was brief and courteous—freezing in its punctilious civility, and prepared without a pang, or a solitary misgiving that its reception would not be philosophically calm. Her design was to intrust it to the footman, to be delivered when Mr. Hammond called; and as the hour approached at which the expectant was to present himself, she took the note from the desk, and started downstairs with it.

The sitting-room door was open, and, aware that Victoria West was in there with Lucy, Sarah trod very softly as she neared it. Her own name arrested her as she was going by. She stopped involuntarily.

"I thought Sarah a girl of better regulated mind," said Victoria, in a tone of censorious pity. "Of course she suffers! It is the inevitable consequence of an unrequited attachment. Such miserable folly, such unpardonable weakness brings its punishment with it. But my sympathies are all yours, my dearest. I only wish you were not so sensitive. You are not to blame for her blind mistake."

"I cannot help it!" said Lucy, plaintively. "It seems so

sad that I should be made the means of depriving her of happiness. I wish I had never known that she was attached to poor Philip. I can't tell you how awkward I feel when any allusion is made in her hearing to the dear fellow, or to our marriage."

"I meant it for the best, dear, in telling you of my discovery," replied Victoria, slightly hurt.

"I know that, my dear creature! And it is well that I should not be kept in the dark as to the state of her affections. I only hope that Philip never penetrated her secret. I should die of mortification for her, if he were to find it out. It is a lamentable affair—and I am sure that he is not in fault. What did you say that you gave for that set of handkerchiefs you showed me yesterday?"

"The cheapest things you ever saw! I got them at Stewart's, and they averaged six dollars apiece! As to Mr. Benson, I trust, with you, that he is as unsuspecting as he seems; but he has remarkable discernment, you know. What I could not help seeing, before I had any other proof than her behavior, is not likely to have escaped him."

Half an hour later the twain were disturbed in their confidences by the sound of wheels stopping before the house, followed by a ring at the door. Victoria, ever on the alert, peeped, with feline caution and curiosity, around the edge of the curtain.

"What is going to happen? Look, Lucy! Mr. Hammond in a handsome light carriage, and driving a lovely pair of horses! I never thought to see him go in such style. How well he looks! Take care! he will see you!"

Both dodged as he glanced at the upper windows; but resumed their look-out in time to see the light that was kindled in his face when Sarah emerged from the front door. He was at her side in a second, to lead her down the steps, and his manner in this movement, and in assisting her into the carriage, the more striking in one generally so self-contained and deliberate, inspired the pair of initiated observers with the same conviction. As the spirited horses disappeared into the Avenue, the friends drew back from their loop-hole, and stared each other in the eyes, with the simultaneous exclamation—"They are engaged!"

They *were* engaged! Lewis felt it with a glad bound of the heart—but a minute before sickening in deadly suspense: felt, as he seated himself by *her* side, that the sorrows of a lonely and struggling youth, the years of manhood's isolation and unsatisfied longings, were swept from memory by this hour of abundant, unalloyed happiness.

And Sarah felt it! As her hand touched his, at their meeting upon the steps, a chill ran through her frame that told the consummation of the sacrifice which was to atone for past folly; to silence, and brand as a lying rumor, the fearful tale that bruited abroad the revelation of that weakness. In her mad horror at the knowledge of its discovery, she had rushed upon this alternative. Better an estate of honorable misery, than to live on, solitary, disgraced, condemned and pitied by her meanest foe! Now that the irreversible step was taken, she experienced no sharp regret, no wild impulse of retreat, but a gradual sinking of spirit into hopeless apathy.

Her veil concealed her dull eyes and stolid features, and to Lewis's happy mood there was nothing surprising or discouraging in her disposition to silence. With a tact for which she had not given him credit, and did not now value aright, he refrained from any direct reference to their altered relation until they were returning homeward. Then changing his tone of pleasant chat for one of deeper meaning, he said:—

"I have dared to hope much—every thing—from your consent to become my companion for this afternoon. Before I ventured to address you directly, I had a long and frank conversation with your father."

"What did he say?" asked Sarah, turning towards him for the first time.

"He referred me to you for my answer, which, he said, must be final and positive, since he would never attempt to influence your choice. In the event of an affirmative reply from you, he promised that his sanction should not be withheld."

Sarah was silent. She comprehended fully her father's warm interest in his friend's suit, which the speaker was too diffident to imply, and how this expression of his wishes set the seal upon her fate.

"We are poor and proud! Mr. Hammond is rich and seeks to marry me!" was her bitter thought. "It is a fine bargain in the eyes of both my parents. It would be high treason in me to dispute their will. Mr. Hammond has conceived the notion that I am a useful domestic character, a good housekeeper and nurse, and he is willing to bid liberally for my services. It is all arranged between them! Mine is a passive part, to copy Lucy's sweet, submissive ways for a season, for fear of frightening away the game, afterwards to attend to my business, while he looks after his. I have chosen my lot, and I will abide by it!"

"Have I your permission to call this evening and inform your father of my success—may I say of our engagement?" asked Lewis.

"It is best, I suppose, to call things by their right names," replied Sarah, in a cold voice, that was to him only coy. He smiled, and was about to speak, when she resumed: "Since we are virtually engaged"—she caught her breath as she brought out the word—"I see no reason why we should hesitate to announce it to those whose right it is to know it."

"Thank you! That was spoken like the noble, unaffected woman you are! Will you always be equally sincere with me—*Sarah?*" His accent trembled with excess of emotion in calling the name.

Is it, then, an easy lot that you have chosen, Sarah Hunt? You, whose pride and glory it was to be truthful, who spurned whatever assimilated in the least degree to deception, what think you of a life where a lie meets you on the threshold, and must be accepted and perpetuated, if you would preserve your name and position in his eyes and those of the world. "It is the way two-thirds of the married people live!" you were saying to yourself, just now. It may be so; but it is none the less a career of duplicity, perjury—*crime!*

"I will endeavor to please you!" she faltered, her face in a flame of shame and confusion.

And this was the hue that met Lewis's eye, as her veil was blown aside, in her descent to the pavement, a blush he interpreted to suit his own wishes. Mr. Hunt appeared in the door-way as she alighted, and read in Hammond's smile and joyous salutation all that he most desired to learn. When the door was closed upon the departing suitor, the father drew his best-beloved child to him, and kissed her, without a word of uttered blessing.

"It would break his heart were I to recede now!" thought Sarah, as she bore hers—heavy, hard—up to her room.

That evening was the proudest era of Mrs. Hunt's existence. Two daughters well engaged — unexceptionably paired off! What mother more blest than she? Where could be found other children so dutiful? other sons-in-law so acceptable? By breakfast time, next day, she had arranged every thing—Sarah's trousseau, her house, and the double wedding.

Lucy expostulated here. "But, mother, this is the first of November."

"I know that, my dear; but the ceremony will not come off until Christmas, and much can be done in six weeks for your sister—your work is so forward. Then, again, 'tisn't as if Sarah couldn't get every thing she needs right here, if she shouldn't have enough. It will be tremendously expensive—*awful*, in fact; but we must make sacrifices. We can live economical after you're married and gone, and save enough to meet the bills."

"If you please, madam, I prefer a plain outfit, and no debts," said Sarah's most abrupt tones.

"If *you* please, my dear, I understand my affairs, and mean to do as I think proper," retorted the no less strong-willed mother.

Sarah was not cowed. "And as to the time you set, I cannot agree to it. I presume that in this matter I have some voice. I say six months instead of six weeks!"

"Very well, my love." Mrs. Hunt went on polishing a tumbler with her napkin. She always washed her silver and glass herself. "You must settle that with your father and Mr. Hammond. They are crazy for this plan. They were talking to me about it last night, and I told them that I would engage to have every thing ready in time; but you must be consulted. I never saw your father more set upon any thing. He said to me, private, that he did hope that you wouldn't raise any squeamish objections, and upset their arrangements."

Mrs. Hunt took up a handful of spoons as composedly as if she had never stretched her conscience in her life.

Sarah's head drooped upon the table. She was very, very miserable. In her morbid state of mind she did not dream of questioning the accuracy of her mother's assertion. That a marriageable single daughter was a burden to one parent,

6*

she knew but too well; that to this able financier the prospect of getting two out of the way, with the *éclat* of a double ceremony that should cost no more than Lucy's nuptials would have done, was a stupendous temptation, she also perceived. But that the father whom she so loved; whose sick-bed she had tended so faithfully; whose lonely hours it was her province and delight to solace—that he should acquiesce—nay, more, rejoice in this indelicate haste to get rid of her, was a cruel stab.

"Very well," she said, raising an ashy face. "Let it be as you say. The sooner it is over, the better."

This clause was unheeded by her mother and sister. Had they heard it, they might have understood it as little as they did the composure with which she joined in the work which was begun, without an hour's delay. In this trying juncture, Mrs. Hunt came out in all her strength. Her sewing-machine (she was one of the earliest purchasers of these inestimable time, labor, and money savers) went night and day; she shopped largely and judiciously, giving orders to tradespeople with the air of a princess; "Jewed" her butcher; watched her pantry, and served up poorer dinners than ever. Jeannie's winter outfit was ingeniously contrived from her sisters' cast-off wardrobe; Mr. Hunt's and the boys' shirts and socks were patched and darned until but a trifling quantity of the original material remained; and this pearl of mothers had her two-year-old cloak and last season's hat "done over" for this year's wear.

Foremost among the visitors to the Hunts, after this latest engagement was made public, was Mrs. Marlow, the wife of Mr. Hammond's benefactor and partner. Sarah was out when she called; so Mrs. Hunt received her, and discovering very soon that, in spite of her husband's wealth and her splendid establishment, she was not, as Mrs. Hunt phrased it to her daughters, "one mite proud, and thought the world and all of Lewis"—the mother opened her heart to her so freely, with regard to the prospective weddings and her maternal anxieties, that Mrs. Marlow was emboldened to introduce a subject which had taken hold of her thoughts so soon as she heard from Mr. Hammond of his expected marriage.

She had a daughter, resident for the winter in Paris, whose taste in female attire was unquestionable, and her good-nature as praiseworthy. If Miss Sarah Hunt would prepare a memorandum of such articles as she would like to have selected in that emporium of fashion, she would promise, for her daughter, that they should be forwarded in time for "the occasion."

"Some friends of mine, now abroad, have kindly offered to bring me over any quantity of fine dresses with their baggage," said the complaisant old lady; "and, as I do not need their services for myself, I can smuggle in whatever your daughter may order. You would be surprised at the difference in prices here and there—to say nothing of the superior excellence and variety of the assortment from which one can choose. My friends will return early in December. Therefore, should you like this arrangement, I ought to have the list and write my letters to-morrow."

Energetic, fussy, snobbish Mrs. Hunt! She stood an inch taller in her shoes at the imagination of this climax to the glory of the dual ceremony. "Trousseau ordered directly from Paris!" She seemed already to hear the envious and admiring buzz of her set; saw herself the most blessed of women—her daughters the brides of the season. She would order for Lucy, also; for the longer the list the more importance would the future Mrs. Hammond acquire in the sight of her husband's friends. They could not know that it was not for her alone. Then, as Mrs. Marlow intimated, it would be a saving. Here, like a cold shower-bath, came the agonizing query—"Where was the money to come from?" It would never do to run in debt to such people as the Marlows. If they were hard-pressed shopkeepers, who needed the money, it would be another thing. No! the cash in hand, or its representative, must accompany the memorandum.

Sarah was secretly pleased at this obstacle, for she despised the ostentation and extravagance going on in their hungry household. Strive as she did, with wicked pertinacity, to conform herself to the world's code, there was as yet too much of the ancient and better leaven left to permit more than an outward obedience to the dictates of customs so irrational and tyrannical.

That very evening there arrived a letter that settled the question, and inflated Mrs. Hunt's collapsed spirits to an expansion hitherto unequalled. It was from Aunt Sarah to her namesake niece; a guileless, fervent expression of good wishes and unabated affection, and a request from "husband" and herself that she would accept the enclosure as a mark of that hopeful regard.

"Since our daughters died"—wrote this true and gentle mother—"we have always intended to give you just exactly what we would have done one of them, as a wedding-present—as you were named for me, and I had nursed you before your mother ever did, and you seemed in some way to belong to us. But since you paid us a visit we have felt nearer to you than ever, and seeing that the Lord has prospered us in this world's goods, we have made up our minds to give you a double portion, dear, what both of our girls would have had, if it had pleased our Father to spare them to have homes of their own upon earth. Living is high in New York, but we have calculated that what we send will buy your wedding-clothes and furnish your house."

The enclosed gift, to Sarah's astonishment, was a check upon a city bank for a thousand dollars!

"Was there ever such a child for luck?" exclaimed Mrs. Hunt, clapping her hands. "What a fortunate thing we sent you down there when we did! That was one of *my* plans, you remember, Mr. H. Really, Lucy, our little Sarah understands how to play her cards, after all! I never did you justice, my dear daughter. I ain't ashamed to confess it. This puts all straight, and is real handsome in sister Benson—more than I expected. Go to work right away upon your list, girls! We'll have to set up the best part of the night to get it ready. Ah, well! this comes of putting one's trust in Providence and going ahead!"

Sarah thought, with aching heart and moistened eyes, of Aunt Sarah's mind-pictures of the neat apparel and snug dwelling she deemed proper for a young couple just beginning house-keeping, and rebelled at this waste, this frivolous expenditure of her love-portion. Mr. Hunt sided with her, so far as to urge the propriety of her doing as she pleased with what was her exclusive property; but, as in a majority of former altercations, their arguments and powers of endurance were no match for the determination and mind of the real head of the family. With a sigh of pain, disgust, and despair, Mr. Hunt succumbed, and, deserted by her ally, Sarah contended but a short time longer ere she yielded up the cause of the combat to the indomitable victress.

CHAPTER X.

The bridal day came; frosty and clear, dazzlingly bright, by reason of the reflection from the snow, which lay deep and firm upon the ground.

"What a delightful novelty this is, coming to a wedding in a sleigh!" lisped one of the triad of bridesmaids, who were to do double duty for the sisters. "How very gay it makes one to hear the bells outside! Have they come, Vic.?"

Victoria, whose marriage was but one week off, was, true to instinct and habit, on the lookout behind the friendly curtain.

She nodded. "Yes—both of them, but not together. What a magnificent sleigh that is of the Marlows! They brought Mr. Hammond. See the bridegrooms shake hands on the sidewalk! That looks so sweet and brotherly! They will be up here almost directly, I suppose."

The attendants immediately began to shake out their robes and stroke their white gloves. They were collected in the sitting-room so often mentioned, and the sisters were also present. In accordance with the ridiculous custom of *very* parvenu modern marriages, although the ceremony was to take place precisely at twelve o'clock, daylight was carefully excluded from the parlors below, gas made its sickly substitute, and the whole company was in full evening costume.

"Am I all right?" inquired Lucy, with a cautious wave of her flowing veil. "Look at me, Vic.!"

"You are perfect, my dearest!" replied the devoted parasite. "How I admire your beautiful self-possession! And as for you, Sarah, your calmness is wonderful! I fear that I should be terribly agitated"—blushing, and casting a meaning smile at Lucy.

Sarah's statuesque repose was broken by a ray of scorn from the eye, and a slight disdainful smile. Whatever were the feelings working beneath her marble mask, she was not yet reduced to the depth of wretchedness that would humble her to accept the insolent pity couched under the pretended praise. She vouchsafed no other reply; but remained standing a little apart from the rest; her gloved hands crossed carelessly before her; her gaze bent downwards; her whole posture that of one who neither waited, nor hoped, nor feared.

"Who would have thought that she could be made such an elegant-looking woman?" whispered one of the bridemaids aside to another.

"She has actually a high-bred air! I never imagined it was in her. So much for a Parisian toilette!"

"I am so much afraid that I shall lose my color when we enter the room," said Lucy, surveying her pink cheeks in the mirror. "They say it is so trying to the nerves, and I am odious when I am pale."

"Never fear, my sweetest. It is more likely that the unavoidable excitement will improve your complexion. There they are!" returned Victoria, hurriedly, and—unconsciously, no doubt—the three attendants and one of the principals in the forthcoming transaction, "struck an attitude," as the sound of footsteps approached the door.

Lucy had only time for a whisper—a last injunction—to her faithful crony. "Remember to see that my veil and dress hang right when we get down-stairs." And the masculine portion of the procession marched in in order.

Sarah did not look up. She bent her head as the formal

exchange of salutations was executed, and yielded her hand to the person who took it in his warm pressure, and then transferred it to his arm. It was one of the freaks, thus denominated by her acquaintances, in which she had been indulged, that she desired to have her marriage ceremony precede her sister's. She assigned what Lucy at least considered a sufficient reason for this caprice.

"Nobody will care to look at me after you stand aside, Lucy. Keep the best wine until the last. My only chance of getting an approving glance lies in going in before you attract and fix the public gaze."

She had her way. A limited number of select friends were admitted to behold "the ceremony;" yet the parlors were comfortably filled, excepting in the magical semicircle described by an invisible line, in the centre of which stood the clergyman in his robes.

Still dull and calm, Sarah went through the brief rôle that fell to her share. "Behaved charmingly," was the unanimous verdict of the beholders, and surprised other people, as well as the complimentary bridemaid, by her thorough-bred air and Parisian toilet. Without the pause of a second, so perfect was the drill of the performers, the wedded pair stepped aside, and made way for the second happy couple. Lucy's solicitude on the score of her complexion was needless. As the solemn words were commenced, a rosy blush flickered up to its appointed resting-place—another and another—until, when Philip released her to the congratulatory throng, she was the most enchanting type of a radiant Hebe that poet ever sang, or painter burned to immortalize on canvas.

Philip stood beside her and sustained his portion of the hand-shaking and felicitations until the press diminished, then stepped hastily over to where Hammond and his bride were undergoing a similar martyrdom. Until this moment Sarah had not looked at, or spoken to him—had never met him face to face since their parting in the summer at Aunt Sarah's. Now, not aware who it was that approached her, she raised her eyes with the serious dignity with which she had received all other salutations, and met his downward gaze—full of warm and honest feeling.

"Sister!" he said, and in brotherly fondness he bent towards her, and left a kiss upon her mouth.

A hot glow, the lurid red of offended modesty or self-convicted guilt, overspread her face; the lips parted, quivered, and closed tightly, after an ineffectual effort to articulate; the room swam around her, and Mr. Hammond caught her just in time to save her from falling. It was Nature's vengeful reaction for the long and unnatural strain upon her energies. She did not faint entirely away, although several moments elapsed before she regained perfect consciousness of her situation and surrounding objects. She had been placed in an easy-chair; her head rested against her father's shoulder, and on the other side stood Lewis, almost as pale as herself, holding a glass of wine to her lips. Around her were grouped her mother, Lucy, and Philip. The guests had withdrawn politely to the background, and maintained a respectful silence.

"What have I betrayed?" was her first coherent reflection; and, with an instinctive perception of the quarter where such disclosures would do most harm, her eye turned with a sort of appealing terror to Lewis. His heart leaped at the movement, revealing, as he fancied it did, dependence upon his strength, recognition of his right to be with and nearest to her.

"You are better," he said, with a moved tenderness he could not and cared not to restrain.

The words, the manner, were an inexpressible relief to her fears, and trying to return his smile, she would have arisen but for her father's interposition.

"Sit still," he advised. "Mrs. Hunt, Lucy, Mr. Benson, will you entertain our friends? She will be all right in a little while, Mr. Hammond."

"*Tableaux vivants!*" said Lucy's soft, rich voice, as she advanced towards the reassured guests. "This is a part of the performance not set down in the programme. Quite theatrical, was it not?"

It is very possible that Philip Benson would not have regarded this as an *apropos* or refined witticism, had any one else been the speaker; but as the round, liquid tones rolled it forth, and her delicious laugh led off the instant revival of mirth and badinage, he marvelled at her consummate tact, her happy play of fancy (!), and returned devout thanks to the stars that had bestowed upon him this prodigy of grace, wit, and beauty. Sarah rallied speedily; and, contrary to the advice of her father and husband, maintained her post in the drawing-room during all the reception, which continued from half-past twelve to half-past two.

It was a gay and shifting scene—a sparkling, murmuring tide, that ebbed and flowed to and from the quartette who formed the attractive power. Silks, laces, velvets, furs, and diamonds; faces young, old, and middle-aged; handsome, fair, and homely; all decked in the same conventional holiday smile; bodies tall and short, executing every variety of bow and courtesy; voices sweet, sharp, and guttural, uttering the senseless formula of congratulation—these were Sarah's impressions of the tedious ceremonial. Restored to her rigid composure, she too bowed and spoke the word or sentence custom exacted—an emotionless automaton in seeming, while Lucy's matchless inflections lent interest and beauty to the like nothings, as she rehearsed them in her turn; and Philip Benson, having no solicitude for *his* bride's health or ability to endure the fatigue, was collected enough to compare the two, and, while exulting in his selection, to commiserate the proprietor of the colder and less gifted sister.

At last the trial was over; the hospitable mansion was closed; the parlors deserted; the preparations for travelling hurried through; and the daughters went forth from their girlhood's home. Philip had cordially invited Sarah and Lewis, by letter, to accompany Lucy and himself to Georgia; but Sarah would not hear of it, and Lewis, while he left the decision to her, was not sorry that she preferred to journey instead with him alone. It was too cold to go northward, and the Hammonds now proposed to proceed with the others as far as Baltimore, there to diverge upon a Western and Southern tour, which was to occupy three weeks, perhaps four.

CHAPTER XI.

During the month preceding his marriage, Lewis Hammond had spent much time and many thoughts in providing and furnishing a house for his wife. His coadjutor in this labor of love was not, as one might have expected, Mrs. Hunt, but his early friend, Mrs. Marlow. His omission of his future mother-in-law, in his committee of consultation, he explained to her by representing the number of duties already pressing upon her, and his unwillingness to add aught to their weight. But when both girls were married and gone, and the work of "getting to rights" was all over, this indefatigable woman paid Mrs. Marlow a visit, and offered her assistance in completing the arrangements for the young housekeepers.

"There is nothing for us to do," said Mrs. Marlow. "Lewis attended to the purchase of every thing before leaving; and the orders are all in the hands of a competent upholsterer whom he has employed, as is also the key of the house. I offered to have the house-cleaning done, but Lewis refused to let me help him even in this. He is very methodical, and rather strict in some of his ideas. When the premises are pronounced ready for the occupancy of the future residents, you and I will play inspectors, and find as much fault as we can."

Mrs. Hunt went around by the house on her way home. It was new and handsome, a brown stone front, with stone balconies and balustrades; but three stories high, it was true, yet of ample width and pitch of ceiling, and—as she discovered by skirting the square—at least three rooms deep all the way up. The location was unobjectionable; not more than four blocks from the paternal residence, and in a wider street. On the whole, she had no fault to find, provided Mr. Hammond had furnished it in such style as she would have recommended. She had her fears lest his sober taste in other respects should extend to these matters, and hinted something of the kind to her husband.

"I have confidence in Mr. Hammond to believe that he will allow his wife every indulgence compatible with his means," was the reply.

Mr. Hunt did not deem it obligatory upon him to state that his son-in-law had conferred with him upon numerous questions pertaining to Sarah's likes and probable wishes; that he had examined and approved of the entire collection of furniture, etc., selected for her use. Why should he, how could he, without engendering in his wife's bosom the suspicion that had accounted to him for Lewis's choice of the father as an adviser? namely, that the newly-made husband had gained a pretty correct estimate of this managing lady's character, her penny-wise and pound-foolish policy, and intended to inaugurate altogether a different one in his house.

Regardless of Mrs. Marlow's polite insinuation that their room was preferable to their company until all things should be in readiness for inspection, the ambitious mother made sundry visits to the premises while they were being fitted up, and delivered herself of divers suggestions and recommendations, which fell like sand on a rock upon the presiding man of business.

On the day appointed for the tourists' return, Mrs. Marlow's carriage drew up at Mr. Hunt's door, by appointment, to take the mistress of the house upon the proposed visit of criticism of her daughter's establishment. Mrs. Marlow was in a sunny mood, and indisposed to censure, as was evinced by ejaculations of pleasure at the general effect of each apartment as they entered, and praise of its component parts. Mrs. Hunt was not so undiscriminating. The millionnaire's wife must not imagine that she was dazzled by any show of elegance, or that she was overjoyed at the prospect of her child's having so beautiful and commodious a home.

"The everlasting oak and green!" she uttered, as they reached the dining-room. "It is a pity Mr. Hammond did not select walnut and crimson instead! Green is very unbecoming to Sarah."

"Then we must impress upon her the importance of cultivating healthy roses in her cheeks, and wearing bright warm colors. This combination—green and oak—is pretty and serviceable, I think. The table is very neatly set, Mary," continued Mrs. Marlow, kindly, to the tidy serving-maid. "Keep an eye on the silver, my good girl, until your mistress comes. Mrs. Hunt, shall we peep into the china-closets before we go to the kitchen? I have taken the liberty, at Lewis's request, of offering to your daughter the services of a couple of my *protégées*, excellent servants, who lived for years with one of my own children—Mrs. Morland, now in Paris. They are honest, willing, and, I think, competent. The man-servant, if Lewis sees fit to keep one, he must procure himself."

The china, glass, and pantries were in capital order; the kitchen well stocked, light, and clean, and dinner over the fire.

"You will be punctual to the minute, Katy, please!" was the warning here. "Mr. Hammond is particular in the matter of time."

"And you will see that *my daughter* has a cup of clear, strong coffee!" ordered Mrs. Hunt, magisterially. "She is delicate, and accustomed to the very best of cookery."

And, having demonstrated her importance and superior housewifery to the round-eyed cook, she swept out.

To an unprejudiced eye, the whole establishment was without a flaw; and, undisturbed by the captious objections of her companion in the survey, Mrs. Marlow saw and judged for herself, and carried home with her a most pleasing imagination of Lewis's gratification, and Sarah's delighted surprise with the scene that was to close their day of cold and weariness.

By Mr. Hammond's expressed desire to his father-in-law, there was no one except the domestics in the house when they arrived. As the carriage stopped, the listening maid opened the door, and a stream of radiance shot into the misty night across the wet pavement upon the two figures that stepped from the conveyance.

"In happy homes he sees the light." The mental quotation brought back to Sarah the vision of that lonely evening, ten months before, when she had moaned it in her dreary twilight musings at the window of her little room. "Dreary then, hopeless now!" and with this voiceless sigh, she crossed the threshold of her destined abode. With a kindly greeting to the servants in the hall, Lewis hurried his wife onward, past the parlor doors, into a library sitting-room, back of the show apartments, warm and bright, smiling a very home welcome.

Here he placed her in a deep cushioned chair, and, pressing her hands in his, kissed her, with a heartfelt—"May you be very happy in *our home*, dear wife!"

"Thank you!" she replied. "It is pleasant here, and you are too kind."

"That is impossible where you are concerned. Sit here, while I see to the trunks. When they are carried up-stairs, you can go to your room. Throw off your hat and cloak."

He was very thoughtful of her comfort—too thoughtful, because his love made him watchful of her every look, word, and gesture. She was glad of the brief respite from this vigilance, that allowed her to bury her face in her hands and groan aloud. She had no heart to look around her cage. No doubt it was luxurious; the bars softly and richly lined; the various arrangements the best of their kind; still, it was nothing but a cage—a prison, from which death only could release her.

The trim maid came for her wrappings, and directly afterwards Lewis, to take her up-stairs.

"Not a very elaborate toilet, dear," he said, as he left her for his dressing-room. "You will see no one this evening but our father and mother, and they will remember that you have been travelling all day."

When she was ready, it lacked still a quarter of an hour of dinner-time, and she acceded to Lewis's proposal that they should go over their dwelling. By his order, there were lights in every room. The graceful furniture, the well-contrasted hues of the soft carpets, the curtains and pictures showed to fine advantage. Every thing was in place, from cellar to attic; not a symptom of parsimony or cheapness in the whole; and all betokened, besides excellent judgment, such conformity to, or unison with her taste, that Sarah, with all her heaviness of heart, was pleased. She was touched too with gratitude or remorse; for, when they were back in the cozy sitting-room, she laid her hand timidly on that of her husband, and said, falteringly:

"I do not deserve that you should take so much pains to gratify me, Mr. Hammond."

Over Lewis's face there flushed one of the rare smiles that made him positively handsome while they lasted. He grasped the shrinking fingers firmly, and drew his wife close to his side.

"Shall I tell you how to repay me for all that I have done, or ever can do, to promote your ease and enjoyment?"

"If you please." But her heart sank, as she foresaw some demands upon a love that had never existed—a treasury that, to him, was sealed and empty; yet whose poverty she dared not avow.

"Call me 'Lewis,' now that we are at home, dear. I cannot realize that you are indeed all mine—that our lives are one and the same, while you continue that very proper 'Mr. Hammond.'"

"It comes more naturally to my tongue, and don't you think it more respectful than—than—the other?"

"I ask no such form of respect from you. I do not fear lest you should fail to 'honor and obey' me, you little paragon of duty! Believe me, dearest, I fully understand and reverence the modest reserve, that has not yet ceased to be shyness, in the expression of your sentiments towards me. You are not demonstrative by nature. Neither am I. But since you are my other self, and there is no living being nearer to you than myself, ought we not to overcome this propensity to, or custom of, locking up our feelings in our own breasts? Let me begin by a confession of one uncomfortable complaint, under which I have labored ever since our engagement. Do you know, darling, that I absolutely *hunger*—I cannot give any other name to the longing—I hunger and thirst to hear you say that you love me! Do you remember that you have never told me in so many words what you have given me other good reasons for believing? I need but one thing this evening to fill my cup with purest content. It is to have you say—openly, fearlessly, as my wife has a right to do—'Lewis, I love you!'"

"It need be a source of no unhappiness to be married to

a man whom one does not love, provided he is kind and generous!" say match-makers and worldly-wise mothers. Perhaps not, after one's conscience is seared into callosity by perjuries, and her forehead grown bold as brass; but the neophyte in the laudable work of adaptation to such circumstances will trip in her words and color awkwardly while acquiring this enviable hardihood.

Sarah's head fell, and her face was stained with blushes. One wild impulse was to throw herself at the feet of him whom she had wronged so foully, and, confessing her mad, wicked deception upon his holiest feelings, pray him to send her away—to cast her adrift, and rid himself of a curse, while he freed her from the gentle, yet intolerable bondage of his love.

"Dinner is ready!" announced the servant. Sarah's senses returned, and with them self-control. With a strange smile, she glanced up at him—a look he did not understand, yet could not guess was born of anguish—and said, with a hesitation that seemed pretty and coquettish to him—"*Lewis!* do you hear? May it please your worship, I am very hungry!"

"Tease! I will have my revenge yet! See if I do not!"

Laughing lightly, she eluded his outstretched arm, and sprang past him into the hall leading to the dining-room. She assumed the seat at the head of the table with a burlesque of dignity, and throughout the meal was more talkative and frolicsome than he had ever seen her before. So captivated was he by her lively discourse and bright looks, that he was sorry to hear the ring, proclaiming the coming of the expected visitors. The dessert had not been removed, and the girl was instructed to show them immediately into the dining-room.

A toast was drunk to the prosperity of the lately established household, and the gentlemen went off to the library.

"Always see to putting away your silver, Sarah!" counselled the mother. "And you had ought to get a common set of dinner and breakfast things. This china is too nice for every-day use. Of course, Mr. Hammond can afford to get more when this is broken; but it's a first-rate rule, child, as you'll find, to put your money *where it will show most.* That's the secret of my management. Mr. Hammond must give you an allowance for housekeeping and pin-money. Speak to him about it right away. Men are more liberal while the honeymoon lasts than they ever are afterwards. Strike while the iron is hot. You can't complain of your husband, so far. He has set you up very handsome. If I had been consulted about furnishing, I would have saved enough off of those third-story chambers and the kitchen to buy another pair of mirrors for your parlors. The mantels has a bare look. I noticed it directly I went in. To be sure, the Parian ornaments are pretty and tasty, and expensive enough—dear knows! but they don't make much of a display."

"I do not like the fashion of lining walls with mirrors," said Sarah, in her old, short way; "and am satisfied with the house as it is. Shall we join the gentlemen?"

Nothing had ever showed her more plainly the degradation of her false position than the confident air her mother wore in making her coarse observations, and instructing her as to the method of managing her generous, confiding husband. It was the free-masonry of a mercenary wife, whose spouse would have been better represented to her mind by his money-bag than his own proper person, towards another of the same craft, who rated her lawful banker by corresponding rules.

"Will I then really grow to be like her and her associates?" Sarah questioned inly. "Will a fine house and its fixtures, will dress and equipage and pin-money so increase in importance as to fill this aching vacuum in my heart? Will a position in life, and the envy of my neighbors, make up to me for the loss of the love of which I used to dream, the happiness which the world owes me yet? Is this the coin in which it would redeem its promises?"

Mr. Hunt's mild features wore their happiest expression this evening. He arose at the ladies' entrance, and beckoned his daughter to a seat on the sofa beside him.

"You are a little travel-worn!" he said. "Your cheeks are not very ruddy."

"Did you ever see them when they were?" asked Sarah, playfully.

"She was always just that pale when she was a baby," said Mrs. Hunt, setting herself in the arm-chair proffered by her son-in-law. "Lucy stole all the roses from her." Sarah may have thought that other and more grievous thefts had succeeded this doubtful one, but she neither looked nor said this. "And that reminds me, Mr. H.! Did you bring Lucy's letter for Sarah to read?"

"I did." Mr. Hunt produced it. "Keep it, and read it at your leisure, Sarah."

"They are supremely happy, I suppose?" remarked Lewis, with the benevolent interest incident to his fellowship of feeling with them.

"For all the world like two turtle-doves!" Mrs. Hunt rejoined. "Their letters are a curiosity. It is 'Phil.' and 'Lucy' from one end to the other. I mean to save them to show to them five years from now. Hot love is soon cool, and by and by they will settle down as sensible as any of the rest of us. You don't begin so, I see, Sarah, and I am pleased at it. Between me and you, it's two-thirds of it humbug! There is Victoria West that was! She looks ready, in company, to eat up that lean monkey of a George Bond. I don't believe but she shows him the other side of the pictures in private."

Sarah heard her father's suppressed sigh, and felt, without looking up, that her husband's eyes sought hers wistfully. The unobservant dame pursued her free and easy discourse. Mr. Hammond was "one of the family" now, and there was no more occasion for choice grammar or fine sentiments before him.

"Not that I blame Victoria for taking him. He was a good offer, and she wasn't much admired by the gentlemen—rich as Mr. West is. Mr. Bond is twenty-five years older than she is, and wears false teeth and a toupee; but I suppose she is willing to overlook trifles. She watches out for the main chance, and will help him take care of his money, as well as spend it. Vic. is a prudent girl."

"Lucy—Mrs. Benson—was at home when she wrote, was she not?" interrogated Mr. Hammond.

"Yes, at his father's. His mother keeps house, and Lucy has nothing to do but ride, visit, and entertain company. She says the house is crowded the whole time, and she has so many beaux that Philip stands no chance of speaking a word to her. She is perfectly happy."

Notwithstanding the various feelings of the listeners, none of them could resist this picture of a felicitous honeymoon, so naively spoken. Lewis's laugh cleared the vapors from his brow, and the pain at Sarah's heart did not hinder her from joining in.

"And the ousted bridegroom, perforce, seeks consolation in the society of his fair friends?" said Lewis. "If this is the way young married people show the love-sickness you complained of just now, Mrs. Hunt, I am content with our more staid ways—eh, Sarah?"

"Quiet ways suit me best," was the answer.

"'Still water runs deep,'" quoted Mrs. Hunt. "I used to worry over your stay-at-home habits and eternal study of books, Sarah; but I'm ready to say now that you was sensible to behave as you did, as it has turned out. I don't mean to flatter Mr. Hammond, but I'd ten times rather you had taken him than a dried-up widower like George Bond."

"Thank you!" bowed Lewis, desirous of diverting attention from Sarah's growing uneasiness beneath her mother's congratulations.

Mrs. Hunt held on her way. "I never had a fear lest Lucy shouldn't marry well. She was pretty and attractive, and knew too much about the world to throw herself away for the sake of love in a cottage. But now the danger is over, I will allow that I used to mistrust Sarah here sometimes. You was just queer enough to fall in love with some adventurer with a foreign name, and never a cent in his pocket—yes, and marry him, too, in spite of all that could be said and done to prevent it. I was forever in a 'feaze' about you; fancying that you was born to make an out-and-out love-match—the silliest thing a girl can do, in my opinion."

"You never dreamed of her 'taking up,' as the phrase is, with a humdrum individual like myself," said Lewis. "Nor, to be candid, did I, for a long time, Mrs. Hunt. Yet I cannot say that I regret her action, disadvantageous to herself though it was. I wrote to you of our visit to New Orleans, did I not, sir?" he continued to Mr. Hunt, inwardly a little disgusted by the frank revelations his mamma-in-law was making of her principles and plans.

The subject so interesting to most wedded people, so embarrassing to one of the present party, was not again introduced during the elder couple's stay. When Lewis returned to the library, after seeing them out, Sarah sat where he had left her, her hand shading her eyes—deep in thought, or overcome by weariness.

"You had better go up to your room, dear," said Lewis. "I wonder you are not worn out completely."

She arose to obey; walked as far as the door, then came back to him.

"It may appear strange to you that I should speak openly of such a suspicion; but I must beg you not to suppose for an instant that in my acceptance of your offer of marriage, I was actuated by mercenary motives. You look surprised"—she hurried on yet faster while her resolution lasted—"but I could not rest without doing myself this act of justice. Much that mother said to-night might—must have led you to this conclusion. I would not have you think worse of me than I deserve, and of this one act of baseness I am innocent."

"My precious little wife, how excited you are! and over what a nonsensical imagination! Suspect you—the noblest as well as the dearest of women—of selling yourself, body and soul, for money? Listen to *my* speech now, dear Sarah!"

He sat down and pulled her to his knee. "I esteem you, as I love you, above all the rest of your sex—above any other created mortal. I know you to be a pure, high-minded woman. When I part with this persuasion, may I part also with the life that doubt on this point would render wretched! Judge, then, whether it be possible for me to link this holy realization of womanhood with the thought of another character, which I will describe. I hold that she who enters the hallowed state of wedlock through motives of pecuniary interest, or ambition, or convenience—indeed, through any consideration save that of love, single and entire, for him to whom she pledges her vows, stands, in the sight of her Maker and the angels, on a level with the most abandoned outcast that pollutes the earth she treads. I shock you, I see; but on this subject I feel strongly. I have seen much, too much, of fashionable marriages formed for worldly aggrandizement—for riches; sometimes in pique at having lost a coveted lover. With my peculiar sentiments, I feel that I could endure no heavier curse than to contract an alliance like any of these. I repeat it, I believe in *Woman* as God made her and intended she should live, if for no other reason than because I recollect my mother, boy as I was when she died; and because I know and have you, my true, blessed wife!"

CHAPTER XII.

A YEAR and five months had passed away since the evening when Lewis Hammond held his conscience-stricken wife upon his knee, and told her—in fervid words that singularly belied his calm and even demeanor at other times—of his faith in and love for her, and his abhorrence of the sin she felt in her trembling soul that she had committed. Yet she had not the superhuman courage required to contradict a trust like this. There was no alternative but to keep up the weary, wicked mockery unto the end.

"But in all these months she must have learned to care for him!" cries Mrs. Common Sense. "There is nothing disagreeable about the man. He is not brilliant; yet he has intelligence and feeling, and is certainly attached to his wife. I have no doubt but that he indulges her in every reasonable request, and comports himself in all respects like an exemplary husband."

Granted, to each and every head of your description, my dear madam! But, for all that, his obdurate wife had not come to love him. I blush to say it; but while we are stripping hearts let us not be squeamish! There had been seasons, lasting sometimes for weeks, when her existence was a continual warfare between repugnance to him and her sense of duty; when she dreaded to hear his step in the hall, and shrank inwardly from his caress; watched and fought, until strength and mind were well-nigh gone. Mark me! I do not deny that this was as irrational as it was reprehensible; but I have never held up my poor Sarah as a model of reason or propriety. From the beginning, I have made her case a warning. The fates forbid that I should commend it to any as an example for imitation! A passionate, proud, reticent girl; a trusting, loving, deceived woman a hopeless, desperate bride—whose heart lay like a pulseless stone in her breast at the most ardent love-words of her husband, and throbbed with wild, uncontrollable emotion at the fraternal tone and kiss of her lost and only love—I have no plea for her, save the words of Infinite compassion and Divine knowledge of human nature and human woe: "Let him that is without sin among you cast the first stone at her!"

The highly respectable firm of which Mr. Hammond was the junior member, was adding, if not field to field, thousand to thousand, of the wherewithal for the purchase of fields, or, what was better still, city lots. Mrs. Lewis Hammond had set up her carriage about a year after her marriage; said equipage being a gift from her generous husband on the occasion of the first airing of the little "Baby Belle," as she was always called in the family. Not until subsequent events had endowed it with deeper and saddest interest did Sarah read Aldrich's beautiful poem bearing the above title. Lewis's mother's name was Isabella. Her grandchild received the same, which became "Belle" on the mother's tongue, and then, because it was natural to say "Baby" too, the pretty alliteration was adopted.

To a man of Lewis's domestic tastes the advent of this child was a source of the liveliest pleasure, and the tiny inmate of his household was another and a powerful tie, binding him to a home already dear. But to the mother's lonely life, so bare of real comfort or joy—haunted by memory and darkened by remorse—the precious gift came like a ray of Heaven's purest light, a strain of angel music, saying to care, "Sleep!" to hope, "Awake, the morning cometh!" Beneath the sunshine of so much love, the infant throve finely, and without being a greater prodigy than the nine hundred and ninety-nine miracles of beauty and sprightliness who, with it, composed the thousand "blessed babies" of the day, was still a pretty, engaging creature, whose gurgling laugh and communicative "coo" beguiled the mother's solitude, and made cheerful the lately silent house.

It was late in the June afternoon, and arrayed in clean white frock, broad sash, and shoulder-knots of pink ribbon, the small lady sat on her mother's lap at the front window, awaiting the appearance of the husband and father. Sarah had altered much since her marriage; "improved wonderfully," said her acquaintances. There was still in her mien a touch of haughtiness; in her countenance the look that spoke profound thought and introspection. Still, when in repose, her brow had a cast of seriousness that bordered on melancholy; but over her features had passed a change like that wrought by the sculptor's last stroke to the statue. The mould was the same—the chiselling more clear and fine. Especially after the birth of her child was this refining process most apparent in its effects. There was a softness in her smile, a gentle sweetness in her voice, as she now talked to the babe, directing its attention to the window, lest the father's approach should be unnoticed, and he disappointed in his shout of welcome.

"How affected! gotten up for show!" sneered the childless Mrs. Bond, as she rolled by in her carriage, on her way to her handsome, cheerless home and its cross master.

"She has chosen her position well, at all events," rejoined her companion, a neighbor and gossip, who had taken Lucy's place in Victoria's confidence.

"Ridiculous!" She spat out the ejaculation from the overflowing of her spleen. "I could laugh at her airs, if they did not make me mad! One would think, to see her as she sits there, that she had decked herself and the child to please a man that she doated upon—like the good wives we read of in novels."

"And why shouldn't she be fond of him? He is a good-hearted fellow, and lets her do pretty much as she pleases, I imagine, besides waiting on her like any lover. I often meet them riding out together. That is more than your husband or mine ever does, my dear."

"They go quite as often as we desire their company, I fancy. Mine does, I know. Perhaps if we had the reason for parading our conjugal devotion that Mrs. Hammond has, we might wheedle our lawful lords into taking a seat alongside of us, once in a while. There's nothing like keeping up appearances, particularly if the reality is lacking. If Lewis Hammond knew some of the pretty stories I could tell him, about his Sarah's love-scrapes, he would not look so sublimely contented with his three-story paradise. The elegant clothes he piles upon that squaw of his are preposterous, and she carries them off as if she had dressed well all her days. I tell you, she never looked decent until she put on her wedding-dress. You have heard of the fainting-scene that took place that morning, I suppose? Old Mother Hunt said it was 'sensibility,' and 'nervous agitation;' the company laid it to the heat of the room; and I laughed in my sleeve, and said nothing. If that woman aggravates me much more, I will remind her of some passages in her experience she does not dream that I know."

"Do tell me what you mean? I am dying of curiosity! Did she flirt very hard before she was married?"

"She never had the chance. Lewis Hammond was her only offer."

"What was the matter, then?"

"I can't tell you now. It is too long a story. The next

time she frets me, as she does whenever she crosses my path, maybe you will hear the romance. Shall I set you down at your door, or will you enliven me by spending the evening with me? I do not expect other company, and George falls asleep over his newspaper as soon as he has despatched his dinner. Come in, and I will show you the loveliest sofa-pillow you ever beheld; a new pattern I have just finished."

"Thank you! I would accept the invitation with pleasure, but I have not been home since breakfast, and James makes such a fuss if he does not find me in the nursery, tending that whimpering baby, when he comes up at night, that it is as much as my life is worth to stay out after six o'clock. Any thing for peace, you know; and since we wives *are* slaves, it is best to keep on the blind side of our masters."

The day had been warm down town, and as Lewis Hammond stepped from the stage at the corner nearest his house, he felt jaded and dispirited—a physical depression, augmented by a slight headache. A business question which he had talked over with Mr. Marlow, before leaving the store, contributed its weight of thoughtfulness, and he was not conscious how near he was to his dwelling until, aroused by a sharp tap upon the window-pane, he glanced up at the animated tableau framed by the sash—the smiling mother, and the babe leaping and laughing, and stretching its hands towards him.

"This is the sweetest refreshment a man can ask after his day of toil," he said, when, having kissed wife and child, he took the latter in his arms. He was not addicted to complimentary speeches, and while his esteem and attachment for his chosen partner were even stronger than they had been in the heart of the month-old bridegroom, he was less apt to express them to her now than then. In one respect, and only one, his wedded life had brought him disappointment. Unreserved confidence and demonstrative affection on his side had failed to draw forth similar exhibitions of feeling from Sarah. Kind, thoughtful, dutiful, scrupulously faithful to him and his interests in word, look, and deed, she ever was. Yet he saw that she was a changed being from the fond, impulsive daughter, whose ministry in her father's sick-room had won for her a husband's love. Her reception of his affectionate advances was passive—a reception merely, without apparent return. Never, and he had ceased now to ask it, had she once said to him the phrase he had craved to hear—"I love you!" Yet he would as soon have questioned the reality of his existence as that she *did* love him. He held inviolate his trust in the motive that had induced her to become his wife, and in this calm confidence he was fain to rest, in the absence of protestations that would have gladdened his soul, while they could hardly have strengthened his faith in her affection.

Few wives, however loving, have been more truly cherished than was Sarah, and of this she was partially aware. If she had remained ignorant of Lewis's sentiments and wishes with regard to herself, until the grieved and unrequited love had subsided into the dull aching that does not, like a green wound, create, by its very smart, a species of excitement that helps one bear the pain; had he glided gradually into the joyless routine of her life's duties, and bided his time of speaking until he had made himself necessary to her comfort and peace, he might have won a willing bride. But what omniscient spirit was there to instruct and caution him? He met and loved her, supposing her to be as free as himself; like an honest, upright man, he told that love, and, without a misgiving, placed his honor and his happiness in her hands.

Sarah could not have told why she revolved all this in her unquiet mind as he sat near her, playing with their child; yet she did think of their strange sad history, and from the review arose a feeling of pity, sincere, almost tender, for him, so worthy and so deceived. She remembered with abasement of spirit how often she had been ready to hate him as the instrument of her bondage; how wrathful words had arisen to her lips at the moment of his greatest kindness; how patiently he had borne her coldness; how unflagging was his care of and for her. Over the dark, turbulent gulf of the unforgotten past that sundered their hearts, she longed, as she had never done before, to call to him, and confessing her sin against Heaven and against him, to implore pardon for the sake of the spotless babe that smiled into the father's face with its mother's eyes. Would he be merciful? Slowly and emphatically memory repeated in her ear his denunciation of the unloving wife, and courage died before the menaced curse.

"Fudge! Fiddlesticks! what frippery nonsense!" cry out, in a vehement storm of indignation, a bevy of the Common Sense connection. "Are we not staid and respectable matrons all? Do we not rear our daughters virtuously, and teach our sons to honor father as well as mother? Yet who of us troubles herself with raking in the cold ashes of her 'long ago' for the bones of some dead and gone love —a girlish folly of which she would be ashamed now? What cares Mr. Common Sense, among his day-books and ledgers, in his study or in his office, how many times his now correct helpmeet pledged eternal fidelity to other lovers before she put her last crop of wild oats into the ground, and settled for life with him? What if some of us, may be all, if driven hard, should admit that when we stood up before the minister we underwent certain qualms—call them pangs, if you like—at the thought of Tom This, or Harry

That, or Dick The Other, who, if circumstances had permitted, we would have preferred should occupy the place of 'The man whom we actually held by the hand!' While men can choose their mates, and women can only take such as propose to them, these things will happen. After all, who is hurt?" You aver that none of you are, mesdames, and we would not call your word in question. Ladies so conscientious must, of necessity, be veracious, even in love affairs.

"I am a thoughtless animal!" said Lewis at the dinner-table. "There is a letter from Lucy! Open it—don't mind me! I will crack your nuts for you while you read it."

There was a troubled look in Sarah's eye when she laid it down. "Lucy says they are certainly coming North this year—that we may look for them in a week from the date of this. This is rather sooner than mother expected them. Her housecleaning is late this season, in consequence of her rheumatic spell in May."

"Let them come straight here! What should prevent them? There is an abundance of room for them—baby, nurse, and all. It will be a grand arrangement!" said Lewis, heartily.

Sarah was backward in replying. "Father and mother may object. I would not wound them by interference with their guests."

"I will answer that mother will thank us to take care of them until her scrubbing and scalding are done. And Lucy would not be willing to risk her baby's health in a damp house."

"I will go and see mother to-morrow about it," concluded Sarah. She still appeared dubious as to the expediency of the proposed step, a thoughtfulness that did not wear away during the whole evening.

The Bensons had not visited New York the preceding year. They were detained at the South by a combination of causes, the principal of which was the long and fatal illness of Philip's mother. Lucy had written repeatedly of her intense desire to see her home once more, declaiming against the providences that had thwarted their projects, like an impatient, unreasonable child.

"Philip says it is not convenient for him to go just yet," said her letter to her sister, "and that our part of the country is as healthy as *Saratoga itself;* but I have *vowed* that I will not wait *one day* beyond the time I have set. It sets me *wild* to think of being in Broadway again—of visiting and shopping, and seeing you all. We have been so dull here since Mrs. Benson's death, and Philip is as *solemn* as a judge. One of his married sisters will stay with the old gentleman while we are away. O Sarah! I am *sick* of housekeeping and baby-nursing! It will do well enough for me when I need spectacles and a wig; but now, while I am young enough to enjoy life, it is *insufferable!*"

"Not very domestic, is she?" observed Lewis, folding up the letter, which Sarah had handed him. "Ah! it is not every man who has such a gem of a wife as I have! It appears to me that the married women of these days are not satisfied unless they have a string of beaux as long as that of a popular single belle. How is it, little one? Do you ever catch yourself wishing that your husband were not such an old-fashioned piece of constancy, and would give some other fellow a chance to say a pretty thing, when you are in company?'

"I do not complain," said Sarah, demurely.

"Not in words, perhaps; your patience is wonderful in every thing. But how do you feel when you see your old neighbor, Mrs. Bond, waltzing every set with the gayest gallant in the ball-room, while your jailor does not like to have you 'polk' at all, and favors your dancing only with men whom he knows to be respectable."

"I feel that Mr. Hammond is a sensible man, and careful of his wife's reputation, even in trifles, while Mr. Bond—"

"Go on! finish your sentence!"

"And his lady are a well-matched pair!"

Much as she disliked Victoria, and knowing that she was hated still by *her*, Sarah deemed it a necessary and common act of courtsey to her sister's friend to call and apprise her of Lucy's probable visit.

"It is not convenient for mother to receive them for a week yet, on account of certain household arrangements," she stated, in making known the object of her visit to her ancient enemy. "So you will find Lucy at our house, where her friends will be received as if they were my own."

"You are very polite, I am sure!" replied Mrs. Bond, smothering her displeasure at Sarah's studied civility, and noting, with her quick, reptile perceptions, that she was to be tolerated as she fancied Sarah would imply, merely as Lucy's early associate. "And the Bensons are to be with *you!* I shall call immediately upon their arrival. Poor, dear Lucy! I long to see her. She has had a vast deal of trouble since her marriage—has she not?"

"Except the death of her mother-in-law, she has had nothing to trouble her that I have heard of," answered Sarah, rising to go.

"My dear creature! what do you call the wear and tear of managing a husband, and a pack of unruly servants, and looking after a baby? And she was such a belle! I wonder if she is much broken!"

"Come and see!"

Mrs Hammond was at the parlor door.

"I will—most assuredly! How do you like their being

quartered upon you? What does that pattern husband of yours say to this?"

"Madam!" said Sarah, surprised and offended by the rude query.

"Oh! I don't mean that it would not be very delightful for you to have your sister with you; but there was a foolish rumor, about the time of your marriage, that you and Mr. Benson had some kind of a love-passage, down in the country; and I thought that Mr. Hammond, with his particularly nice notions, might retain an unpleasant recollection of the story, which would prevent him from being on brotherly terms with his old rival. Men are terribly unreasonable mortals, and perfect Turks in jealousy! We cannot be too careful not to provoke their suspicions."

Not for the universe would Sarah have betrayed any feeling at this insolence, save a righteous and dignified resentment at its base insinuations; but the ungovernable blood streamed in crimson violence to her temples, and her voice shook when she would have held it firm.

"Mr. Hammond is not one to be influenced by malicious gossip, Mrs. Bond, if, indeed, the report you have taken the liberty of repeating was ever circulated except by its author. I cannot thank you for your warning, as I recognize no occasion for jealousy in my conduct or character. I am accountable for my actions to my conscience and my husband, and I release you from what you have assumed to be your duty of watching and criticising my personal affairs. Good-morning."

"I struck the sore spot! no doubt of that!" soliloquized Mrs. Bond, recalling Sarah's start of pain and blush at the indelicate allusion to Philip Benson. "That woman stirs up all the bile in my system if I talk two minutes with her. If there were half the material to work upon in that vain, weak Lucy, that there is in this sister, I would have my revenge. As for Lewis Hammond, he is a love-sick fool!"

Sarah's cheeks had not lost their flush, nor had her heart ceased its angry throbbings, when she reached home. In the solitude of her chamber, she summoned strength and resolution to ask herself the question, so long avoided, shunned, as she had imagined, in prudence, as she now began to fear, in dread of a truthful reply.

When she married Lewis Hammond, she loved another. Fearful as was this sin, it would be yet more terrible were she now to discover a lurking fondness, an unconquered weakness for that other, in the heart of the trusted wife, the mother who, from that guilty bosom, nourished the little being that was, as yet, the embodiment of unsullied purity. It was a trying and a perilous task, to unfold deliberately, to pry searchingly into the record of that one short month that had held all the bloom and fragrance of her life's spring season; to linger over souvenirs and compare sensations—a painful and revolting process; but, alas! the revulsion was not at memories of that olden time; and as this appalling conviction dawned upon her, her heart died within her.

The nurse was arranging Baby Belle for the possible reception of her unknown aunt and uncle, that afternoon, when Mrs. Hammond came into the nursery, her face as pale and set as marble, and silently lifted the child from the girl's lap to her own. For one instant her cheek was laid against the velvet of the babe's; the ringlets of fair hair mingled with her dark locks, before she set about completing its unfinished toilette. With a nicety and care that would have seemed overstrained, had other than the mother's hands been busied in the work, the stockings and slippers were fitted on the plump feet; the sunny curls rolled around the fingers of the tiring woman, and brushed back from the brow; the worked cambric robe lowered cautiously over the head, lest the effect of the coiffure should be marred; the sleeves looped up with bands of coral and gold, a necklace, belonging to the same set, clasped around the baby's white throat, and she was ready for survey.

"Now, Baby Belle and mamma will go down to meet papa!"

And with the little one still clinging to her neck, she met, in the lower hall, her husband ushering in Lucy and Philip Benson.

CHAPTER XIII.

Breakfast was kept back an hour next morning to await Lucy's tardy appearance. "She was sadly wearied with her journey," apologized Philip, and Sarah begged that she would keep her room and have her meals sent up to her—an hospitable offer, which Mr. Benson negatived.

Lucy did look tired and unrefreshed, and, to speak more plainly, very cross. Her hair, in its dryest state of pale yellow, was combed straight back above her temples; her skin was sallow; her wrapper carelessly put on, and its dead white unrelieved by even a bow of ribbon at the throat. Involuntarily Lewis glanced from the uninviting picture to his household deity, in her neat breakfast-dress of gray silk faced with pink, her glossy hair and tranquil features, and said to himself, in secret triumph, "Which is now the beauty? None of your trumpery ornamental articles for me!"

Philip's eyes were as keen as his host's, and the probability is that he instituted a similar comparison, however well his pride succeeded in concealing the act and its result. Cutting short his wife's querulous plaints of the discomforts of travel, and the horrors of nervous sleeplessness, he opened a conversation with Mr. Hammond in the subdued, perfectly-managed tones Sarah remembered so well, selecting such topics as would interest a business man and a citizen of a commercial metropolis. Lucy pouted, and applied herself for consolation to her breakfast.

With a strange mingling of emotions, Sarah listened to

the dialogue between the gentlemen. She was anxious that Lewis should acquit himself creditably. Brilliant, like Philip, he could never be; but in sterling sense, not many men were his superiors. She had never had cause to be ashamed of him; for one so unpretending and judicious was not liable to make himself ridiculous. Whence, then, the solicitude with which she hung upon his every word? her disappointment when he did not equal the ideal reply she had fashioned, as she heard the words that called it forth? Several times she joined in the conversation, invariably to corroborate Lewis's assertions, or to supply something he had omitted to state. Philip Benson was a student of human nature. Was his mind sufficiently abstracted from his domestic annoyances to divine the motive that Sarah herself only perceived afterwards in solitary self-examination? Not love of, or admiration for the intrinsic excellence of the man whose name she bore; not fear lest his modesty should lessen his merits in the eyes of others; but a selfish dread that his acute interlocutor, discerning in him nothing likely to attract or win the affection of a woman such as he knew her to be, might guess her true reason for marrying Mr. Hammond. The timorous progeny of one guilty secret can only be numbered by the minutes during which it is borne in the bosom. Like the fabled Lacedæmonian boy, Sarah carried the gnawing horror with a fortitude that looked like cheerfulness. Habit cannot lighten the weight of a clinging curse; but strength and hardness come in time, if the burdened one is not early crushed by his load.

The sisters spent most of the day in Lucy's room; the latter stretched upon the lounge, as she declared, "completely used up." Mrs. Hunt came around early in the forenoon, and into her sympathizing ears the spoiled child poured the story of her woes and wrongs; Sarah sitting by with a swelling, rebellious heart. With indecorous contempt for one of the most binding laws of the married state—inviolable secrecy as to the faults of the other party to the momentous compact—mother and daughter compared notes upon their husbands, and criticised the class generally as the most wrong-headed, perverse, and dictatorial of all the necessary evils of society.

Mrs. Benson, the elder, and her pleasure-loving daughter-in-law had differed seriously several months before the death of the former. Philip, while espousing his wife's cause to the rest of his family, had, in private, taken her to task for what he considered objectionable in her conduct; her heads of offence being mainly extravagant love of gay company, and the gallant attentions of gentleman-visitors; neglect of dress and all efforts to please, when there was no company by; and a decided indisposition to share in the household duties, which his mother's increasing feebleness made onerous to her.

"Ah, mother!" sighed the interesting complainant, raising herself to shake up her pillow, then sinking again upon it. "If girls only realized what is before them when they marry, few would be brave enough to change their condition. When I picture to myself what I was at home—a petted darling—never allowed to inconvenience myself when it could possibly be avoided; courted in society; free as air and light-hearted as a child; and then think of all that I have endured from the unkindness of strangers, and the—well—the want of sympathy in him for whom I had given up my dear old home and friends—I ask myself why I did not remain single!"

The prudent matchmaker shook her head. "Marriage is a lottery, they say, my dear; but I am very sure that single life is a blank. You had no fortune, and in the event of your father's death would have been almost destitute. I am sorry that your father did not insist upon Mr. Benson's giving you your own establishment at once. I hope, now the old lady is out of the way, you will have things more according to your notions."

"Don't you believe that! As if there were not two sisters-in-law, living but four miles off, and driving over every other day to 'see how pa is.' That means, to see whether Lucy is letting things go to wreck and ruin. I understand their spiteful ways! Philip shuts his ears when I talk about them; but I am determined that I will not bear much more meddling!"

Decidedly, Lucy Benson married was a woeful declension from the seraphic spinster depicted in our earlier chapters; but, as in time past, so in time present and to come, the sparkling sugar, whose integrity and sweetness appeared indestructible, while it was kept dry and cool, if dampened, undergoes an acetous fermentation, and the delicate sweetmeat, exposed to the air at a high temperature, becomes speedily a frothing mass, evolving pungent gases. The pretty doll who anticipates, in the connubial state, one long *fête*-day of adoration received, and benign condescension dispensed, is as certain to awake from this dream as from any other, and upon the temper in which she sustains the disenchantment, depends a vast proportion of her future welfare and peace.

Lucy's behavior to her babe was a mixture of childish fondling and neglect. Fortunately, the little "Hunt's" special attendant was an elderly woman, long established as "Maumer" in the Benson family, and her devotion to her charge prevented any present evil effects from his mother's incompetence or carelessness. Philip's pride in, and love for his boy were extreme. When he came in that evening, Sarah chanced to be in the nursery adjoining her chamber, watching and inciting the two babies to a game of romps.

She held one on each knee, the nurses standing by in amused gratification.

"That is surely my little man's voice!" said Philip, as he and Lewis came up the stairs.

"Let me see!"—and Mr. Hammond peeped into the play-room. "Walk in!" he continued, throwing the door wide open. "Isn't there a pair of them?"

"And a nurse worthy of the twain!" replied Philip. He stooped to the invitation of the lifted arms, fluttering, as if the owner would fly to his embrace. "What do you say of him, aunty? Is he not a passable boy?"

"More than passable! he is a noble-looking fellow. He resembles you, I think," said Sarah, quietly.

"Do you hear that, Hammond? Your wife pronounces me 'more than passable—a noble-looking fellow!' So much for an adroit hint. Is she given to flattery?"

"Not she!" returned Lewis, laughing. "She never said as much as that for my looks in all her life. I have one consolation, however; the less she says the more she means!" He went into the dressing-room, and Philip, still holding the child, seated himself by Sarah.

"How odd, yet how familiar it seems, to be with you once more, my good sister! What a succession of mischances has made us virtual strangers for many months past! I had almost despaired of ever holding friendly converse with you again. I wonder if your recollections of our visit to Aunt Sarah are as vivid as mine. Do you remember that last sad, yet dear day on the Deal Beach?"

Baby Belle was standing in her mother's lap, her soft, warm arms about her neck; and around the frail, sinking human heart invisible arms, as warm and close, were upholding and strengthening it in the moment of mortal weakness.

"Very distinctly. Many changes have come to us both since then."

"To me very many! I have grown older in heart than in years." Then, evidently fearing that she might otherwise interpret his meaning, he subjoined: "We have had a heavy bereavement in our household, you know. *Your* changes have all been happy ones. The enthusiastic, restless girl has ripened into the more sedate, yet more blessed wife and mother."

Press your sweet mouth to the convulsed lips, Baby Belle! veil with your silky curls the tell-tale features, whose agitation would bewilder, if not betray! Philip was stroking the head of his boy, and did not see the uneasiness of his companion.

"Have you heard of Uncle Nathan's death?" she asked, clearing her throat.

He looked surprised at the inquiry. "Yes! Aunt Sarah wrote immediately to my father."

"Ah! I had forgotten that they were brothers. My memory is treacherous. Excuse me! I am wanted in the dining-room!"

Lewis met her just outside the door, and stopped her to bestow the evening kiss he had not cared to offer in Philip's presence.

"Why, you are as rosy as a peony!" he said, jestingly. "Has Benson been paying you compliments, in return for yours to him? I must look after you two, if you carry on at this rate."

With a look he had reason subsequently to recall, but which only pleased him at the time, she raised his hand to her lips—a look of humility, gratitude, and appeal, such as one might cast upon a slighted benefactor—and vanished.

A merry family party gathered around the Hammond's generous table, that afternoon. All the Hunts were there—

from the father down to Jeannie, who was fast shooting up into a tall girl, somewhat pert in manner, but lovable despite this, at times, unpleasant foible.

"Sister Lucy," she said, after an interval of silence, "Ellen West said, at school, to-day, that you were a great belle when you were a young lady; were you?"

"You must not ask *me*, Jeannie!" The old smile of conscious beauty stole into Lucy's cheeks.

"Was she, sister?" Jeannie referred the case to Sarah.

"Yes, my dear, she was very beautiful," replied the latter, simply.

"She isn't now—not so *very* handsome, I mean—no handsomer than you are, sister!"

"Jeannie! you forget yourself!" interposed Mrs. Hunt.

"Why, mamma, I did not intend to be rude! Only I thought that belles were always the prettiest ladies that could be found anywhere."

"By no means!" corrected Lewis, willing to help his wife's pet out of a scrape. "There are many descriptions of belles, Jeannie: handsome, rich, fast, and intellectual."

"And as papa was not rich, I suppose you were either fast or intellectual, sister Lucy!" persisted the child.

"I thought her pretty fast when I tried to catch her," said Philip.—"Mrs. Hunt, Mrs. Hammond, Mrs. Benson, have you ladies decided in the course of to-day's congress what watering-place is to be made the fashion by our clique next month?"

Mrs. Hunt replied that they inclined to Newport; principally on account of Lucy and the children, who would all be benefited by the bathing.

Lucy was sure that she should tire of Saratoga or the Catskills in a week, whereas she adored the ocean.

"What says Madame Discretion?" said Lewis, merrily, to his wife.

"Except that it would break up the family party, I had rather stay at home as long as it is prudent to keep the baby in town; then, if you could go with us, spend a month at some mountain farm-house or sea-side cottage," she answered.

"Hear! hear!" commanded Philip. "Behold a modern wedded dame who prefers seclusion with her liege lord to gayety without him! The age of miracles is returning!"

"Is the case, then, so anomalous?" retorted Sarah, the red spot in her cheek alone testifying to her embarrassment. "Are your Southern matrons all public characters?"

"I can answer that!" said Lucy. "They are slaves! housekeeping machines—nothing better!"

"How many more weak places are there in this crust of family chit-chat, I should like to be informed!" thought the annoyed and uninitiated Hammond. "Here goes for the spot where there is no danger of anybody's breaking in!" He spoke aloud. "A tempting proposal was made to me this morning. It is considered advisable for one of our firm to go abroad for a couple of months, perhaps longer, to divide his time among the principal manufacturing districts of England, Scotland, and France. Expenses paid by the firm, and the term of absence indefinitely prolonged, if the traveller wishes it. Mr. Marlow is tired of crossing the ocean, and presses me to accept the mission."

"What did you tell him?"

It was Sarah who spoke in a startled voice that drew general notice to her alarmed face. Her concern was a delicious tribute to her husband's self-love, if he possessed such a quality. At least he loved *her* well enough to be pleased at her manifest reluctance to have him leave her.

"I told him that I must ask my wife," said he in a meek tone, belied by the humorous twinkle in his eye, and loving half-smile about his mouth. "See what it is to be one under authority, Benson! A man dare not conclude an ordinary business transaction without the approval of the powers that be."

When Sarah accompanied her sister to her chamber that night, the *passée* belle put a direct question.

"Tell me, Sarah, are you as much in love with Mr. Hammond as you seem to be, or is it all put on for the benefit of outsiders?"

"I am not apt to do any thing for the sake of mere show; nor do I care for the opinion of 'outsiders,' as you call them," rejoined Sarah, amazed at the cool audacity of the inquiry, and disposed to resent Lucy's confident expectation that she would avow the cheat, if such there were, in her deportment.

"You used to be shockingly independent, I know. What a ridiculously honest little puss you were! How you despised all our pretty arts and necessary affectations! How you hated our economical mother's second-best furniture and dinners! I don't believe Victoria West has ever forgiven you for the way in which you used to take to pieces what you styled our 'surface talk and surface life!' I thought, however, that you had discovered by this time, that one cannot live in the world without deceiving herself or other people; *I* prefer making fools to being one. Heigh-ho! this life is a very unsatisfactory business at the best. What a heavenly collar that is of yours! One thing I do wish, and that is—that my husband were half as fond of me, or as good to me, as Lewis is to you!"

CHAPTER XIV.

Lewis Hammond had thrown the whole weight of his influence in the family conclave, into the Newport scale; and to this popular resort Sarah went, in July, in company with the Bensons, her mother and Jeannie, who was made one of the party at Lewis's request and expense. The generous fellow acted in conformity with conscience and judgment in this temporary exile of his treasures; and, consistent in his purpose of rendering it a pleasure excursion to his wife, he made very light of his prospects of lonely widowerhood, representing, instead, the benefit she and the babe would draw from the sea-breezes, and his enhanced enjoyment of his weekly visits, because they *were* so far apart. He went with them to the shore, at their general flitting, and spent two days; saw for himself that those whose comfort was nearest his heart were properly accommodated; privately feed chambermaid and waiter, with hints of future emolument to accrue to them from special regard to the wants of Mrs. Hammond and her infant, and returned to town with the unenviable consciousness of having left at least three-fourths of himself behind him.

A brisk rush of business beguiled him of the aching, hollow void for a few hours after he got back. Not even Baby Belle's accents could be heard amid that roar and whir. But at luncheon-time, while waiting for his order to be filled at a restaurant, the dreary, solitary void overtook him—a fit of unmistakable home-sickness, that yet caused him to recoil at the idea of entering the deserted house up-town, when evening should oblige him to seek a lodging. How were Sarah and baby getting along without him? He was afraid that Lucy was not, in all respects, as congenial a companion as he could have wished his wife to have, and that Mrs. Hunt's undisguised worldliness, her foolish love of fashion and display, would often annoy and mortify her sensible and right-judging daughter. Benson was capital company, though—a gentleman every inch of him! and very friendly to Sarah. But for her reserved manners he would act the part of a real brother to her; in any case, he would be kind, and see that she wanted for nothing.

Then—shot into his head by some unseen and unaccountable machinery—there darted across his mind a fragment of a conversation he had overheard, at entering his parlor, the day before the Bensons left. Philip and Lucy were standing before a miniature painting of Sarah and her child, completed and brought home a short time previous. Although seemingly intent upon the picture, their conversation must have strayed far from the starting-point, for the first sentence that reached the unintentional listener was a tart, scornful speech from Lucy, that could by no stretch of the imagination be made to apply to her sister.

"If you admire her so much, why did you not marry her when you had the opportunity? She was willing enough!"

"Take care you do not make me regret that I did not do so!" was Philip's stern rejoinder as he turned from her.

The change of position showed him that Lewis was present, and for a second his inimitable self-possession wavered. Recovering himself, he reverted to the picture, and called upon his host to decide some disputed point in its artistic execution which he and Lucy were discussing.

"Poor fellow! he has learned that all is not gold that glitters!" mused Lewis to the newspaper he was pretending to read. "Lucy had a high reputation for amiability before she was Mrs. Benson. There is no touchstone like the wedding-ring to bring out one's true qualities."

He sat with his back to the entrance of the saloon, and the table directly behind him was now taken possession of by three or four new arrivals—all gentlemen, and apparently on familiar terms with one another. They called for a bountiful lunch, including wine, and plunged into a lively, rather noisy talk. Lewis closed his ears, and applied himself in earnest to his paper. He started presently at a word he could have declared was his name. Restraining the impulse to look around and see who of the group was known to him, he yet could not help trying to determine this point by their voices. One, a thin falsetto, he fancied belonged to George Bond, who was no more of a favorite with him than was his better half with Sarah. Lewis regarded him as a conceited rattle-pate, whose sole talent lay in the art of making money—whose glory was his purse. "Why should he be talking about me here? Nonsense; I was mistaken!" and another page of the newspaper was turned.

"When I leave my wife at Newport, or anywhere else, in the particular and brotherly care of one of her former flames, publish me as a crazy fool!" said the wiry voice again, almost in the reader's ear.

"He doesn't know old stories as well as you do, perhaps," remarked some one.

"I should think not! When *my* wife pulls the wool over my eyes in that style, horsewhip me around town, and I won't cry 'Quarter!' Sister's husband or not, I'll be hanged if I would have him in my house for two weeks, and he is such a good-looking dog, too!"

He stopped, as if his neighbor had jogged him, as Lewis looked over his shoulder in the direction of the gossip. A dead and awkward silence ensued, ended at last by the pertinent observation that the "waiter was a long time bringing their lunch."

In a maze of angry doubt and incredulity as to the evidence of his senses and suspicions, Lewis finished his meal, and stalked out past the subdued and now voracious quartette, favoring them with a searching look as he went by, which they sustained with great meekness. All the afternoon a heavy load lay upon his heart—an indefinable dread he dared not analyze; a forboding he would not face, yet could not dismiss.

"You are blue, Lewis!" said Mr. Marlow, kindly, as they started up town together. "This is the worst of having a wife and children; you miss them so terribly when they are away. But you will get used to it. Make up your mind at the eleventh hour to cross the water, and stay abroad three months. You will be surprised to find how easy your mind will become after a couple of weeks."

"I am satisfied, sir, without making personal trial of the matter, that men become inured to misery, which seemed in the beginning to be insupportable."

Mr. Marlow laughed, and they separated.

Lewis sighed as he looked up at the blinds of his house, shut fast and grim, and still more deeply as he admitted himself to the front hall, that echoed dismally the sound of the closing door. His next movement was to walk into the parlor, throw open a shutter, and let in the evening light upon the portraits of the dear absent ones. There he stood, scanning their faces—eyes and soul full of love and longing—until the mellow glow passed away and left them in darkness.

The comfortless evening repast was over, and he betook himself to the library, Sarah's favorite room, as it was also his. Her low easy-chair stood in its usual place opposite his at the centre-table, but her work-basket was missing;

likewise the book, with its silver marker, that he was wont to see lying side by side with some volume he had selected for his own reading. But one lay there now, and there was an odd choking in his throat as he read the title on the back. He had expressed a wish for it in Sarah's hearing some days before, and her delicate forethought had left it here as a solace and keepsake, one that should, while reminding him of her, yet charm away sad feelings in her absence. Even in the exterior of the gift, she had been regardful of his taste. The binding was solid and rich; no gaudy coloring or tawdry gilt; the thick smooth paper and clear type were a luxury to touch and sight. Lewis was no sentimentalist, in the ordinary acceptation of the term, yet he kissed the name his wife had traced upon the fly-leaf ere he sat down to employ the evening as she by her gift tacitly requested him to do. But it was a useless attempt. The book was not in fault, and he should have read it intently, if only because she had bestowed it; still, the hand that held it sank lower and lower, until it rested upon his knee, and the reader was the thinker instead.

The most prosaic of human beings have their seasons of reverie—pleasing or mournful, which are, unknown often to themselves, the poetry of their lives. Such was the drama Lewis Hammond was now rehearsing in his retrospective dreams.

The wan and weary mother, whom he remembered as always clothed in widow's weeds, and toiling in painful drudgery to maintain herself and her only boy; who had smiled and wept, rendered thanksgivings and uttered prayers for strength, alternately, as she heard Mr. Marlow's proposal to protect and help the lad through the world that had borne so hardly upon her; who had strained him to her bosom, and shed fast, hot tears of speechless anguish at their parting—a farewell that was never to be forgotten in any meeting on this side of eternity; this was the vision, hers the palladium of love, that had nerved him for the close wrestle with fortune, guarded him amid the burning ploughshares of temptation, carried him unscathed past the hundred mouths of hell, that gape upon the innocent and unwary in all large cities. Cold and unsusceptible as he was deemed in society, he kept unpolluted in his breast a fresh living stream of genuine romantic feeling, such as we are apt to think went out of fashion—aye, and out of being—with the belted knights of yore; wealth he had vowed never to squander, never reveal, until he should pour it, without one thought of self-reserve, upon *his wife!* He never hinted this to a living creature before the moment came for revealing it to the object of his choice. He was a "predestined old bachelor!" an "infidel to love and the sex," said and believed the gay and frivolous, and he let them talk. His ideal woman, his mother's representative and successor—the beauty and crown of his existence—was too sacred for the gaze and comment of indifferent worldlings. For her he labored and studied and lived; confident in a fatalistic belief that, at the right moment, the dream would become a reality—the phantasm leave her cloudy height for his arms.

Love so beautiful and intense as this, like snow in its purity, like fire in its fervor, cannot be won to full and eloquent utterance but by answering love—a sentiment identical in kind, if not equal in degree; and Sarah Hammond's estimate of her husband's affection was, in consequence of this want in herself, cruelly unjust in its coldness and poverty. His patience with her transient fits of gloom or waywardness in the early months of their married life; his noble forgetfulness of her faults, and grateful acknowledgment of her most trifling effort to please him; his unceasing care; his lavish bounty—all these she attributed too much to natural amiability and conscientious views of duty; too little to his warm regard for her personally. In this persuasion she had copied his conduct in externals so far as she could; and applauding observers adjudged the mock gem to be a fair and equitable equivalent for the rare pearl she had received.

Lest this digression, into which I have been inadvertently betrayed, should mislead any with the idea that I have some design of dignifying into a hero this respectable, but very commonplace personage, return we to him as he hears eleven o'clock rung out by the monitor on the mantel, and says to himself, "Baby Belle has been asleep these three hours, and mamma, caring nothing for beaux and ball-room, is preparing to follow her."

Beaux and ball-room! Pshaw! why should the nonsensical talk of that jacknapes, George Bond, come to his mind just then? The whole tenor of the remarks that succeeded the name he imagined was his disproved that imagination. But *who* had left his wife at Newport in the care of a "good-looking" brother-in-law? *who* had been domesticated in the family of the deluded husband for a fortnight?

Pshaw again! What concern had he with their scandalous, doubtless slanderous tattle?

"Why did you not marry her when you had the opportunity? *She* was willing enough!"

Could Lucy have spoken thus of her sister? Sarah was barely acquainted with Philip Benson when Lucy wedded him, having met him but once prior to the wedding-day at the house of her aunt in the country, from which place his own letter, penned by her father's sick-bed, recalled her. How far from his thoughts then was the rapid train of consequences that followed upon this preliminary act of their intercourse!

Did that scoundrel Bond say "Hammond?" It was not

a common name, and came quite distinctly to his ears in the high, unpleasant key he so disliked. A flush of honest shame arose to his forehead at this uncontrollable straying of his ideas to a topic so disagreeable, and so often rejected by his mind.

"As if—even had I been the person insulted by his pity—I would believe one syllable he said of a woman as far above him in virtue and intellect, in every thing good and lovable, as the heavens are above the earth! I would despise myself as much as I do him, if I could lend my ear for an instant to so degrading a whisper! I wish I had faced him and demanded the whole tale; yet no! that would have been rash and absurd. Better as it is! By to-morrow, I shall laugh at my ridiculous fancies!"

"Scratch! scratch! scratch!" The house was so still in the approaching midnight that the slight noise caused him a shock and quiver in the excited state of his nerves. The interruption was something between a scrape and a rap, three times repeated, and proceeding, apparently, from the bookcase at his right. What could it be? He had never seen or heard of a mouse on the premises, nor did the sound much resemble the nibbling of that animal. Ashamed of the momentary thrill he had experienced, he remained still and collected, awaiting its repetition.

"Scratch! scratch! rap!" It *was* in the bookcase—in the lower part where were drawers shut in by solid doors. These he had never explored, but knew that his wife kept pamphlets and papers in them. He opened the outer doors cautiously, and listened again, until assured by the scratching that his search was in the right direction. There were three drawers, two deep, the third and upper shallow. This he drew out and examined. It contained writing-paper and envelopes, all in good order. Nor was there any sign of the intruder amongst the loose music and periodicals in the second. The lower one was locked—no doubt accidentally, for he had never seen Sarah lock up any thing except jewels and money. Their servants were honest, and she had no cause to fear investigation on his part.

Feeling, rather than arguing thus, he removed the drawer above, leaving exposed the locked one, and thrust his hand down into it. It encountered the polished surface of a small box or case, which he was in the act of drawing through the aperture left by the second drawer, when something dark and swift ran over his hand and up his sleeve. With a violent start, he dashed the casket to the floor, and another energetic fling of his arm dislodged the mouse. His first care was to pursue and kill it; his next to examine into the damage it had indirectly produced. The box—ebony, lined with sandal-wood—had fallen with such force as to loosen the spring, and lay on its side wide open; its treasures strewed over the carpet. They were neither numerous, nor in themselves valuable. A bouquet of dried flowers, enveloped in silver paper, lay nearest Lewis's hand, as he knelt to pick up the scattered articles. The paper was tied about the stalks of the flowers with *black* ribbon, and to this was attached a card: "Will Miss Sarah accept this trifling token of regard from one who is her stanch friend, and hopes, in time, to have a nearer claim upon her esteem?"

The hand was familiar to the reader as Philip Benson's. Why should Sarah preserve this, while the many floral tokens of *his* love which she had received were flung away when withered like worthless weeds? The pang of jealousy was new—sharp as the death-wrench to the heart-strings, cruel as the grave! The card was without date, or he would have read, with a different apprehension of its meaning, the harmless clause—"*And hopes in time to have a nearer claim upon her esteem.*" There was a time, then, when, as Lucy had taunted her husband, he might have married her sister! when Sarah loved him, and had reason to think herself beloved in return! What was this sable badge but the insignia of a bereaved heart, that mourned still in secret the faithlessness of her early love, or the adverse fate that had sundered him from her, and given him to another?

Crushing the frail, dead stems in his hand, he threw them back into the box, and took up a bit of dark gray wood, rough on one side—smoothed on the other into a rude tablet. "*Philip Benson, Deal Beach, July 27th,* 1856. *Pensez à moi!*" But ten days before he met her at the wharf in New York to take her to her sick father! but three months before she plighted her troth to him, promised to wed him, while in spirit she was still weeping tears of blood over the inconstant! for he did not forget that Philip's engagement to Lucy preceded his own to Sarah by eight or nine weeks. There were other relics in the box; a half-worn glove, retaining the shape of the manly hand it had inclosed—which, he learned afterwards, Philip had left in his chamber at the farm-house when he departed to seek gayer scenes; a white shell, upon whose rosy lining were scratched with the point of a knife the ominous initials, "P. B.," and beneath them "S. B. H.," a faded rose-bud, and several printed slips, cut from the columns of newspapers. He unfolded but two of these.

One was an extract from Tennyson's "Maud"—the invitation to the garden. Breathlessly, by reason of the terrible stricture tightening around his heart, Lewis ran his eyes over the charming whimsical morceau. They rested upon and reviewed the last verse:

"She is coming—my own, my sweet!
Were it ever so airy a tread,
My heart would hear her and beat;
Were it earth in an earthy bed,

"My dust would hear her and beat;
Had I laid for a century dead,
Would start and tremble under her feet,
And blossom in purple and red."

He did not discriminate now between printed and written verses. These were love stanzas sent by another man to *his* wife, received and cherished by her, hidden away with a care that, in itself, bordered on criminality, for was not its object the deception of the injured husband? The most passionate autograph love-letter could hardly have stabbed him more keenly.

The other was Mrs. Browning's exquisite "Portrait."

And here the reader can have an explanation the tortured man could not obtain. With the acumen for which Cupid's votaries are proverbial, Philip Benson, then at the "summer heat" degree of his flame for the Saratoga belle, had recognized in this poem the most correct and beautiful description of his lady-love. Curiosity to see if the resemblance were apparent to other eyes, and a desire for sympathy tempted him to forward it to Sarah. She must perceive the likeness to her divine sister, and surmise the sentiment that had induced him to send it. A little alteration in the opening stanza was requisite to make it a "perfect fit." Thus it was when the change was made:—

I will paint her as I see her:
—— times have the lilies blown
Since she looked upon the sun."

The poetess, guiltless of any intention to cater for the wants of grown-up lovers, had written "Ten" in the space made blank by Philip's gallantry and real ignorance of his charmer's age. For the rest, the "lily-clear face," the "forehead fair and saintly," the "trail of golden hair," the blue eyes, "like meek prayers before a shrine," the voice that

"Murmurs lowly
As a silver stream may run,
Which yet feels you feel the sun,"

were, we may safely assert, quite as much like poor Sarah, when he sent the poem, as they were now like the portrait he would—if put upon his oath—sketch of his unidealized Lucy.

It was not unnatural then, in Lewis Hammond, to overlook in his present state, these glaring discrepancies in the picture as applied by him. With a blanched and rigid countenance he put all the things back into the box, shut it, and restored it to its place. Then he knelt on the floor and hid his face in his wife's chair; and there struggled out into the still air of the desecrated home-temple, made sacred by his love and her abiding, deep sobs from the strong man's stricken heart—a grief as much more fearful than that of widowhood, as the desertion and dishonor of the loved one are worse than death.

CHAPTER XV.

It was the "grand hop" night at the head-quarters of Newport fashion. Sarah, characteristically indifferent to gayeties "made to order," had determined not to appear below. The air of her room was fresh and pure, and a book, yet unread, lay under the lamp upon her table. Her sister and mother had withdrawn to dress, when Jeannie's curly head peeped in at Mrs. Hammond's door. Her features wore a most woe-begone expression.

"What has gone wrong, Jeannie?" inquired Sarah.

"Why, mamma says that I will be in her way if I go into the ball-room; and it will be so stupid to stay out the whole evening, while all the other girls can see the dancing and dresses, and hear the music. And sister Lucy says that children are 'bores' in company."

"A sad state of things, certainly! Perhaps I may persuade mother to let you go."

"Yes; but if she does, she will sit close against the wall with a lot of other fat old ladies, and they will talk over my head, and squeeze me almost to death, besides rumpling my dress; and I so want to wear my tucked pink grenadine, sister!"

"And you would like to have me go down with you; is that it?"

Jeannie's eyes beamed delightedly. "Oh, if you only would!"

Sarah looked down into the eager face and saw, in anticipation, her own little Belle imploring some boon, as important to her, as easy to be granted by another as this, and consented with a kiss.

"Run away and bring your finery here! Mother is too busy to attend to you. Mary can dress you."

The order was obeyed with lightning speed; and Sarah, still beholding in the excited child the foreshadowing of her darling's girlhood, superintended the toilet, while she made herself ready.

"What shall I wear, Jeannie?" she asked, carelessly, holding open the door of her wardrobe.

"Oh, that lovely fawn-colored silk, please! the one with the black lace flounces! It is the prettiest color I ever saw; and I heard Mrs. Greyling tell another lady the night you wore it, when brother Lewis was here, you know, that it was one of the richest dresses in the room, modest as it looked, and that the flounces must have cost a penny!"

"Probably more!"

Sarah proceeded to array herself in the fortunate robe that had won the praises of the fashionably distinguished Mrs. Greyling. Her abundant dark hair was lighted by two coral sprigs, which formed the heads of her hair-pins, and, handkerchief and gloves in hand, she was taking a last survey of Jeannie's more brilliant costume, when there came a knock at the door.

"Mr. Benson!" said Mary, unclosing it.

"May I come in?" he asked.

The tidy Mary had removed all trace of the recent tiring operations from the apartment, which was a compound of parlor and dressing-room, a necessary adjunct to the small chamber and smaller nursery, leading out of it, at the side and rear.

"You may!" replied Sarah. "Here is an aspirant for ball-room honors, who awaits your approval."

Mademoiselle, que vous êtes charmante! I am penetrated with profound admiration!" exclaimed the teasing brother-in-law, raising his hands in true melodramatic style.

Jeannie laughed and blushed until her cheeks matched the grenadine.

"Mrs. Hunt told me that you had changed your mind, and intended to grace the festive scene with your presence," continued Philip, addressing Sarah. "She and Lucy are there, and the dancing has begun. I came to escort you and our fair *débutante* here—that is, unless some one else has offered his services and been accepted."

"That is not likely, since Mr. Hammond left us in your care. Do not your fourfold duties oppress you?"

"Not in the least. If all my charges were as chary of their calls upon me as you are, my time would hang heavily upon my hands. No one would imagine, from your reluctance to be waited upon, that you had been spoiled at home. If Mr. Hammond were here now, he would tell you to draw that shawl—"

"It is an opera cloak!" interrupted Jeannie.

"A ball-cloak to-night, then, is it not? I was saying that, although the night is not cool for sea air, you had better wrap that mantle about your chest and throat as we go out."

Just outside the door a waiter passed them with a note in his hand. He stopped, on seeing Philip.

"Mr. Benson! I was on my way to your rooms with this, sir."

Philip stepped back within the parlor to read it by the light. It was a line from a friend who had just arrived at another hotel, notifying him of this fact. It required no reply, and leaving it upon the table, he rejoined his companions.

"See mamma! Isn't it just as I said?" whispered Jeannie, as she established herself beside her sister in a comfortable corner that commanded a view of the spacious hall and its gay, restless sea of figures.

Sarah smiled at discovering her mother sandwiched between two portly dowagers; one in purple, the other in lavender silk; all three bobbing and waving in their earnest confabulations, in a style that presented a ludicrously marked resemblance to the gesticulations of a group of Muscovy ducks, on the margin of a mud-puddle, held by them in their capacity of a joint-stock company.

"I see that Lucy has taken the floor," observed Philip. "She will not thank me for any devoirs I could render her for the next three hours. If they get up any thing so humdrum as quadrilles, may I ask the pleasure of your company for the set?"

'If you wish it—and my dress is not too grave in hue—"

"And too decorous in its make, you were about to add, I presume:" he finished the sentence bluntly. "It forms a refreshing contrast to the prevailing style around us."

Lucy here flitted into sight, and her very bare arms and shoulders pointed her husband's strictures. A stool, brought into the room for the use of some child or invalid looker-on of the festivities, now stood empty under Sarah's chair, and Philip, espying it, seized upon and drew it forth. When seated, his mouth was nearly on a level with Sarah's ear.

"This is pleasant!" he said. "We are quite as much isolated from the rest of mankind as if we were sitting among the heathery hillocks on Deal Beach. You do not love the visions of those tranquil sunny days as I do. You never allude to them voluntarily. Yet you have had less to convert your dreams into every-day actualities, tedious and prosaic, than I have. I stand in direful need of one of the old lectures, inculcating more charity, and less study of complex motives and biassed tendencies in the machine we call Man. Begin! I am at your mercy."

"I have forgotten how to deliver them. I am out of practice."

"That is not surprising. Your husband is behind the age he lives in—and so are you. You two would make Barnum's fortune, could he ever persuade the public of your idiosyncrasies."

"What are you talking about?"

"Look around and through this room, and you will understand one part of my meaning. Do you remark the preponderance of married over single belles? and that the most tenderly deferential cavaliers are husbands, and *not* dancing with their wives? I could point out to you three men, leaders of the *ton* in this extremely reputable, eminently moral assembly, who, it is whispered among the knowing ones, are married, and, having left their domestic associations for a season of recreation, boldly attach themselves to certain stylish young ladies here, and challenge observation, defy public censure, by their marked and increasing devotion. I meet them strolling along the beach in the morning; riding together in the afternoon; and when not engaged in this evening exhibition of toilet and muscle, you will find them pacing the moon or star-lit piazza, or, perchance, again sentimentalizing on the shore until the witching hour draws near."

"You surprise me!"

"You have no right to be surprised. You have the same thing continually before you in your city. Every fashionable hotel or boarding-house can supply you with such flirtations by the dozen. A married woman who declines the polite services of all gentlemen, except her husband and near relatives, is a prude, with false scruples of propriety and delicacy. Let her legal partner complain—he is cried out upon as a despot, and you can trust the sweet angel of an abused wife to elude his vigilance—violence, she terms it—for the future, without altering her conduct in aught else. Do you see that pretty woman in blue—the one with the madonna-like face? Her tyrant is here but once a week—from Saturday until Monday—then hies back to the business he loves as well as she does her pleasure. Monday, Tuesday, Wednesday, Thursday, Friday, and the forenoon of Saturday, any mustachioed puppy may walk, talk, drive, and flirt with her—bask in the rays of those liquid orbs. When the rightful lord appears, she is demure as a nun, patient as a saint, dutiful as Griselda, to him and him alone. Do you begin to understand why I congratulated you upon having a husband of the olden stamp? why, I do from my heart felicitate my friend Hammond upon having gained, as a helpmeet, one of that nearly obsolete species—Woman!"

Sarah's embarrassment was painful, and but indifferently concealed. She felt that it was barely excusable, in consideration of his fraternal relation to her, for Philip to speak so plainly of this social blemish; and altogether unpardonable, while he did not, or could not, prevent his wife's participation in the questionable gayeties he assailed so unsparingly. Reply she could not, without implicating Lucy in her reprobation, and he must perceive her difficulty. This was the trouble that lay uppermost. At her heart's core, the uneasy feeling she ever experienced in conversation with him; the stirring of the entombed love, of whose actual death she had horrible misgivings; the incongruous blending of past emotion with present duty, were now aggravated by the enforced acceptance of unmerited praise. Her woman's instinct, her experience as a wife, told her that the cause of the sinful recklessness, the contempt of the true spirit of the marriage tie, was not the fruit merely of the vanity and thirst for adulation, to which it was properly attributed. With the recollection of her own life, the education she had received at home, the hateful, yet, even to her independent spirit, resistless decrees of society, there swelled up within her bosom something akin to Philip's bitter cynicism. Under this spur, she spoke.

"And from these signs of the times, you would argue an inherent degeneracy of womanhood—a radical change in its composition, such as some anatomists tell us has taken place in the structure of our bodies—our blood—our very teeth. A dentist, who filled a tooth for me the other day, imparted divers scientific items of information to me that may illustrate your position. 'Enamel, madam, is not what enamel was in the days of our ancestors!' he affirmed pathetically; 'the color, the very ingredients of the bone, the calcareous base of the teeth, differ sadly from the indestructible molars of fifty years ago.' At this passage of his jeremiade, he chanced to touch the nerve in the unhappy 'molar' he was excavating, and I am persuaded that I suffered as really as my grandmother would have done, had she sat in my place."

She paused, and beat time with her fingers on Jeannie's shoulder to the wild, varying waltz that swept the giddy crowd around the room in fast and flying circles.

"Your analogy asserts, then, that at heart women are alike in all ages?"

"Why not, as well as men?"

"Then why does not action remain the same, if that be true?"

"Because custom—fashion, if you prefer this name—an unaccountable, irresponsible power—owing its birth oftenest to accident or caprice, says, 'Do this!' and it is done! be it to perpetrate a cravat-bow, a marriage, or a murder!"

Another pause—in which music and dancers seemed sweeping on to sweet intoxication—so joyous in their *abandon* were the gushing strains; so swift the whirl of the living ring. The fingers played lightly and rapidly on Jeannie's plump shoulder—then rested on a half-beat.

"Yes!" She was looking towards the crowd, but her eye was fixed, and her accents slow and grave. "Hearts live and hearts love, while time endures. The heart selects its mate in life's spring-time, with judgment as untaught as that of the silly bird that asks no companion but the one the God of Nature has bestowed upon it. But see you not, my good brother"—she faced him, a smile wreathing her lip—a strange glitter in her eye—"see you not to what woeful disorders these untrained desires, this unsophisticated following out of unregulated affections would give rise? It would sap the foundations of caste; level all wholesome distinctions of society; consign the accomplished daughters of palatial halls—hoary with a semi-decade of years—to one-story cottages and a maid-of-all work; doom nice young men to the drudgery of business for the remainder of their wretched lives, to maintain wives whose dowries would not keep their lily-handed lords in French kids for a year; cover managing mammas with ignominy, and hasten ambitious papas to their costly vaults in—as Dickens has it—'some genteel place of interment.' Come what may of blasted hopes and wrecked hearts, the decencies of life must be observed. Every heart has its nerve—genuine, sensitive, sometimes vulgarly tenacious of life—but there *are* corrosives that will eat it out; fine, deadly wires, that can probe and torture and extract it. And when the troublesome thing is finally gotten rid of, there is an end to all obstacles to judicious courtships and eligible alliances!" She laughed scornfully, and Philip recoiled, without knowing why he did so, as he heard her.

"That is all very well, when the nature of the contract is understood on both sides," he said, gloomily. "I doubt, however, whether the beautiful economy of your system will be appreciated by those whose living hearts are bound to the bloodless plaster-casts you describe."

"These accidents will occur in spite of caution on the part of the best managers of suitable marriages. By far the larger proportion of the shocks inflicted upon polite circles arise from this very cause. Pygmalion grows weary of wooing his statue, and wants sympathy in his disappointment and loneliness."

The dance was ended. The fantastic variations of the waltz were exchanged for a noble march—pealing through the heated rooms like a rush of the healthful sea-breeze. The spark died in Sarah's eye. Her voice took its habitual pitch.

"I have permitted myself to become excited, and, I am afraid, have said many things that I had no right to think—much less to utter. If my freedom has displeased you, I am sorry."

"The error—if error there were—was mine," rejoined Philip. "I led the conversation into the channel; you, after awhile, followed. I believe there is no danger of our misunderstanding each other."

"Darby and Joan! good children in the corner!" cried Lucy, flushed with exercise and radiant with good humor, as she promenaded past them leaning on the arm of a young West Pointer, a native Southerner and an acquaintance of Philip's. If his wife must flirt and frolic, he was watchful that she did not compromise him by association with doubtful characters. On several occasions, the advances of gay gentlemen, whose toilets were more nearly irreproachable than their reputations, had been checked by his cool and significant resumption of the husband's post beside the belle, and, if need existed, by the prompt withdrawal of the unwilling lady from the scene. The cadet laughed, and, convinced that she had said a witty thing, Lucy swam by.

"The common sense of our tropes, rodomontades, and allegories is this!" said Philip, biting his lip, and speaking in a hard tone. "The only safe ground in marriage is mutual, permanent affection. You meant to convey the idea that if each of these dressy matrons, humming around our ears, had a sincere, abiding love for her husband—and each of these gallant Benedicts the right kind of regard for his wedded Beatrice, the vocation of us corner censors would be gone?"

"Well said, Mr. Interpreter!" she responded, in affected jest.

"This point settled, will you take my arm for a turn through the room before the next set is formed? They are talking of quadrilles. I shall claim your promise if a set is made up, unless you are not courageous enough to brave the public sneer by dancing with your brother. Come, Jeannie, and walk with us."

Two sets of quadrilles were arranged at different ends of the saloon. Philip led Sarah through one, with Lucy—who considered it a capital joke—and her partner *vis-à-vis* to them, Jeannie, meanwhile, remaining by her mother.

The summer nights were short; and, when the dance was over, Sarah intimated to her younger sister the propriety of retiring. Mrs. Hunt's head ached, and she esteemed the sacrifice comparatively light, therefore, that she, too, had to leave the revels and accompany the child to her chamber. Sarah's apartments were on the same floor, several doors further on. Having said "Good-night" to the others, she and Philip walked slowly along the piazza, light as day in the moonbeams, until they reached her outer room, the parlor.

"I hope you will experience no ill effects from your dissipation," said Philip, in playful irony. "In a lady of your staid habits, this disposition to gayety is alarming. Absolutely eleven o'clock! What will Hammond say when he hears the story? Good-night! Don't let your conscience keep you awake!"

Sarah opened the door softly, that she might not startle the baby-sleeper in the inner room. The lamp was shining brightly, and by it sat—her husband!

CHAPTER XVI.

Lewis had entered his wife's room within fifteen minutes after she left it. He looked so ill and weary that the girl, Mary, gave a stifled scream of fright and surprise.

"Are you sick, sir?" she asked hastily, as he threw off his hat, and wiped his pale forehead. "Shall I tell Mrs. Hammond that you are here? She went down to the ball-room awhile ago."

"What did you say? No!" replied he, shortly.

His frown, rather than his tone, silenced her. He had picked up the envelope Philip had dropped on the table, and his face darkened still more. Too proud to question a servant of her mistress' actions and associates, he believed that he had gathered from this mute witness all that was needful to know. As a privileged *habitué* of the cosy boudoir *he* had been at such pains to procure and make fit for his wife's occupancy, another had sat here and read his evening mail, while awaiting her leisure; careless of appearances, since the deceived one would not be there to notice them, had tossed this note down with as much freedom as he would have done in his own apartment.

Through the open windows poured the distant strains of the band; and, seized by a sudden thought, he caught up his hat and strode out, along piazzas and through halls, to the entrance-door of the ball saloon. As Sarah's ill-fortune ordained it, the piercing glance that ran over and beyond the crowd of spectators and dancers detected her at the instant of Philip's taking his lowly seat at her side. Jeannie's pink attire was concealed by the drapery of a lady, whose place in the set then forming was directly in front of her. Lewis saw but the two, virtually *tête-à-tête;* and, as he obtained fleeting glimpses of them through the shifting throng, marked Philip's energetic, yet confidential discourse, and the intentness with which she listened, until, warmed or excited by his theme, Sarah lifted her downcast eyes and spoke, with what feeling and effect her auditor's varying expression showed.

The gazer stood there like a statue, unheeding the surprised and questioning looks cast by passers-by upon his travelling-dress, streaked with dust—his sad and settled visage, so unbefitting the scene within—while Philip made the tour of the room, with Sarah upon his arm, until they took their stations for the dance; he, courteous and attentive—she, smiling and happy, more beautiful in her husband's eyes than her blonde sister opposite; and he could stay no longer. If Mary had thought him sick and cross at his former entrance, she considered him savage now, for one who was ordinarily a kind and gentle master.

"You can go to your room!" he ordered, not advised. "I will sit up for Mrs. Hammond!"

"I have slept in the nursery, sir, while you were away."

"That cannot be to-night. I will find you some other place."

He had no intention that the anticipated conversation with his wife should be overheard.

"I can stay with a friend of mine, sir, only a few doors off."

"Very well!"

Quickly and quietly the nurse arranged the night-lamp and the child's food, that her mistress might have no trouble during her absence, and went out.

Baby Belle slumbered on, happily wandering through the guileless mazes of baby dream-land; one little arm, bared from the sleeve of her gown, thrown above her head—the hand of the other cradling her cheek. The father ventured to press a light kiss upon the red lips. In his desolation, he craved this trifling solace. The child's face was contorted by an expression of discomfort, and, still dreaming, she murmured, in her inarticulate language, some pettish expression of disgust.

"My very child shrinks from me! It is in the blood!" said the unhappy man, drawing back from the crib.

If his resolution had waned at sight of the sleeper, it was fixed again when he returned to his chair in the outer room. He raised his head from his folded arms when he heard Philip and Sarah approaching, but did not otherwise alter his position. The low tone of their parting words—one soon learned by the sojourners in hotels and watering-places, where thin partitions and ventilators abound—was, to him, the cautiously repressed voice of affectionate good-nights. But one clause was distinct—"What will Hammond say, when he hears the story?" They jested thus of him, then. One of them, at least, should learn ere long what he *would* say.

"Lewis! you here!"

Sarah changed color with amazement and vague alarm—emotion that paralyzed her momentarily. Then, as she discerned the tokens of disorder in his dress and countenance, she hurried forward.

"What has brought you so unexpectedly? Are you sick? Has any thing happened?"

He did not rise; and, resting her hand on his shoulder, she stooped for a kiss. But his stern gaze never moved from hers—anxious and inquiring—and his lips were like stone.

"Lewis, speak to me! If you have dreadful news to tell me, for pity's sake, do not keep me in suspense!"

"I have nothing to say that will be new to you," he said, without relaxing his hard, cold manner, "and not a great deal that ought to have been kept back from *me* when I wished to marry you, believing that you had a heart to give me with your hand."

As if struck in the face, Sarah sank back into a chair, speechless and trembling.

"Yes! had you been sincere with me then, grieved and disappointed as I would have felt, I would have respected you the more, and loved you none the less for the disclosure. But when, after a year and a half of married life, I learn that the woman I have loved and trusted with my whole soul—from whom I have never concealed a thought that it could interest her to know—has all the while been playing a false part—vowing at the altar to love me and me alone, when she secretly idolized another; bearing my name, living beneath my roof, sleeping in my bosom—yet thinking of, and caring for *him*, treasuring his keepsakes as the most precious of her possessions—is it strange that, when the tongue of a vulgar gossip proclaims my shame in my hearing, and other evidence proves what I thought was his vile slander to be true as gospel—is it strange, I say, that I am incensed at the deception practised upon me—at the infamous outrage of my dearest hopes—my most holy feelings?"

She threw herself at his feet, clasped his knees, and implored him, chokingly, to "forgive" her. "Oh! if you knew what I have suffered!"

"What you have suffered!" He folded his arms and looked sorrowfully down at her crouching figure. "Yes! you were not by nature coarse and unfeeling! The violence you have committed upon your heart and every principle of delicacy and truth must have cost you pain. Then you loved him!"

"Once! a long while ago!" said Sarah, hiding her face in her hands.

"Take care!" There was no softness now in his tone. "Remember that I have seen you together day by day, and that glances and actions, unnoticed at the time in my stupid blindness, recur to me now with terrible meaning. For once, speak the true voice of feeling, and own what I know already, that all the love you ever had to give belongs still to your sister's husband!"

"I will speak the truth!" Sarah arose and stood before him—face livid and eyes burning. "I *did* love this man! I married you, partly to please my parents, partly because I found out that by some means my secret had fallen into unscrupulous hands, and I was mad with dread of its exposure! It seemed to me that no worse shame could come upon me than to have it trumpeted abroad that I had bestowed my love unsought, and was ready to die because it was slighted. I have learned since that it is far, far worse to live a lie—to despise myself! Oh! that I *had* died then!" She battled with the emotion that threatened to overwhelm her, and went on. "Once bound to you, it has been my hourly endeavor to feel and act as became the faithful wife of a kind, noble man. If, sometimes, I have erred in thought—if my feelings have failed me in the moment of trial—yet, in word and deed, in look and gesture, I have been true to you. No one have I deceived more thoroughly than Philip Benson. He never suspected my unfortunate partiality for himself; he believes me still, what I would give worlds to become in truth, your loyal, loving wife! It is well that you know the truth at last. I do not ask you how you have obtained the outlines of a disgraceful story, that I have tried a thousand times to tell you, but was prevented by the fear of losing your favor forever. This is my poor defence—not against your charges, but in palliation of the sin of which they justly accuse me. I can say nothing more. Do with me as you will!"

"It is but just to myself that you should hear the circumstances which accidentally revealed this matter to me."

He narrated the scene at the restaurant, and the discovery of the evening. He evinced neither relenting nor sympathy in the recital. Her confession had extinguished the last ray of hope, cherished, though unacknowledged by himself, that she might extenuate her error or give a more favorable construction to the evidence against her. It was not singular that, in the reaction of disappointment, he was ready to believe that he had not heard all; to imagine that he could perceive throughout her statement a disposition to screen Philip, that was, in itself, a proof of disingenuousness, if not deliberate falsehood. She denied that he had ever been aware of her attachment or had reciprocated it. What meant then those words—"hopes in time to have a nearer claim?" what those impassioned verses? what the linking of their initials within the shell? the motto on the wooden tablet? While these subtle queries were insinuated into his soul by some mocking spirit, he concluded the history of the discovery of the casket.

"I have never opened it since the night before I was married," said Sarah, with no haste of self-justification. "I put it into the drawer the day after we went to our house. It has not been unlocked from that day to this."

"Why keep it at all, unless as a memento of one still dear to you?"

"I felt as if I had buried it. I said to myself: 'If the time ever comes when I can disinter these relics and show them to my husband, without a pang or fear, as mementoes of a dead and almost forgotten folly, he shall destroy them, and I shall have gained a victory that will insure my life-long happiness.' "

"And that time has never arrived."

She would have spoken, but her tongue proved traitorous. She crimsoned and was silent.

Lewis smiled drearily. "You see that I know you better than you do yourself. It is well, as you have said, that I know all at last. I pity you! If I could, I would release you from your bondage. As it is, I will do all that I can for this end."

"Never!" cried Sarah, shuddering. "Have you forgotten our child?"

"I have not!" His voice shook for a second. "She is all that unites us now. For the sake of her future—her good name—an open separation ought to be avoided, if possible,—if it be inevitable, *your* conduct must not be the ostensible cause. To quiet malicious tongues, you must remain here awhile longer under your mother's care. To accomplish the same end, I must appear once more in public, and on apparently friendly terms with—your brother-in-law. When your mother returns to the city, you had best go, too, and to your own house. Your brother Robert is now sixteen years old—steady and manly enough to act as your protector. Invite him to stay with you, and also Jeannie, if you find it lonely."

"What are you saying? Where will you be that you speak of my choosing another protector?"

"A very incompetent one I have proved myself to be!" he returned, with the same sad smile. "I have not been able to shield you from invidious reports; still less to save you from yourself. I sail for Europe day after to-morrow."

"Lewis, you will not! If you ever loved me, do not desert me and our child now! I will submit to any punishment but this!" She clung anew to his knees as she poured out her prayer.

Not a month ago she had turned pale with fright at the suggestion of this voyage. It was sheer acting *then!* why not now?

"Objections are useless!" he said. "My arrangements are made. I have passed my word."

"But you will not leave me in anger! Say that you will forgive me! that you will return soon, and this miserable night be forgotten!"

"Shall I tell you when I will return?" He raised her head, and looked straight into her eyes. "When you write to me, and tell me that you have destroyed the love-tokens in that box; when you bid me come back for your sake—*not* for our child's! Until then, I shall believe that my presence would be irksome to you. It is necessary for our house to have a resident partner in England. It is my expectation to fill that place for some time to come; it shall be for you to say how long."

Bowed as Sarah's spirit was beneath the burst of the long-dreaded storm and her accusing conscience, her womanly pride revolted at this speech. She had humbled herself in the dust at the feet of a man whom she did not love; had borne meekly his reproaches; submitted dumbly to the degrading suspicions that far transcended her actual sin: but as the idea of her suing servilely for the love she had never yet valued; of him, indifferent and independent, awaiting afar off for her petition—*hers*, whom he had abandoned to the scornful sneers of the keen-witted hyenas of society; to the cross-examination of her distrustful relatives; the stings of remorse; left in one word to *herself!*—as this picture grew up clearly before her mind, the tide of feeling turned.

"You reject my prayers and despise my tears!" she said,

proudly. "You refuse to accept of my humiliation. Yet you do not doubt me, as you would have me believe that you do! Else you would not *dare* to trust me—the keeper of your honor and your child's fair name—out of your sight! I throw back the charge in your teeth, and tell you that your conduct gives it the lie! I have asked you—shame on me that I did!—to continue to me the shelter of your name and presence; to shield me, a helpless woman, more unhappy than guilty, from the ban of the world; and you deny me every thing but a contemptible shadow of respectability, which the veriest fool can penetrate. I would not have you suppose that your generous confidence in my integrity"—she brought out the words with scathing contempt—"will deter me from sinking to the level you are pleased to assign me. If the native dignity of my womanhood, the principles I inherit from my father, my love for my innocent babe do not hold me back from ruin, be assured that the hope of winning your approval will not. To you I make no pledges of *reformation;* I offer but one promise. If you choose to remain abroad until I, in spirit, kiss your feet, and pray you to receive a love such as most men are glad to win by assiduity of attention, and every pleasing art—which you would force into being by wilful and revengeful absence—you will never see your native land again until the grass grows upon my grave!"

She paused for breath, and continued more slowly. "While your child lives, and I remain her guardian, I will use your means for her maintenance—will reside in your house. If she dies, or you take her from me, I will not owe you my support for a single day more!"

Lewis grew pallid to his lips; but he, too, was proud, and his stubborn will was called into bold exercise.

"Very well! It is in your choice to accede to my propositions, or not. A share in all that I have is yours; not only during the child's life, but as long as you live. Before I leave America, I shall deposit for you in your father's bank a sum which, I hope, you will find sufficient to maintain you in comfort. Your father will be my executor in this matter. I shall not confide to him the peculiar circumstances of my departure, leaving you at liberty to act in this respect, as in every thing else, according to the dictates of your will and pleasure. At the end of a certain term of years specified by law, you can, if you wish, procure a divorce, on the ground of my wilful and continued desertion of you; in which case, the provision for your support will remain unchanged. As to the child—the mother's is the strongest claim. I shall never take her from you. Do not let me keep you up longer. It is late!"

With a silent inclination of the head, she withdrew, and he cast himself upon the sofa, there to lie during the few hours of the night that were yet unspent.

He had arisen, and was standing at the window when Sarah entered in the morning. But for the dark shadows under the eyes, and the tight-drawn look about the mouth, she appeared as usual; and her "Good-morning," if cold, was yet polite.

"I imagine," she said, as the gong clashed out its second call, "that you wish me to accompany you to breakfast, and to preserve my ordinary manner towards you when others are by. Am I right?"

"You are. This is all I ask. The effort will not be a tedious one. I leave here at noon."

Arm in arm they directed their steps towards the great dining-hall—to the view of the spectator as comfortable and happy a pair as any that pursued that route on that summer morning. Together they sat down at table, and Mr. Hammond ordered "his lady's" breakfast with his own. Mrs. Hunt bustled in shortly after they were seated, full of wonderment at having heard from Sarah's maid of her master's unexpected arrival; while Jeannie gave his hand a squeeze as hearty as was the welcome in her smiling face. The Bensons were always late. So much the better. There were more people present to observe the cordial meeting between the brothers-in-law, made the more conspicuous by Philip's surprise. The genuineness of his good spirits, his easy, unembarrassed manner, was the best veil that could have been devised for Sarah's constraint and Lewis's counterfeit composure.

It did not escape Philip's eye that Sarah ate nothing, and spoke only to avoid the appearance of singularity; and he believed that he had discovered the origin of her trouble when Lewis communicated his purpose of foreign travel. When the burst of surprise subsided, the latter tried successfully to represent his plan as a business necessity. Lucy, who never saw an inch beyond her nose—morally and mentally speaking—except when her intuitions were quickened by self-love, was the questioner most to be dreaded.

"Why don't you go with him?" she inquired of her sister. "He should not stir one step without me, if I were in your place. Only think! you might spend six months in Paris!"

"How would Baby Belle relish a sea voyage!" returned Sarah.

"Nonsense! How supremely silly! One would suppose that she was the only member of the family whose comfort was to be consulted. Rather than expose her to the possibility of inconvenience, you will deprive yourself of profit and pleasure, and be separated from your husband for nobody knows how long. This shows how much these model married people really care for one another. When put to the test they are no better than we poor sinners, whom everybody calls flirts. Phil, are those muffins warm? This one of mine has grown cold while I was talking."

"How are the horses, Benson?" inquired Lewis. "Have they been exercised regularly?"

"Yes, and are in capital order. You could have left us no more acceptable reminder of yourself than those same fine bays."

"If you have no other engagement, suppose we have them up before the light carriage after breakfast, and take a short drive."

"Agreed, with all my heart! unless Mrs. Hammond quarrels with me for robbing her of a portion of your last morning with her."

"She will forgive you!" Lewis rejoined, to spare her the effort of reply.

From her window Sarah saw them whirl off along the beach in sight of the hundreds of spectators on the sands and about the hotels, and recognized the ingenuity of this scheme for proclaiming the amicable feeling between the two.

"But one more scene, and the hateful mockery is over!" thought the wife, as she heard her husband's step outside the door on his return.

She snatched a paper from the table, and seemed absorbed in its contents, not looking up at his entrance. Lewis made several turns through the room, sighed heavily, and once paused, as if about to address her, but changed his mind.

Then sounded from without the fresh, gurgling laugh of a child, and the nurse came in with the baby—rosy and bright—from her morning walk on the shore. She almost sprang from Mary's hold at sight of her father, and dismissing the woman with a word, he took his darling into his arms, and sat down behind his wife. Inflexibly sullen, Sarah tried not to listen, as she would not see them; but she heard every sound: the child's soft coo of satisfaction as she nestled in the father's bosom; the many kisses he imprinted upon her pure face and mouth with what agony Sarah well knew—the irregular respiration, sometimes repressed, until its breaking forth was like sobs; and the proud, miserable heart confessed reluctantly that, in one respect, his share of their divided lot was heavier than hers. She was not to witness his final resignation of his idol. Under color of summoning Mary, he carried the infant from the room, and came back without her.

"It is time for me to go now, Sarah!"

His voice was calm, and its firmness destroyed what slender encouragement she might have drawn from the scene with his child, to hope for some modification of his resolution.

"Will you write to me, at regular intervals, to give me news of Belle?"

"Certainly, if such is your wish."

"And yourself? you will be careful of your health, will you not? And, if I can ever serve you in any way, you will let me know?"

"It is not likely that you can; thank you."

There was a silence of some moments. Sarah stood playing with the tassel of her morning robe, pale and composed.

"Sarah!" Lewis took her hand. "We have both been hasty, both violent! Unfeeling as you think me, and as I may have seemed in this affair, believe me that it almost kills me to part from you so coldly. It is not like me to retract a determination, but if you will say now what you did last night—'Do not go!' I will stay, and be as good a husband to you as I can. Shall we not forgive, and try to forget?"

The demon of resentful pride was not so easily exorcised.

At a breath of repentance—a suggestion of compromise, the fell legion rallied an impregnable phalanx. She was frozen, relentless; her eyes, black and haughty, met his with an answer her tongue could not have framed in words.

"I have nothing to say!"

"'Nothing!' The ocean must then separate us for years—it may be forever!"

"It was your choice. I will not reverse it."

"Not if you knew that if you let me go I would never return?"

"Not if I knew that you would never return!"

Without another word, without a farewell look, or the hand-grasp mere strangers exchange, he left her there—the stony monument of her ill-directed life and affections; the victim of a worldly mother and a backbiting tongue!

CHAPTER XVII.

"How gay Mrs. Hammond has grown lately!" said Mrs. Greyling, the fashionable critic of the ——— House drawing-room. "Do you see that she is actually waltzing to-night? She moves well, too! That pearl-colored moire antique is handsome, and must have cost every cent of nine dollars a yard. She is partial to heavy silks, it seems. It gives an air of sameness to her dress; otherwise she shows very tolerable taste."

"I have heard it said that she was a regular dowdy before she was married," observed Mrs. Parton, who was also on the "committee of censure"—a self-appointed organization, which found ample employment in this crowded nest of pleasure-seekers. "Her husband is perpetually making her presents, and she dresses to please him."

"Humph! I distrust these pattern couples! 'My husband doesn't approve of my doing this—won't hear of my acting so!' are phrases easily learned, and sound so fine that one soon falls into the habit of using them. What a flirt Mrs. Benson is! That is the fifth young man she has danced with this evening. I pity her husband and baby!"

"He does not look inconsolable! I tell you what my notion is: he may love his wife—of course he does—but he admires her sister more. See how he watches her! Mrs. Tomes told me that she was standing near him the first time Mrs. Hammond waltzed, and that he seemed real worried. When the set was through, she came to look for a seat, and he got one for her. As she took it, he said something to her which Mrs. Tomes could not hear, but she laughed out in his face as saucy as could be, and said: 'Oh, I am learning when I am in Rome to do as Romans do! Doesn't my elder sister set me the example?'"

"He could say nothing then," said Mrs. Greyling. "Those girls played their cards well. The Hunts have very little, if any thing, besides the father's salary, and the family was very obscure."

Mrs. Greyling's paternal progenitor was an opulent soap-boiler, who was not ashamed, during her childhood, to drive an unsavory cart from one kitchen door to another. But he counted his thousands now by the hundred, and his children ranked, as a consequence, among the "upper ten."

She continued her charitable remarks: "Somehow the old lady contrived to keep up the appearance of wealth, and married both daughters off before their second season. Mr. Benson is reputed to be rich; but for that matter these Southern planters are all said to be rolling in gold. Mr. Hammond is certainly making money. Mr. Greyling says he is a splendid business man."

"He sailed for Europe a week ago, you know."

"Yes; and since then madame has been the belle of the ball. The old story—'When the cat is away, the mice will play.'"

"Sarah," said Philip, an hour later, "will you walk on the balcony with me? You are heated, and the air is balmy as Georgian breezes. It will do you good."

"Are you going to scold me?" she asked, archly, before she would take his arm.

"No. I have no right to do it if I had the disposition."

There was no moon; but the sky was strewed thickly with stars, and the white foam of the surf caught and held tremulously the sparkles from the bright watchers above. Philip did not appear disposed to converse, and Sarah waited for him to begin. Meanwhile, they strolled on and on, until the murmur of the ocean was louder than the music of the saloon band. The sea moaned to the stars, as it had done to the sunless July heavens on that day so memorable in the history of one of the pair—the day of shipwreck stories and a real shipwreck—none the less disastrous, that the treasures and their loss were hidden from all but the bereaved one.

To many it is appointed to lead two lives: to think and feel as well as to act a double part; to separate, as inexorably as human will can decree, past hopes and joys—past sorrows, and, if practicable, past memories from the thoughts and emotions of the to-day in which they exist. Thousands keep up the barrier until death ends the need of watchfulness and labor; the coffin-lid covers the faithful mask that has smiled so patiently and so long above an aching heart. Yet dammed up passion is a dangerous thing. If hearts were so constituted that they could be drained like pestilential marshes, the flood conducted off in harmless and straight channels, then, indeed, might hypocrisy rejoice, and sleek decorum sit down at ease. As it is, genteel propriety and refined reticence are perpetully endangered by the unforeseen swell of some intermittent spring, or the thawing of some ice-bound stream, that is liable to overleap or tear away the dike—ingulfing in an instant the elaborate structures years of toil have cheaply purchased.

Such was the moment when, withdrawing her hand from Philip's arm, Sarah struck suddenly—fiercely—upon her breast, and cried: "Oh! why cannot I die and end this misery!"

"Sarah!"

"I say I can bear it no longer! Others do not suffer thus!

If they do, they die, or lose their reason. I will *not* endure it, I tell you!"

"Sister!"

"Do not call me by that name, Philip Benson! You know better!"

She leaned forward on the balcony railing, her eyes fixed on the sea. Her deep, hurried breathing was like the pant of some worried animal, gathering strength, and, with it, courage for renewed conflict. To her last words the mysterious plaint of the sea lent meaning. Philip, too, remembered that barren shore, the tumbling breakers, the solitary sea-bird's labored flight landward. Was *this* his work? It was but a flicker of truth—dashed out the next second by a blow of indignant will.

"You may forbid me to address you by this title, Sarah; but you cannot hinder me from sympathizing in your sorrow, and trying to befriend you. If my companionship is unwelcome, allow me to conduct you to your room. I cannot leave you alone here, where there is continual passing."

"You are right. Regard for appearances is the one thing needful," she said, mockingly. "I must be a dull scholar, if I have not learned that. I am sane again now—fit to associate with other sane people. If you please, we will go to the ball-room instead of up-stairs. I am not a candidate for solitary confinement yet!"

"Mrs. Hammond, I heard a gentleman inquiring anxiously for you just now!" called out a lady, in passing. "He said that you promised to dance with him."

"I did. Thank you for reminding me. A little faster, my good brother!"

She hurried him into the saloon, where they were met immediately by her would-be partner. Philip, bewildered and uneasy, watched her motions through the evolutions of the dance. She talked rapidly and animatedly, keeping her cavalier in a broad smile, and confirming her lately won reputation of a wit. Her eyes shone; her color was high; she was "really handsome"—as the "censure committee" had occasion to remember at a later day, when it was spoken of in a very different tone from that employed by a member of the distinguished sisterhood in addressing Mrs. Hunt on this night.

"You are a fortunate mother, my dear madam, to have two such brilliant daughters. They eclipse the girls entirely."

"I have nothing to complain of in my children, ma'am. I done—I *did* my best by them, and they have repaid me a thousandfold."

"Now, I am ready!" said Sarah to her brother-in-law. "I release you, Mr. Burley!" waving her hand to her late attendant as a princess might to a courtier.

Vexed and disturbed by her unsettled manner and queer freaks, Philip gave her his arm, and conducted her through the throng.

"Lewis has had fair winds, and must now be nearing the end of his voyage," he remarked, as they sauntered along the piazza.

"Ah! he is on the sea to-night! How strange! I had not thought of that!"

"I see nothing wonderful in the idea, as he has not had time to cross the Atlantic since he left these shores," returned Philip, dryly. "The oddest thing I can think of at present is yourself, Sarah!"

"I am aware of that, Philip. Do not speak harshly to me! You may be sorry for it some day."

They were at her door. Her softened manner moved him, and as she offered her hand, he took it with fraternal warmth.

"Forgive me, if I was rough! I have not understood you this evening."

"It is not likely that you ever will. Time was—but it is folly to allude to that now! Think of me as kindly as you can—will you? You have wounded me sometimes, but never knowingly. I cannot say that of many others with whom I have had dealings. Good-night."

The little parlor was still. Mrs. Hammond never kept her maid up to assist in her disrobing, if she intended remaining out until a late hour. Nurse and child were quiet in the adjacent nursery. Closing the door of communication, Sarah stripped her hair and arms of their ornaments; took off her diamond pin, then her rings, and laid them away in her jewelry case; divested herself of her rich dress, and drew from her wardrobe a plain, dark wrapper, which she put on. Next she sat down at her writing-desk, selected a sheet of paper, and wrote a single line—when a thought struck her, and she stopped. A momentary irresolution ended in her tearing off a strip containing what she had penned, and holding it in the flame of the lamp until it was consumed. "Best not! best not!" she muttered. "Doubt may bring comfort to the one or two who will need it. Let them doubt! Save appearances if you can, my poor mother would say." A smile of unutterable scorn glimmered over her face. She pushed away the desk and walked to the window.

From the distant ball-room the throbbing waves of music still rolled past on the summer air, and blent with them was the solemn undertone of the surf. Did men call its mighty voice a monotone? To her it was eloquent of many and awful things—not frightful. What was there of terror in thoughts of rest, endless sleep, rocked for ages by the rising and falling tide, hushed into dreamless repose by the music of the billows? No more of a vain and wearisome life; no more baffled aspirations and crushed affections; no more disheartening attempts to find and reach the right—

to follow in the steep, rugged path of duty, and shun the easy, alluring way to which heart and memory were ever pointing; no more of stern rebuke and sneering taunt; no more galled pride and outraged womanhood; no more lying gayety, smiles, and repartee, when the spirit was writhing in impotent agony, longing to shriek out its intensity of woe! Only sleep, rest, peace!

"Sleep! rest! peace!" She gasped the words feverishly, as they seemed to come to her on the breeze. Might she not seek these now! *now!* Not yet! The grounds, the beach were still populous with groups of strollers. She would be seen—perhaps recognized—probably frustrated in her purpose. Leaning her head against the casement, she sat there an hour—not debating, still less wavering in her resolve, only waiting until flight would be safe—and thinking! thinking! thinking! until her brain whirled.

A thwarted, warped, disjointed existence had hers been from its beginning. Denied food suitable for her mental and spiritual need; denied sympathy, air, and expression of suffering; under the slow torture of this starvation, every avenue to goodness and liberty hedged up, and, for the future, temptation, repudiation, loneliness, perhaps a sullied name—who could dispute her right to try release by one brief pang she alone could feel? Who would miss her? Not the world that flattered her wealth and wit, her laces, silks, and diamonds; not the mother and sister who worshipped the gilded Juggernaut "Society;" not he who was that night sleeping soundly on the same sea that would embosom her in her sweeter, deeper slumber. Shocked he might be at an event so unexpected and uncommon. His next sensation would be a relief at his deliverance from a burden, at his freedom to come and go as he liked—no longer banished by her obstinacy and his own. He had loved her as most other men do their wives—a bond too weak to bear a heavy blow at their self-love. She had sinned beyond forgiveness in his eyes.

Of Philip she thought with a mingling of tenderness and resentment. His unthinking gallantry had been the root of her sorest trouble; but it *was* unthinking, not wilful wrong. Nor was she the only sufferer. His heart was well-nigh as hungry as hers. Within the past week, she had seen this more clearly than ever before, and *he had felt it!* Lucy's narrow mind, her insipidity, her inordinate vanity, her selfish idolatry of pleasures that wearied him; her dis-relish for intellectual and domestic enjoyments, displayed in its most objectionable form, in her indifference to his company, and her neglect of her child—these were working out their legitimate result in his alienation from her, and attraction towards the once slighted sister, whose large heart and mental gifts he now valued at their true worth. To repel him, as much as to drown her cares, Sarah had plunged into the vortex she had heretofore avoided. She had heard that there was temporary solace in this species of dissipation. The cup was, for her, sparkleless and bitter, from surface to dregs.

She was saving *him* with herself by this final step! He would realize this truth, in the throe that would shake his soul when he found that she was gone; perhaps, even in that anguished hour, would bless her for having showed to him, while she drove him back from, the abyss they were together approaching. It was no idle vaunt she had made to Lewis, that the principles inherited from her father would save her from overt sin. Thus, thus would she flee the temptation, when the heart had left the will to battle unaided.

Her father! the gray old man who was toiling through this summer's heat, in his deserted home, as he had through so many summers gone! he who had never given her an impatient or angry word—whose pride and joy she still was! The stroke would be severe upon him. Yet he would not refuse comfort. There were still left to him his boys—fine, manly fellows; Jeannie and his baby grandchild—his lost daughter's gift. Tears rushed into the hot, wild eyes with this last image, but she would not let them flow.

"Is it not better that I should leave her now, when the parting will give her no pain, when one little week will blot out my memory entirely from her mind, than to wait until she can recollect and miss me?"

The music had ceased. The revellers had dropped away faster than they had collected, when once the movement was made to retire. The murmur of the deep was the only sound abroad; the stars were the only sentinels. Sarah arose, threw a shawl over her head, and cautiously unlocked the door. A strong rush of air blew it from her hold, and as she caught it, to draw it after her, she trod upon some object lying on the floor. Mechanically she stooped to pick it up. It was an infant's shoe, a dainty little gaiter, that peeped, during the day, from beneath Baby Belle's white skirt. To Sarah's touch it seemed that the lining still retained the warmth of the child's foot.

Never, oh, never, was the patter of those baby feet to make glad music for the mother's ear! Others must guide and sustain her trial steps; others smooth her daily path; others direct the inexperience of the girl in the perilous passes where that mother had fallen and perished!

"Oh, may I not bless her before I leave her forever?" she cried to stern Resolution. And Conscience rejoined, with meaning severity: "Is it *you* who would breathe a blessing above her purity?"

"Suffer me, then, to take the farewell look I dared not grant myself before!"

And while Resolution faltered at the impassioned appeal,

she opened the nursery door and stole to the side of the crib. The night-lamp shed a feeble halo over the table whereon it stood. The rest of the room was in darkness. Mary's light bedstead was close to the crib. Was hers that hard, short breathing, that sent a start and chill through the hearer? A touch to the lamp threw a blaze of light over nurse and child. A sharp cry rang through the chamber.

"Mary! Mary! get up!"

The girl sprang to the floor before she comprehended the meaning of the alarm. Mrs. Hammond had sunk into a chair beside the crib, from which she had snatched her infant. Baby Belle's head was strained back; her hands clenched; her limbs stiffened in a deathlike spasm. The eyes were rolled out of sight under the lids; and the four little teeth—her "most precious pearls," the fond mother had called them—were hard-locked within the purple lips.

Terrified as she was, Mary had the presence of mind to run for assistance. Mrs. Hunt and a physician were soon on the spot, and every appliance of the healing art that promised relief to the sufferer was used, but with partial effect. Sarah saw nothing but the child; heard nothing but the doctor's calm orders.

"You do not try to help her!" she said, impatiently, as a convulsion, more fearful than any that had preceded it, seized the delicate frame.

"I could not do more, were it my own child, madam!"

He was an elderly man, whose charity for fashionable mothers was very scant, and, having seen Mrs. Hammond in the ball-room the evening before, he was not prepared for the solicitude she manifested.

"You had better let the nurse take her!" he said, more gently, as Sarah, with difficulty, held down the struggling hands that might do hurt to the head and face.

"No! I will have no one touch her but myself!"

The morning broke, the day heightened into noon, and the paroxysms only abated in violence as the babe's strength declined. Steadfast to her word, the mother had not once resigned her. She had herself immersed her in the warm baths, applied the poultices, and administered the medicines prescribed. Mrs. Hunt was compassionate and active; Mary sorrowful, and prompt with whatever service she could perform; Lucy frightened and idle.

Philip, who had often been in the outer room to make inquiries and offer aid, if any were required of him, was told, just before sunset, that he could go into the chamber. Mrs. Hunt invited him, and the information she added gave to his countenance a look of heartfelt sadness as he followed her. Sarah sat in the middle of the room, so altered that he could scarcely credit the fact of her identity with the being he had parted from the previous night. Her eyes were sunken, her features sharpened, and her complexion had the dead, grayish hue of an old woman's: In her arms lay the babe, and, as she crouched over it, her mien of defiant protection suggested to him the idea of a savage animal guarding her young. He could not say whether or not she was aware of his presence, until he knelt by the dying child and called it by name.

"Baby Belle, do you know Uncle Philip?"

The dark eyes, soft still through the gathering film, moved slightly, and Sarah said—

"Speak to her again!"

"Will Baby Belle come to uncle?"

This time there was no sign of consciousness. The wee hands clasped in the mother's grew colder and colder, and the breath fluttered slowly through the parted lips. The end was near, and Philip's pitying accent expressed his sense of this.

"Give her to me, dear Sarah! It is not right for you to keep her longer."

"She is *mine!*"

The glare that came to her eye with the three words revealed a desperation that would have done battle with the King of Terrors, had he appeared in visible shape to claim his victim.

More faintly, slowly, trembled the life over the sweet mouth, and the hands, like waxen shapes, lay pulseless in the mother's clasp; while through the silent room flowed the dirge of the sea. Shaken by the freshening breeze of evening, the shutters of the western window swung ajar, letting in a golden ray upon mother and child, and along that path of light the untarnished soul of Baby Belle was borne by its waiting angel—home!

CHAPTER XVIII.

AUNT SARAH sat in the wide porch at the back of her house, knitting in hand. It was a still, but not oppressive August afternoon. There was not a ruffle on the bright surface of the river, and the long meadow grass was as smoothly spread out in the yellow sunshine. From the poultry-yard on the left arose a pleasant murmur, and now and then a stray hen tip-toed around the end of the house, singing idly as she rambled. Charley lay on the green mound—his old reading-room—with a book before him, and to him Aunt Sarah's motherly eyes turned most frequently. Those kindly orbs were dimmer than they were two summers ago, and the gentle face was a thought more pensive. A glance into the sitting-room window, from where she sat, would have showed one Uncle Nathan's empty arm-chair in the chimney corner, and above it were suspended his cane and broad-brimmed hat, just as he had put them off when he took his departure for a country where neither shelter nor staff is needed. Aunt Sarah's cap had a widow's border now; and in her faithful heart there was a sadder void than the death of her children had created—loving parent though she was—and yet more plentiful springs of sympathy for others bereaved and suffering.

Her rocking-chair was set near the entrance of the hall that bisected the dwelling; and the front and back doors being open, she had a fair view of the public road, whenever she chose to look up the lane. The Shrewsbury stage met the boat at four o'clock, or soon after; and hearing a rumbling along the highway, which she knew presaged its transit through this end of the village, the old lady leaned forward to catch a glimpse of the trunks upon the roof; this being all she could distinguish with certainty above the fence.

"Why, it is stopping here!" she ejaculated, getting up to obtain a better look. "Who upon earth can it be?"

The coach rolled on, and the passenger for the farm-house came through the gate and down the lane. She was dressed in black, wore a crape veil, and carried a small hand-trunk. With hospitable instinct, Aunt Sarah advanced to the front porch to meet her, still entirely in the dark as to who it could be."

"She has a different look from any of the neighbors; and there's nobody in York that would be likely to come to see me, except Betsey's people, and it can't be either of her girls!"

At this stage of her cogitations, the visitant reached the step on which the hostess stood, and put away the long veil from a face so worn and seamed with grief, so hollow-eyed and old, that the good aunt screamed outright in her distressed astonishment—

"Sarah, dear child! can this be you?"

"What I am now, Aunt Sarah. May I come in and stay with you a little while?"

"Stay with me, poor darling! As long as you like, and welcome! Come right in; you don't look fit to stand!"

She was not; for, now that the necessity for exertion was removed, she was faint and trembling. Aunt Sarah helped her up-stairs to the room she had occupied at her former visit, undressed her, and put her to bed. Sarah submitted like a child, too much exhausted to resist being made an invalid of, or to offer any explanation of her singular apparition. She had not slept an hour at a time for many nights; yet when she had drunk a cup of tea, and tried to eat a bit of toast her aunt prepared and brought up to her, she fell into a profound slumber, which lasted until long after sunrise on the following morning. Unclosing her eyes then, they rested upon the dear face, shaded by the widow's cap, that watched at her bedside. A shadowy phantom of a smile flitted over her features at the recognition.

"It was not a dream, then?" she said, languidly. "But I have dreamed of you often, of late—every night in which I have had any sleep. Aunt Sarah, I must tell you why I came to you!"

"Not now, dear," Aunt Sarah hastened to say, seeing the wild stare and the cloud return to her countenance. "Wait until you are stronger. I will bring up your breakfast, and when you have eaten it, you may try to dress, if you like. There will be time enough for your story, by and by. Charley is in a great fidget to see you."

Sarah submitted to the delay; but it was plain that she was not satisfied with it, and that her mind would be easier when once the tale was told. Aunt Sarah hindered her no longer a time than sufficed for her to take the much needed refreshment, to bathe and dress, and to see and exchange a few sentences with Charley, who supported her down to the sitting-room. There, resting among the pillows of the lounge, Aunt Sarah beside her, with the ubiquitous knitting-work in hand, lest too close observation should confuse her niece, the stricken one unfolded the whole of her sad history.

No more affecting proof could have been given of her prostrated mind and will than this unreserved recital. The secret she had sold conscience and liberty to preserve, she communicated now without a blush. Here—where she had formed the intimacy that had shadowed so darkly her after days—she detailed every step of the wrong course to which this weakness was a key; went over all—the stormy parting with her husband; her conviction of the mutual peril she and Philip were tempting in their daily communion; her resolve of self-destruction,—as circumstantially as if she were relating the biography of another.

Aunt Sarah, horrified and pitiful by turns, struggled with indifferent success to maintain equal composure, and against growing doubts of the narrator's sanity. It was a striking and instructive contrast: the world-weary woman returning for consolation and advice to the simple-minded matron, to whom the artificial existence she now heard depicted—its gilded vices and giddy round of vanities; its trials and temptations—were a wonderful, a monstrous tale, as foreign to her sphere of principles and feelings as if they had transpired in another world. But when Sarah came to speak of her child, her manner changed, her voice was hoarse and uneven, and over the care-worn visage there went such alternations of fierceness and heart-breaking sorrow that the listening mother, upon whose soul the shadow of her own childrens' graves still lay long and dark, could hear no more in silence.

"My poor girl!" she cried, falling on her knees, and throwing her arms around the reclining figure. "Dear child! Our Father in Heaven pity and comfort you! There is no help in man for such trouble as yours!"

Sarah had not shed a tear in the course of her story. She said afterwards that she had not wept since they took her dead baby from her clasp; but at this burst of unfeigned sympathy, this gush of pure love and compassion, the burning rock was cleft, and a blessed flood streamed from it. For some minutes they wept together without restraint, and when the more quiet grief of the elder mourner was repressed, the other still clung, sobbing, to her bosom.

Aunt Sarah held and soothed her as she would have done a sorrowful child; stroking away the hair from her forehead, drying and kissing the tear-stained cheeks, with many an epithet of fond reassurance.

"Let me finish! There is very little more!" resumed Sarah, keeping her aunt's hand fast in both of hers. "We went back to the city, and the next day we laid *her* in Greenwood. We stayed at father's—I would not return to the house that used to be mine. Father was very kind, and mother meant to be; but she tormented me with suggestions and consultations about my black clothes. Lucy was pining to get back to Newport. She said it was hot and dull in New York. Philip wanted to comfort me, but I shunned him, and I think he was hurt by my conduct; but it was best, was it not, Aunt Sarah?"

"Certainly, dear!"

"I had often imagined myself lonely before; but I never dreamed of such a horror of desolation as filled my soul during the two days that I remained there, after all was over. Twenty times each night I would start from a feverish doze, thinking that I heard my baby cry or moan, as she did in the intervals of those awful convulsions; and then would come in upon me, as if I had never felt it until then, the truth that I could never see her again, and that my wicked, *wicked* intention of deserting her had brought this judgment upon me. I could not stay there, Aunt Sarah! I heard other voices besides my child's in the air, and saw strange, grinning faces in the darkness. But the worst was to see that, to every one but me, the world was the same that it had ever been. Father looked grave when I was in his sight; but the children could laugh and talk as if nothing had happened, and I have seen mother and Lucy chatting merrily in the room with the dressmaker over my new dresses, while they were criticizing the crape trimmings. And I had buried my last earthly hope in my baby's grave! Then I remembered you, and how you had talked to me of your lost children, and how you had assured me of a home in your heart and house whenever I chose to claim it, and I believed in you, Aunt Sarah! There are not many whom I do trust; but I was sure you never said what you did not mean. I would not tell them that I was coming, for I feared they would prevent me. I slipped out of the house when none of them were at home, and went to the nearest hack-stand, where I got into a carriage and drove down to the boat."

"My dear, did you leave no letter to let them know where you had gone?"

"No, ma'am. I was afraid they would come or send for me, and I cannot go back."

"But your father—your mother! Did you not think how distressed they would be when they missed you? And your reputation? What will be said when it is known that you have left your father's house, and no one knows where you are? You are very weak and tired, dear; but you must sit up, right away, and write a note home. Tell them that I will take care of you as long as you like to stay with me; but don't lose a minute! You may be in time for the afternoon boat."

Sarah obeyed; and the careful old lady hurried Charley off to the boat, with directions to place the billet in the hands of the captain, who was a personal friend, and could be relied upon to post it directly he reached the city.

Mr. Hunt replied without delay. Sarah's absence had given rise to the most harrowing conjectures, made plausible by her extreme melancholy and fitful behavior since her infant's death. The police had been privately notified of her disappearance, and cautiously worded advertisements inserted in the papers. He regretted to add that Mr. Marlow, who, as Mr. Hammond's nearest friend, was informed of the distressing occurrence, had thought proper to communicate the intelligence to Mr. H. before Sarah's note arrived, and the steamer bearing the letter had sailed. Mr. Hunt expressed himself as entirely willing that his daughter should remain in her present retreat until her health of mind and body was re-established, but did not conceal his disapprobation of the manner of her leaving home.

Aunt Sarah looked concerned as she read this epistle, which her niece had passed over to her.

"I am sorry for your husband, my dear. This affliction, coming so close upon the other, will be a dreadful blow. It is a pity they did not wait awhile, until they knew something of your whereabouts, before writing to him."

"I am more sorry that the news must be contradicted," was the reply. "As we are now situated, the certainty of my death would be a relief to him. This was my reflection that night—" She left the sentence unfinished.

"My dear!" Aunt Sarah removed her spectacles, and surveyed her niece with her kind, serious eyes. "Have you made up your mind to live separate from your husband for the rest of your life?"

"What else should I do, aunt? He will never come back unless I promise to love him, and that cannot be."

"That doesn't alter the fact of your duty, as I look at it. You ought to make him an offer to do right, at any rate. It would have been easier and pleasanter to live with him, if you had felt for him as a woman should for the man she marries; but you *are* married to him, and in the sight of the Lord you ought to cleave to him, and him only. That is a solemn covenant, dear—'for richer, for poorer; for better, for worse!' 'Those whom God hath joined together, let not man put asunder!' It doesn't excuse people, who take these vows upon them when the right spirit is wanting, that they never thought how awful the engagement was. Their obligations are just the same, whether they love or not."

"The responsibility does not rest with me. I performed my duty while we were together. The separation was his act, and he must abide the consequences. I have erred greatly, Aunt Sarah; but ever since the night of our rupture, my conscience has been easy with respect to Mr Hammond. I confessed that I had misled him, and begged his pardon. Could I do more?"

"Put the case to yourself, child! Do not be angry if I speak out my mind, and use against you some things you have told me. When you saw that Philip was growing to like you better and better, and that you felt nearer to him every day, why did you determine to die sooner than to have things go on so?"

"Because it would have been a crime for us to love each other—infamous treachery to my sister, to his wife, for us to name the word between us."

"And how would Lucy have felt, if you had come to an understanding and spoken out the true feeling of your hearts?"

"Hers is a careless, indolent nature, but this insult would have aroused her. She would never have forgiven him or me, had she suspected a warmer sentiment on either side than that of friendship."

"But an honorable, affectionate man like your husband, who thought his wife the most precious thing in the world, was to forget his disappointment, overlook your lack of love and truth towards him, only because you allowed that he had found out your real feelings at last, and all the excuse you could give was that you could not help them! You were the one in fault all the way through, from the day you engaged to marry him, up to the minute when you would not say the word he begged from you to keep him at home. It is right that all the advance should come from you."

High-spirited as Sarah was, she was not angered by this

plain-speaking. "Faithful are the wounds of a friend;" and she felt that she had but this one. Aunt Sarah studied her thoughtful countenance before she renewed' the argument.

"I am an old-fashioned woman, dear—born and bred in the country, where, thank God! I have spent all my life. But I've been thinking about your story of the way people act and feel up there in York, and maybe in all other great, fine, money-making cities, and my notion is just this. I look back of their pushing and straining after riches, and show, and worldly vanities; every man for himself, and the one that climbs highest, forgetting as soon as he gets there that he was ever any lower, and ready to kick over anybody that tries to get alongside of him; and I see that they have lost sight of the second great commandment—'Thou shalt love thy neighbor as thyself.' Then I look back of this too, and I see where the greatest sin is, and—dear, bear with me! I see where *you* have gone furthest astray. Here's a passage I was reading this morning that tells the whole story." She raised the Bible from the table, and laid it upon Sarah's lap, pointing as she did so to these words enclosed in brackets:—

"Because thou hast forgotten the God of thy salvation, and hast not been mindful of the rock of thy strength, therefore shalt thou plant pleasant plants, and shalt set it with strange slips. In the day thou shalt make thy plant to grow, and in the morning shalt thou make thy seed to flourish; *but the harvest shall be a heap in the day of grief and desperate sorrow!*"

Mrs. Hunt would have regarded as an insult any expressed doubt of her religious principles and practice. She had a desirable pew in the fashionable church which was nearest her residence, and, stormy Sabbaths excepted, it was generally full at morning service. When her children were presentable as to looks, very young babies being seldom pretty, they were offered in fine lawn and Valenciennes at the font for the rite of baptism; and not a confirmation had passed since her daughters were grown, that she did not fancy how interesting they would look, kneeling before the surpliced bishop, heads gracefully bowed, and the regards of the whole congregation fixed upon them. Sarah never could be brought to the performance of the commonest act of public worship, unless it was to rise with the rest, when a standing posture was prescribed by the prayer-book; and she shocked her mother by declaring that she only did this because she was tired of sitting! Lucy's serene grace of devoutness was beautiful, if not edifying to behold. Those who occupied adjacent pews involuntarily suppressed their responses as her mellow tones repeated, with melancholy sweetness—"Have mercy upon us, miserable sinners!" And as the melting cadences entranced their ears, the lovely penitent was speculating upon the probable cost of Miss Hauton's Parisian hat, or coveting Mrs. Beau Monde's sable cloak.

If Sarah had ever heard of regeneration, it was as a technical phrase of the church articles and christening service. Of its practical meaning, its inward application, its absolute necessity to the safety of the soul, she had as vague a conception as a Parsee or New Zealand cannibal would have formed. She had read the Bible in connection with rhetorical lectures, and admired it as a noble specimen of Oriental literature. What other associations could she have with it? A handsome copy of the Holy Scriptures, surmounted by a book of common prayer, lay on a stand in Mrs. Hunt's third and rear parlor, and was dusted when a like attention was paid to the other ornaments of tables and *étagères*. An Oxford edition, russet antique, formed one of the wedding-gifts of each of the sisters, and in due time was laid in pious pomp on its purple pillow in the library corner. It was hardly strange, then, that the quotation, so apposite to the case in point, should fail to impress her very strongly. Aunt Sarah had gone out, deeming solitary reflection the best means of enforcing the lesson she had tried to inculcate, and, after re-reading the two verses, without further appropriation of their meaning, Sarah turned leaf after leaf of the volume, catching here and there a sentence of the large print, so grateful to the failing sight of her who was its daily student.

"David said unto his servants—'Is the child dead?' And they said, 'He *is* dead!'"

The smitten chord in the mother's heart sent out a ring of pain, and her listless hand paused upon the open page. It is a simple story—the royal parent's unavailing wrestle with the Chastener, the dread end of his suspense, and the affliction, made manifest in the calm resignation, the sanctified trust of the mourner. But when received as Sarah read it, with the vision of a similar death-scene intermixing itself with its unadorned details, the fresh blood still welling from the wound made by the tearing away of a portion of one's own life, every line is fraught with truth and pathos.

"Can I bring him back again? I shall go to him, but he shall not return to me!"

"Go to her! Oh, if I could! My baby! my baby!"

To the low, sad cry succeeded a season of yearning and of tears. It was an echo of the wail of the heathen mother who, centuries ago, having seen her babes slain before her eyes, cried aloud, in unselfish agony, as the sword, reeking with their blood, was plunged into her own bosom—"Oh, my children! where are ye?"

Sleep on, in thy lowly bed upon the hillside, sweet Baby Belle! Like the pale buds that are fading with thee in thy narrow resting-place, thy mission on earth is accomplished.

Joy, young freed spirit, if, stealing through the melodies of Heaven, there comes to thee the whisper of that mother's call! Fair lamb! the love that folded thee in the Shepherd's arms designed likewise, in recalling thee, to lure the wandering parent home!

CHAPTER XIX.

"MY DEAR LEWIS: Before you receive this letter, you will have had the explanation of my disappearance from New York. A merciful Providence directed me, in my partial derangement, to this peaceful retreat. Here I have found rest for body and soul—peace such as the world could never give the heart, even were it not bowed down by a sorrow like mine. Not that I forget past errors; nor that the review does not humble me in the dust. I confess, with shame and bitterness of spirit, my wasted years, my unsanctified affections, my evil passions. But for the assurance of the Father's pardon, the Saviour's loving pity, the black catalogue would strike me dead with horror and anguish. It is a fearful thing to be made to see one's self as she is; to scan in terrified solicitude the record of a life, and find there nothing better than pride, misanthropy, falsehood, hatred of men—rebellion against God. It is a sweet experience to taste, however tremblingly, the consolations of the Friend who invites the weary and heavy-laden to draw near and learn of Him. In His strength—not in that feebleness I once called power—have I resolved to lead a new life. Of the causes which have contributed to produce this change, we will speak more at length when we meet.

"'When we meet!' Lewis, will you, can you forget your manifold wrongs and come back to me? I do not plead, now, 'for the sake of our child.' Her sinless soul henceforth can know no pain or woe. God saw that I was not worthy of her, and He took her. In the earlier weeks of my selfish mourning, I had no thought of *your* bereavement. Latterly, I have longed to comfort you, for I know that your heart is riven by this stroke. She was your joy, as she was my angel of peace. Her loss is our common sorrow. Shall it not draw us together? Yet, as I have said, our estrangement cannot now affect her. Thoughtless of evil, she passed away. Had she lived, the Omniscient only knows what grief and mortification might have darkened her pathway. Nor do I desire a reconciliation as a shield from the world's sneer or ban. I hold its applause and its censure alike cheaply. In prosperity, its favors were painted, tasteless fruit; in adversity, it would have fed my starving heart with husks. But for *my* sake—by the thought of my late and sore repentance; by the remorse that must gnaw my spirit, when I remember your noble trust in me, your unswerving fidelity, your generous love and my base requital of it all; by the sorrow that never leaves me by day or by night—forgive me, and return to the home we have both forsaken! I will serve you very faithfully, my husband! I have gained other and higher views of the marriage relation within a short time past. However presumptuously I may have assumed its responsibilities, however unworthily I performed its duties in former days, I would enter upon our re-engagement with a solemn sense of what I owe to you and to Him who united us. You must have despised me at our parting, and since. Perhaps you have come to think of me with dislike as well as contempt. I will bear this—grievous though the burden will be—as a part of my righteous punishment. I will never murmur—never, even in thought, accuse you of unjust harshness, if you will grant me the opportunity to make what amends I can for all you have lost and suffered through my fault."

Sarah was still far from strong; and wearied as much by

the intensity of her feelings as by the manual effort of writing, she laid the pen down, and leaned back in the cushioned chair. Her table stood in the parlor beneath the window overlooking the river. The room was prim and clean, as of yore, with its straight lines of chairs; its shining specks of mirrors; the grim black profiles above the mantel, and the green boughs in the fire-place. The outer scene was in its general features that which the girl had surveyed, with pleased surprise, the July evening of her arrival here two years ago.

Only two years! The sufferings and life-lessons of twenty had been crowded into that brief space. The meadows were growing sere, as if scorching winds had swept over them, and the stream reflected truthfully, yet, one could have fancied, sadly, the changing foliage fringing its borders. But the sky, with its tender blue and its fleecy clouds, ever shifting, yet ever retaining their likeness to one another—the river's smooth, steady flow, were the same; fit emblems both of them of counsels which are mercy and truth through all their workings; of love that abideth forever!

The train of thought was replete with refreshing to the spirit that was striving, in prayer and watchfulness, to adhere to the right, to accept, with meek submission, all that her cup yet held of pungent or nauseous lees. There was no affectation in the humble tone of her letter. She would not begin it until she had mastered the stubborn remnant of her native pride. It should be nothing to her that her husband had wilfully separated himself from her, and refused her overtures of reconcilement. If this was unkindness, it was all she could reproach him with in the course of time they had spent together. He had been a true friend, an honorable protector, and dimly still, but more justly than ever before, she perceived that into his love for her there had entered none of the merely prudential considerations, the cool calculations, wherewith she used to account for his choice of herself as a helpmeet. Where, in the world's heartless circles, could she point out another wife as much indulged, as much honored in public and in private, as she once was by him? Mournfully, if not lovingly, she dwelt upon the countless evidences of his cordial fulfilment, in letter and in spirit, of his part of their mutual engagement, with something of the sinking of heart the alchemist may have felt when, after he had, by a mechanical and habitual fling of his arm, tossed the eagerly-sought philosopher's stone into the sea as a worthless pebble, he discovered that the divining steel he held had been changed to gold by its touch.

To whom of us has not an experience similar to this come? It may be that the eyes which once besought affection with dumb and disregarded eloquence are closed and rayless for all future time; the lips that told, with modest frankness, how dear we were to hearts we cared not then to win, are now but silent dust. Or, perchance, grieved by indifference, repelled by unkindness, those hearts have sought and found in other loves solace for the pain we, in our blindness, inflicted. It matters little whether they be dead to all the world, or only to us. In either case, the longing and despair of our lonely lives are rendered the more unendurable from the flash of tardy truth that shows us, side by side with our actual poverty of heart riches, the tranquil beauty of the pictured "might have been."

Aunt Sarah had gone on a visit to a neighbor; the hired girl was in the distant wash-house; and Charley considered it his duty to linger within easy reach of his cousin, should she need him for any purpose. To guard her from all chance of intrusion, he stationed himself on the front porch steps, with his book on his knee. For an hour, he read on uninterruptedly; then, glancing up as he turned a leaf, he saw a gentleman coming down the gravel-walk. He looked thin and anxious, and his restless eye wandered from door to windows, as in expectation of seeing some one besides the boy. With a ready apprehension of his infirmity, only to be accounted for by some prior knowledge of the person he saluted, he took from his pocket a card, which he presented before he shook hands with the silent host. Charley's intelligent face was one beam of pleasure as he read, and his warm grasp showed his sympathy in the happiness he fancied was in store for his cousin. Inviting the guest by a gesture to follow him, he went softly to the parlor-door, tapped lightly—too lightly, indeed, to attract the notice of the musing occupant of the room, then drew back the bolt, admitted the stranger, and delicately withdrew.

Sarah heard the door open and Charley's retreating footsteps, and, supposing that he had peeped in to see that she was comfortable and wanted for nothing, she did not look around. The intruder stood still one step within the room, as if unable to advance or speak. The languid attitude of the figure before him, so unlike the self-poise and quiet energy of her former deportment, her black dress, even the wasted hands dropped so wearily upon her lap, told of the storm that had passed over her, the utter revolution in her life and nature. A struggling sigh he could not repress broke from the gazer's breast, and Sarah turned hastily towards him. She did not swoon, as he feared she would. A thrill, like an electric shock, shook her from head to foot; a wild inquiry looked from her eyes; a question of the reality of the appearance, succeeding so closely to—did it grow out of her revery?

Lewis put this imagination to flight.

"Sarah!" he said, pressing in his the hands she extended mutely. "They told me you were lost, and I hurried home to find you. I could not wait for your permission to come to you, when I learned in New York that I had a living wife! The loss of the child was heavy enough; but this—" He could say no more.

"I am thankful! I am glad that you are here!" A faint, beautiful smile shone over her wan features. "And our baby, Lewis! We must remember that she is an angel now!"

CHAPTER XX.

To no one except Aunt Sarah were the facts of the estrangement and reconciliation of her relatives ever revealed, and within her faithful bosom the secret was hidden as securely as in a tomb.

Great was the chagrin of gossips, male and female, when it was known that Mrs. Hammond's strange flight from her father's house, which had leaked out nobody knew how, and been variously construed into an elopement, a freak of derangement, and a deliberate intention of suicide, according to the degrees of charity possessed by the theorists, was a very innocent and unromantic journey to the country home of her favorite aunt and godmother, a lady of ample fortune and benevolent heart, who would, in all probability, make her namesake her heiress. Under her care, and for the benefit of the seclusion so congenial to one in her affliction, and the salt air so necessary for the restoration of her impaired health, Mrs. Hammond had remained until her husband's return from abroad.

Mrs. Hunt had told Mrs. A., who had told Mrs. B., who repeated it to Mrs. C., how he had not stopped in New York an hour after he stepped ashore from the Adriatic. He hurried to the bank, and ascertained from Mr. Hunt that his wife was with her aunt, and that a boat which would land him near Shrewsbury was to leave in fifteen minutes. So he drove down post-haste, and jumped on board of her after the plank had been drawn in and the wheels began to move.

There never was a more devoted husband or a more attached pair, Mrs. Hunt affirmed.

"More than she could say for that flirting Mrs. Benson and *her* other half," agreed A. B. and C., unanimously.

"Her conduct at Newport was scandalous, and would have been outrageous if he had not watched her like a lynx!" said Mrs. Beau Monde, who had never been able to secure one-half as many admirers as had Lucy, and hated her as honestly as if they were a couple of Biddies pulling caps for Patrick or Murphy.

"I don't see why he should have felt jealous, I am sure. He wasn't dying of love for her! That could be seen with half an eye. They say he loved Mrs. Hammond before he addressed her sister, and married this one out of spite," rejoined Mrs. Townes, who had made *beaux yeux* at the *distingué* Southerner for three whole evenings, and won only the most indifferent glances in requital.

"Mrs. Hammond behaved very prudently!" pronounced Mrs. Greyling, "and dressed very well. I suppose Mr. Hammond brought her some elegant things from abroad. Pity she is in mourning, and must dress plainly at present! If I were in her place—as it was only a baby—I would not wear black more than six months, unless it was *very* becoming."

"She has become very religious, you know," said Mrs. Parton.

"Indeed! People are apt to, I think, when there has been death in the family," concluded Mrs. Greyling, pensively. "I remember, when my poor sister died, I used to look forward to church and Sunday with real pleasure. I could not go anywhere on week-days, you know, although there were piles of tickets lying in my card-receiver, and we had just taken a box at the opera that very winter! I declare, I should have lost the run of the fashions entirely, and forgotten people's faces, if I had not gone to church. I dare say, too, that she finds some comfort in religion—poor woman! if what the preachers and good books tell us be true."

Had Sarah found comfort?

Look we, for reply, to the chastened lustre of the eye, where once burned restless fires, like the sunward gaze of the imprisoned eagle; to the holy serenity struggling through and finally dispelling the clouds of memory and regret that, at times, would roll in between her soul and the bright, sustaining hope upon which Faith would have its regards forever fixed; to her daily life, sanctified by prayer, beneficent in good works, and by its unostentatious loveliness winning others, first to admire, then to imitate; to the wifely submission and loving kindness of her bearing to her husband, her grateful estimate of the affection he lavished upon her, the deep, true tenderness growing up in her heart for this fond and noble companion; look we, lastly, to the snowy marble guarding that tiny mound in Greenwood, where the mother once believed that hope and joy were buried to know no awaking.

"BABY BELLE,"

INFANT DAUGHTER OF

LEWIS AND SARAH HAMMOND.

SHE WENT HOME

July 16, 1858, *aged* 8 *months.*

"*Is it well with thee? Is it well with thy husband?*
Is it well with the child?" *And she answered,*

"IT IS WELL!"

COLONEL FLOYD'S WARDS.

BY

MARION HARLAND.

NEW YORK:
SHELDON & COMPANY, 335 BROADWAY.
1863.

COLONEL FLOYD'S WARDS.

CHAPTER I.

"Yes?" said Aunt Ruth, with kindling interest.

This important monosyllable was, in the mouth of this excellent lady, susceptible of an infinite variety and numberless gradations of meaning. Wooing encouragement; hearty and unequivocal assent; loving sympathy; lively curiosity and civil indifference; sometimes, upon sufficient provocation, a mild species of sarcasm or contemptuous incredulity—all these were habitually expressed by the gentle spinster through the medium of the little word, defined by mistaken masculine lexicographers as "an affirmative particle opposed to *no*." Opposed to "no," indeed! As if Aunt Ruth could not, and did not, make it mean "no"—and no uncertain negative, at that—every day of her life!

She sat now in a well-cushioned Boston rocker, dressed in a gray merino, and a cap trimmed with dove-colored ribbons, swinging slowly to and fro, knitting a lamb's wool sock. Upon the other side of the round candle-stand was her eldest nephew, Mr. Alexander Lay, yclept by his intimates and the community in general, "Aleck," lounging in lazy content against the stuffed back of a great easy-chair, covered with black leather, polished to shining sleekness by constant service during many years. His nether limbs were supported by the brass fender, and a meerschaum was between his teeth. He was a fine-looking young fellow of four-and-twenty, with a well-developed, sinewy figure, black hair, and a beard whose length, while it would have given an *outré* air to the visage of most men, was yet highly becoming to his bronzed complexion and marked physiognomy. He had arrived unexpectedly, but three hours before, at his patrimonial mansion, after an absence of two years from his native land, most of which time he had spent in a German University.

"The neatest people upon the globe!" he had said, pursuing a description of a tour through Holland.

And Miss Ruth Massie, his maternal aunt, whose forte was housewifery, and who was famed, far and near, for the scrupulous cleanliness of her establishment, forgot the yawn lodged in her throat, provoked by his incidents of travel through Switzerland and Italy, and rejoined by the "particle" quoted above.

"I wished most for you when I visited Broëk," continued the tourist. "The streets are scoured as frequently and carefully as you wash your plates and dishes; the iron railings enclosing the little patches of brick pavement they denominate door-yards, are ornamented by brass knobs, brought, by dint of diligent friction, to the brightness of mirrors; and the fronts of the houses are deluged every morning by jets of water from a hose or syringe. Not an atom of dust or a cobweb is anywhere visible. They even tie up the tails of the cows when they have combed and brushed them, lest they should trail upon the ground, and be afterwards accidentally used to whisk their smooth sides."

"Yes?" Miss Ruth's eyes opened more widely.

"The chickens' nails are cleaned and pared each day, and I have heard, although I cannot vouch for the truth of *this* statement, that the hens' teeth are scrubbed at the same time, with a brush invented solely for this purpose."

"Yes!"

The "particle," this time, was equivalent to—"You don't tell me so! I never heard the like!"

"I felt sorry for the children," Aleck went on with the veracious narrative—"rosy, roly-poly, pudding-faced Dutch babies that they were! Fancy a childhood—above all, a boyhood—passed in ignorance of the glories of paddling in mud-puddles, with one's trousers rolled above his knees, and the delight of manufacturing mud pies! I never longed, before or since, to be an instructor of youth, but I did covet the privilege of initiating the unfortunate little wretches into such practices as used to enrapture Robin's soul and mine!"

"I don't believe their mothers would have thanked you! I recollect the trouble you boys used to give me by such tricks."

Aleck laughed. "Don't bear malice, aunty, since we have put away childish things—more's the pity! But I was going to tell you about the Dutch girls. Such complexions! such roses and lilies! such plump dumplings of forms—suet dumplings, you could not doubt! It made a fellow's mouth water to look at the angels!"

"Ah, yes!" Miss Ruth's slight nod heightened the significance of her arch, knowing tone. "Now you are coming to the point!" she meant to imply.

"Then, you should see them skate in winter! Ten or a dozen miles they fly down the canals to market, to sell their eggs and butter, and back again the same day. They have regular balls upon the ice. Shall I ever forget a day's sport upon skates, which I enjoyed with a blue-eyed beauty—

fleet of foot as a grey-hound; lips like cherries; cheeks like the sunny side of an apricot, and waist like a firm roll of butter! Ah, me! 'Joys that we've tasted!' That is one of the never-returning kind, I am afraid!"

"*The* one—was *she?*" interrogated Miss Ruth.

"One of them!" said the male coquette, heartlessly.

"Yes! yes!"

Which was, being interpreted—"Aleck! Aleck! you are a sad fellow!"

"Can't help it, aunty! If the girls will be fascinating, they must take the natural consequence of their behavior, and endure my devotion with the best grace they can."

"I thought you were going to bring her home to America with you?"

"I would have done so, assuredly, had I known that you desired it, and if I could have decided which 'her' you expected me to elect to that supreme felicity."

"Yes!" said Miss Ruth, in affectionate ridicule of this conceited speech. "The 'her' I meant was that Gret—Gretna—or some such name you went crazy about, six months ago. It's queer I can't remember what you called her."

"Gretna Green, perhaps?" suggested Aleck, with praiseworthy gravity.

"You didn't mention her surname, but I think it more than likely that's the one—the beautiful German girl, whose singing and dancing, you said, had carried you into the seventh heaven—and all that sort of nonsense."

"Gretna Green is of Scotch extraction. Perhaps Gretchen was the word you could not recollect."

"Yes. Where is she?"

"I really cannot say. Probably married to some lager-loving Herr Von Something, making his sauer-kraut and brewing his bier. I have not thought of her in five months, that I know of. I do remember, however, since you have alluded to the subject, that she was quite a pretty girl, and sang tolerably."

Aunt Ruth shook her head again—now, in sorrowful deprecation of the criminal trifling he avowed so carelessly.

"I was in hopes you meant to settle down for good and all! Not that I fancied over-much your marrying a foreigner; and of the two girls you've spoken of, I'd rather you had brought home the Scotch than the Dutch."

"German!" corrected Aleck.

"It's all the same—ain't it? Aleck! what possesses you to smoke that dirty-looking pipe? Maybe you haven't noticed how the amber is staining it through and through?"

"Aunt Ruth! I am ashamed of you! This is a genuine meerschaum, and cost more money than Robin could get for the best horse in his stable!"

"Yes? Let me see it!"

She inspected the shining black bowl, with its curious cloudy veins, and the curved stem.

"A *mere sham*—did you call it?"

"Yes, ma'am. There are so few of the real articles among the many that pass with the verdant purchasers for valuable, that the contemptuous title deserved by the counterfeit has gradually been applied to all. There's a moral in the fact, if you will take the pains to study it."

"It wants burning out badly!" said his aunt, disregarding his philosophizing, and handing back the vaunted "real article," with an unmistakable contortion of the nose and upper lip. "It would be the sweeter, and so would your mouth, for that matter, if you would leave it under the back-log there, all night. I could caution Marthy to be careful not to crack or break it when she takes up the ashes to-morrow morning."

Managing his facial muscles with considerable difficulty, the fun-loving nephew explained that the discoloration she condemned was the prime beauty of the pipe, adding divers reminiscences—authentic, of course—of the high estimate set upon long-used and well-blackened meerschaums by discriminating Teutons.

"Reckon they are not such overly clean people, after all!" was Miss Ruth's conclusion, enunciated with disdainful emphasis. "But seriously, my boy, what has become of this girl? not Miss Green—the other one! What broke off the match? You as good as told me you were going to marry her right off."

"I did! When and how?'

"In a letter, crammed from beginning to end with her praises, which you wrote me half a year ago."

"Ah! that was the end of the matter, I fancy. The flame burned itself to ashes in that epistle. I cannot remember certainly what disenchanted me. I have an idea that it was Gretchen's immoderate fondness for cabbage in an advanced stage of decomposition—so-called sauer-kraut."

"Yes!" Aunt Ruth sighed.

"You don't think that a sufficient cause for a breach of promise, I see," said her nephew, in pretended anxiety.

"I am afraid you will never marry, Aleck!"

"If I ever do, my wife's favorite dish shall be neither cabbage nor onions."

"You are as bad as Colonel Floyd! When he has bacon and cabbage for dinner, he won't allow Mrs. Floyd and the girls to come to the table. He says it is only fit for men to smell. Once in a while he has an old-fashioned neighbor there, to whom he wants to be polite; and since his rich friend must have the dish, it is prepared, and the ladies don't make their appearance until the cabbage is removed. I've heard, though, that Helen will not submit to this nonsense since she came of age—that she will take her place at table and entertain the company in her aunt's absence."

"They are all well at Belleview, are they?" questioned Aleck, puffing away rather faster at his meerschaum.

"Yes."

Mr. Lay turned at the hesitating tone, enwrapping so much of mysterious meaning, and ominous of ill-tidings.

"Why, what's the matter there? Has any thing gone wrong?"

"Nothing new—nothing but what has been wrong from the start, and that was more years ago than most people dream of. Only—from all I can gather from people's sly whispers—nobody dares say any thing aloud—things are *looking* crookeder of late than they used to."

She stopped to count the rounds in her sock, preparatory to turning off the heel. Aleck said nothing, and seemed to watch the briskly-rising rings of smoke.

"This marriage is a serious business—one that is generally entered upon too carelessly," resumed Miss Massie, oracularly. "I don't know but you are right to be cautious about risking a chance in the lottery; but there are many worse faults in a wife or husband than a breath scented with cabbage or garlic. Colonel Floyd always reminds me of the men of old who used to tithe mint, anise, and cinnamon, while they neglected the weightier matters of the law. If he had been as careful of his wife's property and happiness, and his children's real good, as he is to spare them a few trifling annoyances that nobody else would ever think of, they'd be better off in mind and estate. They say he gambles awfully—worse than ever—and that if half his debts were paid, he would not have a dollar or an acre of land left that he could call his own."

"Nobody is surprised at that, I imagine. People have prophesied that for years past;—although, as you say, the real condition of his affairs may be more generally known, and spoken of more openly than it used to be," said Aleck.

Miss Ruth's needles rattled nervously against one another.

"Yes; but there's one thing that worries me more than all the rest. While I am, of course, very sorry for poor Mrs. Floyd and the children, still it's natural to feel most uneasy about one's own flesh and blood, and—well—maybe I ought not to speak of it, even to you—but I'm very sure that Robert has lent him money, and a good deal of it, and I am doubtful whether he will ever be paid."

"You need not be. There is a moral certainty that he will never see a cent of it again. No man ever did yet, who was so foolish as to lend any thing to the colonel. You can set your mind at rest upon that score."

"Yes, I suppose so; but it is a pity and a shame, Aleck! I wish you could put Robert upon his guard. He's so soft-hearted and open-handed that he can't say 'No' to anybody, much less to a friend. And he always defends Colonel Floyd when he is attacked; says he's not so bad as the world is disposed to think, and has some fine traits of character, and has always been very kind to him, and all such talk. You know Robert, and how easily imposed upon he is; and the colonel certainly puts himself out to be polite and attentive to him, and, Robert told me, gave his consent in the most handsome manner to his engagement with Helen Gardner. Gracious, Aleck! you might have broken it all to pieces!"

Aleck stooped to pick up the pipe that had slipped from his fingers, and remained in that position for a minute, busily brushing the ashes from the gayly flowered hearth-rug—a manifestation of care and neatness which, if Aunt Ruth remarked, she attributed to the effect of his residence among the cleanly Hollanders.

"Ugly and dirty as it is, it would have been a pity to break what cost so much money, and is so hard to replace in this country!" continued the thrifty housewife. "'Tisn't cracked, is it?"

"No! But I interrupted you! What were you saying?" Aleck refilled and relighted his pipe, after seeming to examine it solicitously, and stretched out his feet as before. "You were talking about the Floyds."

"Yes! so far as I can judge, there is no love lost between Helen and her guardian. I don't think there ever has been. He has always found her an unruly charge, I reckon. So it isn't to please her that Robert let him have money, when he asked for it. It's just his own good-nature, and he will suffer for it."

"They have been engaged for some time, have they?"

"Who? Robert and Helen? Four or five months. They seem very happy together, as contented a couple as I ever saw. They expect to be married at Christmas; but I suppose Robert has told you all about that."

"At Christmas! and this is the first of November!"

There was a dreary echo in his tone that reached even Miss Ruth's apprehensions, and elicited a responsive sigh.

"Yes! it will be a change for us all—for you and me, as well as them! But I hope it is for Robert's good. He will make one of the best husbands alive; and she has steadied surprisingly—sobered down more than I once thought she ever could, since they were first engaged. Do you recollect how wild she used to be?"

"Yes!"

And after this musing articulation of his aunt's favorite monosyllable, there was an interval of silence. Miss Ruth plied her knitting-needles assiduously, and looked over her spectacles into the crackling fire. The nephew smoked slowly, and seemed to study the same blazing pile of hickory logs. What were her motherly and housewifely meditations, it concerns us not to inquire. The central figure in his dream-pictures was a young girl, with flashing, laughing eyes, and dark chestnut locks wound in heavy braids about her nobly-shaped head; form erect, yet pliant; dancing feet whose rapid beat was sweetest music to his ears.

"*Did* he recollect how wild she used to be?"

Mrs. Floyd, sober and shocked, had oftentimes expostulated with him for aiding and abetting her harum-scarum niece in her hare-brained pranks and lawless proceedings. He had taught her to sit firmly his most spirited hunter, in leaping fences and ditches; to fish, and, most barbarous of all pursuits for a young lady—to hunt! to carry her fowling-piece and bring down her game with the coolness and address of a veteran sportsman. This last named accomplishment was rather practised in secret, than alluded to in public. It was doubtful whether Mrs. Floyd was ever quite sure that Helen had really acquired it. Many a day had she spent in the woods in company with Aleck and Robert, when governess and guardians had granted her permission to pay a proper, hum-drum visit to Miss Ruth. An unfortunate accident finally cured her of her Nimrod proclivities. The three were out turkey-hunting, one day, and Aleck, having stationed Robert with Helen behind the blind of brushwood and bushes, to await the coming of the frightened and scattered flock, grew impatient of the tardiness of the dogs sent to "flush" the birds, and started off himself to seek and direct them. He was not long in discovering a fine gang of turkeys, and after assuring himself that many of them had taken the direction he desired, undertook to regain the covert by another route. Crouching low, that his head might not appear above the undergrowth of the wood, he made his way rapidly and stealthily towards the ambuscade. He was within twenty yards of it, when the crack of a gun rang out upon the forest stillness. Helen, excited and impetuous, had mistaken the slight motion created by his passage among the bushes, for the advance of the expected game, and fired before Robert could interfere to prevent her rash action. The charge from her weapon lodged in Aleck's shoulder and the upper part of his chest, inflicting a severe, and, as they, in their inexperience, feared, a fatal wound.

Bleeding and suffering—ignorant as his companions of the extent of his danger, the elder brother still retained his habitual power of resolve and command.

"Leave me here—both of you!" was his order. "Robert! you will see her home! then ride over to Greenfield and bring a couple of men back with you. And, my dear fellow! mind! *I did it myself!*"

Helen interposed with a passionate burst of self-accusation. It was all her work—her unpardonable stupidity! her cruel, cruel blunder! and she alone should be blamed for it! She deserved the most severe things that could be said of and to her!

"Nelly!" The wounded youth looked up with his own saucy smile. "Do you remember what that old Hebrew king—Abimelech, I believe it was—said to his armor-bearer, when a woman cast a piece of millstone from the wall of the besieged city, and cracked his crown? 'Draw thy sword, and slay me, that men say not of me—'*A woman* slew him!' Robert, you will do as I said!"

Robert hastened away in quest of help; but Helen's will was not to be borne down in this matter. For two hours—long in their anguished suspense to her;—short and delicious as a dream of Paradise to the injured boy,—she lingered beside him in the heart of that lonely forest; stanching the blood with such appliances as were within her reach; making him a pillow of leaves; fanning him; gently wiping his brow, when the pain, that could not extort groan from the manly heart, or dim his grateful smile, forced great beads of sweat through the pores. Nay, more! when the sound of voices was heard approaching the spot, and he besought her for both their sakes to make good her retreat before she was perceived by curious or unfriendly eyes, she gazed long and earnestly into his face, a look that awoke a new thrill of life in the fainting heart, and, the tears raining down her cheeks, bent over and kissed him.

When Robert and his attendants arrived at the scene of the accident, Aleck was alone, lying quietly upon his leafy couch, more than serene, with a happy light upon his countenance that glorified and elevated every feature. It was but the commencement of a splendid hunting season—the finest that had been known in years—when he was shot, and he lost the whole of it. Miss Ruth marvelled at and lauded his patient endurance of his tedious confinement; his comrades were affected with equal surprise at the cheerful equanimity with which he received their raillery upon his awkwardness in hitting himself,—he, the best shot in the country!

"Merely a difference of game, boys!" he said, gayly. "I went to look for turkeys, and brought down a great goose instead!"

Robert carried daily health bulletins to Colonel Floyd's, and never returned without some token of remembrance or sympathizing message from Helen. Sometimes she wrote to the invalid. Every one of these hastily penned notes—incoherent, girlish, extravagant—was treasured up to this day—locked away, as too sacred for other eyes;—perfumed with the roses she had sent by his brother's hand. The three guarded well their secret; but Helen never hunted again. If she had not lost her unfeminine hankering for a personal participation in the amusement, she shrank from its practice with trembling.

She was but fifteen then,—scarcely more than a child. Robert was two years older, and Aleck his senior by eighteen months. He was twenty-two when he went to Germany, and it was still "Aleck" and "Nelly" between them. Still they laughed, danced, rode and sported together, the acknowledged ringleaders of every frolic—the wilder the better—and Robert was the balance-wheel to their impetuosity. He was mirthful, and loved fun as dearly as did either of the others, but he exhibited a gentle steadiness of demeanor, a graceful propriety of action, that caused him to be extolled by all the matrons of the region as a "pattern young man, and a safe chance for any girl." Nobody called Aleck Lay an unsafe chance, yet his popularity never equalled his brother's. He was too unscrupulous in speech, often reckless and imprudent in manner. The weak-minded and timid feared his lash of ridicule; hypocrites and pretenders, his fearless exposure of their true characters. Little cared he for popular judgment, for public favor, or public reprobation! Aunt Ruth petted him; Robert loved him; and Helen was his willing ally, his fast friend, his confidante upon all subjects save one.

Their farewell, prior to his departure for the Old World, was spoken in the interval of the dance, at a large party given at Colonel Floyd's in celebration of Lily Calvert's—a niece and another ward of the colonel's—birthday.

"It would hardly be honorable in me were I to say to you all that is in my heart," Aleck had said, hurriedly; "for this avowal would force you to a corresponding frankness—and I shall be absent a long time—and we are both very young. It would be basely ungenerous, were I to attempt to bind you by a promise now."

His color came and went almost as rapidly as did hers, and his whole behavior was oddly at variance with his usual easy, self-assured bearing.

"But, if my presumption in daring to speak of this matter—to think of you, to hope and dream, as I have for years, has not offended you; if you will still keep your early play-fellow in remembrance—still permit him to cherish your image where he has always worn it—in his heart of hearts—may I ask you to wear this while I am away? It is no signal of bondage, recollect! It leaves you free as air. When I return, if I do not see it on your finger, I shall, nevertheless, have no right to feel myself ill-treated—shall never molest you by demands for any explanation."

They stood apart from the crowd, at a window partially concealed by a curtain. Without a word—only with one thrilling look into his eyes, that revived the memory of the forest scene, she drew off her glove—his hand touched hers—held it for a second! The next minute a partner claimed her for the ensuing set, and led her away, dreaming as little of the ring hidden by the snowy kid, as did the throng at large of the wild throbbings of the heart—the mingled rapture, pain, and unrest masked by Aleck Lay's laughing face. Helen was never more gay than during the remainder of the revel; and his spirits seemed to keep pace with the rise of hers. Their last dance together was a dashing, sweeping waltz, whose almost frantic swiftness, and the length of time they kept it up, set all the prudes' heads to wagging in holy horror, and drew from kind, loving, charitable Aunt Ruth a deprecating remark to her nephew Robert.

"She's a good-hearted girl, I don't doubt, Robert! And I have great confidence in her principles; she wouldn't knowingly do a wrong thing; but it's a pity the poor child has no mother!"

The rout over, the adieux were brief—a single glance was interchanged, and a hand-clasp, fervent, but not prolonged;—a jesting phrase, intended for the benefit of the bystanders,—

"Good-by, Nelly! Take care of yourself!" and

"Good-by, Aleck! I suppose we shall not see you again until you are a fat Mynheer, whose thick tongue will be unintelligible to untravelled ears."

This was all! As he had said, they were both very young then; it was his choice to leave her untrammelled by the shadow of a pledge. The ring might have been a friend's parting gift. She was a woman now—more grave, more thoughtful, more judicious than in the days when she seemed to prefer his society to that of other admirers—even to Robert's; a woman who had chosen for herself a life partner, and who would, in seven weeks more, be his brother's wife!

He thought all this over, without the change of a muscle or an audible sigh. His will was strong, and his pride stubborn; himself one of the men who can meet death, however horrible its form, with a steady or smiling front, if it be proved to be inevitable, and there are others looking on to mark how they sustain the trial.

His voice, cheery and unfaltering, ended the protracted pause.

"Ah, well, aunty, you and I need not stay here to embarrass the movements of the rightful master and mistress of this establishment. Greenfield is a dear and lovely spot to us both, but duty and expediency unite in forbidding my longer residence here. Maple Hill is sadly in want of a tenant, and I have always looked forward to a settlement of myself and worldly goods there when I should be ready to begin life in earnest. But I cannot keep house by myself, you know. It would be a doleful and disgraceful Bachelor's Hall, that would cause you to disown me forever. I must have somebody to scold the maids, to pour out my coffee and lecture me occasionally. You will not mind the change of home so much as if I invited you to be my companion in a strange neighborhood and unfamiliar house, will you?"

"I was born there, lived there until your mother and grandfather died, and your father begged me to come here and take charge of you boys!"

A tear found its way from beneath the spectacles.

"And you have no idea what an exemplary character I mean to become," pursued Aleck. "Not quite so good as Robin, to be sure, but a very decorous and decent young man, notwithstanding beard and meerschaum."

Miss Ruth smiled up at him affectionately. Scapegrace though she was often obliged to consider him, he had ever been her favorite of her adopted children; and the vision of an independent home with him was far more pleasant, more in consonance with her tastes, than the thought of resigning the insignia of authority, *i. e.*, the keybasket, into the hands of Robert's wife, and the meek acceptance of a secondary position in the court where she had reigned supreme for upwards of twenty years.

"You were always kind-hearted and generous, Aleck! one of the sort whose worst side is the outside. I hope you'll get a good wife of your own some day."

"Don't trouble your brain with such useless wishes and unprofitable imaginings, aunty! *I* do not! Why! it is ten o'clock! Is Robert generally so late in returning from court?"

"No! I'm afraid he went home with Colonel Floyd! He often does. It is naturally hard work for him, now he is in love, to pass the Belleview gate on his road, especially when he thinks that there is nobody here but me, and knows that I am never lonesome. We had not an idea of seeing you for a fortnight to come. How stupid and selfish it was in me not to think sooner of sending a boy to the colonel's to inquire if he was there. But, you see, I kept expecting him every minute."

"Exactly! I understand! I am glad your after-thought came so late. I would not have him disturbed from his present agreeable quarters on my account. You think that he will not be home to-night, then?"

"Hardly. He usually stays at the colonel's all night when he goes there from court. I suppose that, like most other courting couples, they sit up till past midnight, and he doesn't like to trouble me by coming in so late. I should think they would have talked it all out before this time, but that is always the way. Engaged people never seem at a loss what to say to one another."

"Theirs is a theme which is exhaustless, until after marriage!" said Aleck, yawning and rising. "I feel tired after my journey, and it is already long past your bed-time. Good-night!"

His chamber was the same he had shared with Robert until their separation, two years before; the same in which he had lain, helpless and suffering, during the weeks that followed the accident already described. There was a bright fire on the hearth; his mother's picture, the object of his boyish idolatry, still smiled down at him from its place above the mantel; every article of the old familiar furniture was endeared to him by its associations of a happy childhood and joyous, hopeful youth, yet the place was inexpressibly cheerless and desolate; awoke a sensation of homesickness, more acute than any he had felt in the way-side inns of foreign lands.

He looked through the window. The moon shone with fitful lustre between flying clouds; the high autumn wind roared through a pine-grove to the right of the house, and tore showers of leaves from other trees—the dismantled boughs groaning in every fibre as they gave up their summer treasures. It was a weird, dreary night to a solitary and sad watcher, whether his lonely vigil were kept above a dead form or a dead hope; a night to make friends draw closer the ring surrounding the social blaze, and talk more earnestly and frankly; a night to cause lovers to cling more nearly and fondly to one another, to feel, as they had never done before, the warmth and blessedness and glory of that heart sunshine which beamed the fairer for the rush and crash of outward storms.

"This is my welcome home!"

He left his look-out; went to a trunk which, with the rest of his baggage, stood against the wall, unstrapped and opened it, and took from its depths a pretty casket. The lid of this was raised, and a subtle perfume stole through the apartment—the odor of rose-leaves. Then, the entire contents of the box were emptied upon the table: notes, dried flowers, a knot of blue ribbon—lastly, a lady's cambric handkerchief, with dark-red stains upon it. With this, the rude compress of moss and bruised herbs had been bound upon his shoulder on that memorable day. One corner bore a name. He tore this off and threw it into the fire, turning his back that he might not see it burn; the rest, cambric, papers, withered stalks and petals, were rent into small bits, not impatiently, but carefully, deliberately, as one performs a solemn duty, re-collected and returned to the casket. The November blast screamed hoarsely past his ear as he lifted the sash. In a second it caught the pile of fragments; whirled them aloft; dashed them downwards; scattered them far and wide over plain, hill, and grove.

"So let it be!" was all Aleck said, as he lowered the window.

CHAPTER II.

THERE was no lack of cheerful company in Colonel Floyd's parlor that evening. The colonel himself read the papers he had taken from the post-office in the afternoon—seated by a round stand at the warmest corner of the fire-place. So real was his absorbed interest in the sheet he held, that his presence imposed less restraint than it was wont to exert upon the innocent hilarity of the junior portion of the party. He had enjoyed in his younger days the reputation of being the handsomest man, the best rider, and most graceful dancer in the county; and the years which had frosted his hair, and made rigid the once flexible lines of his face, had not bowed the stately form, robbed the eye of its fire, or the limbs of their strength. He looked proud and resolute, and he was both of these, and more,—proud, with a haughtiness that inspired dislike and fear, rather than respect; arrogant and overbearing to an extent which made him popular throughout the region where he would have ruled with absolute sway. In his family, he was an autocrat; upon his plantation, a despot, whose laws were Draconian in severity; everywhere, in theory and in practice, he was an aristocrat of the sternest type. It was a common saying among the working classes, that it was almost as much as a poor man's life was worth, to press Colonel Floyd for the payment of a just debt; yet no tradesman or mechanic durst refuse him unlimited credit. It is a sight that may be seen every day in other communities, North, East and West, where the feudal system has never prevailed as it did at the date of our tale, in this old Potomac county of Maryland,—I mean the supremacy accorded to a single individual by those, his equals and betters in all respects—merely because he, out of the pride and mightiness of his inflated heart, chooses to proclaim himself a prince and a lord over them. Some of those whom he counts his vassals are too indolent, others too cowardly, others still too amiable, to dispute his reign, and, unchecked, he flaunts his dictatorship in the eyes of his amused or disgusted fellow-citizens, until a Tyrant, stronger and grimmer yet than he, forces him to discharge the last humiliating debt of Nature; proves him to have been, after all his pomp of place and circumstance, but common clay.

The Floyds had, from their family seat of Belleview, governed the adjacent county for three generations back; and distasteful as was the bearing of the present proprietor to his well-born, well-bred, and wealthy neighbors, they never thwarted, very rarely contradicted him. Behind his back, he was stigmatized as violent, unscrupulous, and dissipated—a *roué* and a gambler; a bully and a swindler; yet, not one of his uncomplimentary friends ever thought of testifying his disapproval of a course so disreputable by declining the hospitalities of Belleview, and obliging his wife and daughters to do the same; none withheld from him the grasping hand and hearty salutation of delighted civility; few there were who did not feel and express themselves as pleased and honored by his visits to their houses.

Upon the opposite side of the hearth was Mrs. Floyd, mild, inane, and faded, as might have been predicted of the sweet-tempered, spiritless beauty and heiress, who had, at eighteen, wedded this imperious partner. She feared her husband, loved her children, and found her chief pleasures in housekeeping, gardening, and the participation in an occasional weak and innocuous dish of gossip with some congenial visitor. At the period of her marriage, she had represented several ciphers, prefaced by a more important figure, and these, it was surmised, had formed her principal recommendation, *malgré* her bright eyes and peachy bloom, in the sight of the bridegroom. But beneath his hot, hasty fingers, the sum of which she was the sign and seal had melted away, until the total and her consequence to her spouse had dwindled, in a like proportion, to a forlorn 0. Yet they maintained the state they had borne when cash was plenty, and houses nor lands were overshadowed by cumbering mortgages. In mansion and farm and stables, there was no symptom of the decay of wealth or gentility. People said that they were going down hill, while all agreed that, during the colonel's lifetime, his family would never be allowed to soil their dainty feet with the mud; that to those, reared as they had been, lies a dread and hopeless quagmire,—filthy and unfathomable, in the vale of Poverty. As for Mrs. Floyd, it may be safely affirmed that the idea of such a descent, the bare prospect or possibility of this terrific fall, had never occurred to her mind.

She was half dozing now over a knitted edging she was manufacturing of fine spool cotton—a vacant smile upon her features, a meaningless smirk, that was supposed to indicate excessive amiability, which brightened mechanically, as, now and then, a merry out-burst from the group of young people reached her drowsy senses. This was her usual style of entertaining her nieces' visitors.

This group, consisting of six persons,—three ladies and a corresponding number of gentlemen,—were gathered about a table in the middle of the large room, engaged, evidently to their own most lively gratification, in the game of "Consequences." The table was littered with the folded slips of paper, so well known to the lovers of the play, and each one held a pencil. The member of the little band who would soonest have attracted the notice of a stranger, was Lily Calvert, the younger of Colonel Floyd's wards, and his own niece. Her chair was set in the full glare of the lamp that lighted the scribblers in their employment. She was nearly nineteen years of age, but not taller than many girls are at ten, with pale gold curls floating loosely upon her shoulders; exquisitely shaped and extremely small feet and hands; large, melancholy blue eyes, with drooping fringes, and a voice clear and sweet as that of a bird. But her complexion, to which she owed her pet name, now the only one by which she was ever called, formed the marked peculiarity of her appearance. It was white as the purest wax; never warmed by a tinge of color, whatever were her feelings; and her lips had, usually, a bluish tinge. The most obstinate unbeliever in the reality of such phenomena could not, in surveying her, help crediting the explanation of this one, commonly reported among those who were conversant with the family history.

Egbert Calvert had married Colonel Floyd's only sister, and settled with her upon the estate bequeathed to her by her father. One night, less than a year from the wedding-day, he was brought home a corpse, stark, cold, and bloody, having been picked up from the roadside by some belated passers-by. He had not a known enemy in the world; no man was more popular and respected, and, in the absence of all testimony tending to prove human agency in producing his death, the ghastly cut upon the back of his head, which had crushed in the skull, was somewhat lamely accounted for by the supposition that his horse—a fiery and imperfectly broken colt,—had thrown him with violence against the rocky road on which he was lying when found. The poor wife never smiled again; seldom spoke a voluntary word after recovering from the swoon into which she fell at the fatal spectacle; but it was not until Lily's birth that she manifested unmistakable signs of derangement. Lunacy was not reckoned a disgrace in this patrician community. On the contrary, its frequent appearance in the best, that is to say, the wealthiest and proudest classes, caused it to be recognized as an aristocratic complaint, produced, as it undoubtedly was, by the need of an admixture of fresh, new blood with the thin, blue current cousin had poured into cousin's veins, from one generation to another, for a hundred years and more. The Floyds had, like the rest of those who plumed themselves upon being of "good old stock," been pertinacious in the practice of intermarriage. Grandfather, father, and son had espoused first cousins, and the State Asylum was the more populous by reason of their adherence to ancient customs.

So Charlotte Calvert, bereaved of husband, and, more mercifully, of reason, was consigned by her affectionate relatives to the safe and comfortable retreat where others of her race were enjoying a peaceful home; her brother assumed the control of her property, as guardian of her child and trustee for herself, and Mrs. Floyd opened her motherly arms to the worse than orphaned babe. She had no daughters of her own,—had been, as the phrase is, "unfortunate" in her children. Her eldest boy was born an idiot, and, at the time of our story, was an inmate of the same asylum in which his aunt, Mrs. Calvert, was confined. The second, a beautiful, intelligent child, lived to be two years old, and was then snatched from her within a day after the commencement of the disorder by an attack of croup; the third, a girl, died a few hours after its birth. This event occurred almost simultaneously with the little Lily's advent, and the latter gained, by means of this association and her own sad helplessness of condition, such a hold upon the heart of her foster-mother, that the subsequent arrival of four sons, three of whom were still alive, could not dispossess her of the first place in the good lady's affections. Her uncle did not pet her; he never petted any thing, not even his most valued racer; but neither did he scold and rebuff and cuff her, as it was his habit to treat his own offspring, and thus she grew to regard herself, and to be regarded by others, as a favorite with him. She was a spoiled child from the beginning of her existence; but more self-indulgent than selfish; exacting of notice and love, and disposed to be jealous of superior attentions bestowed upon others; yet it was so natural to admire and humor her; she was so pretty and *petite*, and her naïve, winning ways so like those of a gleeful, graceful little girl, that it was not often she had reason to complain of being overlooked.

Her supporters on either hand at the table were Tom Shore and Junius Dickson, beaux from the vicinity, who had made this their halting-place on the way homewards from the county court-house—quite a fashionable practice with the young men for twenty miles around. Facing her sat Virginia Shore, Tom's sister, an intimate friend of the cousins and a gay-spirited rattle; next her, Robert Lay, and beside him, his betrothed, Helen Gardner, looking very much as Aleck's yearning heart was then picturing her in his fireside visions, only with a richer maturity, a ripeness of womanhood upon her, that Miss Ruth may have had in her mind, when she essayed to describe the change that had taken place in the girl since her engagement. Robert was a trifle shorter than his brother, but still a well-made, tall figure, with pleasant hazel eyes, light hair, clear complexion, a mouth that betokened sweetness of disposition and delicate sensibilities, a voice at once manly and gentle, and a full, curling auburn beard. He was a handsome fellow; companionable to a charm; easy-tempered to a fault; and universally beloved by high and low. By unanimous acclamation, he was chosen reader of the party; and in his manner of collecting the folded slips, as each writer pronounced his or hers ready, there was a frank, smiling courtesy, so natural and customary with him, that he was unaware of its manifestation, but which wrought its effect upon those he addressed.

"Are you ready, Miss Helen?" he said to his right-hand neighbor, when all the others had given in their contributions.

"Not quite! I am stupid to-night!"

"I believe you are!" retorted Lily, with a slight spice of pettishness in her manner. "You have been behindhand in every round. If you will write what you are dreaming about it will interest us, I have no doubt."

"Never mind! There is time enough, and to spare," observed Robert, kindly, as Helen bent down, her face crimsoning with shame or impatience, and scribbled away desperately at the limited space remaining for her to fill.

He pretended, further to relieve her, to be busied in sorting the narrow strips of paper deposited in his care.

"There!" Helen pushed hers towards him, and threw herself back in her chair. "My invention is exhausted! I shall retire at the next round."

"Do as I do, and write whatever nonsense first occurs to you," replied young Lay. "I should never progress beyond a single line if I attempted to be brilliant!"

The game of "Consequences," I may as well state, for the information of those who, from the misfortune of ignorance, or the wilfulness of superior wisdom to such frivolous amusements, need enlightenment upon the subject, is conducted after this wise. A half sheet of note-paper is furnished to each person who desires to take part in the entertainment, and he or she writes at the top of this a character or personal description applicable to a lady—as "the fair and witty," or the "homely and shrewish"—folds this down so carefully that no part of the writing is visible, and passes it to the one sitting next the said him or her, on one side, receiving at the same moment a similarly prepared page from the neighbor on the other hand. Next comes the lady's name, usually that of some friend or acquaintance of the writer; then, a description masculine, and a name; the place of meeting; what he said, and her reply; the consequence of the interview, and, as a finale, the world's opinion upon the matter. The best fun of the performance is the marvellous and oftentimes ludicrous coherence of the narrative, written piece-meal by so many hands, each scribe being perfectly ignorant of a single word that precedes his own addition to the story. There were a few blushes and a great deal of laughter upon the present occasion, as various good hits and strikingly appropriate allusions were given to the auditors in the reader's best style.

At length came a tale that awoke different sensations in the breasts of all, that was felt acutely by at least one member of the company:—

"The graceful and winning Miss Lily Calvert and the refined and chivalrous Mr. Robert Lay met in Colonel Floyd's parlor. He said,

> "'How happy could I be with either,
> Were t'other dear charmer away!'

"She answered, weepingly,

> "'The moon looks on many brooks;
> The brook sees but one moon.'

"The consequence was, that the loss of her wits followed upon that of her heart, and his comfort and happiness were not at all damaged thereby. The world said—'Poor thing! what else could have been anticipated from her antecedents!'"

One or two tried to raise a spasmodic laugh, and nobody looked at Lily, whose forced mirth jarred upon every ear, while her taper fingers interlaced each other tightly on the table.

"Bah!" said Helen. "That is the flattest thing we have heard yet! Give us another, if you please, Mr. Lay."

No one, unless it were himself, in their private interviews, ever heard her call him "Robert" now-a-days.

"This looks racy!" remarked he, catching a glimpse of the names heading the one he was unfolding.

"The witty and accomplished Miss Helen Gardner, and the learned but cynical Mr. Alexander Lay, met behind a turkey-blind. He said—'False as fair! did you not plight your troth to me? Was not this ring the seal?' She said—'Alas! it is too late! They told me you loved another!' The consequence was that she married his brother, and he lived and died a crusty, rusty, fusty old bachelor. The world said—'It is dangerous, this playing with edge-tools!'"

Robert's smile was free of all unpleasant meaning, as he flashed a merry glance at his betrothed.

"Reefs ahead!" he said, in a playful "aside," inaudible to others, amidst the chattering that succeeded the reading of this, the last paper. "I must be on the look-out! You know that we expect this dangerous rival of mine in the course of a week or two, do you not?"

"No—I had not heard! Let me look at that nonsense!"

She took the slip he was twisting between his fingers, perused it scrutinizingly, probably to assure herself that no two sentences were penned by the same individual, cast it down contemptuously upon the pile with the rest, arose, and left the room.

The entrance of a servant with a tray of refreshments diverted the attention of the others, and Robert was not long in finding and improving a favorable opportunity for following Helen. They often met, when there was company in the parlor, in the dining-room just across the hall, where the fire was never suffered to go out in cold weather; and since he had signified to her, earlier in the evening, his wish to see her alone by-and-by, it argued no unreasonable vanity on his part that he fully expected to find her there awaiting him. But the room was deserted. The fire had been recently replenished, doubtless by some sagacious servant, in anticipation of the conference he hoped for, and the ruddy shine showed him distinctly every object in the spacious apartment. An unlighted candle was on the table; two comfortable chairs were set in affectionate and suggestive proximity to one another, in front of the hearth.

"She will be in presently!" was his mental comment upon the disappointment, and he sat down to bide her pleasure or convenience.

Five—ten—fifteen minutes went by, and while he chafed less at the delay than a more irritable man would have done, he yet experienced a growing and disagreeable sentiment of impatience.

"At last!"

Footsteps approached along the corridor. He stood up to welcome the late-comer, with no intention of offering her a reproach, or even a remonstrance. True gallant that he was, he never thought of assailing her with such. If he were her knight, he was her vassal likewise; bowed to her will in glad humility, as in courtly grace. His countenance changed as he listened. Helen's light foot never trod the floor with that lazy shuffle; nor was it her habit, even in the days when she "used to be so wild," to proclaim her coming by whistling—

"Possum up a gum-tree,
Raccoon in a hollow."

But it was a melodious whistle, and deftly executed; the

original melody being artistically varied by fantastic trills and cadenzas; and it was a good-humored face which was illumined by the candle borne in the intruder's hand.

"Beg pardon, Mars' Robert! Come for Marster heavy boots! He want 'em, byme by!"

He was a negro lad of fourteen or thereabouts—boot-black, errand-boy, and assistant waiter; a knowing, saucy imp, who stood in awe of but two living creatures, his master and his father.

"Dey ain't in here, arter all!" he ejaculated, in well-feigned surprise, having made an exploration of all unlikely and impossible hiding-places for the required articles, such as the sideboard, knife-box, and plate-warmer. "Dat's too bad!"

"I saw a pair in the hall when I came through just now," said Robert, whose instinct it was to help every one, no matter how lowly his station, out of trouble, whatever might be its nature.

"Thank you, sur! I'm obleeged to you!"

He halted, in backing towards the door, as if just struck by an idea.

"If you please, Mars' Robert, would you mind asking Miss Helen if she will have a fire made up in de office? It's cold for her to be a-settin' thar to-night—and damp besides. To be sure, the chimbly has what you may call a 'different deliverer, and does smoke pretty bad for a while arter the fire is kindled—but, ef she likes to set thar, she ought to have one, and I'm 'tirely at hur survice—ef you'd be so kind as to say so to hur, sur!"

"I will! Here, Gabriel!"

He tossed the boy a coin, which was caught dexterously, and, without advancing to hear the profusion of thanks that ensued upon the receipt of the gift, Robert entered the long, dark hall by which Gabriel had come to the dining-room. This led to a wing of the building which was mostly taken up by store-rooms and closets, and at the farther end by what was termed "the office." Not that any of the Floyds had ever professed to practise law or medicine, unless it had been some obscure younger son, whose very name had passed away from family traditions. No one now upon the earth knew from what usage or circumstance the apartment had derived its name—only, it had always been called "the office" within the memory of this generation, and innovations upon former customs were not popular in the connection. There were scores of ancient volumes, with yellow pages and worm-eaten bindings, packed into two book-cases on different sides of the room; in one corner was an antiquated spinet, its keys dumb or discordant, its gayly ornamented top cracked and defaced; in another a dusty spinning-wheel, minus a leg, leaned against the wall. There were chairs in various stages of dilapidation—legless, backless, and bottomless; and a spindle-shanked, rickety table or two; a general flavor of mustiness and cobwebs, the chilliness of a vault and the choking dryness of a disused garret pervading all.

Any thing more ill-suited to be the bower selected by beauty for lovers' tryst could hardly be imagined, yet Robert Lay saw and thought of nothing except the figure that started back from the moonlighted window, as he unclosed the creaking door. He spoke promptly, to reassure her.

"Nelly! Darling! why are you here all alone?"

No answer; but there was light enough for him to perceive her further recoil into the darkness behind her; to note the drooping head and arms crossed upon her breast.

"Are you unhappy? Is there any thing which I can do for you? Or, had you rather I should not interrupt you at present?" he pursued, not offering to advance from his position at the entrance.

"No! no!" she laughed, and came forward to meet him.

"This is my old Cave of Melancholy—the grotto of Trophonius; my chosen resort in my earlier and more haughty days. Oh! the tears that have watered these dusty boards! the bursts of angry and pathetic declamation to which these stained walls have lent patient ears! But you see I can laugh now in reviewing those—my callow days!"

Robert was not deceived by this show of high spirits. He had taken her hand and drawn her to the window, while she was speaking. Her cheeks were flushed, her hand hot in his.

"And the naughty world has dared to use you ill again, has it, although you *are* now a full-fledged bird?"

"Did I say so?" she asked, in quick evasion.

"I infer as much, from finding you in the depths of your sorrowful grotto."

"Oh! my visit to-night was a whim. Not that I have not had a touch of the blues all day—"

"I have observed this evening, that you were hardly in your usual spirits—a trifle below concert pitch, I should say. Will you not let me share your trouble or annoyance? relieve it, if I can?"

He ventured to steal his arm around her! the love and sympathy depicted in his countenance were plainly to be read by the brightness of the moonbeams, pouring over them at that instant. She did not repel him, albeit she was generally shy of caresses from her betrothed. She even looked up, as his soothing, lovefull accents saluted her ears; then, meeting that eloquent gaze, burst into a stormy flood of tears, and buried her face in her hands.

"Robert! Robert! if I could only tell you all!"

"Perhaps that 'all' is not so profound a secret to me as you imagine, dearest!"

He clasped her more firmly, as she would have started from his side.

"Love's eyes are very keen, and mine have discerned much that you, from an overstrained, unreasonable sense of honor, would have concealed."

Her sobbing had ceased, but her head was bowed more lowly still, and she trembled violently.

"In this respect, and in this alone, I have been disposed to accuse you of injustice to me, Nelly. When I gave you my love, or, to speak more accurately, when you accepted it—for I cannot remember the time when my heart was not yours!—when you accepted my love, I gave you my whole confidence, and entreated that you should be equally unreserved with me. While I cannot fail to admire and appreciate the delicacy that has restrained you upon this point, for it is both a difficult and a delicate matter to bring a charge of unworthiness against one who is so nearly related—"

She threw off his arm; raised a pale, haughty face, whose flashing eyes fairly appalled him.

"You are laboring under a strange misapprehension, Mr. Lay! I have no accusation of any kind, certainly none of unworthiness, to bring against the person of whom you speak. Your information is utterly incorrect, or your imagination has wandered wildly, if you believe the contrary."

"Nelly!" articulated the astonished lover, "listen to me! It is not *my* imagination that wanders now. Surely, the bond which unites you to him who hopes, in less than two months, to call you his wife, is as strong as that binding you to Colonel Floyd—your guardian, indeed, but merely your uncle-in-law! I ask your forgiveness, if I have erred in supposing that this house was an uncongenial home, from which you have often longed to escape; if I have fancied that Colonel Floyd was, at times, a harsh, and, to one of your disposition, an unwelcome protector. But, while sympathizing with you in the many trials you bear so beautifully, I do not pretend to deny that, out of this bitterness, has sprung some sweetness to me. I have loved to picture to myself how different shall be your daily life when you are all mine, the queen of my home, partner of my fortunes, as you are now of my affections. Again let me entreat your pardon, if I have offended or grieved you by this my first allusion to a subject concerning which you have heretofore avoided speaking. But, my pet—does it not seem preposterous in us, situated as we are, to cherish these foolish, petty reserves?"

"It is I who should sue for your forgiveness. I was petulant, unjust! I did not understand you! Will you pardon me?"

His answer was a fervent kiss upon the hand she extended.

"It is as you have said!" she continued, in the same altered tone—gentle—pleading—almost humble. "This has never been a happy home to me. I will be as frank as you can desire upon this theme; will discard the reserve you deem foolish and childish. My aunt is kind and means well. She could not treat any thing unkindly, you know; but although my father was her brother, she loves Lily far better than she does her niece by blood. I try to please and to be dutiful to her; I am sincerely grateful for all she has done for me; but she and Lily assimilate more nearly to one another than she and I ever can."

"I understand!" Robert smiled, a little queerly—a gleam that was not complimentary to Mrs. Floyd's favorite.

"I do not murmur at this," added Helen. "I have never experienced a moment's jealousy of Lily. She is lovely and engaging, and was born to win affection. She used to call me her sister, and seemed to esteem me as such; yet she has changed greatly within the past six months. She does not mean to be unjust; still, she treats me coldly, and will assign no reason for the revolution in her feelings or manner. Colonel Floyd, my uncle, never professed any regard for me; in fact, I have seen, from the time I came to live here, that he disliked me. He is more irritable now than ever before—sometimes says things that are very hard to bear. Oh, Robert! but for you I should be driven to the belief that I have not the power of retaining the love of any one! The scanty share of this, Life's best gift, which Providence ever bestowed upon me, seems all to have slipped away. Nobody cares for me now—nobody!"

She wrung her hands and moaned much.

It was a moment of the most exquisite pain the listener ever endured. Blest—rich beyond all possibility of spirit-need—in the consciousness of possessing her affection, he could not comprehend this agony of poverty of which she complained. He would fain have hoped to fill her heart, if not so full as she had his, yet, so well as to leave her no cause for such repinings. Repressing the expostulation he felt would be selfish and cruel, he told her anew, in words whose fervor was not diminished by the sadness in which they were uttered, of his devotion, single and entire; his trust that coming years had in reserve for her, sunshine that should beguile her into forgetfulness of the gloomy Past.

She heard him with calming pulses and more composed mien. Presently, the bowed face was uplifted, and her eyes sought his again—a look that was reverence, admiration—was it love? So it seemed to his sanguine apprehension, as he laid the unresisting head upon his breast, and bent to the still quivering lips.

"My own Nelly! my precious Love! my *Wife!*"

A cloud, crossing the moon's disc, wrapped every thing in obscurity for some moments. The room was upon the ground floor, the window-sill low, and, as the moonlight broke forth again and suddenly, there fell upon, or between the lovers, the shadow of a man—a long, dark figure, with a gun in its hand.

Helen started, with a terrified ejaculation.

"Hush!" whispered Robert, smiling. "You know who it is?"

"Yes—but it was so unexpected! so like an evil thing! Come back here, where he cannot see you! He may look in."

"What if he does?" returned the young gentleman, bravely. "I hope he will be edified by the spectacle!"

But he retired into the shade of the interior of the apartment at her reiterated entreaty.

The master of the mansion, for he was the startling apparition, remained motionless and sentry-like, his back towards the window, for perhaps three minutes, when his shadow was joined by another, shorter, stouter, and less erect. This belonged to his only confidential servant, the head man in the field, and sub-manager of the estate,—a negro named Booker, who was sire to the redoubtable Gabriel, and to the rest of the slaves not only a taskmaster, exacting and pitiless, but a veritable tyrant, a meet tool in the hands of his unscrupulous owner. He, too, had his weapon, a thick cowhide, and, after a brief conference, the pair moved on.

"Do you patrol your plantation in person?" questioned Helen, abruptly.

"Neither in person, nor by proxy! On the contrary, I have never permitted any patrolling gang to enter or search my servants' quarters, except upon very rare occasions, when they had a warrant to examine my premises, together with those of others in the neighborhood, for stolen property."

"I am very glad! I cannot describe to you the sensations of disgust and dread which I experience, whenever I happen to espy those two upon their nightly round. They go at irregular hours, sometimes as early as nine o'clock, at others not until midnight, that they may take trespassers by surprise. Every person is expected to be in his cabin by ten, and if a visitor be discovered, he is peremptorily ordered off if he has a pass—punished if he has not. You must have heard that Colonel Floyd shot a poor fellow, one of the Reverdy servants, last year?"

"I did! But he caught him thieving, did he not? That is the popular version of the transaction."

"That was the story set in circulation to palliate the act, for Mr. Reverdy is not a man to submit to wanton injury, as Colonel Floyd well knows. But the facts of the case are just these:—The negro who was shot, a very decent, well-behaved young fellow, was in love with Sally, my maid. For some reason, best known to himself, Colonel Floyd conceived a dislike for him, and forbade his coming upon the plantation, 'with his master's permission or without.' I was aware that they still met clandestinely, in spite of this prohibition, and several times warned Sally of the danger they incurred by so doing. One night they were straying along the edge of the melon-patch, when Colonel Floyd hailed them by name, and demanded what they were doing there. The girl ran one way, the man another. Unfortunately, he went directly across the field of melons. When midway, he was fired at and severely wounded. Appearances supported the statement of his pursuers—Booker was in attendance upon his master—that he was in the act of purloining the melons, and 'on the side of his oppressor there was power.' Poor Sally! it nearly killed her! She is a good girl, and sincerely attached to Thomas, her admirer."

"We will make up the match again, and give them a grand wedding at Greenfield, when Christmas is over," was the reply. "Would *you* be very seriously afflicted if some evil-minded or careless hunter were to shoot me in like manner, wing me, as a certain fair damsel of my acquaintance once served poor Aleck?"

"Don't, please!" she begged, in a tone whose distress touched, while it flattered him.

"I am a selfish dog! inconsiderate and unkind, to permit you to stay in this cold vault of a place so long!" he said, anxiously. "Your hands are like two icicles, and you are positively shivering! There is a fire in the dining-room, and I want to read you Aleck's last letter. Won't he be overwhelmed by the pleasant surprise we have in store for him?"

"Do you mean that you have never told him—"

"That we were engaged? Never! It was hard work to keep the delightful secret, but I could not do the subject justice upon paper, and then again I owed him a Roland for the Oliver he gave me, in writing the pretty tale of his German betrothal to Aunt Ruth, and never whispering it to me! He ought to be shot for the trick—the dear old fellow!"

It was at this moment the shower of paper fragments was given to the bitter wind. The brothers each took his last look at the stormy moonlight at the same time.

CHAPTER III.

Helen Gardner sat sewing with her maid, in her chamber upon the following day, when Virginia Shore and Lily burst in upon her quiet. They had just returned from a shopping expedition to the neighboring hamlet, dignified by the name of a village.

"Guess who has come at last!"

"Whom *do* you think we met at the Post Office!" they cried in concert.

"The queen of England, or a peer of the realm at the very least, if one may judge from the state into which the encounter has thrown you both!" responded Helen, with provoking coolness.

"Pshaw! nonsense! make a real guess!" insisted Virginia.

"The Great Mogul, or the Emperor of Timbuctoo—possibly, the Lord High Chamberlain of her majesty, the Empress of Borrio-boola-Gha!" was Helen's next attempt. "Sally! take these young ladies' bonnets and shawls, and set chairs for them!"

She went on with her needlework, which was a portion of her trousseau.

"A more interesting personage than any you have yet named!" Lily walked up to her cousin, and slipped her little hand under her chin, that she might better study her expression as the news was communicated: "Alexander the Great!"

"Certainly the most distinguished *lay*-man of this region!" Virginia supplied an additional hint.

If there were suspicious scrutiny in the gaze which Lily

would have had convey only the impression of arch mirthfulness, its end was foiled for that time. Helen calmly released her face from the hold of the pretty hand.

"Indeed! he has arrived unexpectedly! His friends did not look for him until next week, at the earliest. I hope he is in good plight."

"Superb! magnificent! irresistible!" rejoined Virginia, clasping her fingers and rolling up her eyes in tragi-comic earnestness. "Oh, my poor stricken heart!"

"Let Sally unhook your dress, so that the afflicted organ can thump more freely!" recommended Helen. "Or, if the palpitation is very alarming, try a little hartshorn and lavender!"

"Is that what you take when you are thus affected?" questioned the young lady, plaintively.

"Always!" Helen answered, gravely.

"Then, Sally! if hartshorn be the cure of love, bring it on!" She actually made the amused handmaiden pour out a few drops of the sedative mixture into a glass, and dilute the potion with water; then drank it off, and executed a grimace. "Faugh! what stuff! the remedy is worse than the disease!"

Lily looked supremely disdainful of all this nonsense.

"How can you act so ridiculously, Virginia? And you have not once thought to deliver your Irresistible's message to Helen!"

The needlewoman's complexion did vary slightly at this, and the swift motion of her hand was less even.

"Message! he sent none by me! It was Mr. Robert Lay, who said that they intended riding over this afternoon."

"I beg your pardon!" said Lily, positively, "but my ears are unfortunately quick, and assuredly heard him begin a sentence to you, *sotto voce*, with, 'And my quondam playfellow, Helen'—I was too honorable to listen any longer."

"Indeed, my dear child, your ears deceived you for once. I have no recollection of any such language, or if it was used, I said that myself!" denied the rattle. "I was talking about Helen, part of the time, but there was only a single sentence spoken on the subject, I am sure."

"That was what you two were whispering about, at the carriage-door, was it?"

"I shall not tell you!"

Virginia's color arose suspiciously, although she still laughed. Helen set her teeth and held her peace, while Lily sneered significantly.

"Oh, well! it is none of my business! I introduced the matter because I supposed that Helen would be glad to get the affectionate greeting which I supposed was committed to your trust by her brother-in-law, that is to be. Nelly, dear! we, Virginia and I, have been talking heresy on our way home. We have decided that you did not display your best taste in your selection. The elder and dark-haired brother is unquestionably the handsomer man of the two."

"Tastes differ!" replied Helen. "Yours and mine often do, Lily!"

There was nothing on the surface of this speech to call forth the gasp and wince of surprise or pain with which Lily drew in her breath, yet Helen remarked these, and also the sudden quietness of manner with which she next spoke.

"I am very negligent! I must go and see if I can give mamma" (so she always called Mrs. Floyd), "any assistance in her preparations for dinner. I am growing heartily tired of dining-days!"

Helen sewed on in silence when she had gone, and her sedate, almost stern composure was an uncomfortable damper upon Virginia's merry mood.

"Do give me some sewing, Nelly! something that will keep these idle hands out of the mischief which somebody, who must not be mentioned, always finds for such to do!"

"I have nothing ready besides what we are doing, thank you!"

"Your dresses are to be made in Baltimore, are they not?"

"Yes."

"That is the only decent and comfortable way of getting up a trousseau—to commit it to the profession."

"It is the least troublesome."

A protracted silence, ended by a desperate effort at renewed liveliness on the part of the chatter-box.

"Dear me! I don't wonder you grow sober and thoughtful and matronly before your time, sitting here, stitching eternally upon your wedding-clothes! The very sight of mine would frighten me out of courage and wits together! If I am ever married, it must be upon half an hour's engagement. I should change my mind, if I had leisure to reflect seriously upon what was before me. Honor bright, now, Nelly. (Sally! Mrs. Floyd is calling you!) There is nobody but our two selves here now, dear, and I can be the soul of secrecy when I choose—don't you sometimes get a little, just a *tiny* bit out of the notion of marrying even so charming and lovable fellow as Robert Lay—if he does adore you? It must be nice to be adored, though! I wish somebody would help me to a personal experience upon the subject!"

"If it were only a 'notion,' I have no doubt that I should, now and then, waver in my intention,"—said Helen; "probably reverse it completely."

"You mean, then, that it was something more substantial than a fancy for his sweet smile, his beautiful eyes and matchless whiskers, that induced you to say 'yes' when he popped the question?"

"I do!"

Helen sustained the saucy examination unflinchingly.

"And you really—excuse my impertinence! but I am an humble, sincere, and earnest inquirer after truth, particularly since I have seen the resplendent Alexander—and you really and truly love this man, whom you are to take by the hand, with all your heart, soul, and strength, and are resolved, henceforward, forsaking all others, to cleave to him and him alone; to love, honor, and obey, so long as you both shall live?"

"When the proper time for putting that question arrives, I shall be prepared with an answer."

Another freezing silence.

"Have I offended you? It is only poor, foolish, rattle-pated Ginnie, remember," pleaded the visitor at length. "I am going off to dress for dinner now. I have a new dress which is perfectly heavenly! The effect upon Aleck's heart must be great, but I shall not enjoy it one whit unless you assure me that you are not angry with me."

"Have I ever been out of temper with you?" Helen's iciness thawed as she saw the half-roguish, half-penitent face. "I know what valuation to put on your words, Ginnie. You would never give your worst enemy a sly thrust in the dark, or stab one to the heart under pretence of a friendly jest!"

"Of course I wouldn't be guilty of any such shocking things! And we are quite friends now, aren't we? I'll never try to put you through Cupid's catechism again so long as my name is Virginia Shore, and yours Helen Gardner. I will wait until you exchange it for Helen Lay. My! isn't that beautiful? Kiss me, and I am gone!"

Helen locked the door after her.

"I could not have borne it two minutes longer! Poor, weak, pitiful fool that I am! whom straws like these can pierce to the quick! Oh! how I hate myself!" She struck hard upon her breast with her clinched hand. "And he *dared* to send a light message to me! could speak jestingly of our former intercourse to that heedless, giddy creature! It was like him! His behavior has the merit of consistency, to say no more!"

She took a note from her work-box. Robert had sent it to her that morning, and thereby prepared her to expect the tidings brought by the girls.

"My dearest Helen:

"Picture, as your affectionate heart will teach you to do, my surprise and happiness at finding Aleck here when I returned home! I think I have never been happier (excepting once) in all my life than I am at this moment, as I scribble this, and the blessed old fellow sits, smilingly, watching my nervous, wayward fingers—unmanageable through very joy. He is well, and better-looking than ever; true as steel; good as gold! the same noble, generous soul whom we parted with so sadly when our trio was broken two years ago. What do you think of his having divined our secret so far as to provide himself with a wedding-present for you before leaving Paris? So, the surprise *bonbon* I have treasured up against his arrival, is all thrown away. I always knew that his instincts were unusually fine. I suppose you will slyly insinuate that maybe I am deficient in the art of keeping a secret. I do not deny it, when the person to be kept in the dark is one I love.

"I write to notify you that you may expect a visit from us to-day—if agreeable to yourself. We shall probably be with you at dinner-time. Aleck is naturally impatient to see you again; and when did I fail to avail myself of any and every opportunity of seeking your presence?

"In haste, but none the less fondly, your own,

"R——."

She went over it twice; she had read it many times before, the proud lines of her features hardening at each word; refolded it, and deliberately thrust it into the fire. Then she unlocked the door, rang up her maid, and began a studied toilette for dinner.

There was other company expected to partake of that repast. The Floyds kept an open house from one year's end to the other, and these impromptu dinner-parties were, at the lowest computation, of semi-weekly occurrence. One or two families from the neighborhood were bidden on this occasion, as the nominal nucleus of the social gathering; and to this Lily and Virginia had, in the course of their morning's drive, added several other cavaliers besides the brothers Lay. When Aleck and Robert presented themselves in the parlor, their ears were saluted by the hum of many voices, and they beheld divers knots of talkers scattered about the room. Mrs. Floyd entertained four or five matrons, seated upon a sofa and in rocking-chairs in one corner; the colonel had his cluster of politicians and fox-hunters upon the hearth, at the far end of the apartment; Virginia Shore was "carrying on" in her most extravagant style, standing in the middle of the floor, surrounded by a bevy of beaux; and Lily Calvert—more ethereal than was common, even with her, in her blue silk robe, her sloping shoulders veiled thinly by a tulle cape—had her coterie, at a little distance from her vivacious friend.

Upon none of these personages, individually or collectively, did the eyes of the fresh arrivals rest for more than a second. Robert was quick to observe that Helen stood by the western window, chatting with Tom Shore, and that she was very beautiful, as seen in the rich glow of the sunshine, streaming through the crimson curtain; and having made his bow to hostess and host, waited impatiently for the subsidence of the buzz of welcome and congratulation that swelled towards and around Aleck. The traveller received his old friends with great apparent heartiness and a subdued show of joviality; had a cheery word and a hand-grip for the gentlemen, and a pretty speech for each lady, young and old. Virginia Shore began to think, as she marked his progress from one to another of the fair ones, who vied with their fathers and brothers in the warmth of their greetings, that she had acted very foolishly—verdantly, she expressed it to herself—in hoarding up, as something too beautiful and precious to be told to Lily and Helen, the sugared nothings he had breathed into her willing ear at the carriage-door, that forenoon.

All this time Robert did not approach his betrothed; made his smile and bow from afar off, the testimonials that he acknowledged and rejoiced in her presence. He wished to present his brother with himself before her. Nor did she stir from her position, or manifest the slightest agitation at their entrance. She looked at Aleck, as politeness advised and curiosity seemed to dictate, when Tom Shore remarked aside upon his tanned cheek and hirsute ornaments; assented naturally, yet nonchalantly, to that youth's refined asseveration, that "Lay was a blamed handsome fellow, in spite of his dark skin and Turkish beard." This was generous, for Tom thought himself an Adonis, and *his* skin was like milk and roses, his hair fair and curly, his "love of a mouth" tinct as with carmine; his cleft chin innocent of whiskers, or, sooth to say, any promise of the same. At last, patient waiting had its reward in Robert's bearing off the prize, and the two neared Miss Gardner. She advanced a step—a queen could not have done less—and held out a hand that was neither chill nor tremulous, to salute the wanderer.

"We are glad to see you at home again, Mr. Lay! You have taken all your friends by surprise. Had you a pleasant voyage?"

And yet she was standing, her hand in his, upon the spot where she had heard his hasty, passionate farewell; where he had pressed the pledge-ring upon her finger! Involuntarily he glanced down. It was not there! In place of the plain gold circlet there sparkled a diamond hoop—his brother's gift. What else could he have expected? If she noticed the look—quick as a flash of light—no one else did, nor did other ears detect the faintest shade of sarcasm in his rejoinder.

"Very pleasant, thank you, swift and smooth—as time seems to have flowed for the old acquaintances I meet here to-day. I cannot realize that twice twelve months have passed since I left the homestead and my boyhood's companions—since the evening of our parting, Miss Helen! By the way, it took place in this identical room, did it not?"

"I believe it did!" as calmly courteous as himself.

"Here you shed the parting tear,
To cross the ocean foam,"

said Tom Shore, who, like his sister, was addicted to quotation from latter-day poets, or, more correctly speaking, rhymesters and song-writers.

"Exactly—with the trifling difference that ours was dry-eyed mourning," answered Aleck.

"You cannot take exception to the concluding lines of the verse," said Helen.

"'Now, I'm once again with those
Who gladly greet me home.'

Your 'Home again' is too obviously an occasion of unfeigned and general rejoicing for you to question its heartiness."

"Thank you!" He bowed profoundly. "I do *you* the justice to believe you sincere at all times, and in all that you do!"

At this juncture, Tom Shore—albeit his constitutional infirmity was not an overplus of modesty—was seized by the impression that the part allotted to him by existing circumstances, in this particular locality, was that of second fiddle, and walked off in quest of less distinguished company. Simultaneously with his withdrawal, Robert obeyed the imperious beck of Lily Calvert's fairy forefinger, and, to Helen's consternation and Aleck's chagrin, they found themselves the only occupants of the window recess.

Consternation nor chagrin outlived the shock of the discovery of their situation. Both would have done all in their power, consistent with outward propriety, to avoid the tête-à-tête; but, now that it was forced upon them, each experienced an interest in its progress and results, painful, yet not devoid of a certain strange sweetness. They talked of common-place topics; of neighborhood changes and foreign travel. The most jealous lover might have heard every word, noted and weighed the import of every intonation and glance, and felt no misgivings as to the standing of the colloquists with regard to one another. The past—as *theirs*—was not referred to in the most remote manner, yet it was not practicable for Aleck to continue the cruelly significant badinage which was, to Robert and young Shore, but pleasant trifling between old friends. It seemed unmanly and irreverent—a thing of which he was ashamed, as he looked at, and listened to her; as if, while they talked, the bier, holding the shrouded corpse of his boyish hope and manhood's aim, lay between them.

Whether or not the pride and bitterness passed away, likewise, from Helen's spirit, all trace of either disappeared from her demeanor. She ceased to question and reply with the elaborate show of strained civility that had hailed his approach, and characterized her conversation while others were by. It was no longer easy to meet his eyes with steady, haughty gaze; to fling back retort for innuendo; to repay counterfeit courtesy with lofty indifference. The truth was that neither had, in his or her anticipations of the interview, taken into account the subtile and sure effect of the personal presence; the wondrous magnetism of voice and look and action; the indescribable fascination lingering in each and all of these; every one bringing up its swift train of memories, and each link in the chain reuniting, as by magic, with the rest, to draw their hearts once more together. The awakening, and anguish, and shame, and renewed resolves for future conduct with it, would come by-and-by; for the present, they saw nothing beyond the tumultuous joy of being again with one another, after the dreary blank of absence. When dinner was announced, Aleck offered his arm, which was silently accepted. Robert walked before them, in attendance upon Lily. Devoted in appearance to his fair companion, he yet found a favorable opportunity for throwing back a smile to his brother and Helen. Its gleam of affectionate meaning, its guileless trust and hopefulness, were not lost upon them. When they took their seats in the dining-room, Helen's cheek had lost its blush, and her eye its softness, and beyond offering her the ordinary civilities of the occasion, Aleck paid her no attention while they remained at the board.

It was after sunset when the gentlemen rejoined the ladies in the drawing-room. Robert, having seen that Helen was not there, bethought himself, as was his wont, of the least admired or least courted person of the company; and finding her in the shape of a shy school-girl, ensconced in the nook between the piano and wall, sat down in front of her, and tried to draw her into conversation. The barrier of bashfulness and nervous timidity was being rapidly undermined by his sedulous tact, when Gabriel wormed his way through the talkative groups, dispersed irregularly about the room, up to the two in the corner.

"Was you de lady what asked for a glass of water, ma'am?" presenting a salver, with a goblet upon it.

"No!" said the girl, in surprise.

"Beg a thousand pardons, ma'am! sorry for de mistake, I'm sure, ma'am!"

He bowed himself backwards—a bit of court etiquette, upon whose acquisition and practice he plumed himself mightily, and steered off in another direction; but not before he had adroitly dropped into Robert Lay's hand a folded paper. Although the latter divined intuitively and through his recollection of precedents the authorship of the wee note, hidden so soon as it fell in the hollow of his palm, and burned with desire to learn its purport, he retained his position some minutes longer, until he could signal Tom Shore to come and occupy it. Tom was dandified and conceited, but he was kind-hearted withal, and, to gratify Robert, would have undergone ordeals yet more trying, if that were possible, than expending his time and fascinations upon a girl who was neither pretty, witty, nor rich, nor yet "knowing" enough to appreciate him; "smacking," as he decided, "rather too much of school bread and butter."

Robert read his precious billet by the hall window. It was, as he had supposed, from Helen, and a simple request that he would meet her at "the spring," where she would wait half an hour for his coming. Hastily taking down his overcoat and hat from the row of pegs in the wainscot, he was in the act of putting them on, when he heard through the dining-room door, which was ajar, Lily's voice, sharp with pettishness, yet silvery still.

"Where did you get the note I saw you give Mr. Lay, just now?"

"'Twouldn't be honorable in me fur to tell what I'm ordered not to, Miss Lily!" said Gabriel, respectfully but stoutly.

"Don't answer me in that way, sir!"

It conflicted sorely with Robert's feelings and sense of justice to leave his Eboe ally exposed to the assaults of womanly pique and curiosity; and, not waiting to hear more of the dialogue, he stepped across the hall, making as much bustle as he conveniently could, and tapped at the door.

"Miss Lily!" he called.

"Come in!" said the clear tones, with a perceptible change of key.

Gabriel took advantage of the diversion, and vanished, like a shadow, through another portal. Lily started at sight of her guest's great-coat, and the hat in his hand.

"You are not going yet, surely!"

"Only for a walk with Helen." He smiled, and hesitated in pronouncing the name. "I wanted to ask you—our dear little sister—to contrive that our absence should not provoke the criticism of gossiping tongues, if there are any such instruments of mischief among the good people in the other room. I will do the same for you some day, when you are situated as we now are!"

She made no reply, except a nod of acquiescence—stood looking down into the fire with her great sorrowful eyes, so large and mournful—and there was such an air of desolation expressed in her fragile figure and pale face, that Robert felt impelled to say some comforting or friendly word before leaving her there alone.

"I am afraid that we—your cousin and myself—may appear selfish to your apprehension sometimes, Lily; but it is only your imagination that leads you to believe that there is any real diminution of our regard for you. You must not bear me a grudge because I am happy in the thought of taking her away from you. Our home will always be yours; for she loves you as fondly as ever; and, for myself, I can truly say that you were never dearer to me than you are now, while I have in view the blessed prospect of the closer tie soon to be formed between us."

He spoke caressingly, for he had known Lily from her babyhood, and petted her to this day and hour, as did nearly everybody else.

One of her hands—scarcely larger and quite as soft to the touch as a petal of her name-flower—lay passively within his fraternal grasp; his head was bent towards her in protecting tenderness, that looked lover-like, when the door at the side of the fire-place was pushed back, and in walked Colonel Floyd!

In confusion or alarm, his niece snatched her hand away from Robert, with a faint "Oh!"

"I thought that you were both in the parlor," said the guardian, his dark features gathering additional grimness from his corrugated brow.

Robert's pleasant tones answered the reproof he knew was aimed at Lily.

"So we were, three minutes ago, sir! I was on my way out to take an after-dinner stroll—the 'constitutional' one is apt to need after Mrs. Floyd's dinners, Colonel! and hearing Miss Lily's voice, as I passed that door, I stepped in to engage her kind offices in covering or excusing my temporary absence."

"The precaution was needless, Mr. Lay! It is my wish and request that my friends should be free to come and go at pleasure, in my house."

"No one knows that better than I do, sir. Still, my withdrawal from society, such as is collected in the parlor, might subject me to the charge of moroseness, or a want of gallantry. I shall not be gone long. The bracing air will soon clear my brain from the fumes of that last glass of champagne."

He bowed, with his frank, boyish laugh, and went out.

Lily also moved, as if to go to the parlor, but her uncle prevented her.

"Lily!"

"Sir!"

"Is this fine story true, or has that smooth-tongued beau-general been making love to you? One girl at a time is enough for most men."

"Love to me, sir!" Her eyes glittered, as polished steel does in the sunlight. "Do you, then, think that I would submit to that insult? for insult it would be from an engaged man!"

"You might do worse, girl! Why did you let him slip through your net in the first instance? You angled badly."

"I never had any hold upon him, sir. If I had—"

Colonel Floyd's smile was one of sinister gratification, as he studied her face and translated the language of the gesture that finished the sentence.

"If you had, you are no true Floyd if you allowed him to stray with impunity. If you possessed your mother's spirit you would not give him up alive. I have watched him and her, too, and I tell you, on the authority of one who is seldom mistaken in his judgment of character and feelings, that he may still be yours, if you care to make the effort to lure him back."

"Uncle! You forget that he is to marry Helen next month!"

"Tut, child! Matches have been broken off at the altar before now! You have a stout will of your own, and a quick wit—*and he is worth having!*"

She was left alone—the girl so early and so terribly orphaned—left with the fiery Floyd blood, of which her tempter had reminded her, swelling and boiling in her veins, and his strange, artful insinuations working in her mind, revolving in the brain he had truly described as quick and shrewd. She had little respect for her guardian, and few loved him except the wife he daily trampled in the dust; but Lily had confidence in his boasted acquaintance with men and the world's ways—his penetrative discrimination of action and motive. He had evidently divined a secret she had imagined was buried from all mortal ken, in the depths of her own mourning heart. Might it not be that he was equally sagacious in reading those of the betrothed pair?

She roamed up and down through the firelit room, her hands chafing one another, and the colorless cheeks whiter still than before—if that could be—under the strivings and insidious promptings of the passions he had so cunningly aroused. She spoke once, with energy and fire that seemed to threaten the rending of the slight, shaking frame. It was an appeal to Divinity—not the cry of a soul that felt the danger of the impending shipwreck among the billows of lawless affections—"Save! or I perish!" or the lowlier prayer of the tried, yet faithful heart, "Leave me not to temptation!" but a sudden, insane-sounding ejaculation:—

"'Worth having!' Oh, Heaven! do I not know that too well already!"

CHAPTER IV.

"The spring" was between three and four hundred yards distant from the mansion-house, at the foot of the hill on which the building was situated; and beyond the arch of rude masonry covering the fountain arose another eminence, thickly wooded and cleft with ravines—the outskirts of the extensive forests attached to the plantation.

The night was cold, but there was no wind stirring, and far up towards the zenith the moon rode in unclouded majesty. The frosted earth and brittle grass crackled under Robert's tread as he sought the trysting-place. The walk was a familiar one, and a favorite with him; doubly dear since the scene of four months agone that had hallowed the rustic fount forever. With the gurgling flow of its waters had been blent the first vows of love he had breathed in the ear of her who now sat awaiting him upon the gray stone that had been their resting-place then. She was not alone. Withdrawn to a respectful distance behind her mistress stood a woman, whom Robert recognized with a kindly "How do you do, Sally?"

Helen rose immediately and took his proffered arm. Until he spoke she had remained quietly seated, her head resting upon her hand, apparently buried in absorbing thought.

"Have I kept you waiting?" he asked. "I was afraid that I should. Gabriel may have met with unavoidable delays in delivering your note, fertile in ruses though he is, nor could I get away directly it reached me without attracting attention."

"You came sooner than I expected. You may have thought my message a singular one, but I wished to talk with you, and I knew that we could not procure the opportunity for uninterrupted conversation anywhere within doors this evening."

"Not in the 'grotto?'" asked Robert, smiling. "Do not apologize, I entreat you! Your suggestion—it was too modest to be called a request, much less an appointment—was highly proper, and eminently acceptable. The most starched prude in America could not condemn it, especially as Sally is in attendance," casting a backward glance at the girl, who, with her shawl wrapped about her head—in true Dinah fashion—had seated herself in the shadow of the stone arch.

Helen tried to imitate his mirthful tone.

"You surely know why I brought her along!"

"To keep away the bugaboos until I should make my appearance, I presume."

"To prevent molestation from bugaboos, indeed—but not of the species which children dread. Time was when I was careless of forms and customs, for I had only myself to consider. Now, as my good aunt will certify, I am growing prudent, very like other people. You and I need no one to play propriety, but since others would advise the attendance of a duenna—a somniferous one is better than none—I bow to the decree. But not to postpone the discussion of the subject which I wished to broach to you, I have heard two pieces of news since dinner that have disquieted me. One was, that your aunt intends leaving your house and taking up her abode at Maple Hill. Is this true?"

Robert fairly whistled with astonishment.

"She does contemplate such a change, but the matter is yet in abeyance; and inasmuch as the proposition originated with Aleck, the thought never entered her mind until last night. It baffles me to guess how the story could have reached you so soon. Why, the busiest tattler of whom we have any record—the renowned little bird of the air, could hardly have borne the tidings in this time!"

"Mrs. Catlin mentioned it as a settled thing to another lady, and in my hearing. She had it directly from Miss Ruth, she stated, having stopped at Greenfield on her way to Belleview. But, Robert! please dissuade her from this step! It has been a serious and constant fear with me, that I may not contribute so much to your happiness as you anticipate, for I know my grievous shortcomings. Do not add to your disappointment the loss of your aunt—your second mother. Beg her from me to stay with you! You will miss her more than you dream of; you will need her gentle offices, her unfailing consideration for your feelings and comfort, her steady affection! You cannot exist without these. Say to her that I am miserable in the thought of causing any change in her household; that I will never interfere with her plans; that matters shall be conducted according to her wishes, not mine; that I will endeavor to accommodate myself to her just ideas in every thing; study to be dutiful—I cannot but be affectionate to her—if she will continue to live with you."

"My precious girl, what an impulsive creature you are! You plead like a frightened child, who fears to be left alone with me! Am I such an ogre that Aunt Ruth must not abandon you to my tender mercies? Before we go any further, dear Helen," he continued, dropping his jesting tone, "I must say one thing. Whether Aunt Ruth remains an inmate of my house or not, you, and not she, must be its mistress, its irresponsible controller. She understands this. It is no novel idea to her, and she has the good sense to admit the wisdom of the arrangement. If she goes to Maple Hill, it will not be to avoid the necessity of taking what would be her proper place in my family, in the event of my marriage, but at Aleck's instance and earnest solicitation. He will be very lonely there without her, he represents, and no man of my acquaintance is less fitted than he to be happy in a veritable bachelor establishment."

Helen brought out her next sentence with an effort.

"But, in time, he will have no need of her in the capacity of housekeeper or companion, if what we have heard be true."

"An important '*if!*' Taking it for granted that he means to install his Fraulein as Mrs. Lay, in the course of a year or less, I question her ability to undertake the charge of an American *ménage*. He has not showed any disposition to speak upon this point since his return, and I would not force his confidence. Aleck is a queer fellow in some respects. The very depth and might of his feelings seem to deprive him of the power to express them fluently. I can divine them; yet, loving one another as we do, there are many reserves on both sides. If he marries a true, loving woman, who can enter into the peculiarities of his disposition, she may unseal the tide. I hope that his Gretchen, if she be indeed his, may bring him one-half the heart satisfaction, the fulness of joy, that my love has brought me."

There was no "Amen" from the figure at his side. They were rambling along a narrow footpath, which wound about the slope of the wooded hill, and her regards were bent upon the ground.

"You will speak to your aunt—tell her what my earnest desire and petition is, however—will you not?" she said, abruptly recurring to the original topic.

"Assuredly, if you still wish it!"

"I do!"

They stopped under a large oak tree, whose far-reaching branches cast fantastic shadows upon the whitened turf of the hill-side. Helen withdrew her hand from Robert's hold, and, folding her arms, leaned against the giant trunk of the forest monarch, and appeared to be lost in the contemplation of the landscape.

"Colonel Floyd has the finest site for a house that can be found on this side of the Potomac," observed Robert. "It crowns that knoll grandly."

"That reminds me that I have another matter on my mind," replied Helen, arousing herself. "I was so fortunate or unfortunate, as the event will decide, as to overhear, awhile ago, a part of a conversation between two ladies, that was not intended for the ears of any member of Colonel Floyd's family."

"It was delicate and kind in them to introduce such matters while partaking of his hospitality!" was Robert's ironical interruption.

"His extravagance and gaming propensities," said Helen, "were animadverted upon in one sentence, for I heard but two. The other imparted the, to me, unpleasing intelligence that he was heavily in your debt, you having, it was said, lent him money at several different times. I trust this is a mistake or a fabrication."

Robert laughed.

"The meddling gossip was partly correct, but I am sorry that you troubled yourself about her story. We should have no secrets from each other, and I do not see why those pertaining to money matters should be an exception to this rule. I *have* let Colonel Floyd have a small sum now and then, but not enough to beggar me, should he never return any part of the amount."

"It was very unwise in you," replied Helen, reprovingly. "You should have remembered what reputation he bears among his creditors. They say that he never pays debts that honest men consider sacred and confidential, unless forced to it by the strong arm of the law. He is thoroughly conscious that you will never resort to this means of recovering what you have advanced. Now, answer me frankly; were his applications to you for assistance out of his difficulties made prior to our—our—to the formation of our present relations?"

"What terrible 'relations' they must be, to require that tremendous amount of stammering and circumlocution! I have a wretched memory for dates!"

"I am answered! It is as I have suspected! He has taken a base and unwarrantable, a most indelicate advantage of your attachment to his ward to extort money from you! He is no stranger to your generous and pliant temper! He reckoned shrewdly upon his customer. It is infamous!"

"Gently! gently, Nelly, dear! Do not tilt too ferociously with your windmill before daylight is let in upon it! There was no extortion in the affair. He was 'hard up'—excuse the slang! I was easy in purse, and felt it to be a privilege, not a hardship, to help a neighbor in his embarrassment."

"I comprehend fully! My opinion is unchanged, Robert! I have a favor to ask of you in *my* turn. It is not fair that Colonel Floyd should enjoy a monopoly of this kind of business."

"Make it a hundred, and consider them all granted!"

Helen was not to be beguiled out of her earnestness.

"Never lend Colonel Floyd another dollar! Learn to say 'No!'"

"I will—to everybody excepting a little lady of my acquaintance, who cannot ask an unreasonable thing!" rejoined he, in playful, yet tender gallantry.

She went on, gravely as before.

"Furthermore—and upon this I have a right to insist, since it more nearly concerns me—if he should propose a marriage-contract to you, refuse positively to accede to its provisions—reject them utterly!"

"Why, my beauty! who has been vexing your brain with legal lore? Don't you know that every marriage is a contract—civil and religious?"

"I know from your tone, and evasive replies, that there have been intimations, if nothing more definite, made to you already, touching the expediency, the moral righteousness, of securing my property to myself. I know it as well as that upon my twenty-first birth-day, months ago, I was entitled to the entire control of all that I am worth; that Colonel Floyd had no further authority over it or my actions; yet I have been repeatedly put off with surly promises of settlement at some future date, and am treated more like an imbecile minor than ever before,—know it as perfectly as that I have rightly interpreted the drift of my aunt's frequent and prosy harangues to me, within a couple of months—ill-contrived expositions of her husband's tenets, respecting the manifold benefits arising from contracts of marriage. How I despise the name and the idea!"

"Windmills again?" interposed Robert's gentle raillery.

"Not so! I can tell you the exact terms which Colonel Floyd has sketched to you—commended to your consideration, by appealing to your sense of honor and justice. All that I have inherited from my father is to be settled upon myself, and my late guardian, an incorruptible Spartan, who could not be betrayed into the least violation of my rights! is to be appointed my trustee."

"You are a witch!" exclaimed the amazed listener.

"I am a woman whose training has taught her vigilance and distrust! hard lessons—and hardly learned by one of my age and sex. If all men with whom I have had to deal were like you, I should not have mastered the alphabet as yet! You may think me unfeminine, sordid, calculating, in thus obtruding pecuniary matters upon your consideration. I suppose that most women leave these arrangements to parents, guardians, and friends. I am an orphan; I have no near relations; no friend, who can aid me, excepting yourself; I had better never have had a guardian. You have invited and urged my confidence, and you see how eagerly I take you at your word!" She broke off her rapid, passionate speech to say, with an attempt at gayety, "Do you feel as poor Tarpeia did, when she asked for bracelets and got a shower of shields instead?"

Robert was embarrassed. "Your confidence can never be burdensome!" he answered, sincerely. "But, Nell, darling! there was nothing preposterous in Colonel Floyd's plan of settlement. The most affectionate fathers propose the like, continually. I rather glory in the chance thus afforded me of showing that my love for you is purely disinterested. You will not discredit my declaration, that, until your guardian made reference to your fortune, the thought of it had never crossed my brain in connection with my attachment to yourself. Whatever is yours, now, shall remain your own. I cheerfully relinquish all claim that the law would give me upon it, with one proviso—all that I possess must be added to it."

"I believe in your sincerity, but not in the word of any other man alive. I am gratefully alive to the generosity, which the world would deem unsafe and romantic. But, Robert! in this one thing you must let me have my own way. I have reasons, weighty and sufficient, for pressing my request. I will have no deeds, no settlements! They will not be valid without my consent, and that shall never be given!"

This was a strange conversation for a moonlight tryst between lovers, and she was an uncommon type of a betrothed maiden; her every resolute lineament discernible by the white moonbeams; arms sternly crossed, and feet planted hard against the gnarled roots of the oak, apparently as impassive and immovable to expostulation as the tree itself.

Some minutes of troubled reflection passed before either spoke again. Then Robert resumed the discourse.

"I cannot disregard your wishes in this matter, Helen, however they may war with my inclination and judgment; for, as you say, you are the person who will be most nearly affected by the disposition of your property. I *did* tell your guardian that I acquiesced heartily in his views, and would shape my course accordingly, and he may misinterpret my altered purpose; but let that pass! So long as you and I are agreed, and understand one another, what matter the opinions of others?"

"I thank you for the sacrifice you make to please me; for, paradoxical as it would be to many—to most vulgar minds—the acceptance of wealth with your bride, in these circumstances, *is* a sacrifice, and no light one to you. I take it upon myself to guarantee that Colonel Floyd shall learn to whose influence your change of intention is attributable—upon whom he is to charge the frustration of his holy design. What is it, Sally?"

Engrossed in their talk, the young couple had not thought of the girl—had not seen that for some time past her motions had been indicative of extreme restlessness. Her crouching figure had become erect; the shawl dropped from her ears to her shoulders; her head moved uneasily from side to side, as if she were watching or listening intently. When Helen addressed her, she had arisen from her seat by the spring, and approached within a few feet of her mistress and her lover.

"I'm thinking you'll be missed at the house, Miss Helen! I'm sure I've heard Gabriel calling me two or three times—and—and—it's getting colder, 'seems to me."

Helen eyed her more attentively.

"It is too bad to have kept you sitting there all this while, my poor girl! We have been walking, and have not felt uncomfortable; but your teeth are absolutely chattering!"

"I reckon I must ha' been asleep!" rejoined Sally, with a foolish, ashamed laugh. "I didn't know we'd been out long."

"I think it very likely!" said Helen, smiling, as did Robert, in recollection of the "somniferous duenna." "Run on, now, and get yourself in a glow. We will follow."

As they were ascending the hill upon the other side of the spring-stream, she subjoined an explanation of the request she had urged with regard to her fortune.

"I was put upon my guard against Colonel Floyd's probable machinations, by a story told me by my cousin, Miss Rogers, when she paid us a visit in October. She was an intimate friend of Lily's mother, and having taken quite a fancy to my society, confided to me certain incidents of the family history, which I had never heard until then. Among others, she mentioned that Colonel Floyd, as his father's executor and sister's guardian, had her share of the estate secured to herself prior to her marriage with Mr. Calvert, and, as seemed natural and proper to most people, assumed the trusteeship of the same. Either Mr. Calvert resented this as an imputation upon his honor, or an implication of his inability to manage his wife's property, for, shortly after the wedding-day, a coolness grew up between the brothers-in-law, which greatly distressed Mrs. Calvert. There were serious threats made by her husband of a lawsuit to recover that which, he alleged in Miss Rogers's hearing, had been dishonestly abstracted by Colonel Floyd from his sister's portion; proceedings which were suspended by his own tragic death. It is always best to avoid litigation by having these questions settled beforehand."

"What a business head you have!" replied Robert, much amused. "I had not supposed that you knew how many cents make a dollar. Very few of the Floyds are endowed with arithmetical talents. Your uncle, for example, is utterly ignorant of the value of the prime idol of the Yankee nation."

"He understands the rule of subtraction, as your pockets can attest. You are mistaken as to his regard for money. He is an odd compound of extravagance and covetousness."

At the yard-gate she stopped.

"Do not judge me harshly for to-night's talk!" she said, almost sadly. "I suppose that I must appear to you wofully common-place and practical; censorious in judgment and rigorous in action, for you are charitable and lenient to a proverb. But I have only your good at heart; desire to do that which will be best for us both. I do endeavor conscientiously to study your interests, Robert!"

He made some comforting response, and there the subject rested.

He was not, however, so blindly in love, that the substance, no less than the tone of this last sentence, did not fall gratingly upon his sensitive ear. It was, of course, pleasant, or ought to have been, to know that she looked upon their interests as identical; to see that her manner of speaking of these was characterized by the clear-sighted zeal and prudence of the wife, rather than the bewitching hesitancy of the blushing bride. Yet, in his heart, he felt a lack of something, a deficiency that was at once indefinable and painful. Her bearing was not too free—that could never happen—still, a trifling diffidence, a dash of coyness would have imparted to it an additional charm. The fruit—ripe, rich, and round—was his, and he was proud and thankful in its possession; but he could have wished that the downy velvet, shading and softening its bloom, had not been so carefully and thoroughly rubbed off before the treasure was given. He could not resist a ridiculous preference for the "Loves of the Angels," as a lover's text-book, above ledger or bank-account, let them be never so accurately balanced, and largely in his favor.

Above all, that word, "conscientiously," offended his spiritual nervous organization. Regard unmeasured, because immeasurable,—Solictiude,—loving and anxious-eyed Aphrodite, born out of the waves of this boundless love;—these would have been to him as the waters of the river of Life and the fruit that grows thereby. But he did not want to be loved "conscientiously." He did not care to be informed that there was, on her side, a "conscientious endeavor" to think of and to do whatever would conduce to his happiness.

Moreover,—but this was a secondary and very inferior consideration,—he could not divest himself of a disagreeable expectation of an unpleasant, if not a violent scene with Colonel Floyd, when they came to the question of the final settlement; feared lest the retraction of his partial pledge that all should be done in consonance with the guardian's desire, would place him, the bridegroom, in a false and humiliating position.

Keeping these misgivings and his dissatisfaction to himself, he parted from Helen in the hall, with the fond, gentle smile she alone of all women ever had from him, and repaired to the drawing-room, whence had proceeded the sounds of music and laughter the outdoor promenaders had heard ere they reached the house.

A lady, elderly, and who had never been pretty, a governess in one of the aristocratic families there represented, was at the piano, playing a lively waltz; and six or eight couples were whirling around the room, in the exultant swing of that entrancing dance. Making a wide circuit to avoid collisions, Robert succeeded in stationing himself by the side of the musician. The piece she was playing was an unfamiliar one to her, and, dexterous and true as were her fingers, she dared not remove her eyes from the sheet. There was no need for her to see his features to assure herself who turned the leaves with a *volte subite* movement, bespeaking an intelligent eye and a hand trained to the like gallant offices. She knew who had won for himself the appellation of "the wall-flowers' friend," and shunned not to maintain his right to the title by rendering attentions as graceful and assiduous to the neglected children of beauty and fortune, as to the most pampered darlings of both. Poor Miss Carter's lank, starched figure and dyed silk dress covered a heart slightly indurated and withered by twenty years' thankless drudgery in her present profession; but there were hidden away there, in shady, jealously-screened recesses, kept green by the dews and occasional freshets of sentiment and memory, stray blossoms and modest mosses of romance and feeling, whose existence would have been scoffed at by the patrons and acquaintances of the "old maid teacher." And never did these bits of verdure and bloom quiver with more vitality than beneath the sunshine of Robert Lay's smile. She was not in love with him; she never deluded herself with the chimera that a single thought of her visited him when she was out of his sight; but in her mental, or rather heart portrait-gallery—how scantily furnished, it would have given *you* a heart-ache to see!—he was enshrined—a stainless hero.

He offered her a glass of water when the tiresome round of variations was at an end, and advised that she should rest her strained fingers for a time. But no! the dancers were ready to begin again, and so must she be also, or give offence. Automatons and ill-paid governesses are not expected to complain of fatigue in the service of their masters.

"At least, play something that you know," said Robert. "That will be less exhausting to the head—only finger-work! You can talk then!"

With himself, he meant, for every other available masculine specimen of humanity had a partner. He hardly merited all the credit for self-denial she inwardly heaped upon him, as his pleasant sayings enlivened the monotony of her occupation, for it cost him little trouble to keep aloof from the dancers, so long as Helen did not appear. He did not witness her entrance. The first intimation he had of her presence was the sight of her at Miss Carter's back, when this set of waltzes was likewise concluded.

"You should not have been appointed to this work to-night, Miss Carter!" she said. "You are not well enough. Does your head ache very badly now?"

"Thank you! it is about the same."

With a gesture and three words, Helen swept her from the piano-stool and established herself upon it; shook her head in smiling wilfulness in response to the grateful lady's remonstrances, and drowned their continuation in a pealing march. Robert conducted Miss Carter to an easy-chair; found a fan and a bottle of sal-volatile for her, and went back to the instrument.

The pale, weary governess watched the pair with deep and affectionate interest. They were so young and noble; so admirably adapted each to the other, in virtues, manner, and disposition, and their mutual attachment so beautiful to behold, it was not marvellous that the romance into which she wove their united lives had not, in its bright texture, one sable thread. If the sigh which heaved her bosom was an inaudible and hopeless lament over her barren life and departed youth, it was untainted by envy of their different and more blessed lot. Presently Helen glanced up at her betrothed, and said something, briefly and positively. He made reply, seemingly, by an interrogation, and upon receipt of her answer turned away, and joined himself to the band of revellers. He went directly up to Lily Calvert, offered his hand, which was smilingly accepted, and they took their position in a cotillion that was just forming.

The music flowed out in a bolder, quicker measure, and light feet beat time over the floor. Still the silent, unnoticed governess kept watch upon the now lonely performer—free now, moreover, to indulge at will in the enchanting maiden visions that attend—brilliant-winged and willing sprites—upon the meditations of the "young, loving, and beloved." Yet Miss Carter saw the fine, mobile features subside into pensiveness; then, fixed sadness; the eye settle into melancholy steadiness—a sort of introverted look which told plainly enough that the source of her grief was not far away, nor beyond herself. While the spectator was taxing the meagre stores of her experimental knowledge of Love's mysteries for a solution of this enigma, Aleck Lay drew near, deputed by his partner to convey some message to the dreaming pianist. A red tide rushed over Helen's face as he spoke to her; she started; lost time, skill, and tune, her hands crashing heavily down upon the keys; and a harsh, loud discord from the thrilling wires brought the dance to an untimely pause.

"What is the matter?" "Go on!" cried a chorus of voices.

"It was my fault!" Aleck's sonorous tones quelled the Babel of inquiry. "I interrupted her and did all the mischief. I ask a million pardons!" he pursued laughingly, to the drooping and abashed musician. "It was thoughtless and awkward in me to accost you so abruptly, when I might have seen that you were intent upon your music. It shall be a wholesome lesson to me for the future. I was about to ask you to play a little faster—a very little, if you please."

An irrepressible impulse of gratitude made her lift her eyes to his, and he saw that they were full of tears. This might be the effect of nervous agitation merely, but the sight sent him back to his place with a madly throbbing heart. Helen struggled valiantly with the rising softness, superinduced by a passing vision of the olden days, when he interposed to ward off every annoyance from her; met, with scathing retort, each sarcastic or unfriendly retort that had her for its object. For the rest of the evening they kept far apart,—did not exchange another look or word. "A wholesome lesson for the future!" They would do well to remember and profit by the warning!

Helen refused to dance at all that night;—she "preferred to play for the entertainment of the rest;" and when she would not let him hover near her, Robert Lay's most frequent companion was Lily Calvert. She was very pretty and charming; so winning in her childlike, confiding ways; so kind and amiable with him, and apparently so gratified by his attentions, that he could not resist the temptation presented by all these, and quite forgot his duty to the wall-flowers in waiting upon a belle. She was really a sweet girl, he reflected, despite some unimportant foibles; and a warm-hearted friend of his, who would make the dearest little sister imaginable, one of these days, when she and Helen understood one another again.

Aleck danced, flirted, and flattered, with a reckless grace no one else could emulate; was the life, as he was the lion of the company. Half the girls in the room went home in love with him; two-thirds of the beaux wished devoutly that he had never quitted the "Faderland" until he was ready to bring a wife to the western continent with him.

At twelve o'clock, the last carriage, with its cortége of gallant outriders, left the door of the hospitable abode, and Helen, wearied and dispirited, sought her chamber. The faithful Sally was in wakeful attendance, and, disobedient to her mistress's recommendation, that she should betake herself to bed without further delay, began, with alert hands, the task of disrobing her. It may have been that fatigue and dissipation had rendered Helen indolent, or that, in her depressed state of feeling, the society of this attached dependent was more tolerable than solitude and her own musings; for she did not repeat the order: submitted languidly to her maid's pleasure.

"Miss Helen!" she said, as she kneeled to untie her slipper-string; "I hope you did not think it *un*proper in me to hurry you home from the spring to-night. I deceived you about the reason, then. I didn't like to tell you there, for fear you might be frightened, and Mars' Robert get angry, and go to search into the matter, and so get you both into trouble; so I made the excuse I did, to start you up to the house."

"What are you talking about, Sally?" asked Helen, somewhat sharply; "you have been dreaming, and are not quite awake yet, I believe."

"I'm broad awake, ma'am, and so I was then, for all I had to pretend to be sleepy and cold, to hinder you from mistrusting the truth. And I saw him, Miss Helen, as plain as I do you, this minute! I wouldn't move till I was sure."

"Saw him! Saw whom? Why do you tell your story in such a queer, blundering way? Go on!" urged her mistress, as the girl bent lower over the foot resting upon her knee, and tugged and picked at the hard knot she had made in the string.

"The man behind the tree, ma'am! the big oak you was leaning against."

"Nonsense! you mistook the shadow of the limbs for a man! How could any one be there, and I not hear him move or breathe? How could he get there without making any noise?"

"Tree shadows don't move of a still night, as this one did," persisted the girl. "As to how he got there, I can't say, nor how long he'd been standing close up against the trunk of the tree when I first noticed him. I didn't see him until he poked out his head—this way—as if to hear better what you two were saying."

"Pshaw! why should he care to hear? why stay there, if he could get away?"

"That isn't for me to say, ma'am. I only know that I saw him, and that he behaved just as I've told you."

Helen pondered for a moment upon this strange tale. The maid was unusually sensible and discreet for one in her station, and not superstitious or cowardly. Her mistress did not question that she really believed all that she had said; but the more she thought of it, the more unlikely it appeared that Robert and herself had been dogged by so bold an eavesdropper, or that any chance vagrant of the forest could have remained for any length of time in the position Sally had described, without being discovered.

"Could you see who he was? or whether he was white or colored?" she inquired.

"He kept well in the shade, ma'am, and I wasn't very near, you know. Maybe he was a runaway. There's a good many 'out,' I hear, more than common for this season of the year," returned the girl, still averting her face, and putting away the slippers in a drawer.

"Perhaps it was Lem!" exclaimed Helen. "Poor fellow! he need not have been afraid of us! We would never have betrayed him."

This was a field-hand of Colonel Floyd's, who had run away six weeks before, goaded to desperation by the brutal oppression of the driver, Booker, whose authority was invariably supported by the master. Lem had married Sally's sister, as Helen now considered, and the probabilities were manifestly in favor of the supposition that he was lurking about the plantation, in the hope of seeing his wife. Sally was not certain that she recognized him, yet that she had some misgivings on the subject was clear. She might feel it to be her duty to put her mistress upon her guard against a repetition of the nocturnal stroll, while she was cautious not to commit her brother-in-law. Acting upon this hypothesis, which she imagined was fully sustained by Sally's silence after Lem was named, Helen forbore to prosecute her inquiries, and her thoughts strayed of themselves back to the more pressing cares and disquietudes that weighed heavily upon her young spirit.

In ten minutes after the servant's story was concluded, her auditor had forgotten the runaway and his woes.

CHAPTER V.

"A WHOLESOME lesson for the future!" Aleck Lay had said, and he conned it to such profit, that, during the month immediately succeeding his arrival at home, he paid but two visits at Colonel Floyd's, and they were made in decorous compliance with special invitations. He spent most of each day, and often stayed over night, at his plantation of Maple Hill, a fine old place, which had come into the family through the female line; having been bequeathed, at his grandfather's death, to his mother. Active and judicious preparations were being made there now, for the reception of his aunt and himself. "He went to as much pains and expense in fitting it up, as if he were expecting to take thither a beautiful wife, and not an old maid sobersides like herself," Miss Ruth affected to complain, while, inwardly, she was happy and proud that he did so. The paternal mansion, Greenfield, was meanwhile in a state of disorder unparalleled in the previous annals of Miss Massie's reign. Cleaning, repairing, painting, and refurnishing were all going forward at once, under the superintendence of that painstaking housewife. Mrs. Robert Lay should find every apartment in every story, every closet and stair, even the "cuddy-holes" in the garret, irreproachable, if she, the indefatigable present incumbent, perished in the laudable attempt to attain this end. She naturally believed that Robert's love-making was prosecuted as diligently, and that its results were likely to prove as satisfactory to all concerned, as she hoped those of her labors would be; justly considering the sentimental—in metaphysical jargon, the "subjective" branch of the nuptial arrangements as quite out of her province.

Mrs. Floyd pursued a similar line of thought and action, as she overlooked seamstresses, laundresses, and chambermaids; set aside a goodly reserve of her finest sweatmeats, and oldest pickles and liquors; bespoke eggs, far and near, to be delivered a week before Christmas at Belleview; tested the golden rolls of butter packed away for the "occasion;" inspected her poultry-yards, and, like the celebrated William O'Trimmerty of the nursery rhyme,

"Gathered her hens,
And put them in pens,"

to be fattened against the great day. She had private personal trials, in addition to household cares, and the two classes of perplexities thoroughly engrossed every faculty of a mind which was none too capacious at its best estate.

Never, in the whole course of her wedded life, had she beheld her lord in a worse humor than now held complete possession of him. His household words were one perpetual growl—not loud, but deep; and their connubial confabulations, which always partook more of the nature of monologues from him, than a reciprocation of ideas and feelings, were uniformly so stormy now, that she trembled in heart and body at the anticipation of them. When, with simple and wifely guile, she tried to divert him from his sombre brooding over his grievances, unknown as yet to her, by small domestic details, and deferentially begged his opinion upon the momentous topics of invitations, and the numberless etcetera pertaining to the grand wedding,—for no Floyd was ever married without a large and magnificent party,—he swore at her, at the guests, and the supper; as Gabriel reported in the kitchen, "cussed up-stairs and down, and all 'round the lot;" reserving his choicest imprecations for the unconscious bridal pair, whom he anathematized as "a brace of the most ungrateful and unmannerly villains, the most barefaced cheats, that ever conspired to effect a man's ruin!"

"But how, dear?" mildly questioned his spouse, after one of these philippics. "Helen has her fits of temper, I know, but she is much quieter than I ever saw her before. Yet it must be confessed that, even now, she does get awfully stubborn about some things. Now, for instance, I've been scolding her to-day about a senseless notion she has taken. You know that Alexander Lay brought over for her a superb set of pearls, for a wedding present, and sent them to her by Robert, soon after he got home. She has a pearl-colored satin, trimmed with lace, among her new things, her 'second-day's dress,' and anybody, with half an eye, can see that it was made to go with these—"

"Confound your satin and pearls! The twaddle of you women is enough to drive one to distraction!" roared the colonel, kicking over a stand that opposed him in his heavy tramp about the floor.

"Yes, dear! I am sorry!" Meek Mrs. Floyd let fall a shivering tear upon her stitching.

Her husband muttered a dozen or so of hotter oaths before he dropped again into his arm-chair. When he did sit down, it was with a force that made the windows rattle. Then, picking up the tongs, he poked the fire furiously.

Mrs. Floyd mustered a faint heart of grace to endeavor to repair her mistake.

"What I wanted to say was this, my love; Robert Lay always seemed to me to be a most amiable, obliging young man. This is his reputation all through the neighborhood, and has been ever since he was a boy. I supposed that he would do pretty much whatever you asked him to—he is so ready, generally, to grant favors to his friends. Hasn't he behaved handsomely about the settlement, or whatever you call it? You told me you thought he would."

"So handsomely that he has backed out of every thing that he promised to do, Mrs. Floyd! He has lied like a dog, madam! He is obliging enough to give me to understand that he will grab every dollar of your brother's estate upon the wedding-day you are preparing for—if he can! That's your amiable, popular saint, madam!"

Another volley of oaths, accompanied by a shower of coals upon the hearth, and sparks up the chimney.

"You don't say so! After all the advice I've tried to impress upon Helen, about letting you manage her property! I should think she might have had some little confidence in my judgment, and tried to persuade him to act differently! I declare I am quite hurt by such disrespect and ingratitude!"

"It's her work! I'll take my oath of that—the brazen minx! She can twist him around her finger, if she likes."

"Well! well! well!" ruminated the matron, and returned to her former plaint; "I can't tell when I've been so much hurt!"

"Hurt, madam! You'll begin to know what has hurt you, when you are turned out of house and home; your last stick of furniture gone; your very clothes sold from off your back, in order that your affectionate niece may flaunt in her husband's mansion in her satin and pearls!"

"Good gracious, colonel!" The lady twitched back her skirts briskly, to avoid the stream of fiery embers that bounced from under the forestick in her direction, at the conclusion of this comforting prophecy.—"It can't be so bad as *that*, I'm sure!"

"You are sure, are you? Much you know about it! It

is an easy thing for a man with an extravagant family like mine, hung like a mill-stone about his neck, to hand over some fifty thousand dollars' worth of property, and, may-be, a matter of five thousand in ready money, upon a month's notice, is it? I would be obliged to you if you will inform me where it is to come from!"

"Why, I don't know any thing about business, dear."

"You need not trouble yourself to tell me what is self-evident, madam!"

"But I supposed that Helen's fortune was put away safe somewhere, against she came of age—in the bank, or—"

"Or tied up in a stocking-foot, or carried loose in my breeches pocket!" interrupted her husband, with an ugly sneer. "That is as much sense as you have about any thing outside of your dirty kitchen!"

He got up, still snarling, put on a shaggy great-coat, took his gun from a closet, and made ready for his nightly patrol.

"And see here, my lady, keep your tongue inside of your teeth when you think of what I have been fool enough to say to-night—or it may be the worse for you!"

Mrs. Floyd gave a weak sniff of wounded sensibility when the door banged to after her lawful protector and loving liege;—then fell to work upon a mental calculation of the number and variety of the loaves of cake, whose manufacture she was to begin the following week.

One used to ebullitions of temper akin to that she had just witnessed, seasoned by years of endurance to the peltings and reverberant peals of such thunder-storms as were any hour liable to break upon her head—was not apt to remark or inquire into the cause of lesser variations in the family barometer. If Helen grew graver each day, and was often moodily taciturn for hours together; if Lily were fretful, restless, and capriciously gay by turns, without any visible reason for these humors—the good aunt winked at these fluctuations of temper and spirits, and, when winking did not suffice to shut out the unseemly exhibitions, closed fast eyes and ears, and minded her own business. She was not, therefore, the person who could have been expected to discern other signs of the times—such as affected her ease and comfort less than the behavior of her husband and adopted daughters towards her personally. She never bethought herself that Robert Lay's handsome, sunshiny face was at times worn and haggard, and his manner oddly *distrait;* that, while he never failed to follow Helen's every movement with his eyes, and sought out occasions of divining her wishes and forestalling their expression by immediately gratifying them, he as frequently had long, confidential talks with Lily as with her, and treated the younger cousin with a warmth of familiarity he had not manifested formerly.

Nor did Helen's quicker vision appear to discover this change in her lover's bearing, or imagine that there was peril in his increasing intimacy with Lily. Whether she had other food for thought, so much more important in her estimation, or was incapacitated from feeling jealousy, through perfection of confidence, or, what was surely very unlikely, a calm indifference, was not to be learned from her demeanor. Certain it was that she pursued the avocations so replete with stirring interest to most women with a mechanical fidelity, a diligent drudgery, that looked more like a conscientious performance of allotted duty than desire; more like an abstraction of ideas and absence of feeling than loving zeal. Occasionally she aroused her torpid conscience to the examination of the contrariety of emotions that alternately depressed and agitated her, questioned herself sharply, and censured unsparingly. It might be an indication of a noble trust in Robert's truth and affection that she did not object to see him sit, for an hour at a time, beside Lily's piano, or promenade with her on the lawn for the same period, both talking earnestly and continuously, as friends whose interest in one absorbing theme is a bond of union between their hearts. But did she sin when she wondered what was the source of the relief she experienced in the discovery that, while his kindness to herself remained unabated, he was yet less demonstrative; made fewer demands upon her time and love than of yore; let her alone when she was inclined to indulge in pensive revery, instead of trying by cheerful arts and tenderwiles to dispel the cloud? She had outlived her age of romance, she was in the habit of saying, and perhaps it was better that he should also learn to look at Life's prosaic side;—to view feelings, as well as facts, as they were, without the dangerous and deceptive glamour cast about them by a loving idolatry. They would be happier for the disillusion when their lots were united.

She did not palliate the folly and crime of the unutterable sadness that would, combat it as she might, steal over her in the contemplation of this prospect. Was she not going, of her free will, to marry a man who had loved her from her childhood in spite of her faults, her many frailties and foibles of disposition and errors of conduct? who loved her purely and wholly, as few other women were ever esteemed? Was he not the non-such of his sex, in his spotless life, his engaging deportment, perfect temper, and singleness of purpose? She was a fortunate, a happy woman, and, if ungrateful as fortunate, unreasonable as happy, she might blame herself and no one else. What if she had, in childish folly, once hearkened and thrilled to another's vows, as she had never done to Robert's manly fervor of protestation? What if, for many months, she had nursed a beautiful shadow of bliss, in the belief that this other was hers—hers only and forever—as she was keeping herself for him? That was a weary, weary time ago! It seemed as if years of wretchedness had gone over her head since the summer evening—but one month prior to her betrothal—when she had heaved, torn with desperate strength, the great stone by the spring away from its bed, and buried in the moist black mould the ring she had worn, in credulous faith, for a year and a half—worn hopefully, joyously, proudly! then rolled back the rock to its place—a tomb that hid a grave!

These trifles belonged to the girl's history; as a girl she had judged falsely of their nature, and consequently overrated their value. She had grown into a woman now, rational, strong, resolute! Was she resentful and despairing as well? It might be, for she had no memory of a mother's gentle rectitude of conscience and action; a father's wise counsels. A wild, undisciplined childhood had not laid the kind of foundation from which would spring, in spontaneous growth, moderation of judgment and dispassionate conduct at the age of maturity. She knew her temperament, and what were her besetting sins; and she firmly believed that Robert Lay, of all others, was best acquainted with these, and that his influence would exert the most salutary effect in restraining whatever was objectionable and fostering the few germs of good. He had said that she only had the power of making him happy; that Life would be bare and joyless if he were deprived of the hope of winning her; and with tender sympathy, born more of her own intense suffering, her aching, bleeding heart, than out of the sisterly regard she had ever felt for him, she listened, and promised to be his wife.

"There's many a heart caught in the rebound!" says a time-honored maxim we see daily exemplified in the drama of Life. With regard to the quality and volume of this reflex tide of affection the oracle is mute.

I heard once of a simple, true-hearted girl, a novice in the world and its ways, who was cruelly deserted by the man she had loved and trusted for years. She "bore it wonderfully," said curious lookers-on. Some went so far as to express a doubt whether her attachment had ever been so strong as was generally supposed. Cheerfully and quietly—none guessed how heroically—she went through her round of duties; neither in her home, nor in society, ever yielding, for an instant, to visible depression of spirits. Two or three years had elapsed since the event that had changed the whole tenor of her inner life; the recreant lover had wedded another, and it was considered that she had, in common phrase, "quite gotten over her trouble," when she was addressed by another suitor, a noble fellow, who could appreciate aright her rare excellence, and was, in himself, entirely worthy of her love and respect. She was greatly moved as the tale proceeded, and, when he paused for her answer, hid her face and wept abundantly. Encouraged by this evidence of softness, the wooer pressed his suit yet more warmly.

"Please do not," she sobbed, putting both her hands into his, and looking up at him with an expression of grieving pity. "Do not go on, or I shall promise that which will render us both miserable for life. I know how hard it is to endure the pain of wounded affection. Do not make me too sorry for you!"

Had the nature of Helen's former relations to Aleck Lay been such as could be avowed, and Robert not his brother, she would have made a like answer to his confession of love.

It wanted just three weeks to the wedding-night, and the brothers had accompanied the Floyds home from morning service in the church, to partake of their Sunday dinner. Aleck had joined the party sadly against his will; but Lily had seconded her aunt's invitation so pressingly, declaring that she believed he had some secret and cogent reason for his dislike of Belleview or its inmates; that the whole county had observed his neglect of his old friends, and that divers queer rumors were in circulation explanatory of his behavior —that he complied, to avoid discussion and check scandal. Lily had a meaning accent and look, moreover, while she delivered this lively tirade, that piqued and puzzled him. Had such a thing been possible, he would have felt assured that she was no stranger to the true cause of his consistent avoidance of Helen.

He was not an admirer or friend of Miss Calvert. When a boy, he had mortally offended her by pronouncing her "a whey-faced witch," which observation, by means of some kind tongue, reached her ears. The feud was further increased by his invariable championship of Helen, in the petty quarrels between the girls. Lily professed to like him at this date. It had even been slyly and gratuitously suggested to him, by disinterested young ladies and prudent mammas, that he, the elder and richer brother, was regarded by the Floyd connection as a *bon parti*, and probable suitor of the colonel's younger ward, now that the other was "out of the market." This benevolent warning he received with profound carelessness, and did not trouble himself to controvert the theory. It was not fear of these tattlers that kept him away from the home of the elfin beauty. Yet it might be expedient to throw them yet farther off the right scent, besides showing his contempt for their impertinent gossip, by riding fearlessly by Robert's side, behind the Floyd carriage, when it rolled away from the church door on this bright day, and his officious friends were looking on, in rows and squads, awaiting the arrival of their respective vehicles.

For a wonder, the Lays were the only persons present besides the family at dinner, and all found the repast a dull and cheerless ceremony, although the cookery did ample credit to Mrs. Floyd's kitchen. The poor lady's eyes were red and watery. She had a headache and catarrh, she said; but the initiated members of the company, and this included the entire number, recollecting that she had returned from church in her usual spirits and bodily condition, were not slow in assigning a more plausible reason for these signs of discomfort, in viewing the knit brows and hearing the gruff tones of her sovereign master. He carved savagely, and wasted as few decent words upon his guests as he could, taking no share whatever in the conversation that Lily, Robert, and Aleck tried to keep up, to cover his surliness and Mrs. Floyd's tremor. He broke a goblet, in pushing it roughly against the dish before him; swore audibly at the quaking servants; and finally ordered his second son from the table in a voice of thunder, for spilling water on the cloth.

The colonel seldom went to church except in summer-time, when he could pass the hours of service out of doors, under the trees shading the sacred edifice, talking politics with neighbors as graceless as himself. He had spent the forenoon of this Sabbath in examining his account-books—"business papers," his wife styled them, in a lame apology she offered in the drawing-room for his "being out of sorts;" he having finished the meal he had succeeded in spoiling for every one else, and stalked off up to his chamber for his Sunday afternoon nap.

"It always gives him the blues to look over these tiresome papers!" she sighed, while she tried to smile at the absurdity of allowing such trifles to mar one's happiness. "I often wish there were no money matters in the world. I don't pretend to understand them myself!"

"Few ladies do!" said Aleck. "They are among the ills of life which are confined almost exclusively to us unhappy men."

Helen met Robert's eye with a forced smile, which was returned by one yet more mirthless.

"Can he be so unjust, after all my frankness, as to imagine me mercenary?" she thought, indignantly.

His uncomfortable cogitations were, in reality, dwelling upon the strong likelihood that the "business papers" which had stirred up the colonel's bile appertained to the records of his stewardship over his niece's estate, and the certainty, if this were so, that there were vexatious trials of patience in store for himself, when he and the guardian came to the dreaded final settlement.

The diversion was not unwelcome when Lily called him into her green-house, to inspect a plant he had sent her some time before. It was drooping and yellow, from some cause, whose discovery was beyond the reach of her horticultural acumen. Robert was a zealous and accomplished amateur florist, and his decision, after a minute examination of the flower, and inquiry into the course she had pursued towards it, was, that she was killing it with kindness.

"You pet it too much; water it too abundantly; and dress the earth about the roots too often. Plants require rest, like animals. This needs a little wholesome neglect; a judicious letting alone, with plenty of sunshine. That will bring it around, if it is not too far gone."

Lily bent over the fading favorite in silence, until the large drops gathered in her eyes, and one fell upon the plant.

"My dear child!" ejaculated Robert, in surprise, "I will procure a dozen more of the same kind for you, if you want them, sooner than you should shed a single tear; and this may revive yet!"

"I am *not* a child!" said she, passionately, "although everybody sees fit to treat me like one! And it is not the flower, for the flower's sake, that I grieve over! I was just thinking how every thing that I love best is taken from me.

I did care for that geranium, because you gave it to me, and I have always believed that you were one of the very, very few who really liked me!"

She plucked a rose and rent it apart, petal by petal, her lip pouting and trembling; the tears yet hanging, like pearly dew, upon the gold fringe of her eyelids. She looked perilously pretty, Robert acknowledged, in his conscious innocence of every thing except brotherly kindness, and his great, tender heart yearned at the sight and confession of her artless distress. What a guileless babe she was! How sinless and free her attachment for her early playmate!

"And you thought right, Lily! There are not many people whom I like better than I do you—as I have often told you."

"Only a couple of dozen or so!" returned the beauty, petulantly.

Robert was obliged to laugh.

"Hardly a single couple, I can assure you! You know who comes first upon the list, and would not dispute her right. Then there is Aleck! He is the only brother I have in the world."

"And Miss Ruth is your only aunt; and mamma is Helen's father's only sister, so she ought to come next; and Mam' Becky is your only mammy, and Hero is your best horse, and Dash your best dog—and they all take precedence of a nobody like me, who has no claim upon you!" cried Lily, snatching at another rose, and bringing it away, stem and all. "I don't thank you, or anybody else, for a seventh, or even a third rate place in his regard. Thank goodness! if I am insignificant, I have too much pride for *that!*"

"Don't try to pick a quarrel with me, little sister! I have enough sources of disquiet without this one—disquiet which your sweet sympathy has done much to alleviate. You wrong me by affecting to misunderstand my meaning. You know the sincerity of my attachment for you, Lily!"

"Forgive me!"

Her head fell upon his arm. Whether he would have released himself from this position, or awaited the recovery of her composure, was not to be seen.

"A letter for you, Miss Lily!" said Aleck's voice behind them. His face was stern—his eye and accent penetrating. "Your aunt was going to bring it in to you, and I took charge of it to spare her the trouble."

He bowed and withdrew, before either of the twain, whom his abrupt address had started, could find breath or words for a reply.

He was not surprised, on returning to the parlor, to perceive that it was deserted. The stiff and labored dialogue carried on by himself and Helen, after they were left together by the floral connoisseurs, was so difficult and painful to both the participants, that he had seized upon the circumstance of Mrs. Floyd's entrance with a note for Lily as an opportune pretext for ending the miserable pretence. Helen understood his eager politeness to her aunt, and contributed her share towards their mutual relief by leaving the coast clear before he reappeared. There was a dark flush of passion upon Aleck's brow as he strode over to the window, and his mouth worked convulsively under his heavy moustache while he remained there, looking out upon the wintry landscape, blasted and sere, like his own hopes. He was displeased with Robert—more than displeased with the miniature siren, whose enticements were operating upon the senses of her cousin's affianced husband.

"He can love twenty women—I but one! If *she* were mine, I would have shrunk with loathing from the touch of that little serpent! Instead of enduring her subtlety and fond twinings about me, would have cast her from me as a hateful thing! How different was the scene transpiring in here! Have I, then, more regard for his rights and honor than he has himself?"

It was a hasty and unjust aspersion of his brother's fidelity and delicacy of affection for his betrothed; but his wrath glowed yet more hotly as he reviewed, in detail, the illustration of rigid self-control, amounting to coldness, his manner to Helen had afforded; his absolute reticence of even friendly warmth towards the woman he nevertheless adored; the extreme circumspection he exercised over each glance and word, lest Robert's bride should chance to read in any of these that which it would be dishonorable in him, who was soon to be her brother, to show; and contrasted this line of conduct and principle with Robert's passive, if not fond reception of blandishments, such as he had interrupted.

He was too angry to look around when Lily's clear voice was heard at the door connecting conservatory and parlor.

"Helen! Helen! Why, Mr. Lay, I thought she was entertaining you all this time!"

"You were mistaken, you see!" he answered, curtly.

"Don't you know where she has gone?"

"I do not!"

"Then I must hunt her up! It was very uncivil in her to leave you here all alone. I shall scold her well for it!"

Away she ran, singing in her bird-like tones as if she had never shed a tear in her life. Robert, who had come in with her, silently took a seat by the fire.

Without having the remotest conception of the hidden reasons that exasperated into deep displeasure Aleck's righteous disapproval of the supposed flirtation, the younger brother yet felt that he had placed himself, or been placed by another, in a false light in his mentor's eyes. Unwilling to make a serious affair of an occurrence so trivial, or to impute forwardness and levity of deportment to Lily, he was nearly as reluctant to sustain in his own proper person the weight of the blame Aleck ascribed to one or both of them. That he did blame somebody for what he had seen, Robert did not need his present behavior to convince him. He knew his ideas of a lover's honor—his delicate fastidiousness upon some points relative to this—scruples for which none save those who were most intimately acquainted with him ever gave him credit. Gay rattle and reckless flirt as he was generally esteemed, his chivalrous respect for true womanhood amounted to reverence; his recognition of innate purity was instinctive. Had he been betrothed, he would have expected—not exacted—a whole-hearted devotion, not of the affections merely, but of the mind. If he scorned to exercise the slightest espionage upon the movements of his *fiancée* or wife, left her, as free as air, to obey the bent of her inclinations, it would be because he believed, with a faith more powerful than the convictions produced by sight, that she was as pure as the freshest air ever breathed from Heaven; that she was *his*—heart, body, and imagination, incapable of cherishing a thought she would not impart to him; and he would have given as much as he asked. His teasing talk with his aunt about the fabulous Gretchen, and his fine compliments to heedless butterflies like Virginia Shore, were the veriest lip-play, and every one who knew him understood the badinage and flattery. No girl could accuse him of more culpable trifling, of the most distant approach to unwarrantable familiarity in language or touch.

Robert was conscious that he was sinless in respect to that whereof he feared his brother held him to be guilty; yet, he said to himself, that he wished, since Lily's unguarded, because artless action, was destined to have another spectator besides himself, that it had been Helen, and not Aleck. She would have judged of the case more charitably, approximated the truth more nearly. But something must be said to undeceive the real judge, and there was no time to be lost.

"Aleck—old boy!" He passed his arm over his brother's shoulder, who stood like a statue of ice under the embrace. "Are you thinking hardly of me?—blaming me for the little scene you happened to behold just now?"

"You are master of your own conscience and actions," rejoined the other, freezingly. "I do not presume to sit in condemnation upon either."

"I require no stronger evidence that you have arraigned me already—condemned me unheard," Robert said, in a hurt tone. "You should know me better, Aleck! If you had heard the rest of the conversation you would be more lenient. I wish you had!"

He waited for a response, but none came.

"It was the simplest, most innocent of gallant farces, Al!" Robert resumed, in a lighter tone.

> "'When a pretty woman shows her rings,
> What can a fellow do?'

"That is an analogous quandary to the one in which you saw me—for which you are inclined to have me hanged, drawn, and quartered."

"The question is," said Aleck, turning to face his brother, and speaking slowly, with no softening of his severity, "the question is, whether a man, situated as you are, has a right, or ought to have the disposition, to think of the beauty of any other woman?"

"Pshaw!" replied the other, still determined to turn the affair into a jest, "that dogma belongs to a former generation; the Grandisonian race of swains and shepherdesses; the age that painted Cupid blind."

"That is very possible. My ideas upon this subject are decidedly antiquated, I admit; somewhat deficient, moreover, in tolerance of this 'dear passion for many' that modern lovers find so delightful!" answered Aleck, crossing to the fireplace, and throwing himself upon the sofa.

Nothing further passed between them for that time. Even Robert's sweet temper was ruffled by the unmerited sneer. Their disputes were of such rare occurrence that reconciliation was an awkward undertaking, if either were disposed to attempt it.

"Excuse me for leaving you!" cried Lily, floating into the room—her airy motion could hardly be called walking—"but Nelly and I have been arranging a frolic for this evening. Won't you, gentlemen, aid and abet us?"

"The better the day the better the deed?" said Robert, playfully interrogative.

He would not allow Aleck's unjust imaginings to influence his demeanor to this unsophisticated, warm-hearted child.

"Yes—but this is really and truly a Sunday frolic. Mr. Sheppard, the new circuit-rider, is to preach to the servants at Mr. Shore's to-night, and Ginnie has written to say that we must all come. She knows you came home with us to dinner, so she will expect both of you, certainly. I dearly enjoy these colored meetings—don't you, Mr. Robert?"

"That depends upon their hue. I have found them very blue, and a dingy indigo at that, sometimes—taking blueness and dulness as synonyms."

"Oh! you know what I meant! Why will you be provoking? Mr. Lay, I wish you would take him in hand, and teach him how to behave as you do."

Aleck did not raise his eyes from his book. He would

not be a party to this deceitful trifling. Lily gave him a stare of inquiry, and returned to the more complaisant Robert.

"They say this Mr. Sheppard is a stirring speaker, a thorough-going revivalist; and the ride home by moonlight will be splendid!"

CHAPTER VI.

SEVEN o'clock found the quartette from Belleview in the revivalist's audience, at one end of Mr. Shore's long dining-hall.

The white population of the neighborhood was principally made up of Episcopalians, with a slight sprinkling of Roman Catholics; but Mr. Shore wedded for his second wife a devout Methodist, whose example and precept had wrought great, and, it was hoped by the reformer, radical changes in the religious habits of the slaves upon her own and certain of the surrounding plantations. The clergymen of her denomination, whose itinerant habits brought them within range of communication with her, were urgently invited to visit at, and most hospitably entertained in, her house; encouraged to establish meetings for public and social worship among the negroes, innovations which were not opposed, but rather forwarded, by her indulgent, irreligious husband. The gathering on this occasion was made up, for the most part, of colored people, a goodly assembly in number, seated in close rows upon benches manufactured for such purposes by Mrs. Shore's orders. The room was narrow in proportion to its length, and had a fireplace at each end. Around the upper one of these were ranged chairs, for the accommodation of the family and neighbors. There were about thirty in all; and while the younger portion of the company had undoubtedly been attracted thither by the consideration that had moved Lily's inclination to attend, namely, the love of a frolic, let the day be what it might,—they behaved with due decorum, preserved the semblance of respectful attention. It would not have been safe to act otherwise under Mrs. Shore's watchful eyes.

Mr. Sheppard was suffering from hoarseness, having already delivered two sermons and conducted a class-meeting that day, besides riding twenty miles on horseback. He therefore the more gladly committed the preliminary and closing exercises of singing and prayer to those of the congregation who were able and willing to lighten his labors by taking their part in the same. Mrs. Shore joined in the familiar choruses, endeared to her by so many early and sacred associations, and her husband, to gratify her, added his assistance, which was, to say the least, of doubtful value, since his voice was cracked, and he knew neither tune nor words. But the best feature of this portion of the service was the grand, rich tones of the negroes, surging in thunder-peals of exultation, or sweetly plaintive in the pathetic strains of penitential lamentation.

"Did you hear any thing finer than that in Germany, in the fatherland of sacred music?" whispered Helen to Aleck, who sat a little to her right, behind her.

"Nothing that sounded so delightful to my ears!" was his response. "It is like the music of Carryl and the memory of departed joys, pleasant and mournful to the soul."

He had leaned over, his hand resting upon the back of her chair, to hear and to answer her, and in the self-forgetfulness of the moment, both had looked and spoken naturally, with the cordial ease that had once signalized them in their bearing, the one to the other.

As Aleck resumed his former position, he caught sight of Lily's face; saw that she was on the alert to hear what was passing; met a covert side glance, which was quickly withdrawn; and his blood boiled anew. His distrust of the girl was becoming intense and irrational, and in exact ratio with its increase was augmented his loving compassion for Helen, whom, he honestly believed, her cousin was endeavoring to supplant in her lover's regard.

"Can it be that she sees nothing to excite her jealousy?" he speculated, and while the sermon engrossed the attention of the crowd at large, his watch upon her was keen but furtive.

She sat quietly; a casual observer would have supposed that her thoughts were, with her external organs of vision, fastened upon the speaker; but Aleck divined, or imagined that he did, that this immobility of feature betokened any thing but interest in the orator's impassioned appeals and vivid descriptions; that she found other and more prolific material for reflection in her own thoughts. There was nothing to awaken surprise in this abstraction in one who was to become a bride in less than one short month from that night; but it was remarkable that he did not succeed, in the course of that hour of close scrutiny, in detecting one stolen look at Robert, who was in full view, and whose eyes repeatedly wandered to her statuesque face.

"Perhaps love has taught her to practise concealment, a prudent vigilance over look, no less than word and action!" mused the spy. "Yet I should not have expected it!"

While revolving these trifles lighter than air in his mind, and more ill at ease on account of his restless meditations than he was himself aware of, he omitted to pay the requisite degree of attention to the passage of other events; was so lost to the consciousness of where he was, and what was the nature of the services, that he sprang to his feet, in uncontrollable bewilderment, when the sable congregation fell simultaneously, and not very noiselessly, upon their knees, at the invitation to prayer. Lily laughed, audibly to his sensitive ear, although she tried to smother the cachinnation with her pocket-handkerchief; and Mr. Alexander Lay, self-contained man of the world as he was, sinking again to his seat with a tingling sensation about his bronzed cheeks, mentally and fervently devoted her to the infernal gods.

His confusion had time to abate during the prayer. The instrument, in his own phrase, "the humble tool," selected to convey the petitions of the assembly, was a servant belonging to Aleck himself, one of the field-hands upon the Maple Hill farm, a pompous, pragmatical Boanerges, distinguished above his fellows by his "wonderful gift of speech." He gave this talent full play now, beginning with constrained moderation and deliberate utterance, and gradually waxing louder and warmer, incited to greater vehemence by the groans of assent from his brethren, until the gusts of sound escaping from his surcharged lungs, presumed to represent equal vigor of heart, threatened to bring the ceiling down upon his head and those of the audience; as if, Samson-like, he meant to involve them with himself in one common ruin. He was "a mighty man in the Scriptures," said his admirers; and the majority of those of his own caste heard, with a glow of pride in their representative but inadequately expressed by long-drawn "Amens," and sepulchral "Ahs!" his mention of the preacher to whose exhortations they had been called to listen on that occasion.

"Be pleased to pour out Thy plenteousest blessin's 'pon de great and notable man of de Lord who has spoken to us dis blessed arternoon, from de rivers to de ends of de earth. Strengthen him in his weakly body and diminished mind; bless him abroad and in his home, from de rivers to de ends of de earth. Grant him, in Thy mussiful and undesarved kindness, a superabundance of souls as de purchase of his hire. Make him fur to grow up before Thee, and in de sight of all mankind, from de rivers to de ends of de earth, like a calf of de stall; dat at last he may be worthy to become *meat* for de kingdom of Heaven. May he soon cease from his labors, and den, his works—may dey follow him!"

There was hardly a serious face in the semicircle of young ladies and gentlemen, when this remarkable effusion was brought to a peroration and final "Amen." Mrs. Shore, scandalized by their irreverence, yet derived some satisfaction from the spectacle of Aleck Lay's sombre visage. She had heretofore secretly accused him of scoffing at religious subjects, but she recalled now the gratifying fact that she had never really heard any blasphemous talk or unseemly jesting from him; only knew that he was sarcastic, and had studied in Germany, where she had been taught to believe that heresy was rampant, and orthodoxy unknown. Who could tell what leaven of Brother Sheppard's discourse might not be working in his unsanctified nature? Infinite then was her disappointment and speechless her horror, when, service being over, as the negroes were filing out of the doors upon the right and left of the room, and Boanerges swaggered past the patrician group, bowing graciously, his master sternly bade him, "Stop!"

"Sar!" said the amazed orator.

"I want to know what you meant by insulting a minister of the gospel to his face?" said Aleck, authoritatively.

"*Me*, marster?"

"Yes, *you!* Do you know, you rascal, that you have not only declared here, in the hearing of us all, that Mr. Sheppard's mind was failing, but called him a calf—made butcher's meat of him, and then prayed for his speedy death?"

The negro gaped in dumb and sheepish astonishment.

Aleck, like many other and better men, now that he had found an object upon which he might justly vent some of his pent-up wrath, was disposed to deal more unmercifully with the offender against sense and decorum than he would have felt in a moment of less irritation.

"All that I have to say to you is this, my fine fellow," he pursued. "If I ever hear of your making a prayer in public again, before you have learned to perceive that most of what you say is outrageous profanity, I will have you transported to the South, as sure as your name is Petronius. While you belong to me you shall not be guilty of such scandalous impertinence in the name of Heaven, that is, if I can hinder it. You can go!"

"Really, Mr. Lay," Mrs. Shore recovered herself sufficiently to say, when the man had sought a refuge for his "diminished" head outside the door; "you were unnecessarily severe upon the poor fellow. We all understood what it was that he intended to say, and he is a person of great influence among our colored people, a leader of a class-meeting, and high authority in all religious matters."

"So much the more reason for putting a stop to such balderdash, madam! I must apologize to you, sir," addressing himself courteously to Mr. Sheppard, "for the seeming disrespect of his language with regard to you. I will see that the like does not occur again."

"The poor ignorant slave needs no apology to be made for him," answered the minister's solemn tones, doubly hoarse and deep by reason of his cold. "I would rather hope that his master will make amends to him, for the mortification he has sustained on account of his desire to perform his duty in a becoming manner."

"Our ideas of becomingness differ," said Aleck, with admirable temper. "I call such vile and ridiculous garbling of Scripture sacrilege; consider its effect pernicious in the extreme upon the minds of his simple and superstitious followers."

"It may be made, nevertheless, the sword of the Lord and

of Gideon, even in unpractised and weak hands, my young friend. There is One, who is not limited by circumstances; who deigns to make use of feeble instruments in the accomplishment of His work. In this land the use of the Scriptures and the quotation of the same are allowable to all."

Aleck smiled. "It is dangerous to meddle with edge tools!" he rejoined, turning away to end a profitless discussion.

"So the world said!" cried Lily.

Tom and Virginia Shore, like a couple of giddy pates, burst into a fit of laughter.

"We must tell Mr. Lay that pretty story some day," said the latter, merrily. "It was too funny!"

"I have the original document at home. He shall see it, this very night, if he wishes to consult the Fates," replied Lily. "It was the strangest coincidence I ever heard of, and its happening upon the day of your return was not the least wonderful part of it."

"Don't look so disconcerted, Nelly," said Virginia, teasingly. "If one portion of the narrative is likely to be fulfilled, it does not follow that the rest is not a false prophecy."

Aleck looked from one to another, in real curiosity and well-assumed indifference.

"You deal in mysteries!" he said.

"In nonsense, I should say, and very witless fun it is, according to my perception of humor," returned Helen. "Lily! it is time we were gone. The carriage is ready, and we ought not to keep the horses standing in the cold."

"Wait!" Lily was fumbling in her pocket. "This is the dress I wore that evening, and I recollect putting that paper into an envelope, that I might preserve it as a curiosity. Here it is, I declare! Isn't that splendid?"

"Read it! read it!" was the popular acclaim.

"It is Sunday, remember!" cautioned Mrs. Shore.

"Lily!" said Helen, in distressed expostulation. "This is not kind."

"Why, what a serious matter you would make of it!" replied her cousin. "Of course we all understand that it is a pack of foolish fiction, from beginning to end. You see, my friends, we were playing 'Consequences,' and this is what was written upon one of the papers. I shall give it *verbatim et literatim.* You didn't suppose that I knew that much Latin, did you? Ahem! 'The witty and accomplished Miss Helen Gardner,'—watch her, Mr. Shore! don't let her snatch it!—'and the learned and cynical Mr. Alexander Lay, met behind a turkey-blind—' "

"Fire!" rang out Aleck's trumpet tones in her ear. "Look behind you, Miss Lily."

She gave a jump and a scream, catching hold of her skirts at the same moment.

"Mercy upon us! Where is it?"

"In the fireplace!" returned Aleck, provokingly. "Where else should it be?"

There was a roar of laughter, and Lily's pout was one of real chagrin when she discovered that the paper was gone. Whether it had escaped from her fingers in her fright, and been drawn by the current of heated air into the mouth of the chimney, or been abstracted by some clever trick of legerdemain, she could not determine, and no one could or would tell her.

She shook her curls in pretty viciousness at Helen and Aleck.

"I will be even with you two conspirators yet! see if I am not!"

"I do not question your skill in plotting and counterplotting," responded Aleck. "If practice makes perfect, you should be an adept in cunning manœuvre."

15*

Belleview was about five miles distant from Mr. Shore's, and when half the distance was traversed, our party of four had the highway all to themselves; the little cavalcade of horsemen and vehicles that had started from the house with them having dropped off, a few at a time, at branch and cross-roads leading to their respective homes. The waning moon arose while they were still on their way, casting long shadows from hill and tree upon the light covering of snow that enwrapped the untrodden fields, showing the muddy road like a black serpentine river, winding between high banks and extended lines of fences, and giving to the landscape an aspect of melancholy ghostliness. The sickly rays broke fitfully across Lily's face, white as a phantom's, with unsteady, gleaming eyes, and Helen's, nearly as unearthly in its sad fixedness of thought. It was not a social cortége. The girls leaned, fatigued or out of spirits, against the cushions of the back seat in the carriage, and their cavaliers rode silently in the rear or beside the vehicle.

"What a doleful hour and scene!" complained Lily, at last. "If one of you gentlemen does not summon up gallantry enough to say something pretty, witty, or interesting, I shall expire with the blues. One would think that 'Brother Sheppard' had frightened all the fun out of us. Mr. Robert! are you asleep?"

Thus challenged, the individual accosted rode up to the window.

"Not drowsy, only accommodating myself to the prevalent taste for moonlight meditation, ha!"

They were upon a bridge or causeway of primitive construction, consisting of a few rails laid upon trestles, spanning a rill that crossed the road. One of these slipped, or broke under the foot of Robert's horse, and his leg went through the aperture, up to the knee, so violently and suddenly as to throw the rider quite over his head upon the half-frozen ground. A shriek of anguish broke from Lily, so wild and piercing that it chilled Aleck's blood, as a maniac's scream would have done. Quickly as he alighted, she reached the earth as soon, and when he lifted the head of the insensible man to his knee, she was up on the other side, one hand passed under Robert's neck, while the other put back the hair from his brow.

"Robert! Robert! if you love me, speak to me, my darling. Don't you know me, your own Lily!" she called, in her frenzy.

"Is he seriously hurt?" demanded Helen, in accents that, full of feeling, were yet calm in comparison with her cousin's ravings.

She assisted Aleck to loosen his cravat and collar, and chafed his temples and hands.

"He lives!" screamed Lily, rapturously, as a sigh fluttered through the pale lips, followed by a groan.

"Where am I?" asked Robert, struggling to sit upright, holding his head between his palms, as to steady the giddy brain.

Aleck checked Lily's incoherent ejaculations of joy and explanation.

"Be still, Miss Calvert—if you please! You have had an awkward fall from your horse, Robert, and been slightly stunned. That is all! Can you stand?"

"Simon! Simon!" called Lily to the coachman, who had addressed himself to the work of extricating the unlucky horse, and was now examining into the nature of his injuries, "come help lift Mr. Lay into the carriage!"

"Do not make him more ridiculous than you have already done, Miss Calvert!" retorted Aleck, sharply. "He is not a sick baby, or a fine lady, but a man, in size and age at least! Well, Robert! is your head strong enough for the saddle? You have had many a harder fall before now, and hunted all day after it. I trust you have not degenerated."

Robert's rallying senses were acute enough to enable him to comprehend intonations as well as words, and a feeling of shame came over him at what sounded like unfeeling sarcasm.

"I am quite well, entirely recovered!" straightening himself and speaking cheerfully "I never did a more awkward thing in my life! You used the right word in speaking of it, Aleck. How is he, Simon? not lamed, I hope."

"It's a blessed wonder he ain't, sir, for his hoof was rammed tight in de hole,—but he is all safe and right, 'parently."

"It is not right for you to exert yourself beyond your strength," remarked Helen, with the gentle kindness of a sister, as the horse was led up, and Robert laid his hand on the pommel.

Aleck softened on the instant.

"I can easily lead your horse home, if you think that you will suffer any inconvenience from the too violent exercise of riding. You will certainly be more comfortable in the carriage. A little prudence may save you trouble hereafter."

"Thank you!" replied his brother, proudly, somewhat stiffly. "As you say, I am a man, who has had many worse falls in the course of my lifetime. It is cold for you ladies to be standing here. Allow me to see you to the carriage. I am more uneasy on your account than my own."

When they were shut in, he mounted, rejecting Aleck's offer of assistance silently, as it was tendered, and gathering up his reins, gave the signal for starting.

One would hardly have anticipated that the sequel of an adventure, replete with danger to one of the actors, and which had drawn largely upon the sympathy of the others, would be general distrust and acrimony of feeling, or that the silence that resumed its reign over the party would be the expression of grief in some, shame and disappointment in others. Robert's emotions were a mixture of all these. An expert in manly accomplishments, famed for his agility and daring, he was mortified at his downfall, and grieved, no less than ashamed, at the ridiculous light in which Aleck had set his misfortune. Having been partially insensible for the first few minutes after the accident, he had understood Lily's lamentations very imperfectly; was doubtful whether he had not dreamed of her distressed accents and tender adjuration. He was consequently greatly at a loss what reason to assign for Aleck's cold contempt. Helen's composure had struck him as unnatural, and piqued him unaccountably. There were limits even to his loving charity.

"If I judged from the manner of the two, I should decide that Lily loved me best," he meditated, in his vexation. "Presence of mind in such exigencies may be a very useful virtue,—highly commendable and heroic, but, to my taste, there are others more lovely."

Lily was in tears all the rest of the way. She had betrayed her secret to the last persons in creation whom she would have had penetrate it, Helen and Aleck; her imprudence and lack of self-control had frustrated her cherished plans by premature development. Aleck would assuredly consider it incumbent upon him to impart the discovery he had made to his brother—unless—unless—she said, with trembling hope,—Aleck himself reciprocated the sentiment she fancied Helen entertained for him. This was but a transient ray of comfort, for, upon examination, the supposition appeared chimerical and preposterous. Why, if she nursed a preference for the absentee, had Helen engaged herself to Robert? That she might, and would have accepted him, or any eligible suitor, in a moment of pique or despair, the little schemer could readily have imagined; but what provocation had there been for either feeling?

It was a tangled skein—an invisible web, whose mazes each of the four felt knotted about him or her, and still was powerless to break. The young men saw their fair companions to their guardian's door, and bade them "good-night" upon the porch. Lily said nothing; Aleck only the briefest and most coldly polite formula of parting; Helen's voice was sweet and steady in speaking to Robert.

"Must you go home? Do you feel no uneasiness from your fall?"

"None whatever; and I cannot stay—thank you!"

"Then, at least, come in for a moment, and let me get you a glass of wine, to prevent a return of faintness."

"You are very kind, but there is no danger. Good-night!"

He pressed her hand, and perhaps Lily's likewise, but held neither longer than was demanded by politeness, and the brothers returned together to their horses.

They rode on for more than a mile, side by side, before either spoke.

"Is your head at all affected by the shock you sustained? Were you bruised, do you think?" then queried Aleck, kindly.

"I am unhurt *in body*—I am obliged to you!"

The last rejoinder was indicative, Aleck knew, of wounded feeling—not temper.

"I am sorry that you have sustained injury of any kind," he said. "Who inflicted it—may I ask?"

"Yourself more than any one else. I cannot be sullen with you, Aleck. Your conduct towards me, this day, is inexplicable to my mind. If you have any just grounds of complaint against me, speak it out, and give me a chance to clear myself. At any rate, I request you, as one gentleman has the right to ask of another, to refrain, in future, from insulting me in the presence of others—particularly when those others are ladies."

Here was an opportunity for full confession, yet Aleck discovered that he was unable to avail himself of it. So much of his overwrought disapprobation of what he had seen that day had its origin in feelings he could not disclose, that it was a difficult undertaking to make out an indictment against the offenders. Hampered by this conviction, his tone was an unfortunate contrast to Robert's, and jarred sorely upon the listener's heart.

"We can hardly hope to agree upon this topic, Robert. Our views respecting the expediency, not to say the morality, of certain practices, are radically different, I fear. Not that I believe that you would wantonly indulge a dishonorable thought, much less commit a dishonorable deed; yet there is a looseness of principle and conduct in these matters whose harshest name in the vocabulary of society is 'levity,' or 'flirtation,' that often works consequences as disastrous as deliberate villany."

"'Dishonor' and 'villany' are words hard to be borne, even when the speaker is a brother. Please remember that!" said Robert, moving restlessly in the saddle. "In Heaven's name, man, say plainly what I have done, and let there be an end of innuendoes! My patience is worn threadbare."

"I have no objection to plainness of speech. Unless I am greatly mistaken, you have won the love of two women, while you are bound by every law of honor and feeling to hold faith to one alone," said Aleck, bluntly.

"I am not responsible for your visionary conclusions," returned the other, struggling with his rising choler. "What proof have you to substantiate this extraordinary charge?"

"The evidence of my eyes and ears in the scene of this morning, and in the remarkable one of to-night. Lily Calvert would have thrown herself upon your bosom if I had not pushed her back by main force. She called you by name in a tone of passionate devotion, such as a beloved wife only has the right to employ, and entreated you to speak to her—'to your own Lily—if you loved her!' One of two inferences is inevitable. She is either a criminally fond and foolish woman—false alike to her cousin and every instinct of feminine modesty—or you have trifled with her affections."

"I reject the alternatives you lay down so arbitrarily! Lily is innocent and pure-minded. She is not to be judged as you would other girls."

"It seems not, indeed!" interrupted Aleck.

"She is not! She is a simple-hearted, affectionate child, whose very ignorance of evil makes her confiding and fearless. She has been accustomed to petting and indulgence from her infancy, and her sad history, her early orphanage, should commend her to the love of every feeling heart—the protection of every true man."

"I do not know that she is entitled to a more bountiful share of these than is her cousin. She has no recollection of her bereavement, and Mrs. Floyd is shamelessly partial to her. She has never felt the need of any other mother."

"We will not introduce Miss Gardner's name in this connection, if you please!" said Robert, haughtily. "If that lady has any cause of dissatisfaction to allege against me, I hold myself in readiness to hear and answer it when she shall bring it forward in person. I will have no go-between in this matter!"

"You wrong her by the insinuation that she would stoop to employ a 'go-between,' were her wrongs ever so great!" Aleck schooled himself to reply quietly, but forcibly.

"Wrong her more foully than you do me by applying the base title to me! I am neither her confidant nor champion. I deemed it my duty, when you inquired the reason of my altered bearing, to utter a fraternal warning. I have done so in sincerity, with a single desire for your happiness and reputation. From this time henceforth, since you desire it, let the subject be untouched by either of us in our daily intercourse. It is devoid of charms to me, and, it would seem, obnoxious to you."

"Agreed!" returned Robert, spurring on his horse. "I am willing to abide by the results of my actions in this, as in every thing else!"

For the first time in their lives, the brothers separated that night with a cold nod and lips locked in stern displeasure; lay down to rest heart-sore at thought of their alienation; yet each smarting under a sense of injustice and indignity received from the other; each stubborn in his own opinion, and unrepentant of his own hasty words and irrational anger.

CHAPTER VII.

HELEN had her explanation scene with Robert also, as he had foreseen; but it was conducted in a spirit totally diverse from the unsatisfactory and intemperate conversation he had held with Aleck.

She had had many misgivings since that memorable Sabbath night, she frankly avowed; misgivings excited by Lily's agitation and singular language.

"I have doubted whether, after all, we had not acted unwisely in entering into this engagement, Robert; whether you may not have mistaken your feelings for me," she said, raising a clear, searching eye to his.—"If this is so—if this marriage will bring sorrow to Lily and yourself, I entreat you to tell me the truth now, while there is still room for retreat. You shall never be blamed,—your character suffer no tarnish from the annulment of our contract. If you love her,—if you would address her, were you not bound by your promise to me,—trust me with your secret, and all shall be as you wish. I have feared, among other things, that you and I were not so well adapted to one another as you suppose."

"I am not worthy of you, Helen, yet I love you, you alone! The day in which you forbid me to hope for a return of that love, and the gift of your hand, will be to me the darkest of my life. I regard Lily as I would your younger sister, if you had one, and I honestly believe that her affection for me is of a like nature. She is addicted to the use of extravagant expressions, as you know, and has as little command of her feelings as the merest child. I am her elder brother, her counsellor and friend. She would shrink at the mention of any nearer relation. So much to exculpate her! As to yourself,—"

He stopped, and a sad, wistful gaze attested the change that had come over his fervent spirit.

Helen sustained the scrutiny without faltering or blushing.

"What of me?" she asked.

"Will you imitate my candor? Is your love for me the same, in quality and degree, that it was when you first pledged yourself to become my wife? I, too, have had my fears; fancies of your growing coldness; imaginations that my society was becoming irksome to you. Helen! my only love! my almost bride! if you knew the anguish such thoughts bring to a heart that is bound up in you; that cannot live, except in the sunshine of your smile and presence, you would not chide me for being jealous sometimes."

"Jealous!" Helen's head was uplifted in regal pride. "Of whom have you the shadow of a right to be jealous? What room has my conduct afforded for the birth of such a passion on your part?"

"None! I own with shame that my uneasiness had no foundation of that kind. Yet I find myself eying with jealous apprehension every man that approaches you, my own brother not excepted. Do not despise me, Helen!"

She withdrew from the arm he would have cast about her; her face was averted; her breath came thick and fast. Supposing that he had offended her, Robert implored her forgiveness; declared the complete restoration of his confidence; engaged that it should never again be interrupted.

"Only do not take your love from me!"

"My love!" she repeated, in a strange, far-off tone, as

if communing with some phantom of the past; "you do not know for how poor a gift you sue!"

He eagerly asseverated that it was to him the highest of earthly prizes; that it alone could content a heart that had never for a moment turned to any other than herself.

"I have tried you sadly of late, dearest; have not seemed like myself to you, or to any one else," he continued, penitently. "But I have been on the rack many, many times. I blush to confess it! I do not deserve your esteem or affection."

"There!" With a bright smile she put her hand before his lips. "We will have no more self-criminations; no more cross-examinations of one another! no more unavailing sighs over the never-to-be-recalled past! When I plighted my faith to you, we said, solemnly—'until Death shall part us!' I have meant from that hour to this to keep the vow, and I must believe you when you assert that you have never desired to violate it. A vow is a fearful thing!" She turned paler and shuddered slightly. "An awful thing! and ours was not a light one, or lightly spoken. Mine shall stand until you say to me, of your own accord, 'I wish to be free!' or, as we said that day, the day of our betrothal—'until Death itself part us!'"

Ere the last word quite left her tongue, the shaded lamp upon the table behind them burst with a report that sounded terrifically loud in the quiet room, and the inflammable fluid that fed the wick flew in lurid jets over the floor, the furniture, their clothing, over every thing within a radius of eight or ten feet. The explosion, and the scream Helen could not repress, alarmed the whole household—were distinctly heard at the negroes' dwellings in the yard. In half a minute the apartment was filled with a frightened, questioning throng. The fire had caught Helen's dress in several places, which were extinguished by Robert before the flame could spread; the surface of the mahogany stand was blistered by the blazing stream; and there were scattered, here and there, scorched and smoking patches upon the carpet and wall-paper.

When Helen recalled her senses with sufficient clearness to take note of surrounding objects, several servants were upon their knees, picking up bits of broken glass; Mrs. Floyd was sobbing hysterically upon the sofa; Lily standing by, laughing violently; and the colonel was cuffing Gabriel to and fro like a rubber ball, for his carelessness in having left the top of the lamp unscrewed when he filled it; "else, how could the fire have touched the camphene?"

"'Deed, marster, and I screwed it on tight as tight could be, sur, 'fore ever I lighted it, and sot it on de table thar', keerful!" blubbered the boy.

"No amount of care can prevent accidents of this nature, colonel!" ventured Robert, in respectful corroboration of Gabriel's self-vindication. "Camphene is a dangerous invention, neither a decent servant nor a merciful master.

"Not another drop shall ever be burned in this house while I am alive! I'm determined on that!" sobbed Mrs. Floyd. "It is hateful stuff, and I've always said so, for all it gives a good light!"

"You will burn it until doomsday, madam, if you live so long!" was the civil response of her husband; and giving Gabriel a parting kick, responded to by a dismal howl, he recommended all present to go about their business, and himself set the example.

Helen acceded to her aunt's proposition that they should adjourn to the parlor--the accident had occurred in the dining-room—but stepped back after she had reached the hall, to look for a handkerchief she had lost. Two negro women were still searching for fragments of glass under the table.

"De wust sign dat could 'a happened!" Helen heard one mutter to the other. "Death and partin', sure!"

"Dat's so!" assented her crony. "And it couldn't mean nobody but one 'o dem—for wasn't dey a-settin' close by it? Ah, well! poor young things! if so be—"

The other touched her to be silent, perceiving the young lady's presence, and Helen pretended not to have listened to their prognostications. Nevertheless, her nerves were sadly discomposed, and although devoid of superstitious dreads, she could not help thinking of the odd coincidence between the servant's prophecy and her own words, interrupted in their utterance by the startling incident. So hard was it to shake the impression from her mind, that she related the circumstance to Robert, when he was about leaving her that night.

His spirits had arisen rapidly since the conversation in the former part of the evening; he had never been more tender in manner, more hopeful in picturing their future, and his answer to her story was a hearty laugh.

"You regard this shabby trick of that detestable camphene as an omen, do you? 'Death and parting, sure,' as Nancy says?—Breaking glass signifies fractured vows—and what is the significance of the fiery baptism, of which you had the largest share?"

"A blazing temper, perhaps!" said Helen, saucily. "Take care!"

"Then your uncle is predestined to enact a volcano, and not you! What has gone wrong with him lately? He has not spoken a pleasant word in my hearing for a month and more."

Helen shook her head. "He is angry with you—more incensed at me, because we will not be puppets in his hands. We shall soon be independent of his humors, so we will not be miserable about them now."

"Why do you sigh? Is the anticipation of liberty so dreadful? For myself, I have not been so buoyant and light-hearted in weeks and weeks—if I ever was before. I had hoped that you felt the same."

"I am happier! There is always a sure peace in the consciousness of having done right."

Whence, then, the large slow drops that followed one another down her cheeks, when she went back to the parlor, after bidding him "good-by?" The rest of the family had retired long before, and she sat down on the rug and looked at the two chairs standing so close together in front of the fire. Whence came the sense of desolation that crept over her, in the recollection that her fate was now doubly sealed? that no mortal power could prevent the consummation of the engagement she had that evening ratified? Had she secretly expected—guiltily hoped for—a different sequel to the momentous interview?

"I have done my duty—kept my word to myself and to him. I only told the truth when I reiterated the assurance of my attachment. I love him as much, and in the same way, that I did when we were first betrothed. I have counted the cost, and I will abide by my decision. After a while I shall conquer this foolish weakness. Then we shall be happy together—quite happy!"

And at this comforting assurance she lapsed into an agony of weeping.

Aleck was reading in his chamber when he heard his brother gallop into the yard on his return from Colonel Floyd's, and a minute afterwards his running step upon the stair, and a knock at the door.

"Come in!" he said, surprised at the unseasonable visit.

Robert entered, blithe and glowing, after his swift ride in the cold.

"Al! old boy!" he began, without preliminary, walking

straight up to his brother, his hand outstretched, "I have made all right with her, have told her that I have acted like a brute and a villain, and she, like an angel--by-the-way, she doesn't fall far short of one!—and now I've come to beg your pardon for my shameful treatment of your friendly advice—to ask that we may stand once again upon our old footing. Quarrelling is a new and unpleasant business to us, my dear fellow!"

"It is!" Aleck wrung the proffered hand. "I thought you would understand me better when you came to think over the matter. You can never know how dear your happiness is to me, Robin, or the pain this estrangement has cost me."

They sat down, side by side, and talked freely and affectionately—one of them happily, until the clock struck three.

"Never mind the march of Father Time!" said Robert, as the other exclaimed at the lateness of the hour. "The faster he gallops, the better pleased am I! We shall not have many more such seasons of dissipation either. The habits of a staid Benedict and householder, such as I hope soon to be, must be, perforce, diametrically opposed to irregular hours, and I fancy that your Gretchen will knit her pretty brows at these propensities in her husband. Ah! Aleck! you have not acted quite fairly with me in that affair. Here I have turned out the lining of my heart to you, and you have been keeping your most precious secret locked away from my brotherly eyes."

"I do not understand!" answered Aleck, inquiringly.

"You hypocritical rascal!" Robert collared him, and searched his face with his mirthful eyes. "Do you persist in your deceit? Is Aunt Ruth the only worthy depositary for your confidences? Do you dare to deny that you are every whit as deeply in love as I am? still to keep up the flimsy pretence that the improvements going forward, with such un-German velocity, at Maple Hill, are designed for your personal delectation and our good aunt's comfort, you dutiful dog?"

"Soho!" Light beamed over Aleck's puzzled visage. "I begin to comprehend! And you were blessed with a perusal of the private and confidential missive directed to Aunt Ruth, and crammed with eulogies upon the little German beauty? *You* were so verdant as to swallow the hoax I intended as a reward for her monthly epistles upon the dangers to which a marriageable young man is exposed when he has no aunt near to guard him from temptation, and the passing importance of making a judicious choice of a 'pardner,' as she pronounces it? Gretchen, forsooth! The jade never cared three straws for me, nor I one for her!"

"I am glad, and sorry too!" replied Robert. "Pleased that I am not to have a foreign sister-in-law; very sorry that the high place in your heart is yet vacant. My happiness makes me sympathize the more keenly in your poverty in this regard. You could love warmly and truly, Aleck; and if you had that *summum bonum* of earthly blessings, Aunt Ruth's well-chosen 'pardner,' would prove yourself a capital husband."

"Thank you! If I ever summon courage to try the experiment, I will apply to you for a certificate to that effect," Aleck promised, with a laugh, as they separated with another warm clasp of the hand.

He was off to Maple Hill the next morning; spent every day and nearly every night there, until Christmas.

Thorough as was the revolution in the appointments of the long-disused mansion, it scarcely exceeded that going on at Greenfield, or the tumult which prevailed at Belleview. Seamstresses plied hot needles; hot ovens disgorged loads of cake and every imaginable species of delicious home-made confectionery; the din of scrubbing, polishing, and hammer-

16

ing, was lively and incessant; fires burned in every chimney all day, and piled the hearth-stones over night with huge beds of live embers; and two teams of stout oxen found abundant occupation in hauling wood to feed the throats of the voracious smoking monsters. Mrs. Floyd was too busy to heed her husband's "tempers," and nothing can be cited that would prove more strongly her absorption in the great work she had in hand.

Christmas eve came. The sun set gloriously behind the dark, interminable line of forest bounding the view in all directions, and the stars glittered dazzlingly as they were kindled in the clear, frosty sky. Every thing gave promise of a fair day for the approaching festival. In Helen's chamber was collected a bevy of chattering girls, the bridesmaids, busy in the discussion of the important duties before them. Of course, all talked at once, and each strove to drown her neighbor's voice, yet Virginia Shore contrived to make herself heard above the clamor.

"Isn't it a shame?" she called in her highest key. "Helen declares that she is in sober earnest in refusing to be married in that elegant set of pearls Mr. Aleck Lay brought her from Europe! I tell her she had better try at the outset to gain the blind side of her husband's relatives, and that his brother will have a right to feel offended at the manifest slight put upon his gift, which, every one can see, was meant for a bridal toilet."

The cabal agreed that the neglect would be an insult and unpardonable, even were the jewels as tasteless and unbecoming as they were handsome and suited to the owner and the occasion.

"But what ornaments will you wear, Helen?" questioned one.

Virginia interposed her ready tongue. "That is the most nonsensical part of the story! Nothing but a pitiful little tea-rose in her hair, and another in her bosom, and just because Mr. Robert Lay gave her the bush, and this is the first time it has blossomed! Isn't that *too* love-sick?"

Helen remained unmoved by the ridicule and arguments of her finery-loving train.

"My mind is made up!" she said, pleasantly, but decidedly, to their varied and repeated attacks.

"She might have had orange-blossoms from Lily's greenhouse, if she wished," pursued Virginia. "I see that you have a tree loaded with them, Lily. It was very generous and considerate in it to come out in full dress just now, and in you to keep every flower and bud for the benefit of your friends."

"Not one of them shall be gathered by you, or any one else, for to-morrow's frolic!" returned the proprietress of the flowers, curtly.

Virginia stared in blank astonishment.

"Why, Lily! that is downright stinginess, and not what we should have expected from you! We girls expected a sprig apiece for our bouquets, and the bride's should be composed almost entirely of them. What is a wedding without orange-blossoms?"

"You will shortly have an opportunity of seeing, unless you furnish yourselves from some other quarter. Not one of mine shall you have."

Apparently, the diminutive beauty was what would have been termed, in a larger and homelier woman, "desperately out of humor."

"One would think that this tree was a present from *your* true-love—you value its productions so highly!" observed another "friend."

Lily bit her lip, and her blue eyes emitted sparkles of angry light. Only Helen, of all the girls, knew that Robert was the donor of nearly every rare plant in her collection;

that the orange-tree was one of his contributions, she having raised it from a graft set expressly for her by his hand, three years before, in a fine bush that graced the Greenfield conservatory; and Helen did not know how sedulously she had tended it to its present flourishing estate; the kisses she had showered upon its glossy leaves; the tears that had lately gemmed its snow-white petals—but the random hit was stinging.

"Lily is quite right, allow me to say, young ladies!" said the bride, coming to the help of her discomfited rival. "The tree is too beautiful as it now is, to be spoiled by your destructive fingers. The green-house will be lighted to-morrow evening, and the orange be the queen of the floral belles."

"I comprehend! 'Touch not a single bough!'" said Virginia, dramatically. "But I want to ask, my dear Mrs. Lay—Mercy, Helen! don't murder me with your eyes, and upon my word of honor as a lady, I won't give you the title again until the minister grants me leave!" cried the giddy creature, crouching behind the chair of her nearest neighbor, in affected terror.

"What were you about to inquire?" said Helen, recovering herself.

"Only whether you expected Mr. Lay over to-night; whether he is so selfish and lover-like as to deprive us of your society on this, the last evening of your freedom?"

"He will not be here, I think. Do you want me, Sally?"

"No, ma'am,—but your uncle told me to say as how he would like to speak to you a minute in the office."

Sally had never said "master" to or of Colonel Floyd, when she could avoid it, since the shooting adventure in the melon-patch. She did not belong to him, she used to boast, and would not compliment him by the respectful title.

To the office Helen bent her way, leaving her fair attendants to talk over and wonder at her marvellous serenity; as Virginia Shore had it, "her cool style of taking what threw most girls into fits. Surely no other woman ever looked and acted as she does, upon the eve of her marriage-day!"

Helen crossed the dining-room, with its long table set for supper; went along the passage beyond, to the scene of the moonlight talk with Robert, on the evening of Aleck's return. Upon the threshold of this apartment, the wave of renovation that had swept through the rest of the mansion had been stayed. There was more lumber stored there, and it was overspread by a thicker coat of dust, and fringed more heavily with cobwebs, than at Helen's former visit, and the dark, airless smell of the place seemed heightened instead of dissipated by the fire feebly burning upon the hearth. To this uninviting retreat had Colonel Floyd retired with his tormentors—the accounts of his ward's estate, or papers purporting to be such. They were scattered upon a dingy table, from which hung tattered strips of baize that had been green, and whereupon stood also a couple of candles and an inkstand. He was bowed over a great book, yellow and ink-spotted, at his ward's entrance, pen in hand, his countenance grave to dolefulness.

Helen stopped in front of him, keeping the desk between them.

"You sent for me, I believe, sir?"

"I did! Sit down!"

"Thank you! I prefer to stand, unless our conference is to be a lengthy one."

"It need not be. I assuredly have no wish to prolong it. I have prepared and collected a few papers which it is necessary for you to sign, in order that I may proceed in the work of legal surrender of the charge placed in my hands by your father—the care and management of your estate. There is one!"

He pushed towards her a sheet of large dimensions, covered with figures.

"I will take a seat, since this is to be inspected," said Helen, coolly, drawing up a chair with a broken back—the most secure one that offered itself among the unfortunate collection—and dusting it with her handkerchief.

The colonel's brows met ominously.

"You are not required to undertake that task. Mr. Lay has examined it, and is satisfied that it is correct."

"I do not see how that can be. This, as I learn from its caption, professes to be a report of my expenditures since I attained the age of fifteen—bills for clothing, board, pocket-money furnished, etc.,—matters of which Mr. Lay is profoundly ignorant. I am the fittest person to judge of the accuracy of your statements."

Unheeding the muttered curse at her "perversity" and "unbearable insolence," she reviewed the long columns of numerals; dwelt thoughtfully upon particular items, and raised her eyebrows meaningly at the sum total.

"I shall not affix my signature to this, sir!" she said, letting the sheet fall as she finished its study. "I too have a statement to make, which it is proper you should hear. My uncle, William Gardner, was joint guardian with you until his death, which occurred at the date when this account begins. Until then your reports were subject to his examination. When you assumed the entire charge of my property, I opened a private expense-book. He advised me to the measure, upon his death. I have kept it with scrupulous exactness, in anticipation—let me say—of the final settlement upon which we are now engaged. I can prove by it that the sums disbursed by you for my expenses do not exceed *one-half* of the amount you have here set down. I have taken pains to omit nothing in my account. Every school-bill was copied with punctilious care before I passed it to you; every sixpennyworth of ribbon was registered so soon as it was procured. I cannot truthfully certify, as you wish me to do, that I have received, either in ready money or its equivalent, all you declare has been spent by and for me. There is a mistake somewhere, and a great one!"

"Girl' do you know that you are accusing me of swindling?"

"I have used no such word. I have said that there is an error in your computation. We will therefore lay this paper aside for further consideration. Did I understand you to say that there are others to be inspected?"

"Will you have the goodness to 'inspect,' since you are so fond of using the word, *that*—and let me have your ladyship's judgment of it?"

He flung an envelope over to her so rudely, that it wizzed past her cheek and fell to the floor. Nowise disconcerted by his violent tone and action, she stooped to pick it up.

"This is directed to Lily—not to me!" she said, reading the address upon the back.

"I am aware of that. You will find, notwithstanding, that it concerns Miss Helen Gardner very nearly. You recognize the handwriting, I presume?"

"I think that I do."

"It bears a very tolerable resemblance to Mr. Robert Lay's, does it not?"

"It does!" Helen laid the letter down with an air of unconcern.

"It *was* written by him, and intercepted by myself—"

"In that case I shall take the liberty of restoring it to the rightful owner," interrupted she, stretching her hand towards the letter. He secured it before she could touch it.

"You had best not be over-hasty, young lady! You may reverse your decision when you learn the contents of this epistle," tapping the cover meaningly. "This, which came into my possession this very afternoon, confirms what I have long suspected—the fact of Robert Lay's infidelity to my wealthy ward, and real love for her poorer but more beautiful cousin. He tells Lily, here, that his heart has failed him at the eleventh hour; that he cannot and will not, unless driven to it by her cruelty, carry out the projected union with yourself, and proposes an elopement upon his wedding-day. What say you to this pretty arrangement? It offers quite a refreshing variety to the ordinary hackneyed style of entering the hymeneal state, does it not?"

If demon ever wore a more fiendish smile than the sneer that curled his lip and looked evilly from his eye at that moment, it must have been the prince of devils himself.

Helen's features hardened into stone beneath it.

"I have nothing to say to such a tale, sir, except to insist, still, that the letter shall be delivered to the person for whom it was intended!"

"You do not care to read it yourself?"

"Certainly I do not! The act would be dishonorable."

"You may perhaps not object to glance at the signature? It is boldly and well written!"

Before she could draw back, or divine his intention, he thrust the open page abruply under her eyes.

"*Forever your own Robert,*" she could not help reading, in the round comely characters that were traced upon many a note to herself.

"You refuse to take it still! Your principles of honor are invulnerable, your curiosity stagnant?" mocked her companion, as she arose in offended dignity.

"I have seen no reason why I should change my mind," she replied.

"Be it as you will! I shall not transmit this letter to the lady-love No. 2 of this fickle swain—shall uphold Mammon's cause against Cupid's," continued Colonel Floyd, replacing the epistle within the envelope, then putting it, with ostentatious care, between the leaves of his pocket-book. "It is my duty to protect your reputation and your cousin's so long as you are inmates of my house, reckoned by the public as members of my family. Disgrace is a word unknown in the Floyd annals. Mr. Lay's disappointment at not finding his bonny Lily at the place of rendezvous (not a euphonious name for a romance—Rock's Tavern!), his chagrin at her non-compliance with his petition, may produce a reaction in your favor; so, do not despair of seeing him in his appointed position to-morrow evening."

"If he comes I shall marry him, without demanding a word of explanation!" said the low, determined tones he had been used to hear from her, in her obstinate moods, since the days of her wilful childhood.

"Very well! What woman ever let 'a good chance' slip through her fingers? I will oppose no obstacle to your manifest destiny, which is to show yourself to be as grand a fool as he is a knave!" rejoined her guardian, contemptuously. "The remainder of my business may with propriety be delayed until the knot is tied. 'There's many a slip 'twixt the cup and the lip!' I am to meet the amorous bridegroom at the clerk's office at eleven o'clock to-morrow, when he applies for his marriage license. It will then be seen which of my wards he has finally decided to promote to the dignity of favorite in his harem. Fascinating creature! what a pity he was not born in Turkey!"

Nothing but Helen's indomitable pride enabled her to carry an unblenching front up to the last word spoken in this unlooked-for trial, this unprecedented emergency. Pride was her master-spirit. It had impelled her to the destruction of her earthly happiness as a blind for a slighted, broken heart; had bound her fast to the fulfilment of a rash and sinful vow; it came to her aid now; strengthened her to cast back disdainfully this crowning insult.

"If, as I suppose, this is the climax of your choice observations, sir, I will, with your permission, retire!"

She swept him a lofty courtesy in return for his mocking obeisance, and walked erect and haughtily from the room. Once out of his abhorred presence, she quickened her stately gait to a rapid flight; traversed hall and porch, avoiding lighted apartments; gained the little conservatory in the rear of the parlor, shut the door behind her, and sank upon a bench against the wall, panting and exhausted.

"Am I going mad? What am I to think? What can I do? GOD help me in this fearful strait!"

The glimmer of the stars through the glass roof met her agonized upward glance, as the unwonted petition broke from her;—the holy watchers, beyond whose shining bands, HE dwelt whom she blindly invoked.

"Of purer eyes than to behold evil!"

The text came unsought to her mind, and the swift inference followed—"Then HE has neither notice nor compassion for me!"

They still beamed mildly, benignantly, upon her—the eternal sentinels of Heaven! and she could not withdraw her answering regards. Beneath their pure rays, as under the distilment of refreshing dews, feelings trampled, soiled, and crushed by the fierce rush of earth-born passions, began to revive and lift themselves anew. She had sowed the wind;—the whirlwind of humiliation and despair was the legitimate harvest; but her proud spirit prayed in its writhings that she might be spared the direful punishment. Slowly sinking to her knees, she cried out of the depths to the All-merciful; with tears and sighs besought Divine succor and support amid the snares that encompassed her.

"Lead me into a plain path!—however hard and thorny it may be, I will tread it without a murmur! Strengthen me to tell *him* the truth, and then do with me as Thou wilt. Keep far from me all bitter or revengeful thoughts of him—for, oh! am I not the more guilty of the two? Did not my sin of unfaithfulness and deceit precede his?"

She still knelt—still looked upward, in inaudible supplication, accompanied by fast-flowing tears, when the lock of the door, which she thought she had made fast at her entrance, was drawn back, and a figure glided in. The faint starlight revealed enough of the small figure and waxen face to show who was the intruder, if her cousin had not recognized her by the noiseless grace of her movements. Supposing that she had come on some errand that would not detain her more than a minute, Helen crouched lower to avoid being seen, and waited, with hushed breath, for her departure. Every fibre of her frame thrilled to the low cry of agony that stirred the silence of the place. Lily was standing by the orange-tree, which loomed up a pyramid of dusky white in the darkness; bent over and caressed it as if it were a sentient thing, while sobs, mingled with incoherent lamentations, attested the depths and reality of her sorrow.

Helen never afterwards inhaled the scent of orange-blossoms without a return of the heart-sickness, the deathly faintness of spirit, that came over her in that season of painful irresolution. Lily's heart was breaking,—and *she* stood between her and happiness,—she, with her empty vows and failing resolution! and did not Robert approach the altar with a divided, if not a recreant heart?

"Oh, Helen! if you could only know!" said Lily, with a fresh paroxysm of tears.

In the woman's grief there was still a touch of the child's

fretfulness and impatience at being thwarted. Helen seldom denied her any gratification which it was in her power to afford, and this moan appealed to the sympathies of the listener with peculiar and pathetic force. She was the elder of the two—the stronger and wiser;—her own folly and perverseness had brought her trouble upon her; but what had this poor girl done that her life should be blighted?

"She *does* know, my darling!"

Helen put her arm around her neck; would have drawn her to her bosom; spoken words of pity and of promise; but at her voice and touch Lily sprang back with a stifled shriek; in her mad alarm, struck at the speaker with all her strength, and sped away like a frightened hare at the sound of the hunter's horn.

The assault took Helen so entirely by surprise that she staggered against the orange-tree and fell to the floor with it. When she regained her feet, she was alone in the darkness. She would not, she could not follow Lily then! Hers was a generous and not implacable disposition, but it was not in it to recover immediately from the indignation awakened by this unfeminine and uncousinly treatment. She had bruised her shoulder against the flower-stand, and her bosom ached intensely from the effects of Lily's blow. She had not meant to hurt her, Helen knew—perhaps had not recognized the person who accosted her so unexpectedly—but her hand had fallen sharply.

"To morrow!" Helen promised herself.—"By that time she may be ready to listen and I to speak calmly. A night of sober thought will be beneficial to both of us."

Merriment and gamesome entertainment ran high in the parlor that evening, for the bridesmaids were not without their attendant train of admirers. Yule-log and Christmas jokes and wassail-cup were not wanting to enliven the youthful band, who watched for the first hour of the Advent-day;

and no smile was brighter, no voice more ready in laughter and song, no step more elastic in the dance than were Lily Calvert's. Etiquette and inclination for once united in advising that Helen should not appear below, and she had no fear of loneliness. She would be better satisfied if they would leave her to herself.

Lily would have been as extravagantly gay, had her cousin been present in the hilarious gathering, for the blood that never tinged the alabaster skin yet seethed hotly in her veins; rushed, a tumultuous tide, to and from the heart. Says Charlotte Bronte of a certain crisis in her heroine's life—

"It found her despairing—it left her desperate—two evidently different stages of feeling."

The second, and more trying of these, Lily was now learning.

And thus passed the eve of the wedding-day.

CHAPTER VIII.

MISS RUTH had slept but indifferently well the night before Christmas. Her maidenly dreams were vexed by images of bridal veils; jellies that poured from the moulds in splashing, insipid liquids, when she would have had them pellucid, flavorous, and firm; torn kid gloves, that could not be mended; burnt and curdled custards; cakes with sticky icing and streaky interiors; pie-crust heavy with rancid butter, or tough as leather for want of the forgotten "shortening;" nuptial benedictions; showers of tears; hail-storms of kisses, congratulatory and confectionery; jumbled into a confusing, distracting medley, that allowed her tortured brain not one hour of natural sleep out of the six she spent in bed.

"Upon my word," said the good soul, when a ray of red light from the coming sun flecked the gray East, and apprised her that the world would soon be awake—"upon my word, I don't believe I could have rested worse if I were expecting to be married myself to-day—and that is saying a good deal!"

By sunrise she was dressed and had mustered her troop of menials. The happy pair were to come home for the second day's feast, the splendor of which was to suffer no diminution by contrast with Mrs. Floyd's wedding-supper. The same company would be present, and comparisons were inevitable. The dear woman was brave and confident in view of all this. She had not kept the cleanest house in three counties, and the best table in six, for twenty years, to be appalled by the array of any odds of this kind that could be brought against her—no! no! not by the Floyds themselves, whose profuse hospitality was proverbial. So, buckling on her armor, in the shape of an immense check apron, two breadths wide in the skirt, reaching to the bottom of her dress, and with a broad bib attached, which was pinned up to her double chin, she walked, with her prim but brisk little pace, to her cake-room.

Cake, cake everywhere, and not a faulty crumb in the collection! Snowballs whose hearts were yellow sponge, and their surfaces white satin; loaves of "pound," smooth, fluted, and beflowered, conical and hexagon, all rich enough to guarantee, on their own responsibility, a fit of dyspepsia to each rash taster among the expected guests; silver cake that, when cut and heaped in alternate slices with the gold, should present a pleasing sight to the eye and agreeable associations to the mind of the beholder; piles of slender "ladies' fingers" and macaroons, cocoa-nut and almond, light as a feather and sweet as sugar; two immense structures, precisely similar in size and shape, inwardly a toothsome but perilously indigestible conglomeration of currants, raisins, citron, and spices, held together in a not very strong union by a cement of eggs, sugar, and flour, made brittle with butter,—externally, twin mountains of snow, wreathed with garlands of the same material as the icing; and upon the summit of each a pink Cupid—the festoon of roses, his insufficient tunic, offering a self-evident apology for the exaggerated flesh-color of his cuticle, when the thermometer stood, as it did this morning, at the freezing-point. He trode with one foot upon a pair of hearts, also in sugar, spitted together by a red dart, and his bow was drawn at a venture.

Before these her *chefs-d'œuvre*, being the bride and bridegroom's cakes, and destined to adorn the head and foot of her dessert-table, Miss Ruth paused in full satisfaction, folded her hands upon the check apron, and set her head on one side. A minute elapsed before she spoke or moved; then she inclined her head towards the other shoulder, gently rubbed her fat palms together, and sighed, in sublime content—

"YES!"

A shout of laughter from the open door behind her answered. Her nephews, both early abroad on this morning, had encountered each other in the passage leading past the apartment devoted, for the time, to the genius who presides over "good things," and stopped simultaneously to inspect the array, and the chief-priestess of the temple.

"Yes!" repeated Aunt Ruth, in an altered tone, a blush creeping up to her cap-border.

The "particle," as first enunciated, denoted the height of mortal complacency: now it signified—"I know you wicked boys are making fun of me, but I don't care! I am strong in the consciousness of merit."

They came in—Robert foremost—still laughing.

"Aunty? do you mean that Mrs. Lay, who-is-to-be, is to live by cake alone throughout the honeymoon? That would be rather too impressive an illustration of the saying, 'Sweets to the sweet!' Hey, Aleck?"

Aleck smiled, but somewhat constrainedly.

"I believe that caged humming-birds are usually fed upon honey-paste, as the diet best suited to their constitutions and tastes, while in a state of bondage. Aunt Ruth, you have excelled yourself! I can say nothing more complimentary!"

"Wait until you see the jellies, blanc-manges, charlottes, and ice-creams!" replied the housewife, in pardonable vanity. "Or, rather, until you *taste* them! My good things are not show-pieces, fancy articles, to please the eye only, as you'll find out, Robert, when you eat your second day's dinner and supper."

"I do not feel, just now, as if I should ever care to eat another mouthful," said the groom expectant, with a slight grimace. "I was scared with visions last night; tormented by all sorts of hobgoblins, and am appetiteless this morning."

"Yes!" retorted Aunt Ruth, slyly.

"I suppose that it is a common symptom in the circumstances!" answered Robert, coloring a little, "but I had not expected to feel exactly as I do on this, my wedding-day."

"The smell of the cake is sickening to an empty stomach!" said Aleck, retreating towards the door. "I don't see how you can endure it, Aunt Ruth."

Robert overtook him upon the piazza.

"You look pale, Al!" he remarked, linking his arm in his brother's, and falling into step with him, in his hurried walk up and down the long porch. "I wish that I could attribute my uncomfortable sensations to bodily ailment! It may sound ungallant, unloverlike, and pusillanimous, but I must confess that I could, without great repugnance, cast my vote for a postponement of the 'happy occasion,' ardently as I have desired its coming, from the earliest hour of my engagement. I wish it were all over! I grow positively nervous and tremulous in the anticipation."

His laugh did indeed shake, and his complexion, usually clear and sanguine, took a cadaverous tinge.

Aleck gnawed his moustache—a fierce, restless movement he strove to conceal by passing his hand over his mouth.

"I suppose," he said, presently, "that, as Aunt Ruth intimated, this species of stage-fright frequently seizes upon men in your position, and that persons of your temperament are peculiarly liable to fall victims to it."

The latter clause was added involuntarily, as it were, and

Robert flushed up at the latent touch of meaning in the accent.

"It is sheer nervousness—nothing else!" he returned, eagerly—"induced, I verily believe, by the ugly dreams that beset my pillow all night. One vision haunts me wherever I look. I thought that I sat by Helen, holding her hand, and talking earnestly and happily of the life upon which we were about entering, when, all at once, she started up and confronted me, and I saw, instead of her features —ugh! I will not tell you of the horrid sight! Yet I dreamed this three times, and awoke half dead with fright."

"You had the night-mare. The sights and smells of hot sweets that have hung about the premises lately have been enough to give any one dyspeptic visitings. Do not dwell upon such fancies! You are but deepening impressions unsuited to your real feelings and the actual event before you. What a splendid day!"

"Is it not?" With his accustomed elasticity of mood Robert welcomed the change of theme. "Happy the bride that the sun shines on! May this bright Christmas morning be an augury of good to her! I shall try to make her happy! If zealous endeavor and ardent desire of mine can do this, she will never have cause for sorrow. Yet I have not been without my doubts on this head."

Aleck made no reply, and they took several turns in their promenade before the other resumed:

"She is a singular girl—a woman of marked character, and I have often feared, recently, that we did not quite understand one another; asked myself if we ever would attain to that perfection of mutual confidence that constitutes so large a proportion of the happiness of the true marriage. There seems to be a background of motive and feeling to which I am denied admittance. Yet I do love her! I have loved her from the time when we were happy children together —we three, and—Lily Calvert!"

There was a slight hesitancy in his pronunciation of the last name, and Aleck's eyes fell quickly—burningly—upon the speaker's countenance.

"Is she the cause of the misunderstanding you deplore?" he asked, sternly.

"Partly—and yet, no! You wrong poor Lily, Aleck, and I fear that Helen does also. I know the child better than either of you can do. There are many allowances to be made for her."

"You make many, I see! But we will not revive that subject on this day, of all others. A year hence these trivial differences of opinion and feeling between us will be forgotten, will have died a natural death and be buried without parade. And sooner still will fade into empty air the imaginary want of confidence and congeniality between your wife and yourself."

"You are the prince of prophets—the king of seers! Away with bugbears and dreams! Vive l'amour!" called out Robert, swinging his hat around his head, while the early sunshine wove of his fair hair a glittering crown.

Aleck looked at him with a loving, aching heart.

"You are a handsome fellow, Robert; I do not wonder all the girls fall in love with you!"

"Nonsense! You are the right sort of man to play the deuce with the softer sex! tall, dark-haired, dark-eyed, and 'bearded like the pard'—'grand, gloomy, and peculiar,' as that rattle, Virginia Shore, called you in my hearing one day. I have said to Helen several times that it was strange she had not taken you instead of me. You would have made a splendid couple!"

"Don't, Robert! it is both wrong and foolish to run on in that strain," said Aleck, in grave, sad rebuke. "I cannot understand how you bring yourself to jest upon such a theme—how you endure the imagination of resigning her you love to another."

"Because it is an imagination, and nothing else! What a glorious day! Did you ever breathe such invigorating air before—ever see such sunlight? Every beam is clarified to diamond purity and lustre. 'Happy the bride that the sun shines on,' I say again! What is the corresponding adage? There is one, isn't there?"

"'Blessed the corpse that the rains fall upon,' I believe," responded his brother. "It runs somewhat after that fashion."

"For pity's sake, man, keep your death's-heads out of sight when you can!" Robert exclaimed, half-angrily. "I had a surfeit of them last night. What have they to do with daylight and bridals, I should like to know? But isn't that Gabriel trotting down the road? I hope nothing has gone wrong at Belleview."

They walked out to the gate to meet the Cimmerian Mercury. His grin and bow in nearing them, his saucily-deferential "Christmas gift, my marsters!" dispelled whatever anxiety either might have experienced as to any outward calamity in his master's household.

"All well, Mars' Robert," he replied to the inquiry after the health of the family. "I've brung a note for you, sur."

Aleck turned to go back to the house as this was presented, but, against his will, his falcon eye saw the address before he wheeled—so carelessly was the transfer from one hand to the other performed. The billet was directed to "Mr. Robert C. Lay, Greenfield. *In haste*," and the chirography resembled Lily's, he thought. It was assuredly not Helen's. He had paced the porch for perhaps fifteen minutes when Robert joined him. Aleck had seen him scribble something with a pencil upon a scrap of paper, using the gate-post for a desk; fold it, and give it to the messenger; Gabriel, meanwhile, sitting still upon his horse and eying the operation, from under the brim of his old felt hat, with intense interest. When he had deposited the reply in the crown of the said head-covering, he set off on a gallop in the direction of home. Then the bridegroom came slowly up the walk, wearing a very unbridegroomlike aspect, re-reading the gilt-edged sheet. He thrust it into his vest-pocket as he reached the steps; mounted them, and continued the exercise the boy had interrupted. He volunteered no explanation of what Aleck had seen and overheard, although he looked worried and perplexed, and sighed repeatedly, in deep thought or sadness.

Finally, when the breakfast-bell ended their matutinal stroll, and disturbed his revery, he said, with an appearance of frankness, laying his hand upon his brother's shoulder,—

"I am ready to acknowledge that you know my weak points better than I do myself, Al! I wish I were more like you in certain respects."

"You have chosen a sorry examplar!" replied the other. "Act out what conscience and honor dictate, Robin, and you cannot go wrong."

"Is the voice of feeling then to be wholly disregarded?" asked Robert, looking down.

"If it militates against the other and surer monitors—yes—a thousand times, yes!" said Aleck, emphatically.

And, "Ah! brother mine! we are made of different stuff! where you would be adamant, I am very soft wax—a fickle, cowardly dog!" ended the dialogue, for Aunt Ruth, to whom every minute of daylight was now precious, appeared in the house door to expedite their progress to the dining-room.

Robert had, as he had said, little or no appetite for food, but he either was, or feigned to be, in finer spirits than he had been able to summon, an hour previous. He rallied Miss Ruth upon her household arrangements; prophesying all manner of failures in the delicate and critical manufactures that yet remained to be perfected; teased her about an antiquated bachelor planter, a former beau of hers, who had, he affirmed, been fitted by a Baltimore tailor with a bran-new suit of clothes, to be sported that night, in the hope of tempting her to a reconsideration of the discard she had given him twenty-five years ago; condoled with his brother, because of the probable state of utter isolation that menaced him in his sojourn at Maple Hill, in view of his housekeeper's defection and desertion; inquired gravely from whose establishment the marriage would take place, and warmly advocated the claims of Greenfield to that honor; in fine, conducted himself in such a wild, inconvenient manner, that his aunt was heartily rejoiced when he obeyed her commands and quitted the table.

Aleck met him soon afterwards on the stairs, equipped for a ride.

"You allow yourself ample time for your jaunt!" observed the elder brother, taking out his watch. "I meant to ride with you so far as our way remained the same, but I have not ordered my horse yet."

"You are very kind, and I should like to have your company, but I am in a hurry," said Robert, pulling on a tight new buckskin glove, and studiously avoiding Aleck's eye.

"It is but half-past nine, and I understood you to say that you were to meet Colonel Floyd at the clerk's office by eleven."

"Oh! for that matter, twelve would do as well as eleven, if the colonel is faithful to his practice of unpunctuality," replied Robert, with an indifferent effort to speak gayly. "But the truth is, that I have another engagement at ten—one that I ought not to put off. I dare say you might not deem it obligatory upon yourself to keep it, you are such a stone pillar in firmness and fixity, when you will it to be so. I ought not to say more to you about this, much as I would like to make a clean breast to my father-confessor. I believe you never unwarily get yourself into a scrape. I do! and I am afraid I have done it now. Don't look as if you thought me the worst fellow living, please! Be as charitable to me as you can, old boy! If the right time ever comes while you and I are in the flesh, I may explain matters more to your satisfaction than now seems credible to you. Good-by!"

Could the loving kinsman ever judge harshly of him, while the image of that face, with its sweet smile and ingenuous eyes, remained stamped upon the mind's retina?—so long as the pleading tones, gentle and fond, yet not free from mournfulness, continued to sound in his ears? Adamantine pillar though his brother regarded him, Aleck would, if questioned thus at that moment, have replied indignantly in the negative.

"Robert!" called Miss Ruth, hearing the ring of his iron heel upon the frozen walk outside of the window of the pantry, where she was up to her ears—figuratively speaking—in calves'-foot jelly.

She threw up the sash, and he leaned upon the sill.

"Where are you going?" inquired the aunt, without suspending her occupation of whipping into aggravated pallor and foam the whites of a dozen eggs she had just broken into a dish upon the table.

"To the Court House."

"To get your license?"

"Even so. You are a very Yankee at guessing."

"You have put it off long enough."

"Maybe I feared that we might change our minds at the last moment. 'There's many a slip'—you recollect!"

"Yes!" intensely ironical.

"You need not speak as if that were impossible in this case! There is nothing certain in this world."

"Except death," said Aunt Ruth, solemnly oracular—feeling herself in duty bound not to omit an opportunity for dropping in a seed of exhortation.

"And taxes," added Robert. "But I shall not believe that I am really going to commit matrimony, until I find myself face to face with the parson. Aunty, you are looking divinely, to-day! Have you no bowels of mercy, that you can coolly contemplate the certainty of driving old Gales to desperation by the spectacle of your unapproachable charms?"

"Yes!" sneered Miss Massie, in lofty incredulity; but the wintry bloom deepened in her plump cheeks, and the egg-whisk flew like lightning through the stiffening froth.

"I never was more in earnest in my life!" pursued the nephew. "Look at me, as at an imperfect illustration of what his deplorable condition will be. Don't you see that I cannot tear myself from the survey of so much loveliness?"

Miss Ruth set down the dish, and picked up a switch from a bundle that lay near, to furnish rods for beating trifles and creams. Robert dodged the blow—not a heavy one, it must be owned.

"Cruel creature! is this the treatment which all your admirers are to receive?" he complained, at a safe distance. "Alas for Gales's new broadcloth!"

"When are you coming home?" inquired his aunt, dignifiedly. She would have no more of this foolery. "Mind—we must have an early dinner—at two o'clock, anyhow! There's a world of work to be done yet, and I can't be bothered with waiting for you boys. Aleck is always up to time, and if you *are* in love, I want you to remember old habits for this once."

"I cannot promise! My present expectation is to get back in decent season for the ceremony to-night. If any thing should happen to detain me beyond the hour, you and old Gales must be spliced in our stead—*pro bono publico*—which means for the satisfaction of your neighbors. It would never do to cheat the company out of the show they have assembled to behold. They might search far and near, without finding a more seraphic bride than you will make. Only—you ought to wear that bib-apron and enchanting cap, and go bare-armed, as you are now."

A pelting rain of empty eggshells upon his head and shoulders admonished him to retreat, which he did, reeling with laughter, and glancing over his shoulder at Aleck, who had remained upon the end of the piazza—a spectator of the spirited scene. How handsome and light-hearted he looked! Cravens and traitors never wore such innocent and joyous mien!

"He may be misguided by judgment, unduly swayed by his pliable temper and tenderness of heart, but he can never be guilty of actual and deliberate wrong!" was Aleck's conclusion.

"That boy will plague the life out of me yet!" said Miss Ruth, in a tone intended to counterfeit peevishness. "I don't know what has got into him this morning. It's a bad sign for a bird to sing before breakfast. The cat will catch him before night, and Robert has begun the day in too great a glee. I just hope he mayn't change his tune before sundown—that's all!"

"It is not likely that he will!" returned Aleck, soberly. "Gayety is natural to him, and if ever man had an excuse for exuberance of spirit, he has. I am going over to Maple Hill presently, aunt. Can I do any thing for you there, or on the way?"

"No, dear!" She petted her favorite "boy" more than ever now-a-days, from some indefinable maternal instinct that told her he stood in need of love and sympathy. "But I would like to have you come home by two o'clock, if you can, conveniently."

Her manner of suggesting the wish was very unlike the imperious style in which she had laid down the law to Robert.

"Do not wait for me! If I dine here I shall return by that hour."

"You ought not to go at all, I think. You are looking badly. Come back early and take a nap this afternoon. This evening's work will be no trifle to you, seeing you are first groomsman and Robert's brother."

"You are very thoughtful, but I hope that I have strength to do and bear all that lies before me," responded Aleck, walking away.

He nor she dreamed what unforeseen exigencies the evening would bring.

CHAPTER IX.

It was not often that Aleck Lay's eyes played him false; yet, notwithstanding their evidence in this case, Gabriel was Helen's messenger. She had arisen early on her wedding-morn—before the herald ray that ended Aunt Ruth's uneasy slumbers pierced the darkness of the night—and committed to paper the substance of a confession composed during the many sleepless hours she had consumed in prayer and thought. She no longer withheld from her intended husband the secret of her prior attachment, while she sedulously concealed the name of the one she had loved, and all circumstances that might assist in leading Robert to a correct surmise as to his identity with his brother. She had suffered an early disappointment, she said; one that had, she was sometimes led to fear, deprived her of the power of ever loving again with equal fervor. While smarting under this blow, she had precipitately and wickedly received his attentions, and entered into the engagement of marriage now existing between them.

"I beg that you will acquit me of having, in this transaction—culpable as it was—been guilty of wilful wrong to you," she wrote, in continuation. "I was persuaded, when I promised you my hand, as I am now, that I could give you all the heart I have left to bestow upon any man. I love you sincerely, appreciatively, as a friend who is nearer to me even than a brother could be. I can pledge you my faith without a sigh for a happier lot; can take honestly upon me the vows of wedded fidelity. It will cost me no struggle to love, honor, and obey one whom I know to be, in all respects, worthy of my affection and duty.

"Yet before we set the indissoluble seal to a contract that death only can render void, it is best, for both our sakes, that the work of self-examination should be severe and thorough, and its result undisguised from each other. I have unveiled my past history—the saddest chapter of my life—to you, and I have surely a right to expect, if not to demand, a corresponding degree of candor in you. Robert! I charge you by every principle of truth, honor, and manliness, to answer me plainly one question—*Do you love Lily Calvert?* I do not inquire if your conduct to her has been, in every respect, consistent with your engagements to myself; if you have ever given her cause to believe that your attachment for her transcended that which her old playfellow and friend might innocently indulge and manifest. I look deeper; appeal solemnly to the innermost depths of your own consciousness—depths unknown save to yourself and your God. Marriage is a momentous step. I have felt this within the past twelve hours as I never thought to do. I beseech you to give the subject your most earnest consideration. If, as I apprehend, from my knowledge of facts connected with your intercourse with Lily, and my acquaintance with both your characters, you decide that your sentiments for her are more like those a husband should have for his wife than the love you bear me,—your way and mine are plain. Do not act unfairly to yourself and to me—cruelly to her, from the consideration that you have gone too far to retrace your course with honor. I have excellent reasons for believing that Colonel Floyd is already cognizant of your affection for his niece, and that your union with her would be far more acceptable to him than the one you at present contemplate.

"This is my proposition, if the result of your deliberation should be what I expect. Write me a line by the bearer of this, advising me of your purpose: then ride over to see Lily, this morning. Ask boldly for her, and if you gain her consent to the course we have concluded to adopt, afterwards keep your appointment with Colonel Floyd, and have the license filled up with your name and hers. I know what I say, when I assert that there is no likelihood of your meeting impediments in your path.—Even if you should, it is the right one—the only plan you can with rectitude pursue. This done, commit the rest to me. You have often praised my daring and self-possession, and I engage to afford you, in this instance, a notable display of both qualities. Instead of frowns you shall meet nothing but smiles from the witnesses of your marriage ceremony; congratulations upon the cleverness of the *ruse* that has deluded the community into the belief that you were betrothed to one cousin, while you were really, with her knowledge and approbation, plighted to the other. I am aware that this looks like a bold scheme, and that my programme of arrangements is unprecedented in the chronicles of courtship; but, Robert, dear friend! we have had enough of half-confidences and harrowing misunderstandings. Let us, at the very base of the altar, throw off the mask of unworthy deception, that must work out a weary weight of misery to us in the end, and appear in our real characters—dare to tell the truth, and the whole truth! I plead for Lily's sake no less than for ours.

"But if, after all, my misgivings have been groundless, my penetration at fault with respect to your feelings in this affair; if you are still prepared to attest your love for me by marrying me, I stand ready and willing to fulfil my part of our agreement. A line or word sent by Gabriel to the effect that 'all is right' will suffice to convey your intention to me. Since I have confided to no one the step I have resolved to take in the writing of this note, there need be no inconvenient explanations. Matters can go on in their present train, and I shall expect you at the appointed hour. I leave the decision with you. It will be fraught with important consequences to us, and I pray—if indeed my unworthy petitions ever reach Heaven—that you may be guided aright. Whatever your determination may be, believe that I must ever remain

"Yours affectionately and truly,

"HELEN."

If this novel epistle strike somewhat too boldly at the root of established prejudices and precedent in love and match-making, the shocked reader will please bear in mind that the writer was, as her betrothed had affirmed, "a singular girl—a woman of marked character." This was further demonstrated by the exclamation with which she arose from her writing-table, when the departing footsteps of her post-boy had died away in the corridor.

"Now, whatever comes, I can respect myself once more!"

She had borrowed Gabriel privately from her aunt—an accommodation arranged between them the preceding evening—and to insure secrecy on the subject of his errand, rather than to enjoin him to the needful exercise of faithfulness and despatch, she had him summoned to her chamber and herself gave him his orders. The imp was agog with anticipations of "Christmas times," including the wedding, and Helen contributed further to his exhilaration by a bountiful douceur in honor of the day he was prepared to celebrate. But he hearkened with a tolerable semblance of decorous seriousness to her instructions, received the packet, and buttoned it with exceeding care inside of his roundabout, and pledged himself to inviolable discretion. He was very fond of Helen, whose steady favor and kindness were in grateful contrast to Mrs. Floyd's fidgetiness, her lord's harshness, and Lily's caprices. His young mistress did not doubt that she could rely upon him in a matter requiring so much zeal and intelligence.

She enacted her part well at breakfast-time; was not only collected and cheerful in deportment, but vivacious in talk, with sprightliness more real in appearance than was Lily's factitious animation. The latter came down late, as she generally did, and, Helen fancied, avoided her cousin markedly and coldly.

"By and by," was the elder's consolation, "I may be permitted to tell her all, and she will do my affection justice. Until then, the less we say to one another the better. I will not rush into temptation, and I must await *his* warrant for speech."

Altogether, it was a merry party, with the exception of Colonel Floyd, whose settled moroseness did not affect them long, since he ate little, and withdrew from the table before any one else was half through the meal. The bride's room was the popular resort of the young ladies during the day, and Helen could not, without positive rudeness, seclude herself for thought or preparation. The gentlemen wisely dispersed to parts unknown directly after breakfast, most of them not showing themselves again until evening.

Helen was affecting to attend to and bear a part in the frivolous chit-chat rung into her nervous ears by the knot of idle pleasure-lovers about her, when Sally opened the door just wide enough to allow her mistress a glimpse of her face, and made her signal, unobserved by the others. Helen felt the blood curdle suddenly about her heart, and numbness seize upon her limbs, at the apparition for which she had watched so long. The sign notified her of Gabriel's return. With an unintelligible murmur, intended as an apology to her associates for leaving them, she walked totteringly into the entry, where she found her messenger. It did not occur to her then that he looked or acted unlike himself, although his cowed, sulky behavior produced an unfavorable impression upon Sally, who was interrogating him with considerable asperity as to the causes of his dilatoriness.

"You stopped to play 'long the road, I'll be bound!" she was saying when Helen emerged from her chamber, "or, you went out of your way to go by the Court House. That's always the way with you good-for-nothing chaps. So sure as you get a cent to spend, you're crazy till it's gone."

"That will do, Sally!" interposed Helen, faintly. "Did you deliver that letter safely, Gabriel?"

"Yes, ma'am!" dropping his head, with a hang-dog expression, altogether unlike his accustomed pertness.

"And you have an answer for me?"

"No, ma'am. He say dere was none, and tole me jes' fur to tell you dat all was right," answered the page, mustering his briskness, but forlornly enough.

"You are sure? Have you made no mistake? Had you that message from Mr. Lay himself?" pressed Helen, in the earnestness of the dying hope whose existence she had not confessed to herself until this instant.

Annoyed or nerved to boldness by the implied doubt of the accuracy of his report, Gabriel looked up straight at her—an exhibition of courage or forwardness bordering upon effrontery.

"I done tell you de 'xact truth, Miss Helen! He say as how you'd onderstand it, and I must be pertickler to 'peat it jes' as he said it, and I s'posed *you* would be satisfied ef he was!"

"You disrespectful little vilyan?" exclaimed Sally, lending him a cuff upon the ear. "Do you know who you're talkin' to?"

"You lemme 'lone, now! you'd better!" growled the unlucky urchin, doubling up his fists. "I won't be blaggarded by women, and black ones, at dat, nohow!"

"Shame!" Helen's native dignity was aroused at the disgraceful altercation. "You both forget where you are! I am ashamed of you! Gabriel! go down-stairs directly. Sally, I forbid you to speak to him again this day!"

Gabriel was too glad to slink away, wiping his eyes and nose upon his jacket-sleeve; but Sally stopped her mistress, who would have passed her by in offended silence.

"If you please, Miss Helen, I'm very sorry I've displeased you 'pon your weddin'-day, but I mistrusted that boy had been up to some mischief, and maybe lost your letter or the answer—he looked so kind o' guilty, and I spoke sharp to him before I remembered myself—"

"Never mind, my good girl!" Helen interrupted the excuse, that was fast becoming a tearful one. "I know you meant it for the best. We are all apt to act hastily and foolishly sometimes, and, as you have said, it is my wedding-day, and I ought to overlook trifles."

Her smile was positively ghastly as she repeated, musingly —"Yes! it is my wedding-day! There is no doubt of it now—none! none!"

She walked slowly away to the other extremity of the hall; halted by a window, and seemed to look out.

"It is a beautiful day!" she said at length, less dreamily. "I think, Sally, that I should enjoy one more good, long, lonely walk in the woods. Will you bring me my hood and cloak? and take care that nobody sees you! I do not feel like having company."

She succeeded in escaping from the house and yard without being challenged, and took the beaten path to the spring. At the rocky seat beside it she paused a long while, remembering what was buried beneath the rugged tomb, and the binding words—more binding now than ever—so soon to be irrevocable—that had been spoken above it—"Until Death parts us!" Then, stooping and pressing her hand, as in caressing farewell, upon the rough, gray surface, she said firmly—"Let the dead Past bury its dead!" and ascended the wooded eminence beyond.

She stopped again when she reached the great oak where she and Robert had held their "business talk" on that moonlight November night. The first shadow of estrangement had fallen upon them then and there. It was all her fault that the cloud arose—since, while she was striving to act up to the strict requirements of the duty she owed him, her heart was in wild, almost unconquerable revolt.

"No wonder that he was chilled and repelled! no wonder that I have absolutely driven him from me scores of times since then; forced him to seek consolation in another's sympathy, if not happiness in another's love! But we understand each other now—quite well! With our eyes open to the truth, each knowing the other's peculiar temptation, we are ready to unite hands and lives, 'for better, for worse.' Heaven helping me, I shall try to please him in all things; to make him content, that he may not repent his choice!"

How vividly every incident of that evening stroll was stamped upon her memory! Even Sally's sleepy approach, and the reason she had given her mistress, subsequently, for her interruption of the lover's conversation, were not forgotten. The fugitive Lem had never been recovered, but the dread of runaways, so common among the women and childre of the slaveholding States—the bugaboos of nursery ar reside tales—had never had a hold upon Helen's mind. she most feared just now was the society of her fellows; what she sought, in her feverish restlessness of body and spirit, was solitude for reflection—and to gain it she plunged more deeply into the trackless forest. The ravines, whose moss-grown depths and sides, thickly fringed with brushwood, afforded cool and tempting retreats in the summer's heat, offered, at this season, warmer nooks than were to be found upon higher ground. At the distance of nearly half a mile from the spring, Helen espied a resting-place that suited her fancy and purpose. Letting herself down a steep bank, overhung by dwarf cedars, she gained a white stone deeply imbedded in moss and fallen leaves—and, although but a few feet above the frozen rivulet that had worn the chasm to its great depth, forming a dry and comfortable seat. It had been one of her girlhood's tricks to seek out such nooks and take possession of them while she read, studied, or dreamed, as her mood disposed her to do.

She was not studying or dreaming now, she would have said, yet she had matter for thought that kept her there a long while—how long, she never exactly knew. She sat motionless as the stone itself, leaning listlessly against the stout cedar clump that kept off the wind, if there were any stirring. There were not many, and they were exceedingly trivial occurrences, to diversify the monotonous passage of the hours or minutes, whichever they were. A torpor of misery had complete mastery over her; and, with a dull consciousness that after this woesome day it would be crime to yield to its desolate entrancement, she was passive, and let the gloomy spell work unchecked. The penitence and higher resolve of the preceding night were recalled in stupid marvel how she happened to feel thus—what power supported her then, and bore her thoughts and aspirations into a purer, nobler sphere. She could not pray or determine now. She had expended her energy in penning that useless, maybe worse than useless letter, which Robert had not deemed worthy of a line of reply. The die was cast by another's hand, and she must abide by the throw. Ah, well! what was easier, in the abstract, than to do nothing? How arduous she found the practice of quiescence, concerned nobody except herself.

A few winter birds hopped from bough to bough of the cedars, in quest of the blueberries that grew thereupon. She smiled vacantly in perceiving that they were not scared at seeing her. Perhaps their bright eyes were too intent upon their search for food to observe the presence of the intruder, for her green cloak and hood offered no striking contrast to the dark verdure of the evergreens. Once she heard a gun—not very far away it seemed in the still, clear day—but the report did not startle her—only as it served to awaken more poignant reminiscences than those upon which she was meditating when the sharp echo rolled through the leafless woods, was caught and repeated by the ravines, and died away sullenly among the distant hills. Did Aleck ever think of her last hunt? of the watch she had kept beside him in the Greenfield woodlands? Was the scar yet upon his shoulder? What a cruel wound it was! how fast the blood trickled through her fingers as she renewed the compress Robert had applied, when it became deranged by the incautious movement of the injured lad! Had he forgotten all these things? Did he hate and despise her when he looked at the mark left by the shot?

She wished, at times, that he did hate her, and that she knew, for certain, that he felt this aversion. Any active sentiment would be preferable to his unvarying coldness, his studied civility, his constrained address.

"How little I imagined in the dear old times—"

She did not finish the sentence, but a single tear forced its way from under the lid and dropped upon her hand. She shed but that one.

Again, a crow sailed slowly between her and the sun, and the shadow crossing the gully, made her look up. He uttered a hoarse croak, just as the shade of his black pinions fell upon her brow.

"A bird of ill-omen!" she thought, languidly. "Portents cannot terrify me now! I am like the man upon the wheel, to whom has been mercifully dealt the *coup de grace* as the first blow!"

Awhile later, she did not trouble herself to think or care how long afterwards, there arrived another interruption to the sluggish current of ideas. This was the tramp of a horse's hoofs, breaking the dry sticks, and rustling the dead leaves that strewed the ground under the trees.

"It will be time enough to move, or take flight, when I am seen," was her reflection; and her indolence or listlessness prompted her to the wisest plan for avoiding discovery.

The rider was forcing his way through the undergrowth, there being not even a bridle-path in that part of the forest. It could not be the hunter, whose gun she had heard, for the Belleview lands were posted, and no sportsman in the neighborhood was so reckless or intrepid as to trespass upon a domain guarded by the law and a master like the proprietor of this plantation. It must be Colonel Floyd himself or his colored overseer, or, possibly, some other negro belonging to the estate, taking a near cut to the house from the main road. Yet this would be an unusual procedure. In spiritless curiosity, she leaned slightly to one side, where a gap in the bushes promised a sight of the equestrian. It was but a glimpse, and an imperfect one, which she obtained, the head and neck of the horse and the upper part of the rider's body only being visible above the high bank. The animal stepped proudly, and manifested some symptoms of restiveness, curvetting in such a style as to elicit a sharp reprimand from the man who bestrode him.

"Go on, you fool!" he said, angrily.

It seemed that a prick of the spur or a cut from a whip followed, for the mettled creature gave a forward spring and a neigh of pain or viciousness. The human brute was Booker, Colonel Floyd's confidential agent. He was looking right ahead, and was, moreover, too busy with his ill-mannered steed to notice her. She was glad of this, for his intolerable surveillance, and reports based upon it, were not confined to the cases of his fellow-servants, as Mrs. Floyd, his nominal mistress, had occasionally learned to her sorrow, after having covertly transgressed some of the by-laws her lord had seen fit, in his sovereign pleasure, to enact for the government of the household. Helen disliked the man with a heartiness she took no pains to dissemble, and, crafty as he was, he had contrived to express to her, at seasonable opportunities, his reciprocation of the antipathy. It was very fortunate that he had not descried her, hiding like a lost or fugitive thing in that out-of-the-way spot, where no other lady of the family or region would ever think of coming. Her guardian would otherwise have been supplied with a subject for sneering ridicule which he would have improved to the utmost advantage, and whenever she least desired its introduction. She waited, therefore, where she was, until there was no longer any danger of encountering the spy in his forest-beat, or of falling in with one she cared still less to face, Colonel Floyd. Like hunter and hound, they were seldom far apart in their business rounds, by day or by night.

Stiff and chill, from having sat for such a length of time upon the ground, she arose with difficulty, climbed the precipitous side of the ravine; listened for a moment, to make sure that the way was clear, and set out for home. When free of the woods, she was surprised to see that the sun had passed the meridian. Mrs. Floyd, like Miss Ruth, had ordered an early dinner, and Helen was not so careless of what gossiping tongues might say, as wilfully to provoke the hubbub of inquiries and teasing observations to which she would be subjected, should she be missing from the table and the house when the rest were summoned to that repast.

She found Gabriel at the spring, leisurely filling a pail with a gourd.

"Is dinner nearly ready?" she asked.

He jumped up, letting go the gourd, and it splashed back into the spring.

"Oh, is dat you, Miss Helen? How you skeered me!"

She repeated her question.

"No, ma'am, not as I knows on; leastways, marster ain't come home, nohow!"

He raised the pail to his head in a mighty hurry, and began his journey up the acclivity towards the house.

"Has anybody called to see me since I went out?" Helen quickened her pace to overtake him.

"No, ma'am," walking yet faster.

"And no letter or message sent that you have heard of?"

"None as I've heerd on, ma'am!" puffing onwards, the water dashing in great streams from the brimming vessel, down upon his shoulders and sooty physiognomy.

"There is no need of such haste, Gabriel!" said Helen, smiling, in spite of her heavy heart, at this ostentatious celerity in one who had the reputation of being the laziest fellow on the place. "I may not have another opportunity of speaking with you alone."

Gabriel was almost running now, but she kept up with him.

"I want to tell you how sorry poor Sally is for her unkindness to you this morning, and how much I blame her for it. She is disposed to be hasty, but she is a good-hearted girl, and likes you. I do not want you to bear a grudge against her or me when we are gone. You have done me many friendly turns, for which I shall always be thankful, and if at any time I can be of service to you, you must not be afraid to apply to me. Oh! Gabriel! stop! I am out of breath!"

Thus adjured, the hurrying Aquarius stood still in his tracks; but, instead of facing her in respectful attention, he made a feint at digging out his eyes with his wet knuckles, and burst out crying.

"Why, my boy! what ails you?" inquired the young lady, in amazement. "Are you sorry that I am going away?"

"No-o-o, ma-a-a-m!"

"Indeed! I had hoped that you were!" returned Helen, laughingly. "What, then, is the matter?"

"I don't mean I ain't sorry! Boo-hoo!"

Rivulets of salt water mixed themselves with the fresh upon his shining cheeks.

"You scoundrel! what are you fooling there about?" roared a voice from the houseyard, now only some twenty feet distant.

"My gracious! if thar ain't marster!" exclaimed the frightened boy, and he resumed his labored flight along the path, breathless under his burden, and palpitating with fear.

He was not disappointed in the reception he met. Colonel Floyd waited for him at the gate; bestowed a curse and several blows of his riding-whip upon him as he passed through; then glowered at his wife's niece, as if anathematizing the accident of sex that prevented him from saluting her in like manner.

"So, my young lady, this is the company you select upon your wedding-day!" he snarled. "I hope his conversation has edified you!"

Without deigning a reply, she trod past him with her queen-like, elastic step; not hurriedly, but as if she had not seen or heard him.

"You still expect your gallant to-night, do you?" he followed her to say.

"Are you speaking to me, or to Gabriel, Colonel Floyd?" she interrogated, casting a side ray of supreme disdain at him.

His complexion had a purplish flush; his eyes a wild, unsettled glare; his articulation was thick and tremulous.

"He has been drinking!" thought his ward, in disgust. "I may steel myself for any amount of insult."

"I am talking to you! You are hoping to welcome your devoted in season for the ceremony, are you?"

"If you mean Mr. Lay, I expect him, certainly!" walking on.

"He was in no haste to procure his license," her tormentor continued, still at her heels. "I waited for him a good hour and a half."

"You will oblige me, Colonel Floyd, by never opening your lips to me again with respect to the matter officiously brought forward by you last night!" returned Helen, confronting him courageously, and speaking with authority. "I wish you to understand distinctly, now and forever, that there is a complete understanding between Mr. Lay and myself, upon this and every other subject. Your interference is impertinent and unwelcome. I trust that I have made my meaning sufficiently intelligible. Mr. Lay is competent to the management of his own affairs and mine also."

She went into the house, without staying to witness the effect of her declaration of independence.

Virginia Shore assailed her in the lower hall.

"Helen Gardner! you strange, mysterious, provoking girl! where in the name of common sense, and every thing else that is reasonable, have you been traipsing to? Here is the day two-thirds gone, and not an individual thing done. And don't you think? something or somebody upset Lily's elegant orange-tree last night, and snapped ever so many of the finest branches; so we girls have been busy gathering the flowers from them, and putting them in water; and isn't it a mercy they were so little withered, and are reviving beautifully; and we find there are enough to distribute among all seven bouquets, unless you are bent upon having yours composed altogether of orange-blossoms, which isn't in the least necessary, it seems to me, for there are white rosebuds, and candy-tuft, and feather-few, and a lovely camelia, if you must have all white flowers, as I suppose you will, and geraniums and arbor-vitæ for greens; then, too, I am certain that Mr. Lay will send your bouquet from Greenfield; he hinted something of the kind to me,—and, would you believe it? there's Lily gone to bed with a bad sick headache—she always picks the most inconvenient season to have them! and won't let a soul of us come near her room, and Mrs. Floyd is afraid she won't be able to be down to-night; says she has fever and all that; and in that case, what will you do for a first bridesmaid? Dear me! what unlucky things do happen at weddings sometimes!"

This breathless string of talk was rattled out while pursuing Helen up-stairs to the chamber of the latter, where Miss Shore threw herself into a chair and declared that she was "fagged out—half-dead, in fact!"

"I am sorry to hear that Lily is sick!" was Helen's reply, while Sally divested her of her cloak and walking-shoes. "She appeared quite well at breakfast-time, I thought. I am afraid that she has over-exerted herself."

"Between you and me, she has fretted herself sick—if she *is* sick—about the accident in the green-house—if it *was* an accident!" said Virginia, knowingly. "You never saw such a look as went over her face when she heard of it. I found it out just after you took such very cool French leave of us. I was hunting high and low for you, and peeped into the green-house, among other places, and there lay the stand, pot and all, upon the floor! So I tore off up-stairs to tell the news. I really thought that Lily was going to strike me, at first! She grew paler than a corpse, and her eyes blazed like lightning, I can tell you! She caught her breath, like one strangling, when I tried to pacify her by saying that no doubt the mischief was done unintentionally, in the dark, by a dog, or one of the servants.

"'No!' she said, in a sort of choked whisper; 'I know all about it! It was not an accident! I will be revenged for that piece of spite, if I die for it!'

"'Why, Lily,' I said, 'how unkind and unreasonable!' But she would not listen—only took herself off to her room and bed, and there she has been ever since! Who would believe that she could be so peppery a little vixen when she is once aroused?"

Helen thought sadly and deeply for several moments upon what she had heard. In the pressure of anxieties personally so much more momentous, the damage done her cousin's pet shrub had entirely escaped her mind, until it was recalled by Virginia's narrative. If Lily were indeed so distressed at the disaster as her volatile friend represented, she might be conciliated by a truthful statement of the manner in which the misadventure occurred, and Helen's regret at having been innocently the cause of it. As a preliminary step, she despatched Sally to Lily's room to inquire how her headache was, and request the privilege of an audience for her mistress.

The tiring-woman returned in high dudgeon.

"The door is locked on the inside, Miss Helen, and when

I knocked, that impudent Sylvy opened it a little ways, and peeped through the crack, and had the assurance to tell me that Miss Lily had just fallen asleep, and mustn't be waked on no account. Then she shut too the door again, and I heard her with my own blessed ears speak to Miss Lily kinder easy-like, and Miss Lily answer her. Asleep—ha? Humph!"

"There! that will do!" Helen arrested her indignant volubility, and congratulated herself that Virginia had flitted off to some other part of the house before this item could be added to her budget of scandal.

She did not censure Lily for averting an éclaircissement that would be productive of embarrassment to them both; and, moreover, it would be of no avail now. Her destiny, and, so far as a strange fatality had intertwined Lily's with it, hers, also, were no longer in her hands. Robert's laconic, but significant message, and his non-appearance, had settled that matter.

The afternoon wore away all too rapidly to the idle, taciturn bride, as to the fussy, excited bridesmaids, and another starlight evening, as cloudless and colder than yesterday's, came on. The marriage service was to be recited at eight o'clock, which, in the accommodating phraseology and according to the pliant customs of that region, meant any time from half-past eight to ten. The more unpunctual a bridal procession contrived to be, the more aristocratic were the performances esteemed. Nevertheless, at six o'clock Helen cleared her apartment of the chattering, officious sisterhood, who clamored for the honor of assisting at her toilette, rejecting their overtures kindly, yet peremptorily; fastened the door upon the last of the reluctant exiles, who was, of course, Virginia Shore, and sat herself down before the mirror to have her hair dressed by Sally's skilful fingers. The maid's manipulations upon the luxuriant locks were conducted silently. If her heart had not been too full for useless speech, a glance at the grave, settled features, so young in outline and color, so old in expression, which were reflected in the glass, would have sealed her mouth. She comprehended, in some dim and imperfect fashion, that her mistress did not go to her bridal as most other women she had seen arrayed for their nuptials had done; that there was no tremulous joy, no excess of happiness, in the suppressed sighs that, ever and anon, heaved her breast; no delicious dreaming in the thoughtful eyes, that seemed to study the untried Future.

The glossy hair was wound smoothly around the classic head, braided and looped at the back, and Sally was obliged to speak.

"You will not have the flowers put in just yet, will you, Miss Helen? They will droop and wither before you are ready to go down."

Helen aroused herself and glanced at the white buds with their graceful group of leaves, simply beautiful, in spite of Virginia's abuse. They awaited her pleasure in a small vase upon the dressing-table.

"They will! you are right. Perhaps I may not wear them, after all. We will attend to that by and by."

"The young ladies all seemed to admire the pearls most," suggested Sally, timidly. "And don't you think, Miss Helen, that Mars' Aleck—"

Helen raised her hand with a frown. "Not a word more, Sally! When I am at a loss what to do, I shall ask other people's advice, not before."

Further debate was prevented by a knock at the door.

"What do *you* want?" said Sally, snappishly, unlocking it, and, in unthinking imitation of her favorite detestation, Sylvia, opening it far enough to allow the tip of her nose to be seen by the person without.

The reply was in the voice of an under housemaid, whom the brisk Sally was wont to denominate a "stupid, no-account body, who went through the world with her eyes and ears shut."

"Mr. Lay down sta'rs. Want to see Miss Helen, d'rectly, if she can come down. He won't keep her more'n a minute, he say. He in de office."

"The office! what did you show him in there for, you goose? It's dark as pitch, and cold as Christmas, besides being dirty as a pig-sty!"

"Marster made me light a fire dar, to-day, and he's been a-settin' by it, constant, from dinner to supper-time," drawled the woman, "and Mr. Lay, he asked Gabriel to take him somewhar' whar' he could see Miss Helen by sheself. Gabriel he took him in de office, and *sont* me for to let Miss Helen know—"

"Isn't your master in there now?"

"No—he went away somewhar', 'pon horseback—he an' Uncle Booker, nigh 'pon half an hour ago. Dey ain't got home yet."

While this colloquy was going on, Helen had thrown off her white wrapper, and, with the utmost haste her shaking fingers permitted her to use, put on, in its stead, a crimson dressing-gown—part of her bridal outfit—which had been hung over a chair near by.

"Let me pass!" she said, trying to knot the massive cord around her waist as she spoke.

"There's no hurry, dear Miss Helen (you be gone, Judy)! there's not the least hurry in the world, my dear young mistress!" reiterated Sally, soothingly, taking hold of the silken cable, and tying it herself. "Mars' Robert knows you've got to dress, and he's one of the thoughtfullest men that ever was born. It's likely he wants to ask some question about the ring, or the glove, or some sech little thing, and he shows his sense by not trusting his message to any of them harum-scarum young ladies—for, if I may make so free as to speak my mind for once, I never see a wilder set. Here's your handkerchief; and now you are all ready, and pretty as a pictur, and I'll be bound Mars' Robert will tell you so. I shouldn't wonder if he begged you to be married in that dress. I'll go with you to light you through the dark entry."

Encouraged by this homely and cheering strain of reassurance, Helen went quickly down the stairway, and through the dining-room, encountering only servants on the way, to the "dark entry," which was the narrow passage connecting the last-mentioned apartment with the office. The attached maid stood midway between the two rooms, holding her candle above her head, until her mistress, having hesitated for an instant upon the threshold of the farther, to gather breath or resolution, turned the bolt of the door, and disappeared from the loving eyes watching her.

There was a handful of smouldering coals and a smoking log or two in the fireplace. A solitary candle was upon the mantel, but its yellow flame gave light enough to enable Helen to recognize the person who advanced to meet her.

It was not Robert, but Aleck Lay!

CHAPTER X.

"Aleck!"

"Helen!"

In the agitation of the moment they forgot the more formal style of address they had employed towards each other of late. Their hands were joined, too, in a clasp altogether different from the cold, passive touch they were used to exchange at their infrequent meetings. When Helen would have withdrawn hers she found it held fast, nor was it released after Aleck had led her to a chair, and placed himself beside her. Her gaze of wondering confusion was answered by one so intense, so eloquent of love and compassion, that her heart thrilled, while she trembled with apprehension and suspense.

"My poor girl! I am the bearer of sad news to you."

"Does it concern your brother!" There was not a particle of color in her cheek, and her eyes dilated, but she could still articulate the inquiry. "Is he ill? Is he *dead?*"

"Heaven forgive me for saying it! but I could wish that he had died before dishonoring himself so vilely!" exclaimed Aleck, passionately. "Helen! he has perjured himself—brought indelible disgrace upon his own head—upon his family—worst of all—dragged down shame and misery upon *you!*"

"No! no!" The girl's haughty spirit sprang to its arms. "Not shame! no mortal can do that while I retain my self-respect! As to misery—better so—a million times better, than if he had suspended his action for a few days or months! Now—let me hear all!"

"Can you bear it!" he asked, doubtfully, looking in unspoken admiration at the noble face, tintless yet, but pure and serene as a marble image of Peace.

"Yes! unless the reality far exceeds my imagination, and I do not think that it can."

"Robert left home this morning early, shortly after the receipt of a letter which was brought to him by one of Colonel Floyd's servants—"

"Gabriel! Yes, I know!" she assented. "It was from me!"

"Indeed! I thought I recognized your cousin Lily's handwriting in the superscription."

"You were mistaken! I sent it."

Aleck went on.

"He ordered his horse at half-past nine, that he might keep an appointment at ten. I suspected that it was in obedience to a summons from the writer of the letter, both from his behavior, and the circumstance that he had not alluded to the engagement until after Gabriel's arrival. I was confirmed in my surmise by a brief conversation we held just at parting. He confessed that his expedition was not one that I would sanction; said he could not retreat from it with honor; entreated me to be charitable in my judgment of him, and hinted at a satisfactory solution of the mystery at some future day. From that hour to this he has not showed himself at home—but when I reached Greenfield, at five o'clock, having spent the day at Maple Hill, this letter was handed to me by one of my own servants, who had met Robert in the road about the middle of the afternoon."

She took it and attempted to read, but the characters were irregular and the lines blotted. The sheet had apparently been written upon in the utmost haste or agitation, and folded while the ink was yet wet. Aleck brought the candle and held it behind her shoulder while she deciphered it.

"Aleck—old boy! you will never let me call you brother again after you have read this, but it can't be helped! You have done your duty towards me, and the hardest struggle I have had in making up my mind was to conquer my fear of your displeasure. My resolution is taken! It was nailed fast to the mast by the perusal of the enclosed, which you saw delivered to me this morning. The last feather breaks the camel's back, and my feather was not a light one, as you will see. You will agree with me—or ought to—when you have studied this specimen of feminine composition—in the opinion that she who could write thus on the morning of her marriage-day was never designed by the Maker of matches to be my wife—never desired to be! She says, in effect: 'Be free if you long for freedom! Be happy with another if you love her better than you do me—and I am resigned—rather relieved, if the truth must be told!'

"I take her at her word. The direction of my flight I cannot reveal at present, for obvious reasons. There are hot-brained fellows—Harvey Floyd, for example—who would not scruple to chase me down, and pistol me for the slight offered the bride—that-is-not-to-be. I am not certain that you would not undertake the job yourself—you have such Roman notions of honor. I may say to you confidentially, however, that I am not without strong hopes that my journey will not be performed alone; that, at no remote stage of it, I shall be joined by a companion fairer and dearer to me than all the universe beside. I commit to you the awkward task of breaking to Miss Gardner and her family the intelligence of this trifling alteration in the programme of the play for this evening. Perhaps the easiest and safest way for you to accomplish this disagreeable but necessary business will be to forward her letter with this to Colonel Floyd. He is the most proper person to manage the affair. Shun an interview with him if you can. He has a high sense of what is due himself, and all of his blood. I should be sorry to have you embroiled in a quarrel with him on my account.

"The 'daring and self-possession' upon which Miss Gardner plumes herself will have abundant scope for display when the guests are convened to-night. I am not racked by fears lest her heart should sustain any serious fracture. Her pride may bleed a little, but depletion there will do her moral system good. My respects to her, and best wishes for her welfare and happiness. May I trouble you to send to Rock's Tavern for my horse? I shall have him left there until called for. If all goes well, you shall hear from me again before long. Good-by! Love to Aunt Ruth. I hope her cake will not spoil for the want of mouths to eat it, although I suppose the second day's feast must be postponed.

"Believe me, ever (whether you will allow it or no!)

"Your loving brother,

"ROBERT C. LAY."

"Can it be possible!" Helen let fall the letter as though it had defiled her fingers, and sat transfixed; the deep dye of offended delicacy, just anger and astonishment at its contents, and the ungenerous animus of the writer, suffusing neck and temples. "Cruel! unjust! This insult, at least, he might have spared me!"

"You are only too lenient to him," said Aleck, in stern wrath. "Like yourself, I could not have credited the possibility of this baseness without the evidence furnished by that infamous communication. Yet I have seen very much that I considered reprehensible in his intercourse with Lily Calvert; have warned him, once and again, of the evil which might result from the intimacy. He had always a ready excuse or evasion wherewith to ward off my attack—and I believed him! He was wickedly weak—she, subtle—I, blind! This is the end!"

"It is!" Helen arose, erect and calm. "I thank you for the gentleness—the true brotherly kindness with which you have discharged a trust that could not but be abhorrent to you. I am especially grateful that you did not accept the alternative of transferring the unpleasant duty to Colonel Floyd."

"I did not entertain the suggestion for an instant. Here is your letter. You notice that he—Robert, I mean—says that it was sent for my perusal. I need not assure you that I have not read a line of it."

"I wish you had!" she said, impulsively—then, checking herself, a new flood of crimson bathed her face. She had recollected the confession embodied in the earlier portion of it.

"That is"—she resumed, more composedly—"I would like to have you read certain parts. You would then see how faithfully I have striven to be guiltless in this matter; whatever may be my faults, and they are many, I am not habitually insincere. Will you oblige me?"

She proffered the open sheet, designating the top of the second page as the place where he should begin.

"I require no testimony beyond what I already have to convince me that your conduct in this lamentable affair has been irreproachable," replied Aleck, repelling the offer by a gesture.

"But I would have you acquit me intelligently. When

the tale is trumpeted abroad—as it must be"—her lips were whiter in saying this—"as it must be, very soon, it will be a great satisfaction, the best comfort I can have, to know that there is one who, with a full knowledge of the case, from beginning to end, yet pronounces that I have tried, and tried hard, to do my duty; that I would have shielded Robert from reproach at the same time that I secured his happiness by a union with the woman he loved—(for I was sure that he *did* love Lily!)—have spared him the trouble of this flight, and myself the ignominy of being publicly rejected!" She turned her head aside, too proud to let him see how keen was the smart of the last thought, and still extended the letter in mute appeal. Aleck unclosed his lips to speak, then, changing his mind, took the paper with a bow of submission to her requirement.

"Robert! I charge you by every principle of truth, honor, and manliness, to answer me one question!"

This was the heading of the paragraph to which she pointed, and he read the letter through, from that adjuration to the close; with what sensations of pain, love, pity, and marvel, his countenance, varied and marked as were the expressions that succeeded one another upon it, but feebly indicated.

"And this generosity he spurned! this angelic candor, this noble self-renunciation he could despise! could speak slightingly of conduct that should have moved him to worship!" broke forth Aleck, impetuously. "Helen! I cannot ask you to pardon him. The man who could sin thus grossly against the love and forbearance you have exhibited towards him, merits your scorn and the reprobation of the world!"

"Hush! hush! It is not the act, but his manner of freeing himself from the distasteful bonds, that I deplore. As he says, I offered him his freedom, and he took me at my word. Only"—the childlike, troubled look that he had seen before, when she alluded to the public scandal menacing her, came back—"will it be asking too great a favor of yourself and your aunt, if I tell you that it will be an inestimable help to me to have you remain here this evening, and show that *his* friends are still mine? that they, having known me from my childhood, do not cast me off as an unworthy creature, whose heartlessness has forfeited their confidence? For you must recollect that the people who were invited to the—the wedding, will come; that there is not time to send word to a single one of them. The invitations cannot be countermanded, and I *must* see them! the story must be told! He quotes correctly, you observe, when he alludes to my boast of 'daring and self-possession.' Had the event been what I proposed, and for a time expected, I think that he would have found these sufficient for his purpose and mine. As it is, the trial will be far greater!"

She faltered.

"Helen!"

She did not repulse him when he took her hand again. In this dark hour of mortification and perplexity, she had no other adviser; no other friend or comforter; and his tenderness of sympathy was inexpressibly sweet.

"Before I answer your question, let me entreat your indulgence while I unfold *my* plan of action; that which I conceived and matured while coming to you to-night. It is a kindred idea to that which I find sketched in your letter, recommended by you for another's adoption. The coincidence is an encouragement to me to proceed. Will you bear with me if it offends you? You will not shrink from me in horror and loathing?"

"Certainly not!"

She gazed at him in unsuspecting wonderment. The earnestness of his imploring tone; the anxiety with which he hung upon her look and reply, were more of a mystery than his words. Seeing that he hesitated to go on, she added gently, almost affectionately, "Whatever may be my opinion as to the propriety of adopting and acting upon this unknown 'plan,' I should be unjust and unkind were I to resent your goodness in presenting it. I have known you too well and too long to impute to you unworthy motives. You could not propose any thing that would involve the sacrifice of truth or honor, however distasteful its terms might be to me."

"Ah! there is the fear!" He groaned in bowing his head upon his hands.

She laid one of hers on his arm.

"Aleck! will you not be frank with me? Is this a time for mistaken delicacy—false scruples? This should be an honest hour with us both. Will you not tell me what it is that you desire to say? It is your old friend and playfellow, Helen, who asks this of you?"

"I will be a man! will brave every thing!" He started from his dejected attitude. "At the risk of debasing myself in your eyes to the level of a selfish, unfeeling monster, who would take advantage of your distress to win his own ends, I will speak! Helen! I have loved you all my life!—loved you more than I ever have done any thing else on earth! I thought I had made you understand the nature and aim of this affection before I went abroad. Fervent as was my devotion, I had yet the manliness and justice not to bind you by a formal pledge. While absent, I dared to think and dream of you as my own—mine only;—to anticipate a future spent with you as a fair and probable prospect. I returned to find you betrothed to my brother. What I suffered; what I have resigned; what concealed under what must have seemed to you a heartless and repulsive exterior, I have not strength or time to tell you now. I do not offer my love—unabated and unconquerable, after all my battlings with it—as a solace for the pain inflicted by the desertion of your betrothed. But I do tender you my name and my hand as a shield against calumny and insult; ask the privilege of protecting you in this hour of isolation and perplexity. I exact nothing in return save that which you have but this moment informed me is already mine, your friendship and confidence. If you will marry me to-night as my brother's substitute, I pledge you my solemn word that no unreasonable or ungenerous demands on my part shall ever cause you to regret the act."

He delivered this extraordinary proposal in a hard, almost fiercely abrupt fashion; the result of overpowering emotion he tried ineffectually to suppress into the collected, moderate show of earnestness he had resolved on. He did not look at her as he brought the speech to a close. Would she flee his presence as from a moral leper? Would she strike him dead with imperial scorn?

For a whole minute there was a profound stillness throughout the room, except for the quick fluttering pants from the figure at his side. Had his audacity taken from her the power of utterance? Then she spoke—very softly, very musically to his excited senses, that had shrunk in dread of accents so different.

"I thought that you were betrothed to a lady in Germany. They—your aunt and brother—told me so—last summer!"

Aleck made an impatient movement.

"That absurd fiction again! I never loved her—never thought of betrothal to any woman besides yourself; have never breathed a word of affection to any other, at home or abroad. The letter from which my aunt deduced her preposterous conclusion was, as anybody but herself could have seen, a foolish, barefaced hoax, from beginning to end. I have told her this since my return, and undeceived Robert also. Could I be so base as to offer you a hand upon which another had a lien?"

Still he did not look towards her. If he had, he must have been at a loss how to interpret the warmer blush that slowly mantled her cheek; the fervid, yet tender sparkle of the eye.

She reopened the letter to Robert. He heard the rustle, in wondering impatience. What had they to do with that part of the question, now?

"I cannot give you a reply until you have read the first page of this."

She could hardly have enjoined a more irksome task; but he obeyed her behest instantly and without a remonstrance. His mind was not in a condition to be easily receptive of hope, or he might have drawn all the encouragement the most ardent suitor could have desired from the cautiously-worded confession; would not have looked or spoken with such mournful firmness, as he ceased reading.

"I do not love you more hopelessly now than I have done from the moment I heard of your engagement to my brother. You say in this letter that a union with him whom you first loved is forever impossible; that you have only half a heart to bestow upon any man who shall hereafter seek your favor. If I am personally disagreeable to you; if my presence will annoy or displease you, instead of being a comfort, I withdraw my suit. Otherwise—unless, indeed, I can bring about a reunion between yourself and your early love—"

"You do not ask who it was?"

"Nor ever shall! It is your secret—yours alone!"

"But what if I insist upon telling you?"

He gazed upon her now, but in unspeakable amaze. What was the meaning of the playful, yet shy intonation, that impressed even his infidel perceptions; incredulous to whatever seemed to bode happiness and success to himself? Stranger still, she smiled in his bewildered face, a smile radiant as heaven's own light.

"We have both 'played too long with edge tools,' dear Aleck? Suppose we abandon the dangerous trifling, and take to truth-telling for the remainder of our lives! I will set the example, by revealing to you the 'dear, fatal name' of him who long ago gained my whole, undivided heart; whose supposed desertion drove me to the mad, wicked step of engaging myself to another. Shall I?"

"If you will!"

He articulated the monosyllables with difficulty in the tumult that possessed his soul.

"Bow your tall head, then. I cannot say it aloud."

Still mystified, doubting, fearing—any thing but hoping, he bent his head to her lips. They breathed one word in his ear.

Had Colonel Floyd, or his devoted servitor and imitator, Booker, chanced to pass through this retired portion of the grounds just then, upon his nightly patrol, and glanced into the low window, he would have beheld an unexpected and highly interesting scene; one which might possibly have awakened sensations the reverse of delightful in the bosom of the unseen spy.

But it happened instead, that this select and exemplary body of police was, at that important instant, engaged about other business, the nature of which shall be briefly explained in the next chapter.

CHAPTER XI.

SALLY "had the fidgets"—a description of fit that became more violent with every added minute of her mistress's absence. In the adjacent chamber, dedicated to the toilette services of three of the six bridesmaids, she could hear the confused clamor of busy tongues, the patter of slippered feet, and frequent outbursts of such mutual admiration as girls are prone to indulge to their own and one another's delectation, all denoting the forward march of preparations for the great event of the evening. Bells were rung from divers other apartments, upon first, second, and third stories; there was continual rushing up and down stairs, and through entries, of valets, butlers, and ladies' maids, each on the run, and all equally regardless of the danger of collisions; already several carriages had rolled around the drive in front of the mansion, and discharged their freight of unnecessarily punctual revellers, mostly relatives and intimate friends of the family, who liked to preface the public proceedings by a little social talk. Yet she, in whose honor all this commotion was raised, the star actress of the promised performance, without whom the play would, in fact, be a remediless wreck, and a disgrace to all concerned in its announcement and management, was still dallying away the fleeting, priceless moments in love-talk, that could be as well if not better attended to after the ceremony.

"There is a season for every thing!" muttered the tiring-woman, distractedly, shaking out the satin robe and lace veil for the twentieth time. "And this isn't the time for no such boy-and-girl play as they're carrying on!"

Sally was in love herself, and, as a consequence, extremely lenient to the delinquencies of others similarly situated, if said derelictions had Cupid's warrant for their apology; but there was a point beyond which delay became inexcusable negligence, and this she considered, and, it must be owned, with just provocation, that the bride was fast nearing. She went into the hall repeatedly, and listened over the balustrades for the returning feet of her charge—the increasing tumult of arrival and reception below, meanwhile, aggravating her inquietude to the verge of frenzy; once she stole down-stairs, and into the dark passage conducting to the office-door—went near enough to that uninviting room, now consecrated as the chosen retreat of Love, to hear the low murmur of earnest voices; finally, she resolved to sit down in desperate resignation by the fire in the bridal chamber, and "not budge one single inch again until Miss Helen saw fit to show herself—no! not if she had to wait there until midnight!"

Her waiting, albeit it was the reverse of "patient," had its reward shortly after she had taken this sensible resolution. A light footstep her ears were quick to recognize skimmed the floor of the hall, stopped at the door, and the long-looked for personage appeared.

"Sally, my good child! I have kept you waiting a tedious time, I suppose, but there is no haste, none whatever!"

"It's a quarter past seven!" responded Sally, not too amiably.

Generally the most docile and respectful of handmaidens, she yet availed herself occasionally of the privilege, earned, by years of faithful service, to lecture her young mistress.

"I know that, but the—ceremony will not take place for an hour or more."

She had sunk into the chair before the mirror, and spoke breathlessly. This might have been the effect of her haste in climbing the stairs, and her rapid flight through the passages, to avoid being seen abroad at this unseasonable hour; but the sparkling eyes and glowing complexion could hardly have been induced by these influences. Resting her chin in her palm, and her elbow upon the dressing-table, she remained for some minutes, apparently lost in revery, fond, yet agitating. Her lip trembled while it smiled; the fire in the eye shone through a soft haze;—even to Sally's untutored sight, her aspect was refined and elevated by the emotions that rapt her in silent happiness. Then, a change which was even more lovely grew upon her;—a chastened gravity, that mellowed every feature; an upward glance told that thought was rising to yet more exalted themes of contemplation.

She turned kindly to her attendant.

"Sally! I should like to be alone for a little while. Do not be uneasy. I will be ready in season."

"Just as you say, ma'am."

Unwilling to submit to further procrastination of the momentous business yet to be performed, but awed into implicit obedience of action by her mistress's look and manner, the maid withdrew.

Helen's chamber was upon the second floor of the main building, which formed the central pile of the large and irregularly constructed old homestead; and access was had to this, not only by the wide front staircase, but also by a steeper winding flight, leading down to the back door. Sally was near the head of these, on the alert for the summons to her post of duty, when her attention was distracted by the rumble of wheels. This was now a frequent, almost an incessant sound, but the vehicle to which these belonged drove around the right wing of the house, where there was no carriageway over the lawn, and stopped at the rear porch. The listener stretched her head over the railing, with the curiosity characteristic of her class, to obtain a view of the back entrance. What or who was to be introduced into the mansion at such a time, and in this unusual way?

Colonel Floyd pushed the door open from without. He was arrayed in overcoat and hat, and carried in one hand his inevitable riding-whip. The other grasped, and, it would seem, not very tenderly, the arm of a lady, muffled in a large cloak and drooping hood.

"Good Fathers, Miss Lily!" ejaculated the astonished Sally, under her breath. "I thought she was sick in bed!"

Behind the supposed invalid cowered the confidential abigail, Sylvia. She bore a bandbox in her arms, and her mulatto complexion was the hue of ashes with fear. The group was completed by her husband, the family coachman, who brought in a small travelling-trunk, apparently from the conveyance standing without.

"Up! that way!" The colonel thrust Lily upon the lower stair. "And you had better rig yourself in your finery in double-quick time, or I will be along to hurry your smart waiting-maid, here!" He lent Sylvia a cut across the shoulders with his whip, by way of further admonition. "I flatter myself that I have spoilt your fun for this night; and the next time you undertake an elopement, look out that I am not at your heels. Leave that trunk there, you scoundrel!" pointing to a corner of the entry. "I take it for granted that there is no bridesmaid gear in that, and she has changed her mind about playing bride, for the present."

Lily had now gained the top of the steps, leaning heavily upon her maid, and Sally had retreated to a dark corner, not too distant to prevent her from seeing and hearing all that transpired. Finding that her uncle had not ascended behind her, the poor fugitive stopped, and fell back, rather than rested, against the wall, as one half dead with fatigue or fright.

Sylvia urged her, in a frightened whisper, to go on to her chamber.

"I cannot yet! I am so faint!" sobbed the trembling girl, pressing her hand to her heart. "What will become of me? Oh! what shall we do?"

Low as were her accents, the sound reached the savage warder below.

"Are you there still?" He came part of the way up to catch sight of the laggards. "If you want more of my help, you have only to say so, and it is at your service."

The terrified women hurried down a side passage in the direction of Lily's room, and at that instant Sally heard her mistress's bell, and made good her escape.

Helen's pre-occupation of mind prevented her from remarking the queer looks and behavior of her assistant. Apart from the revolution in her position and feelings, there was much that required her most serious meditation; an imperative necessity for self-command, and ingenuity of speech and conduct. The Court House—the universal name applied to the shire-town of each county in the Southern States—was but three miles from Belleview, and the county clerk, to whom application must be made for a marriage license, resided near his office in that village. There would be no difficulty in obtaining this, both the parties to the contract being of age; yet Aleck had deemed it best to take into his confidence, and secure as his companion in his nocturnal gallop, Harvey Floyd, a second cousin of the colonel's, and distantly related to Helen herself. He was a merry rattle of a fellow, kind-hearted as quick-witted, and was to have officiated as second groomsman, according to the original arrangement of the bridal train.

This gentleman, on being summoned from his dressing-room to receive the astounding news of a change of bridegrooms, "supposed," when the shock of the communication had passed off, "that it was all right—indeed, it was a capital joke—the boldest and cleverest thing he had ever heard of—this having hoaxed a whole community, the wedding party included—up to the very last moment! He would relish amazingly carrying out the matter in good style. A splendid Christmas trick!" and he laughed until the mouldy walls of the office threatened to come down about his ears.

This was after Helen had left the two young men together; but she conjectured that his co-operation was obtained without much difficulty, from the fact that she heard the clatter of their horses' hoofs down the road in less than ten minutes from her time of parting from them. Harvey was to ride directly back to Belleview, so soon as the license was granted; Aleck would return by way of Greenfield, and bring Miss Ruth with him. Let them use what speed and diligence they might, there would still be a delay of considerable length in the solemnization of the marriage, and this it was Helen's object to make as little noticeable as possible. By way of beginning, she must confide that to Sally which no one else—not the bridesmaids themselves—was to learn until the final moment. She was explicit, but brief, in her narrative to the petrified tire-woman. She—Helen Gardner—was to marry Mr. Alexander Lay, and not his brother, as was commonly supposed, but the secret was not to be divulged as yet to any other person. Least of all must Colonel Floyd, or any member of his family, receive the slightest intimation that could lead to the discovery of the plot. Certain preparations would detain Mr. Lay for an hour, perhaps more, beyond the time set for the marriage, and, to escape unpleasant comments upon his tardiness, the bride's toilette must not be complete until nearly nine o'clock.

It appeared doubtful, for awhile, whether Sally would ever be equal to the functions of her office,—so staggered was she by the intelligence, coming as it did, before she had entirely rallied from the effect produced by the discovery of Lily's escapade and capture. Helen laughed merrily at her bewilderment—so heartily, that Sally smiled in real pleasure.

"I have not heard you give a laugh like that in ever so many months, Miss Helen. It does my heart good to hear it; it sounds so like old times!"

"I have not been so happy for a long time, Sally. There have been painful misunderstandings that are now cleared away," was the response, sincere and simple.

She never imparted to any one else a more circumstantial account of the dark days of her life, and the sudden burst of sunshine following them.

Below, the apartments appropriated to the use of the company were filling fast; and until some officious individual had the bad taste to discover, and was guilty of the ill behavior of promulgating the intelligence, that it wanted a quarter of nine o'clock, and no bridegroom had yet arrived, every thing went blithely enough. Colonel Floyd was a conspicuous figure in the sight of every one that entered. He was dressed with extreme neatness and elegance, and his commanding stature, and stately grace of bearing, recalled to many of the elder guests the memory of his most palmy days, when no other resident of the region could vie with him in manly beauty and deportment. He had deteriorated since, and, by his evil courses, had latterly lost much of the prestige given him by this earlier reputation, and his family rank; but, to-night, he upheld the dignity of the Floyd escutcheon in a style that constrained his worst enemies to admiration. Mrs. Floyd was a cipher, according to custom; but she did her best to receive her friends cordially and entertain them hospitably, and there were few who were so destitute of right feeling as to be wanting in appreciation of her motives.

At a quarter to nine, then, an unmannerly buzz went hissing, like a serpent, through the crowd, leaving in its track dismayed silence, glances of alarmed inquiry, nods and winks of malicious meaning. The knowing and observant ones began to notice the fluctuations of the host's florid complexion from purple to pallor; that his face was lowering and his eye gleamed ominously as he conferred apart with his wife; and that she, poor soul, looked amazed and disquieted, and could not prevent her regards from straying every instant to the door. At nine o'clock, without any pretence of apology or show of concealment, Colonel Floyd left the apartment,—it was conjectured, to institute official inquiry into the cause of the mysterious and most ungallant non-appearance of the person who should have been one of the earliest upon the ground. No sooner was this plausible supposition reached by a majority of the assembly than there was a general and palpable effort to seem lively and unconcerned,—a commendable and ostentatious display of ignorance that any thing was wrong which deluded no one, failed to impose upon the most single minded creature there, and that was unquestionably the lady of the house.

Colonel Floyd crossed the hall and entered a small cloak-room, occupied, for the nonce, by four very stiff and uneasy gentlemen—the groomsmen—who awaited the signal to join their fair mates and take up the line of wedding march.

"This is a very strange affair, gentlemen!" said the colonel, gravely; "and it is my painful duty to inquire into it, without further delay. It may have been a mistaken delicacy which has kept me silent so long. Has any one of you seen or heard from Mr. Lay to-day?"

Every man looked at his fellow, and there was a unanimous shaking of heads.

"He called on me at noon yesterday, and engaged to meet me at the clerk's office this morning at eleven o'clock," pursued the colonel, visibly moved by some powerful emotion. "This engagement he saw fit to neglect. I waited for him until past twelve, and since my presence there was not a legal necessity, obeyed the call of other duties, and returned home. Since then—"

He was interrupted by the entrance of his relative, Harvey Floyd.

"Well, boys!" said the new arrival, gayly, "how goes it with you by this time? Tired of waiting—hey?"

"They may well be!" returned the colonel, indignantly. "What have you to say, Harvey, respecting this very dilatory groom? The business begins to look very black to us. He is a particular friend of yours, I believe. Are you the bearer of his excuses?"

"Well, not that exactly, sir, but I can answer for him that he will be here pretty soon, sure as a gun!" thrusting his hands into his pockets and strolling to the window, where he commenced a careless whistle, that suddenly, and without apparent cause, exploded into a laugh.

All were startled, several shocked by the sound.

"Beg pardon, colonel! Excuse me, gentlemen, but the truth is, you four look so like pall-bearers at a funeral, and my respected cousin there so like chief undertaker, sexton, and parson combined, that I cannot keep my countenance. Haw, haw!"

He dug his hands down deeper into his pockets, and stamped about the room, rolling and choking with merriment.

"There are some subjects, young man, that are not to be jested upon!" rejoined the colonel, his brow blackening with suppressed wrath, while the veins in his temples stood out like cords.

"No offence intended, sir!" Harvey tried manfully to swallow his amusement. "Only, when a man goes to a wedding, it does seem ludicrous to see every one else behave as if it were a funeral. Actually, a stranger would feel disposed to look for crape upon the left arm of each of this lugubrious quartette, and to listen for your official pronunciation of 'dust to dust, ashes to ashes.'"

"When you can express yourself in a manner becoming your position as a member of the respectable family so grossly insulted by the conduct of your associate, the expected bridegroom—expect*ed*, rather than expectant, it appears—I should like to talk with you upon this very unpleasant matter," said the colonel, with increasing choler.

He walked out with immense stiffness. The door opening upon the back porch, the same through which he had conducted Lily upon her return from her evening jaunt, stood ajar, and the aperture was filled by a dusky figure.

"I would like to speak to you, sir!" it said, in a guarded voice, as Colonel Floyd crossed the hall.

The master started as if the word were a bullet.

"What is it?" he asked, hastily.

Booker retired into the portico, whither the colonel followed him, shutting the door after them.

"The moon will be up before we get there," said the man, in the same cautious key. "It's time we were off."

"Had we not better wait until the moon *does* rise? It will be a dark, rough walk," suggested Colonel Floyd, staring upward at the starry heavens.

His manner was less that of the arbitrary owner than the equal of the one he addressed. But for the absurdity of the idea, one might have imagined that there lurked in his accent a certain degree of respect—of humility. The negro's reply was assuredly positive and familiar, such as few white men would have dared to employ in conversation with the lord of Belleview.

"So much the better! We don't want light until we get to the woods. If you are seen quitting the house when it's full of invited company, folks will wonder at it, and there's a chance of our being followed. Then, the ground 's froze hard as a rock, and the path is a rough one, as you say, besides being a good mile and a half long. We will want every minute of our time. If I'd had my way, we would have been off an hour ago."

"That could not be, you know." Colonel Floyd manifested no anger at the imperative language of his inferior. "It was necessary that I should show myself first to those people in the parlors, and contrive some excuse for leaving them."

"That may be so, but we ought to be off now!" repeated Booker, doggedly. "There's nothing else to be gained, and much may be lost by waiting."

"Are you sure that you have every thing ready?" whispered the master, peering over his shoulder at the lighted windows, blazing all along the rear of the building.

"All's right, so far as I am concerned!"

"Then I will be with you in three minutes!"

He went back into the house, and stopped in the hall to collect thoughts or courage for the next move. His face was curiously changed. A leaden hue had come over it, and he had to clinch his teeth to hinder them from chattering—probably with cold or nervousness, for no living man had ever seen him show fear or presumed to accuse him of cowardice. He felt the alteration in his looks, for he stroked his features to compose them; while his hand shook from the same cause that had induced the discomposure he would conceal. First, he proceeded to the dining-room, unlocked the sideboard, and helped himself to a glass of strong brandy and water; waited a minute to ascertain the potency of the draught, and swallowed a second. Then he again sought the presence of the uneasy groomsmen.

There was a glare in his eye that looked like fierceness; and if his voice were slightly husky, and not so steady as usual, it was attributed to the same, or kindred emotions, and these were regarded as altogether natural and commendable by the spectators, or by four out of the five. Harvey may have had his own ideas upon the subject. He, of the number, seemed least concerned by the announcement that should, in consideration of his relation to the bride, have affected him most.

"Gentlemen! you will oblige me by making yourselves at home in my house, and, so far as lies in your power, allaying the apprehensions that may have been excited in the minds of others by Mr. Lay's extraordinary and utterly inexcusable behavior. For myself," drawing himself up, and speaking hoarsely, yet dignifiedly, "I shall go in person to seek that young man—to call him to account for the dastardly slight put upon my niece. I think that I have a clue which, if rightly used, will enable me to ferret out the truth."

"Better stay where you are, colonel!" interposed Harvey, in some alarm; "or, if it is necessary to make inquiries, let me go in your place. Don't be precipitate! Things may come right without your troubling yourself. Lay is an honorable fellow, and, if he is above ground, I am willing to wager my head that he will furnish in good season a solution, and a satisfactory one, of this puzzle."

"Mr. Floyd!" The colonel wheeled suddenly upon him. "This is my affair, and I warn you, once for all, that I will not be interfered with! The only true kindness you can at present do your cousin, Miss Gardner, is to undertake the painful office of breaking to her, as gently as you can, the unexpected news of Mr. Lay's disappearance."

"Shall I find her up-stairs, sir?"

Harvey was near rupturing a blood-vessel in his frantic attempt to repress another uproarious fit of mirth.

"I presume that she has not yet left her room."

"Then I'll run right up!" said the willing bearer of the afflicting intelligence.

He went up the steps, three at a leap, as the colonel solemnly bowed around to the bewildered quartette, and left the house by the back door.

It was Sally's luck, this evening, to play the undesigning eaves-dropper. While Colonel Floyd and Booker held their cautious colloquy upon the porch, she was within ear-shot of most that was said. She had been to the kitchen upon some trifling errand, and was on her way back to Helen's room, when she espied Booker peeping in at the hall door, either watching or waiting for some one within. Sally instantly crouched, like a hare upon her form, and, inch by inch, crept under the portico steps,—not with the intention of overhearing what might follow, but to keep out of the man's sight, and to avoid the chance of meeting him. She hated and feared him, not without sufficient cause, as the reader will allow, and was panic-stricken by the thought that if she encountered him at this juncture of the plot confided to her keeping, he might drag the whole truth out of her. She believed him to be possessed of the craft, as he was of the depravity, of the great adversary of mankind. She quaked in her shoes when the pair—master and man—in drawing away from the door and windows, walked directly above her head, and there arranged the preliminaries of their expedition. Some words were lost; others but partially comprehended; still, she made out the drift of their purpose, and, while she was greatly mystified by certain expressions which occurred in the dialogue, she blessed the business, whatever it was, which took them out of the way at the moment when her mistress was expecting the real groom.

"Before you get back, the knot will be tied fast and hard, and then let's see you break it!" she chuckled.

Not audibly, for Booker was standing upon the top step, awaiting his accomplice's return. The flight was not a tall one, nor was her position comfortable or desirable, bowed together as she was, and not daring to move a finger, hardly venturing to draw a breath, while she could hear the creak of Booker's boots as he shifted his weight from one foot to the other, on the very plank against which her head rested. Her imprisonment was of brief duration in reality, tedious though it seemed to her. She did not quit her covert until the clang of the iron heels upon the flinty spring-path quite died away; but she had one glimpse of the patrolling party, as they passed through the broad stream of light pouring through the dining-room window. Colonel Floyd carried his gun, his inseparable companion in his nightly rambles, and Booker also bore something, she could not determine what, upon his shoulder.

"There you go!" soliloquized the girl, stretching her benumbed limbs. "Two as great vilyans as ever breathed! Hunting runaways, are you? You've tracked some poor fellow to his den, and mean to have him out, live or dead! 'Tain't the first job you've joined hand-in-hand in—but you won't go unpunished in the end, or the Scripter is mistaken, which ain't likely. Bless the Lord, Lem's hundreds of miles away, anyhow! So you won't catch him! Now, to tell Miss Helen that the cats are away—both of 'em!"

CHAPTER XII.

SALLY had no opportunity for the proposed communication. Outside the door of the bride's chamber stood Helen, in close conversation with her cousin, Harvey Floyd. Both were laughing; for if Harvey attached any importance to the colonel's threat of retribution upon the sinning Robert, he kindly and discreetly refrained from whispering to her a syllable relating to this part of the scene, which he pretended to describe to her with great exactness and evident enjoyment. The consultation was broken off by the outburst, from the adjoining room, of a figure in white robes.

"Helen Gardner! why aren't you in hysterics, or swooning, or something like that—as is suitable and graceful in the circumstances? I should be terrified into convulsions, if I were in your place. An hour after the time set for the ceremony, and not a word from the bridegroom! It's a perfect scandal—or, else, some terrible accident has happened—and in either case, you ought to go crazy!"

"I have just brought her a message that obviates the necessity of parting with her wits," replied Harvey. "The fortunate man is now on his way to happiness. I left him only half an hour ago. Aunt Ruth's newest cap was not ready in season, and he could not, as a dutiful nephew, leave her—while she was conscientiously opposed to wearing her second best. It was trimmed with green, which she said was an unlucky color at weddings. There were twelve yards of white satin ribbon to be furbelowed upon the new one, and the last bow but one was being sewed on when I came away; so they cannot be far behind me. You are divine, to-night, Miss Virginia!"

"Humbug!" with a smile of conscious vanity. "You ought to see Lily now! *She* is heavenly! So pure-looking, so ethereal, so exactly like a snow-flake, that you are positively afraid that she will melt away before your eyes—be exhaled like a dew-drop!"

"I hope she won't melt, or exhale, while *I* am looking at her!" answered the saucy groomsman. "Where is this same snow-drift, or snow-drop, or whatever you call her? I would like to take a parting look at her before she leaves this world for good and all."

"In there, with the rest of them," nodding backwards into Helen's room; and Harvey, taking the hinted invitation, walked himself into the midst of the fair and fluttering group.

There was a little scream of affected horror and surprise at his unceremonious entry; then the girls closed in upon him on every side.

"Mr. Floyd! what is the matter down-stairs?"

"What makes you gentlemen so tardy? We're tired to death waiting!"

"Hasn't Mr. Lay come yet? It's shocking!" and similar inquiries pelted his ears—a confusing volley, even to one of his consummate impudence.

"All right! all right! He will be here shortly!" he repeated, over and over, with slight variations, until the Babel subsided into a satisfied hum.

Lily had remained aloof, looking on with sad contempt, that was heightened into disdain when her cousin accosted her.

"Come, Lil! stand out into the light and let me see you!

Miss Virginia likens you to snow-flakes, and dew-drops, and all manner of other beautiful things."

He pulled her towards him, that he might take a better view.

"Don't, Harvey! you hurt me! Let me alone, I say!" she cried, sharply, trying to wrest her hands from his.

He held her tight.

"The half was not told me," said he, in mock reverence. "You are a gem—a star of the first lustre and sixth magnitude—but not snow! There's too much heat for that!"

If Virginia's simile had any aptness, this external fairness was the snowy crust veiling a volcanic heart. Lily's great eyes glittered feverishly; her skin was hot; her lips had a scarlet tinge.

"You are to walk with me, you know, Queen Mab," continued Harvey. "I shall watch you very closely, lest you unfold a pair of starry wings and fly away."

"I know no such thing!" she retorted, peevishly, and Harvey perceived his blunder when he recollected that Aleck Lay, as first groomsman, was the attendant assigned to her.

The sound of an arrival below relieved him from the necessity of fibbing to hide his *lapsus linguæ*.

"There he is at last!"

He dropped the struggling hands and was off like the wind. Miss Ruth passed him on the stairs, mounting to the dressing-room under the pilotage of a maid. The poor lady looked scared and flurried, and Harvey laughed to himself, in the imagination of her amazement at the recent disclosure made to her. Aleck was in the hall, handsome and self-possessed—a smile of heart-felt satisfaction dispelling every vestige of cynicism from his features.

"All goes well!" was Harvey's salutation, "and I have

served a notice upon Chandler, to take the vacant place in the train. You will find him with the rest of the fellows, in the room over there."

"Thank you!"

Aleck preceded him to the apartment designated, and presented himself to the anxious "fellows."

"I am sorry that I have been unavoidably detained, gentlemen—less on your account, however, I confess, than because I fear my delay has occasioned discontent to the ladies who are awaiting you. Every thing is ready, I believe. Shall we go up and make our peace, as best we may?"

"Is your brother here?" questioned one.

"My brother was called suddenly from home this forenoon, and has not returned yet. Fortunately, his presence is not indispensable, however much we may desire it."

"Not indispensable!" ejaculated Tom Shore. "What do you mean? Who ever heard of a wedding without a bridegroom? unless, indeed, you act as his proxy!" he subjoined, with a half laugh.

"I shall be married on my own account—not in the stead of another," replied Aleck, coolly. "This is a matter which was determined upon between Miss Gardner and myself, more than two years ago. Perhaps you would like to test the truth of my assertion by an appeal to the lady herself."

He led the way to the floor above, and the others, including the "dumfoundered" Tom, followed in his wake.

Helen did not lift her eyes at their approach, but the brilliant carmine of her cheek answered the fervent pressure with which Aleck laid her hand within his arm. Never were voluble girls rendered so mute by astonishment as was the knot of pretty attendants. Lily clung to Harvey for support; searched his face in such agony of inquiry, that he could not help whispering an explanatory sentence or two.

"It's all right! They have loved one another for years

and years. She was always queer, and so is he. The engagement with Robert was a blind. It's the best joke of the season!"

Honestly he believed but half of this tale; but he was pledged to carry the matter through, and he would do it with a brazen face, if not with a stout heart. Lily utterly discredited this account of the sudden reversal of preconcerted arrangements, but it mattered little to her how it had come about, while the evidence of her own eyesight showed her Helen Gardner as the bride of Aleck, and not Robert Lay. Divers editions of the surprising story were breathed by the other gallants to their respective charges during the downward march of the procession; and it spoke volumes for the self-command or aptitude in deception of the feminine part of the band, that when they were drawn up in bridal array, confronting the crowd of gaping and aghast spectators, none of them betrayed the slightest symptom of curiosity or embarrassment; each was competent to the occasion.

Mrs. Floyd uttered an exclamation of dismay or wonder as the clergyman, in obedience to a word from Aleck, and after a glance at the license presented by Harvey, began the marriage service. He paused longer than was needful or customary after the solemn bidding of the charge; bent a gaze, scrutinizing, and not altogether free from severity, upon the youthful couple, while the silence throughout the room became oppressive.

"I require and charge you both (as ye will answer at the dreadful day of judgment, when the secrets of all hearts will be dislcosed), that if either of you know any impediment, why ye may not be lawfully joined together in matrimony, ye do now confess it: for be ye well assured, that if any persons are joined together otherwise than as God's word doth allow, their marriage is not lawful."

Aleck met the penetrating eyes confidently—proudly, while Helen stood firm and calm beside him. The ceremony proceeded; the responses were made promptly and audibly, and Aleck's voice had never been more clear and steady than in articulating the vow:

"I, Alexander, take thee, Helen, to be my wedded wife, to have and to hold from this day forward, for better for worse; for richer for poorer; in sickness and in health; to love and to cherish, till death do us part, according to GOD's holy ordinance; and thereto I plight thee my troth."

It was done! and, regaining breath and speech with one simultaneous effort, the assembly surged impetuously towards the newly wedded pair. Inquiries more pointed than polite; banterings of all descriptions, gay, gentle and ill-natured; reproaches that were meant to be playful, and yet had an angry tone mingled with the laugh; every variety of congratulation was heaped upon the perpetrator of the daring deed, in a fashion that few would have been able to bear. But they were blest with dauntless spirits and strong nerves, and while Helen was suffered to remain by Aleck's side she did not shrink, and he was doubly courageous.

Poor, poor Miss Ruth! She slipped fast and quietly out of the press after kissing her "children," and heaving one little sob upon Helen's shoulder, and betook herself to the darkest corner of the conservatory, where she had her cry out in a comfortable style. She alone, beside her nephew and his wife, knew the secret of Robert's dishonorable defection, and the consequent dénouement between the real lovers; and she acquiesced cordially in Aleck's application of the good old-fashioned doctrines, that "those who truly love one another ought to marry," and that "the sooner a false step is corrected the better;" yet she had been taken so by surprise; her limited range of ideas and conjectures had been so abruptly enlarged; her grief at Robert's inexplicable behavior so sincere; her dread of compromising him and annoying Aleck and his bride so great, that it was no wonder she was, to use her own language, "fairly upset."

Her privacy was soon invaded. She mopped up the streaming tears at sight of a white dress and the sound of light, hurried footsteps.

"I came to look for you, Aunt Ruth," said Lily Calvert, winding her arms about the old lady's neck, and sinking to her knees beside her. "I have nobody else to whom I can speak—and speak I must, or my brain will go wild. You will never repeat what I say, will you?"

"Yes—yes—dear!" murmured Aunt Ruth. "That is, I would say, 'No,' my love!"

"You know every thing, do you not? Robert has often told me that he kept nothing hidden from you. You must know why and where he is gone?"

"Yes!" assented Miss Ruth, distressfully.

"Don't speak so sadly, please! You wound me to the quick. I had looked for charitable judgment from you. Indeed—indeed he could not help it, Aunt Ruth! You would not have blamed him if you had known all he had to bear—for he saw that Helen did not love him, and—*that I did?*"

She whispered the last three words, and buried her face in the listener's lap.

"Yes!"

Despite the objurgations Aleck had, in his aunt's hearing, and the early transports of his indignation, launched against Lily's coquetry and treachery, the charitable spinster could not discard all tender thoughts of the child she had loved from the sad hour of her birth. Mrs. Calvert had been the friend of Miss Massie's girlhood, and for her sake she had first learned to love the daughter. To her Lily was always winsome and loving, and she believed in her still; sympathized in the emotions whose intensity she perceived without fully understanding. Her motherly hand softly patted the curly head as she thought how young the weeper was—how tender and delicate—how unfit to bear the sorrow that pressed out those great choking sobs.

"All may come right, dear, if you love one another—"

"If!" Lily reared her head eagerly. "I have seen that he did love me this long while, and others saw it too! But this morning there came this letter"—taking one from her bosom—"in which he tells me how dear I am, and begs me to meet him this evening—to go with him—to become his wife! And I would have done it—by this time we would have been together, never again to be parted, but for my cruel, cruel uncle! How he guessed my intention I cannot imagine, for only Simon and Sylvia knew of it, and they would never betray me—but he overtook me on the road and forced me back. I can never forgive him—never!" Her eyes glowed, and her fingers clutched the letter tightly. "I am not his slave! I want you to write to Robert, Aunt Ruth. I shall be watched too closely for me to attempt that. Tell him why I failed to join him. I cannot have him think that I was prevented by cowardice or indifference—and say, moreover, that if my life is spared I will yet escape and do as he wishes, in defiance of my uncle's threats."

"Yes," said Aunt Ruth, doubtfully; "but, Lily dear, there is nothing now to keep him away, since Aleck and Helen are married. Doesn't it seem to you that it will be more proper to wait until he comes home, and let things go on naturally and smoothly? Then again I don't know where to direct my letter."

"To Washington! He writes that he will wait there

for tidings of me should I fail to meet him. As to propriety, I detest the word!" cried the girl, passionately. "If you are hindered by such scruples, I will steal time to-night to write to him myself. Will you see that my letter is mailed?"

"Yes!" responded Aunt Ruth, yet more slowly and dubiously.

The equilibrium of her ideas was too effectually destroyed by the strange events of the past few hours for her to offer any decided protest against becoming Cupid's postwoman. When she journeyed homeward at midnight, still dazed and wondering, no one part of the performances she had witnessed was more unreal to her than the fact that in her pocket, nestled among the folds of her immaculate handkerchief, reposed a billet whose superscription, hastily scrawled in a fine feminine hand, was, "Mr. Robert C. Lay, Washington, D. C."

Harvey Floyd proved himself to be the nonpareil of kinsmen and groomsmen on that trying evening. Having, as an indispensable preliminary, exorcised his conscience by a potent adjuration in the names of expediency and good-nature, he gayly assumed the rôle of master of ceremonies; circulated freely among the curious and suspicious guests, joking, laughing, and lying as he moved; "pooh-poohing" at insinuations of unfair play towards the absent brother; declaring that he had been the confidant of all three of the parties concerned in this "capital hoax" ever since its inception; had known that Robert was looking after Aleck's interests, while people believed that he was pleading his own cause; had often laughed with him at the adroit manner in which the wool was pulled over people's eyes, etc., etc.

"But how did it happen that neither Colonel nor Mrs. Floyd was cognizant of the true state of the affair?" questioned the shrewd ones.

"In for a penny, in for a pound!" whispered Harvey to his drugged conscience, as it stirred in its sleep, and he replied *sotto voce*, with a meaning wink—"Colonel never liked Aleck—opposed his marrying his ward. My worthy relative is a trifle 'kinky,' as we all know. Had no objection to Robert. Since he could make no legal opposition to the match, both parties being of age, he vamosed so soon as he was informed who the veritable Benedict was to be. The thing had gone too far for him to stop it, but he wouldn't look on. D'ye understand?"

And even the shrewd ones were so verdant as to believe that they *did* understand. Helen was voted "undutiful," "unfeminine," and "fast," by the sober adherents to custom and form; "spunky," "resolute," and "devoted," by the more youthful and romantic portion of the company.

"You are the biggest story-teller I ever heard of!" declared Virginia Shore to the laughing bride. "And to think of your carrying it so far as to pretend that you were going to wear those contemptible rose-buds as your only ornaments, when you intended to behave like a Christian woman, and sport the pearls! It must be owned that you look like a queen in them. Doesn't she, Mr. Lay? But for all that, if I were your confessor, I would make you walk ten miles with peas in your shoes for such abominable fibbing. And, now, I am just expiring to know one thing. If your tongue can speak the truth, after its long and diligent practice in the other line, I wish you would tell me where Mr. Robert is. It is the one unaccountable circumstance in the unravelled plot—and excuse me, my dear—I must say that it has a queer look!"

Aleck came to Helen's relief so promptly that her hesitation at this very direct question was not noticed.

"Until this morning, Miss Virginia, my brother had

never intimated an intention of absenting himself on this interesting occasion. Before breakfast he received a letter calling him from home upon urgent business. The summons was imperative, and admitted of not even an hour's delay."

Lily was passing when Virginia's mention of Robert's name struck her ear, and she involuntarily stopped to listen. Aleck gained her eye at the beginning of his reply, and did not release it until he concluded—held it by a gaze of such significant contempt that, as he said to himself, if the girl retained one grain of self-respect or shame, she must quail beneath its questioning. She did indeed change countenance, but it was a look of incredulity or surprise, not conscious and detected guilt. He let her alone after that. She had no ground to lose in his estimation, and, whatever might be his opinion of her course and motives, he, of all the world, had least cause to murmur at the result of these.

Mrs. Floyd—as she was accustomed to aver in after days—would never have lived through that evening but for the support of Harvey's unblushing mendacity and Aleck Lay's ready tact. Nor was Helen backward in sustaining her aunt in her difficult position. Laying aside the stiff stateliness, enjoined by etiquette upon the bride, she deported herself as the daughter of the house, who was mindful of her guests' comfort and pleasure, and in considering these lost sight of the novelty of her own position. She did not dance, but she was careful that no lady who wished to do so should lack a partner; she chatted easily and freely with matrons; replied merrily to the badinage of the elderly gentlemen, who were not sparing in their comments upon the extraordinary character of her nuptial ceremonies; privily directed waiters, and as privately suggested forgotten duties to the mistress of the establishment. She was incalculably more valuable to her perplexed and worried aunt than was Lily, who spoke and acted all the while like one in a trance.

Never did hostess, especially one by nature and practice so hospitable as was the lady of Belleview, hail the departure of visitors so joyfully as did she the first stir of leave-taking among those whose coming she had greeted with unfeigned cordiality. The colonel had not yet returned, when, at three o'clock in the morning, she threw her wearied limbs and aching head upon her couch, too tired and full of pain to speculate on her lonely pillow as to the causes of his prolonged absence. She slept soon and soundly, so profoundly that she did not know when the absentee came in, and was awakened at last by the broad light of morning.

"Bless my life, it is eight o'clock!" she exclaimed, springing up, "and I never even heard Amy make the fire! When did you come in, and why didn't you wake me, colonel?"

Her husband was at the toilette-table, shaving himself. Apparently, his hand was not very steady, for the lather he had scraped from his chin was streaked with blood, and the razor inflicted a deep gash as his wife spoke. She had scarcely expected any answer, other than the one which came—a bitter oath! and, to tell the truth, she was much more concerned about the wedding breakfast, and the probable condition of the rooms used by the company the previous evening, than affected by his humor.

He surprised her by a query before her hurried dressing was completed.

"How did your dear five hundred friends take the news that there could be no wedding, for want of a bridegroom?" he growled between his teeth.

"Sure enough! How forgetful I am! You were not here when it all came out!" Mrs. Floyd checked herself in the act of lowering her dress over her head. "I don't know how to tell you, or where to begin. It was all so unexpected, even to me! How she contrived to keep it a secret up to the last minute, I cannot divine; but she did, and fooled us all completely. And to think that Aleck Lay could play the hypocrite as well as she did, and Robert too! I wouldn't have believed it of him! I always thought that he had such an open heart and honest tongue. I declare it beats every thing I ever heard or dreamed of!"

She was interrupted by a profane ejaculation, and an order "to say what she had to say, and to stop that infernal gabble!"

"Why, my love, I was just going to tell you! Did you ever suspect that she was not in love with him? that she was throwing dust in our eyes all this time, even when she was making up her wedding clothes and accepting her wedding presents? When Mr. Bradley commenced the ceremony, I really thought that I should faint outright. And nobody knew it except Harvey, and I must say that he behaved very unhandsomely in not giving me a hint. Mercy on us, colonel! what's the matter?"

He had turned about, his back to the table, leaning heavily against it; the razor in his hand; his complexion nearly as colorless as the foam yet left upon his cheeks.

"Ceremony! what ceremony?" he said, in a guttural whisper.

"Why, the marriage service, to be sure, over Aleck Lay and Helen Gardner. They were married about nine o'clock, and—oh!"

She rushed forward with a scream, in season to prevent his falling to the floor, seating him instead in an easy-chair that was luckily close at hand, and supported the heavy head, swaying helplessly to and fro. Her frightened cry speedily brought help. A gang of bustling, terrified servants collected around him; stripped off his outer clothing, loosened his collar and cravat, and bore him to the bed. By the time they reached this stage of proceedings, he had revived so far as to speak, but so inarticulate was his primary attempt, that his wife begged him to repeat it. He did, with an angry effort.

"Booker!"

"Run for Booker, some of you!" ordered Mrs. Floyd. "Do you want him to go for the doctor, dear?" she inquired, tenderly.

He breathed hard and loudly; his forehead was dark still with the dangerous flood that had rushed up to the brain, yet he scowled at her; lifted his hand menacingly towards the flock of negroes.

"Out! every one of them!" he managed to say, more distinctly now.

The violence of the attack was passing. Booker did not obey the summons with especial alacrity. He was asleep when it was brought to his house, and awoke unwillingly; arose sullen. Mrs. Floyd was banished, as her menials had been, at the entrance of this high and sulky functionary. For half an hour she was kept waiting without the chamber, while a low conference went on inside. Her lord was manifestly better when the janitor permitted her return to the bedside; better in body, but in temper as ill-conditioned as mortal could well be. After an infinite amount of argument and persuasion, she prevailed upon him to admit the physician, for whom a messenger had been despatched two hours before; and since she was not forbidden the privilege, she remained in the room during his stay.

Colonel Floyd had ridden twenty miles the night before, he stated to the medical man, "upon a false scent"—he interpolated, savagely—had eaten nothing, and slept none. The consequence was a rush of blood to the head—a trifle not worth naming but women were such fools!

Convinced, upon examination, that the seizure was really not severe, and his patient in no peril of his life, the doctor recommended a little cooling medicine and a day's quiet; buttoned up his coat, picked up his saddlebags, and prepared to go.

"The weather has moderated," he remarked to Mrs. Floyd, in quitting the apartment. "We shall have snow by night."

She accompanied him down-stairs; received an additional direction or two, and resought her husband's presence. He had shifted his position, and dragged another pillow under his head; raised himself high enough to enable him to look out of the window nearest the bed.

"Didn't the doctor say there would be snow to-day?" he asked, in ill-dissembled eagerness.

"Yes, it is clouding up fast. We shall have falling weather by noon, I think. Aleck and Helen are about going, my dear. Do you feel able to say 'good-by' to them?"

"If I did, they should not cross that threshold!" he said, vehemently. Tell them I say 'begone!' and send my curse after them."

Mrs. Floyd wisely and politely concluded to modify this amiable message in the delivery; so the bridal pair were only told how sorry she was that the colonel was too seriously indisposed to see them, and that the doctor had enjoined absolute quiet.

The dinner party at Greenfield was to proceed, as had been contemplated before the late momentous changes. This was decided upon, partly to gratify Miss Ruth, partly to appease the suspicions of those who obstinately cherished the idea that there was something wrong behind the scenes; the incorrigible skeptics, whom even Harvey Floyd could not lie into belief of the story he promulgated so industriously.

The fields were like unwritten white paper; the roads were growing heavy with drifts, and it was still snowing hard, when, at dusk, a carriage drove up to the ancient mansion of Maple Hill, and Aleck assisted his wife to alight. Neither of them would remain under Robert's roof longer than was necessary for appearance's sake. Both longed for quiet and home. Busy hands had been at work within doors all day. The windows were ruddy with fire-light, and the young husband led his bride from the raw, chill outer air into a large, old-fashioned hall, well lighted and warm, where were ranged a score of family servants, dressed in holiday attire, and profuse of smiles and courtesies to their new mistress.

"The blessin' of Abraham, Isaac, and Jacob be upon em!" groaned a pompous voice from the head of the line.

Helen tried to say "Thank you!" but the effort expired in stifled mirth.

"The egregious blockhead!" said Aleck, fretted and yet amused, as, having spoken a kind word of acknowledgment to his dependents, he conducted Helen into the parlor, seated her in a great chair, and undid her bonnet and cloak. "The preposterous humbug! A padlock for his mouth, to be worn constantly, except at meal-times, would be an admirable regimen for him."

"Petronius, was it not?" asked Helen, still laughing.

"Of course it was! By the way, I must have a talk with him to-morrow. It was he who brought that letter to Greenfield yesterday afternoon. I omitted in my excitement then to ask him at what point of the road he met Robert. I would like to inquire into the particulars of their interview. Why are you shivering, love, are you cold?"

"No! only a passing chill. I have a strange aversion to speaking of yesterday, or of any thing connected with—with—what might have happened."

She was very pale, and trembled visibly. Aleck leaned over to kiss her—put his arm about her.

"Why, you dear little goose! the danger is all over now; your fate is sealed! You are a captive, and your jailer is a perpetual institution."

She smiled mutely; then her head drooped upon his shoulder, and there was silence for a while.

"Speaking of Petronious reminds me of the evening service we attended at Mr. Shore's, some weeks ago," resumed Aleck, cheerfully, to dispel any remnant of unpleasant feeling that might be lingering in her mind. "Do you recollect the bit of paper, the loss of which chagrined Lily so much?"

"Yes. I knew that you had it then, although I dared not thank you for the theft."

He took out his pocket-book. "See here," opening an inner compartment.

"Why did you keep it?" asked Helen, catching at the soiled and creased leaf.

"Because I read there, in your handwriting, that it was 'dangerous to play with edge tools,'" responded Aleck, "and my own disappointed heart responded to the truth of the maxim. I preserved it as a monitor for future direction. The consequence was, that I had made up my mind to live and die a 'crusty, fusty old bachelor!'"

With a gesture of playful petulance, that brought back to him the memory of her girl days, Helen put her hand over his mouth, and tossed the paper into the fire.

"I am glad it storms!" she said presently, looking at the snow-encrusted panes. "It makes our home so much the more cosey and dear."

While they mused, with locked hands, tenderly-smiling lips, and eyes full of happy light, upon the sweetness wrapped up in that little phrase, "our home," Colonel Floyd's chamber was dark, save for a feeble glimmer from the fire he would not allow to be replenished, and the waning gray light from the windows. Upon these his haggard eyes were fixed, as they had been from the commencement of the storm, gloating with a sort of greedy satisfaction, which was enigmatical to his attendants, over its continuance and increasing fury. Not until the last ray of daylight had vanished, and he could no longer discern the falling flakes between him and the leaden sky, would he listen to his wife's solicitations that she might have the curtains lowered, and wood and candles brought in.

At nine o'clock Booker appeared to inquire after his master's condition, and receive his orders for the night. Lily happened to be present at the moment. Her uncle had insisted upon seeing her, on her return from the dinner at Greenfield, as if to assure himself that she was actually in the house. She was a heart-sore and peevish creature throughout that lonely evening, but ungraciously promised obedience to his further command that she should see him again before retiring to rest. It was upon this second visit that Booker encountered her.

"What of the weather?" questioned Colonel Floyd of his retainer.

"Snowing faster than ever, sir. The drifts will be four foot deep by morning."

"Good!" The sick man settled himself in his bed, with a grunt of satisfaction

Booker continued,

"And upon ground so hard froze as it is now, the snow will lie three weeks and better."

"I don't see why that should be so desirable as you seem to think!" said Lily, crossly, shrugging her shoulders. "We will have bad roads all spring."

"Hold your tongue, you jade, and go to bed!" said her uncle, furiously.

"That's because you don't understand, you see, Miss Lily," answered Booker, demurely. "Deep snows are prime for the winter wheat, and for every thing else that's in the ground, for that matter. Good-night, sir ; I hope you'll sleep sound."

CHAPTER XIII.

Two months had passed since the wedding, which had set the tongues of the neighborhood wagging, as only an out-of-the-way marriage or shocking murder can do. It was a mild, soft afternoon, in the latter part of February, and Helen Lay stood at the front window of her pretty parlor, watching the winding road that led up to the house. Aleck had been absent four days, on a business trip to Baltimore, and this evening was to end their first separation. How keenly she had felt it, might be gathered from her restless movements about the room, when her eyes became weary of straining into the unsatisfactory distance; her changeful color and quickened attention at sight of any far-off moving object, or any sound that fancy could construe into the rumble of wheels or beat of hoofs.

"He won't come while you are looking for him my dear," observed Aunt Ruth, with a quiet smile, from her seat at the fire.

But, placid as she looked, and steadily as grew the stocking under her fingers, she was not free from impatience herself, and inwardly rejoiced in the signs of anxiety which the young wife could not conceal. They were tributes to her "boy's" worth, proofs of the affection borne him by his best beloved. Helen blushed, and tried to laugh; then came and sat down beside the diligent spinster.

"I believe that I am 'fidgetty' to-night, as Virginia Shore calls it· but it is not altogether the desire to see Aleck again, although I do not deny that that feeling is strong. I am oppressed by the idea of some impending sorrow—a presentiment that something sad or disagreeable is to befall me. You have felt such, Aunt Ruth, have you not?"

"Yes."

"Then you know how hard it is to shake these off."

"Yes!"

Miss Ruth sighed; a respiration telling of a volume of like experiences.

"Not that I believe in omens or presentiments," continued Helen, bravely, "only when one is a little excited from other causes, a notion of this kind fastens more easily upon the mind. I have not been very happy to-day; not nearly so buoyant of spirits as I should be. Lily's countenance, as I saw it yesterday at church, has haunted me ever since. You must have observed how sadly she has changed."

"Yes, dear!" Aunt Ruth said, in intonation and look; "who could help noticing the poor child! I never saw a sadder wreck in my whole life."

"I wish, for her sake, that Robert would come home," Helen resumed, pensively. "His movements are a complete riddle to me. They vex Aleck grievously, too. He has written to Robert five or six times, but the two letters we have received from the runaway, make no mention of his having heard from us. The suspense is hard for the brother to endure; what must it be to Lily, poor girl! Hist!"

The faint echo that had entered her ear grew louder.

"Yes!" nodded Aunt Ruth, smilingly, in answer to the brightening eyes and uplifted fingers.

They harkened a minute longer. A carriage was certainly approaching.

"I will not stir until it stops!" said Helen, poutingly, her cheeks one flush of crimson. "You shall see how well I can behave!"

She fulfilled her promise to the letter; but there was scanty evidence of the spirit of patient awaiting in her gladsome exclamation and rapid flight to the hall door when the wheels ceased to move. The vehicle, a buggy driven by a negro, was similar in appearance to that which had been sent to the dépôt for the absent master of Maple Hill. It had halted before the porch steps, and a gentleman was alighting when she appeared at the entrance. But his was not the joyous bound of a wedded lover; nor was it Aleck's figure and features that met her dismayed vision. The driver was Booker, his passenger Colonel Floyd. Chagrined and disconcerted though Helen was at the unexpected and unwelcome visit, she could not but remark the change in his person and movements effected by his recent sickness. His step was slow and languid; his hair whiter, and his eye had the furtive, uneasy glance of one disturbed by perpetual forebodings of evil, or harassed by constant physical suffering.

"Aunt was right when she told me, the other day, that he was woefully broken," thought Helen, as with instinctive and lady-like hospitality, she offered her hand and invited him to enter the house.

Not until he had paid his respects to Miss Ruth, seated himself by the hearth and removed his gloves, did he revert to the errand that had brought him hither. That he had an errand, and one which could not be intrusted to another, Helen was assured the instant she saw him, for he had never darkened the doors of her new abode until now.

"I have called to see Mr. Lay upon business," he said to her. "Business which should have been settled before this late day, but for my infirm state of health."

"He left home last Friday for Baltimore," replied Helen, "and has not yet returned. I am expecting him this evening."

She could not force herself to propose that he should await Aleck's arrival. Polite insincerity could not carry her to the length of deliberately concerting such a defeat of her anticipated joyous meeting with her husband. It seemed that Colonel Floyd was not inclined, in this respect, to stand upon ceremony. He leaned back in his chair and crossed his legs, with the aspect of one who had laid in a sufficient stock of patience, and had no intention of removing immediately from his chosen position. Aunt Ruth sat up stifly, lips compressed and eyes riveted upon her work. Helen made another effort to do the honors decently. She would not essay cordiality.

"I hope that aunt and Lily are well."

"I believe they are. I hear no complaints."

"Lily is looking badly, I think. I met her yesterday at church."

"Humph! Three-fourths of her disorder is imagination. Her aunt tells me that she is troubled with dyspepsia and blues this winter. It is fashionable for young ladies to fall into ill-health."

"She is certainly very thin, and coughs a great deal," responded Helen, smothering her displeasure at his contemptuous reply—and there was a tedious pause.

Her face kindled presently, and glancing significantly at Miss Ruth, she left the room. There was no mistake this time. Another buggy had driven to the door—Colonel Floyd's moving on to make room for it, and Aleck Lay leaped to the ground almost before the horse was checked. He came directly up the steps to salute his wife; held her to him in a hasty embrace and kissed her; but his first words were abrupt, his tone harsh

"Is Colonel Floyd here?"

"Yes—in the parlor. I am very sorry—"

"*I* am not!"

He strode into the hall; tore off his over-coat, and tossed it with his hat and gloves upon a table; then moved in the direction of the parlor without another word. Shocked and chilled by his stern face and negligent treatment of herself, Helen yet ventured to follow him.

"Dear Aleck!" she entreated, hanging on his arm. "There is no haste about seeing him. Come to our room and rest awhile—let me brush the dust off! You look very weary, and a bath will refresh you. I am afraid you are not well."

"Oh, yes I am! I must see this man—get this meeting over at once!"

Helen still hindered him.

"You know, dear, that I could not help his being here just now! I did not dream of his coming until he drove up. I am sure I wish that he had stayed away! You are not angry with me, are you?"

The question or the timid tone served to recall Aleck to his senses. He looked down into the loving, pleading eyes, where the tears were already welling.

"My precious wife! could I be angry with you even if I had cause? and that can never happen! Forgive me if I act strangely. My mind is full of other and important things—matters concerning which we will talk together by and by. You know that I am happy in being once more at home, and with you!"

He gave her another kiss more fond than the former; released her, and entered the apartment where his visitor awaited him.

Helen did not go in directly after him. She ran off into her chamber to hide the emotion she would not have others perceive. It was very foolish and wrong to weep over a trifling disappointment like this, but she had pictured to herself such different things! the murmured words of tenderness; the long, close embrace; the thousand inquiries after her welfare and occupations during his absence—especially how she had borne that separation; the ejaculations of delight at their reunion—that were to have filled the earlier moments of their renewed intercourse. How could he leave her so soon and hastily—how speak so coldly—how plead preoccupation with more important things? Up to this hour their married life had glided on like a blissful dream; the lover-husband been all that the most exacting bride could require. Was this the beginning of that settling down into the graver actualities of every day home-life which every one except themselves predicted as their future lot; which they had promised one another should never come to them? It had been easy to tell Robert that she had outlived youthful romance; that she was not a sentimental, unreasonable girl, but a common-sense, matter-of-fact woman. If she had married him he would doubtless have found her to be all that she had described. As it was—

She walked restlessly up and down the floor; now letting the tears flow freely, now drying them in haste, as fancy deluded her with the thought that she caught the sound of Aleck's distant footsteps. Surely he *would* come—he could not stay away when he observed that she had not followed him! Colonel Floyd's business was a matter of no consequence after all. She was certain that it pertained to the settlement of his guardianship accounts, for he could have none other with Mr. Lay. Into these it may be remembered that she had advised—nay, urged Robert to look. The idea of being defrauded was then painful to her. She wanted to bring, as her marriage portion, to the younger brother, property that would justify her in a feelling of thorough independence for the remainder of her days;—that should, in plain phrase, pay her personal expenses, and never oblige her husband to lay out a dollar of his own fortune to insure her comfort or pleasure. She believed, then, that she was actuated, as she had said to her betrothed, by a sincere desire for the advancement of his interests no less than hers. She cared little whether she were dependent upon Aleck or no. All that she had was his, and for the rest—benefits—a livelihood itself from his hand would be all the sweeter because she owed them to his love. Total dependence upon the one truly and only beloved never yet wounded a woman's pride.

She had time to indulge these, and many other meditations in the wearisome half-hour consumed in fruitless waiting and childish fears. Then, with a smack of the old haughtiness she condemned as unworthy, even while she yielded to it, she resolved to cast aside the part of the love-lorn lady, pining in her bower; to show him that she, likewise, could be oblivious of tender weaknesses and alive to rational considerations, such as should govern a sober, right-minded couple, from whose cup of happiness eight weeks of wedded experience had puffed away the sparkling foam. She bathed her eyes, smoothed her hair, added an ornament or two to her tasteful home attire, that he might not construe apparent neglect in dress into proof of an absent or suffering mind, and betook herself, work-basket in hand, to the drawing-room.

Aunt Ruth was no longer there,—a circumstance Helen did not discover until she had advanced half-way down the apartment. But she had seen her husband start and look hurriedly over his shoulder as the door unclosed, and imagined that he frowned at seeing her. If her presence were undesired by him, he quickly subdued any token of displeasure or regret, arising to set a chair near the fire for her, and bowing as he did so, as courteously as to an honored guest.

"Perhaps I had better not stay," said Helen, in an under tone, stopping short when she perceived Miss Ruth's empty seat. "I am afraid that you are engaged!"

"You will be no hindrance," was the reply, spoken in grave politeness; and still doubting which course dignity and expediency would advise, she obeyed his gesture and sat down.

There were candles upon the table, so disposed that they shed a strong light on Colonel Floyd's features, while Aleck, by accident or design, had drawn back into comparative shadow. Helen was nearest him, but could only see his profile. Colonel Floyd almost faced her, and she noticed, mechanically, as it were, that he seemed to be annoyed, or otherwise excited. His hand rested upon several letters and other written papers lying on the table, and shuffled them nervously as he spoke or listened.

"You have had no direct personal communication by mail or in any other manner with my brother, since he left home, I understood you to say, Colonel Floyd?" said Aleck, interrogatively, going on with the conversation his wife's entrance had interrupted.

"None, whatever, sir. The last interview we had was purely one of business, and took place in the forenoon of the twenty-fourth of December. At that time he delivered to me the cancelled bonds I have just shown you. My principal reason in requesting his presence on that occasion was, that I might discharge the debt long due him. He was at my house from ten o'clock until one; our conference was held in the office, for want of a more comfortable place, and continued for nearly two hours, as Mrs. Lay may recollect," bowing and smiling sardonically to Helen.

Aleck waived the reference and Helen's silent bend of assent; did not turn to see whether she had heard or replied.

"You had an appointment with him for the next day,

however," he continued, in a tone that sounded dry and guarded to Helen's ears.

"Which he entirely failed to keep!" interposed the colonel, quickly.

"Without sending you any apology?"

"I received none. I left home at ten or thereabouts, rode leisurely to the clerk's office, where Mr. Robert Lay was to meet me at eleven; waited for him more than an hour and a half, as Mr. Willis can testify; then, supposing that he had been unavoidably detained, and not knowing how long I might be kept there if I undertook to stay until he came, I placed a certificate in Mr. Willis's hands to the effect that my ward, Miss Gardner, was of age, and therefore free to marry whenever and whomsoever she pleased, and returned to Belleview. Mrs. Lay perhaps remembers that I was at the house when she came home after a morning walk,—moreover, that I informed her of your brother's failure to keep his engagement with me."

Again, Helen gave a grudged and unspoken response to his appeal, which was heeded as little by her husband as the former had been. He sat with an elbow resting upon the table; his hand spanning his forehead, and from its shadow his eyes gazed keenly, intensely upon his visitor, never quitting him for a second. Colonel Floyd felt their scrutiny, for he winced at each question, and carefully refrained from looking at his interlocutor during his rejoinder.

"It is growing very late!" he observed, rustling his documents into a bundle, and tying them together with a bit of red tape.

The knot was insecure, as was proven upon trial, and when it gave way at the strain intended to tighten it, the loose sheets were scattered over the table. Aleck assisted in collecting them.

"These are the bonds!" he remarked, pausing in the task

to examine two small pieces of paper selected from the heap. "Excuse me for saying it, but it strikes me that this was an unbusiness-like mode of annulment—merely drawing a pen across the face of the instrument. I am surprised that Robert adopted it. I wonder more that you did not demand a receipt, also."

"If I recollect rightly, I did, and received one," returned Colonel Floyd, very busy with the refractory package; his fingers becoming more awkwardly unsteady every instant. "Have it at home—I can show it to you, if you doubt my word, Mr. Lay," summoning his proudest manner and accent.

"I have not intimated such a doubt," replied Aleck, calmly. "My brother's movements of late are enveloped in so much obscurity, and about many of them hangs such an air of mystery, that I am excusable for examining somewhat narrowly into all that can be ascertained concerning the last day or two which he passed at home."

"Certainly! Certainly! You are quite right, sir!" Colonel Floyd crowded the packet into his pocket. "And I assure you that any information that I can afford you, any light that I can cast upon this unhappy affair, is quite at your command, Mr. Lay. But, to be frank with you, I must say that his conduct is not wholly unaccountable to me. Young blood is hot, and young judgment hasty—and Mr. Robert Lay was young, ardent, injudicious. I have heard rumors of his serious losses at play, and other unfortunate indiscretions, to which I would not allude in your presence, but for my desire to elucidate what appears to be a puzzle to you."

There was a stain of fresh blood on the lip Aleck's teeth let go, at the conclusion of this speech, but he betrayed no other sign of passion.

"If I understand you, sir, you counsel me to discretion in

prosecuting further inquiries:—as a friend to my brother, you would perhaps recommend that I drop them entirely?" he said, with the same steadfast look into the colonel's eyes.

"I! I counsel nothing! As I have remarked, I stand prepared to render you what assistance I can. My deeds are ever open to the day. The arrangement is, then, Mr. Lay, that I meet you to-morrow at the clerk's office, and settle with you so far as is practicable, upon so short a notice. It is fortunate that I chance to have several thousands lying in bank at this juncture, or your fair wife's precipitate action might have taken me at a disadvantage,"—bowing to Helen.

"I do not see how that could be, sir!" she was provoked to reply. "You had several months' notice—"

He interrupted her. "Of your contemplated marriage with Mr. Robert Lay, I grant, my dear lady! But there were certain circumstances I will not now stop to explain that made a prospective settlement with your *bona fide* betrothed and present husband a very different affair from what my reckoning with his brother would have been."

Helen was literally too angry to speak—too much incensed to make any return to the pompous adieus that wound up this impertinence.

Aleck attended her whilom guardian to the door—neither his wife nor himself extending to him an invitation to tea—and remained there after the buggy had driven away, pacing hard and hurriedly to and fro upon the piazza, until the bell rang for supper. Then, he made no haste to answer the call.

"I wish Aleck would come in!" mildly complained his aunt. "The muffins will get solid and the chickens cold. I should think he would be hungry after travelling so many hours."

Helen said nothing, but seating herself at the head of

the board began setting out the cups and saucers upon the tea-tray.

"Ring that bell again!" Miss Ruth ordered, presently, as the last hope of saving her hot fowls and puffy muffins from woeful depreciation; and at this second call the master came.

"He might as well have stayed away for all he ate!" thought Aunt Ruth, despairingly noting the untouched food upon his plate.

He drank a cup of coffee; declined his wife's coolly civil offer to send him another, and sat stirring and inspecting the grounds or sugar left in the bottom of the cup, with assiduity as serious as that displayed by the most accomplished fortune-teller. His brows were bent into settled severity; his mouth compressed into sternness as immovable, and when he answered the two or three queries with which his aunt found courage to ply him, his tone was absent and dreamy. Whatever might be the theme of his cogitations, he studied it with every energy of heart and mind, to the exclusion of every other. Finally he pushed back his chair, hardly vouchsafing a brief "excuse me!" to the ladies, and left the table.

"Is Petronius at home?" he demanded of the servant in waiting.

"I believe he is, sir."

"Go and see, and when you find him send him to me, in the library! I have letters to write, Helen," he added, "several that must go by to-morrow's mail. I am sorry to seem unsocial on the evening of my return, but it cannot be helped." He went out.

Helen, too, arose. "Take more wood into the library!" she said to another domestic. "Your master will probably sit up late."

Not a tone faltered. Her lids were level and dry; but

Aunt Ruth divined something of the storm of feeling waxing to its height, and not unreasonably associated these signs of the times with Aleck's reserved, morose mood.

Left to herself to survey the slighted feast, to whose demolition she had looked forward with such lively and innocent delight, the old lady shook her head at the closing door as Helen vanished through it, and sighed a regretful, but not hopeless—"yes."

Not hopeless—for the dear soul had heard of lover's quarrels and the certainty and sweetness of reconciliation, and believed that she read correctly the symptoms of this famous, but not dangerous distemper, in conduct that would upon any other hypothesis have been inexplicable and unpardonable. Acting upon this persuasion, she lingered not long in dining-hall or parlor. In the last-named room Helen kept her company, sewing steadily, and talking, not freely or continually, but pleasantly, when she did speak; the scarlet spot in either cheek and her curling lip evincing that the inward strife was still far from being quelled.

"Proud! proud!" soliloquized Aunt Ruth, mentally. "Lucifers in pride—both of them! The best thing I can do is to leave her to solitary reflection for awhile; at any rate, to take my old useless body out of the way, in case he should give in first—as I've heard that men are apt to do—and come to look for her. They will never make up while there are others by. Helen, dear!" she said aloud, "I am pretty tired to-night, or else it is this warmish weather that makes me drowsy. I believe I will go to bed if you won't mind my leaving you. Aleck will be in pretty soon now to hinder you from getting lonesome. His letters can't keep him much longer."

"If they do, I shall not be lonely, aunt. Do not let me keep you up a minute longer than is convenient and pleasant for you. I shall retire early myself?"

Yet she sat there for two long, long hours, hoping, listening, longing, and resentful, sullen, desperate, by turns; now half resolved to seek him, to cast herself upon his bosom and supplicate for some demonstration of the affection, so freely and richly lavished upon her heretofore by eye, word and caress; now avowing that she would die of heart-break sooner than she would adopt a course so humbling to woman's pride. At eleven o'clock she folded her work, closed the shutters, fastened down the windows and extinguished the lamp; exercising no remarkable degree of caution in performing the work. The library adjoined the sitting-room, and although there was no door of direct communication between the two, yet the occupant of the former could not well avoid hearing and understanding the meaning of the bustle prefacing her retiring for the night. If he did hear it, he would, if he had any consideration for her wishes and feelings, leave his employment—"important" as it was—and come to their chamber to exchange a few words with her before bidding her "good-night." Therefore, she dismissed her maid, professing that she was too wakeful to sleep, and wished to read awhile; then drew her chair near the fire—again to hearken for feet that did not come, to pine for loving tones and language that were not now to feed her hungry heart.

The hands of her watch pointed to twelve, when, exhausted and disheartened, she lay down upon her pillow, and she tossed there a dreary while before falling into a troubled sleep. Dreams connected and vivid, came with more profound slumbers. She was sitting upon the great rock at the spring, in the soft, summer moonlight with Robert. The story of his long-cherished attachment was still sounding in her ears, awakening the strange, sad heart-ache, the mingled pity and sisterly tenderness she remembered so well; his hand enfolded hers; his arm was about her waist;

when—sudden, stern and sad, up started the form and lineaments of his brother, and the whole might of her heart's love leaped out towards him. She stretched her arms to him; cried in the unutterable agony of her soul for him to come and release her—to take her with him,—that she loved him—him only—him, always! But he turned scornfully away, and Robert's grasp was inflexible as chains of wrought steel, binding her with a pressure that nearly deprived her of breath.

"Mine! mine!" he said, in fierce earnestness—"until death us do part!"

CHAPTER XIV.

WITH a smothered shriek—a last, frenzied cry of "Aleck! dearest Aleck!" Helen awoke from the nightmare.

She was sitting upright; the cold sweat dripping from her forehead; her hands clasped, and her lungs heaving convulsively, as if the imaginary pressure had been real, and but just removed. The room was dimly illumined by the dull, red glow of the embers. She had replenished the fire just before going to bed. Had it burned out so soon? Groping her way to the mantel, she struck a light and looked at her watch.

Ten minutes past two! and she was still alone! Where was he? Was there then truth in the horrible dream that had scared her native bravery from her breast, and had he deserted her? Or, was he ill? Had sudden sickness, or fatal accident befallen him in that far off, lonely room?

Seeking hastily for a wrapper, she took down from the wardrobe the crimson cashmere robe she had worn when summoned to meet Aleck in the office, on her wedding night. She thought of that interview while preparing for this, and the memory strengthened her resolve. Taking the candle with her, she stepped out into the cheerless hall. A ray of light stole from under the library door, but all was still within. Her soft step had not disturbed the student. With a beating heart she turned the bolt and entered.

"Who is there?" cried Aleck, angrily springing to his feet.

Then, as his wife's pale, shocked countenance met his sight, he passed his hand over his eyes, as if to dispel the mists of some horrible illusion, and said more gently,

"Ah! Helen! is it you? You startled me a little; is any thing the matter?"

"Not with *me*, darling!"

She had seen his face, and pride and resentment fled apace. The terrible anguish that had ploughed those furrows in the brow, and left its imprint upon every feature, should not be borne by him alone, while she lived to share the load. She crept up to him like a child to whom perfect love has taught boldness, and wound her arms about his neck; drew down his cheek to hers.

"Aleck! dear husband! you cannot reject my sympathy in your trouble, even while you may not think it best to confide to me its nature. I wish I could bear it with and for you!"

He strained her to his heart, as if he would never let her go.

"Darling! darling!" was all he could say, in accents strangled by the welling of the pent-up flood of feeling.

Then he placed her in the chair from which he had arisen; knelt before her, and still holding her in his arms, buried his face in her lap, while a storm of sobs shook his whole frame. The bewildered and terrified wife strove by every loving art to win him back to composure. Not once did she inquire into the cause of the agitation that could so master his healthy nerves and powerful will. She only implored him to be comforted, for her sake; reminded him that whatever other calamity had befallen him, they were still spared to one another; that their mutual affection remained unchanged.

"You *are* mine! mine only—are you not?" he asked, suddenly lifting himself to look at her. "You gave yourself to me not because you believed another unfaithful, but because you loved me."

"You know that I have always loved you, dearest!"

She pressed her lips to the hot eyes, laid his head upon her bosom.

"Do not think me weak, unmanly," he said gratefully. "But I had sat here all the night, surrounded by images of such horror; beset by reflections so agonizing, that the reaction produced by your blessed companionship was too great. I shall not be overpowered again. You have done me good, my comforting angel! Poor child!" he continued, stroking the pallid face bowed over his. "You are worn out with watching and anxiety. I am a careless brute, who does not deserve such a wife."

Her hand was upon his mouth and stopped the words.

"I am not worn out! I have had a long nap,—and awaking, was alarmed to find how late it was; became uneasy lest you might be sick, or some accident had happened, and came to look for you. This is the history of my intrusion."

"Intrusion! a welcome diversion! I was under a spell, and might have remained here until dawn, without moving, had you not broken it."

He was sitting upon the sofa, now, and pulled her, with gentle force, to his knee.—As she complied with his wish, she saw his eye rest upon a pile of papers heaped in the middle of the table, and that a shuddering anguish, a fearful look of sorrow and rage, went over his visage; felt him tremble violently under her weight.

"I cannot have you stay in this haunted chamber!" she said, in forced playfulness.—"The influence of the unholy spell is upon you still, I see."

"If I could tell you—but no! it would be cruel!"

"To me do you mean? If that withholds you from speaking freely, I can answer the objection. How often have you declared that I was the bravest girl in Christendom? and I am *your wife* now, Aleck!"

"Thank God for that!" was the fervent response. "There have been moments to-night, when I have been ready to call myself a villain—an unscrupulous criminally selfish villain—for having married you at the time, and in the manner I did. But you are my witness, dear one, that passionately as I loved you, I never uttered a syllable that conflicted with Robert's rights until I believed that you were freed—and by him!"

"Aleck! what are you saying? Did he not free me!" exclaimed Helen, growing deathly pale, more at his look and manner than his language.

"Hush, love! As I have said, you are mine—lawfully and forever! There was no wrong in what we did, although a morbid sensibility may discern cause for regret that our action was so hasty; that we relied too readily upon the evidence furnished us. But the result would have been the same had we waited for further developments. Be assured of that! I would have made you my wife at the earliest date to which I could gain your consent—in spite of our sorrow and the opposition of others. What should I do without the consolation of your society—the cordial of your sympathy now?"

"You are talking in enigmas," said Helen, colorless as marble, yet speaking firmly. "And since you have said thus much, I must know all. You wrong me in keeping it back. Every moment of suspense causes me additional and needless suffering. I cannot only be strong, but prudent and secret."

She stood in front of him with composed and resolute mien.

"Not so! You must come back to your old place—to

your home, dearest! only while I hold you fast, and feel the touch of your hand upon mine, can I have courage to go through with the sad tale. I will tell you! my heart aches to pour out its grief before you, and the knowledge must come to you sooner or later. Have you the strength to listen now?"

"I have the strength for any thing—for every thing but this racking suspense."

Carefully and gradually as he could, in his own excited state, he unfolded to her all that he had learned and suspected within the past four days.

While in Baltimore he had gone into a jeweller's in quest of some gift for her, and looking idly into a show-case of watches, espied one resembling so precisely a time-piece he had sent Robert from Europe, a year before, that he had asked leave to examine it. His gift to his brother was inscribed on the inside of the case with a peculiar cipher composed of their joint initials, and, to his astonishment, he found this identical hieroglyph within that he now held.

"This is a second-hand watch, I perceive," he remarked to the proprietor of the establishment.

"It is, sir, but a first-class article. One seldom sees a finer specimen of the kind in this country."

"I think that I recognize it as an old acquaintance," rejoined Mr. Lay, nonchalantly as he could speak. "If I were sure of the fact I should certainly buy it. Will it be any breach of confidence if you tell me the name of the person from whom you had it?"

"None, whatever, sir, provided we know it ourselves. Every thing in our business is conducted fairly and above board," replied the merchant, willing to secure a purchaser.

He referred to his books for the desired information. The watch was brought to the store on the twentieth of January by a gentleman who professed to dispose of it on behalf of another—but, beyond this, Aleck could learn nothing. The clerk who had concluded the bargain was out, and none of the other employés retained any recollection of the customer's appearance or name. Stipulating that he should have the refusal of the watch until a certain hour in the afternoon, Aleck left the shop and went to transact some business at the bank where his account had been kept ever since he reached his majority.

He was personally well known to the officials there, and the cashier, while paying over the amount he wished to draw, observed:—"By-the-way, Mr. Lay, I hope your brother has no cause of dissatisfaction with us. His deposits have usually been heavy, and his drafts so infrequent as to leave a large amount always to his credit. But, one day, about the middle of January, he surprised us by drawing upon us for every cent he had in our hands—for more, in fact, as he has learned from the statement of account we forwarded to him by mail. He overchecked, inadvertently, to the amount of five hundred dollars."

"Impossible!" ejaculated Aleck. "Who presented the drafts?"

"A neighbor of yours, I think—Colonel Floyd."

"What!"

"Unless I was mistaken that was the name by which your brother's letter introduced him," answered the bank officer, in some surprise. "I kept it as a voucher, although the bearer came to us in company with a well-known and highly respectable citizen."

"I should like to see both letter and draft, if you please!" requested Aleck, recovering himself.

They were quickly produced. The note was brief, and dated December 24th; and it, as well as the drafts, bore Robert's signature.

"The genuineness of which I deny!" said Aleck to the

alarmed cashier. "In the first place, I do not believe that my brother would have taken a step so singular and important without consulting me; in the second, I happen to know that Colonel Floyd would not be the individual likely to be intrusted with this business. Mr. Robert Lay is not at home just now, and I ask you, as a favor, to let the matter rest until I can privately investigate it."

The promise was willingly given, and the perturbed Aleck directed his steps again to the jewellers, more anxious than ever to obtain possession of the watch, and unriddle the mystery of its present ownership.

The head clerk was in the store this time, a sharp, quick Yankee, whose wits were always on the alert, and who was, in this case, disposed to be very communicative. He recollected perfectly the incident of the watch being offered for sale, and the physiognomy, form, etc., of the man who brought it to the establishment. His attention was particularly drawn to these by the oddity of the proposed negotiation on the part of a gentleman so imposing in demeanor, and stylish in apparel. He could tell more; for chancing, on the day after the purchase, to enter the office of a certain fashionable hotel, he had seen the same person sitting there, smoking in company with a party of acquaintances—had inquired his name, and learned that it was Floyd.

With the watch safe in his pocket, Aleck thanked the obliging salesman, and hurried off to follow up another clue to the truth of the dark surmise he yet entertained vaguely—almost blindly. This was an inspection of the hotel register of January 20th. He found upon the record of the 18th Colonel Floyd's name, written in his dashing hand. He had been in the city at that date then, although Aleck had never heard of the visit until now. He it was, beyond a question, who had presented the false checks, if false they were, and sold the watch. Could he be acting as Robert's agent? accredited, yet secret? If this were so, there was deep villany somewhere; if not, imagination recoiled at the black abyss of crime unveiled by the doubt. Still undergoing the torments of indecision and never-still suspicions, he set out upon his return journey.

The nearest dépôt to Maple Hill was Rock's Tavern, to which place Robert's farewell letter to his brother had directed him to send for his horse. Hero had been found there, securely stabled, and had now occupied his old stall at Greenfield for many weeks; but motives of delicacy, the principal of which was to shield Robert from public remark, had deterred Aleck from making any inquiries as to who had left the animal in the hostler's care. Dismissing these now as absurd, where issues so momentous were involved, he, upon his arrival at the tavern, made it his business to search out the negro who had charge of the stables, and recalling to his mind the circumstance and the time of its occurrence, asked whether he had himself seen Mr. Robert Lay while he waited at the house for the afternoon train. The fellow professed to recollect every thing connected with the matter, and was positive in declaring that the horse had not been brought to the stable until two hours after the cars had passed, and when it was already dark; that his rider was a negro of gruff speech and few words, who represented that he had been ordered to leave the horse in his, the hostler's, keeping, until Mr. Alexander Lay, of Maple Hill, should send for him, and forthwith departed upon foot. He would be loath, he subjoined, hesitatingly, to get an innocent person into mischief, but one of the stable-boys had recognized the horseman by flashing a lantern into his face as he was leaving the yard. He was, the groom was certain, a free colored man of questionable character, who lived about five miles away.

Aleck diverged from his road on the way home, to call at

this fellow's abode—a mean cabin, situated in a pine grove about midway between Colonel Floyd's plantation and the dépôt, a sequestered, ill-looking spot, fit to be the scene of evil deeds that shunned the light. The owner of this choice habitation was absent, but his wife appeared at the door when the carriage stopped, and manifested signs of extreme trepidation at beholding the visitor. Alighting with a severe, determined countenance, Mr. Lay called her aside, and boldly proclaimed his knowledge of her husband's errand to the tavern on Christmas night—a job that would get him into trouble unless he could show that he came honestly by the horse, or confessed who had commissioned him to perform the act. The woman hung back for a time. She knew nothing of the matter; she had not seen the animal; she was away from home all Christmas week, and a dozen lies more, which Aleck upset as fast as she brought them forward.

At last, as he was turning off with the warning that she and her accomplices might shortly find themselves before a tribunal where means would be devised to extort the truth, she burst into tears, and offered to reveal all she knew, provided he would not betray her to her husband. A horse had been brought to their house about three o'clock on Christmas day, by Booker, Colonel Floyd's head man. She had peeped at him through the window as he talked in the yard with Jeff, her husband, had seen him hand Jeff a bank note, and that the latter led the horse to the rude hut they called a barn, and shut him in, locking the door and pocketing the key. She did not dare to ask questions, or indeed to mention what she had witnessed, unless Jeff should volunteer an allusion to the affair. He made but one remark that could have any bearing upon the subject, and that was at night-fall, just after he had despatched his supper.

"I shan't be home until near midnight," he had said,

"and I've got one word to say before I start. Whatever you've seen to-day, or may hear to-night, hold your tongue, or you'll suffer for it."

With that he went out, and she distinctly heard the tramping of hoofs soon afterwards.

"While anxiety and suspense were wrought to the highest pitch by my endeavors to shape a reasonable theory out of all this," continued Aleck, "I reached home, and the first object I beheld was Colonel Floyd's carriage, with Booker standing by it; heard from you that he himself was waiting to see me. His ostensible business was to ask me to fix a day for the settlement of his guardianship accounts. He offered the intelligence that he could hand over immediately that portion of your estate which was in ready money, and also render satisfactory statements of sales of property; the yearly crops and servants' hire; sums disbursed for your expenses; and a great deal more plausible talk, to which I lent only half an ear. As adroitly as I could in my unsettled state, I forced him to speak of his liabilities to Robert, the proofs of which I told him my brother had showed me in a couple of bonds, executed and signed by Colonel Floyd, covering an amount of nine hundred dollars. Accomplished villain as I knew him to be, I was yet thunderstruck when he produced from his pocket-book the identical bonds, and displayed a long cross-mark on the face of each, made, he averred, by Robert himself, on the day before Christmas, at which date he had paid over the full amount of his indebtedness, and received these in testimony thereof. Now, my darling, do not be too much shocked by what I am going to say. At twelve o'clock, that very Christmas Eve, Robert and I sat in my chamber, talking over his prospects, pecuniary and matrimonial, and he exhibited these very papers uncancelled—told me of the debt still due to him, expressing his doubt as to its final liquidation, and his regret for the weakness that had beguiled him into lending money to an unprincipled spendthrift."

"Can it be!" exclaimed Helen. "Yet I heard Colonel Floyd tell you—"

"You heard him tell me!" interrupted Aleck, with increasing excitement—"like the liar that he is, that he had never held any communication with Robert since the noon of the 24th of December; that the annulled bonds were delivered to him at that time; the papers which I stand prepared to swear I saw twelve hours later in my brother's hands. I purposely made him repeat the statement in your presence, that I might have a credible witness of the astounding falsehood. Now come several grave questions. By what means did he obtain possession of those bonds, and Robert's watch, a prized keepsake, which I have often heard him declare he would never part with on any consideration? If that woman's tale be true, and it is corroborated by the hostlers, Colonel Floyd's man Booker must have seen Robert, and had some transaction with him on Christmas morning; else how came he by the horse he left at the free negro's? What is it?" for Helen clasped her hands with a low ejaculation.

"I do not know that it is worth mentioning," she said, "but on that day I took a long walk in the woods back of Belleview, and while sitting under a clump of evergreens, a mile or more from the house, I saw Booker pass on horseback. I had only a partial view of the horse, but I remember he was dark bay in color, and carried his head high, like a gentleman's hunter. Could it have been Robert's Hero?"

"I believe it," said her husband, emphatically. "In what direction was he going—along what road?"

"That was the strangest part of it! He rode through the thickest heart of the forest, where there was not even a bridle-path. I supposed that he was taking a short cut from the Bryantown to the Maysville road."

"The very route he would have chosen if he wished to go by stealth to Jeff Harris's house. Go on! You heard and saw nothing more while you were there?"

"Nothing—the day was very still. Oh, yes, I did hear a gun! but it sounded some distance off—I should say half a mile."

"Was this before or after Booker passed you?"

"Before—some time before. My idea was, when I saw him, that he had fired it, for there are not many sportsmen daring enough to hunt on Colonel Floyd's grounds."

"Does he allow Booker to carry firearms?" asked Aleck, assuming the composure that was contradicted by the white strain of the muscles on the lower part of his face.

"Not that I know of. I do not recollect ever seeing him with a gun. Colonel Floyd rarely stirs from the house without his. I have told you that it was by this sign that Sally identified him in the eaves-dropper behind the oak at the spring, one night, when Robert and myself were talking together."

Abandoning the effort to look and speak as if no great horror were upon her spirit, she said, gazing tremblingly into her husband's eyes—the more fearfully as she saw them try to avoid hers—

"Aleck! you have not said all yet! Tell me plainly, what is your fear? My brain is in such a whirl that I cannot connect all the circumstances you have enumerated. I only feel that there is some frightful mystery in this."

"Would it be wise or merciful in me to burden you with what may be a mistaken conjecture?" he answered, evasively. "Here are Robert's letters—or those purporting to have come from him since his strange flight. Will you look them over with me?"

The first was dated Washington, D. C., and contained but eight or ten lines. It was, as the writer termed it, "a miserable scrawl," and signed—"in great haste, R. C. L." The second was longer, and date and postmark were Vicksburg, Miss. In it, he spoke of himself as a man wrecked in heart and well-nigh ruined in fortune, and intimated his intention of seeking a residence in some distant land. Dishonored and disappointed, he could not yet face his former associates.

"I have not had one word from you, or from L., since I forsook home, and resigned reputation for her sake. Women are the most faithless of created beings, as even you may find some day to your cost. Love to your wife. I read a notice of your marriage in a Baltimore paper. Are you not obliged to me for stepping out of the way in the nick of time? She was easily consoled, and I am not the person to regret this; yet I should have respected her more if she had paid a decent regard to the proprieties of the case. I wish you joy of your bargain, and often amuse myself by fancying how entirely you agree in heaping contempt upon my devoted head. Ah, well! so wags the world! and I must not complain. It is not likely that you will hear from me again shortly. I leave this place this afternoon, for New Orleans, where, unless I change my mind, I shall take passage for Europe. You don't care for me now, old scamp, and I am fast learning resignation to this conviction. Let Greenfield stand as it is, for a year—within which time I will forward instructions as to the disposition I wish you to make of the property.

"Your's more carelessly than of yore,

"ROBERT C. LAY."

Aleck's earliest perusal of this epistle had been so hasty

and indignant that he had failed to note its irregular characters; been incapable of comparing its coarse, careless language with Robert's gentle and habitually courteous style. That his scrutiny and conclusions on this night had been more searching and correct, was evidenced by his next movement.

"Compare them!" he said, laying down before his wife a letter which his brother had written him while he was abroad.

The clean, clear sheet offered at the first glance such a contrast to the Vicksburg document that Helen changed color with surprise and consternation before her husband proceeded, word by word, letter by letter, to point out the dissimilarity between the two. A general resemblance existed—sufficient to deceive a cursory or unsuspecting reader, but the longer one looked the more bungling appeared the forgery.

"What does it mean?" questioned Helen, in a suppressed voice of awe or fright.

"Just this—" Aleck pressed down his wrath and grief to reply—"just this! our poor brother never wrote either of these communications. They are part of a villanous plot contrived to dupe us into a belief of his unworthiness, and to hide, Heaven alone knows what degree of, treachery and crime. The introductory step in the system of deception that has imposed upon no one more than myself—blind, besotted fool that I was! was that libellous letter delivered to me on Christmas night—which—mark me! that wretch Petronius confessed to me in this room, not four hours ago, he did not get from Robert! The cowardly knave, terrified by my manner into the belief that I had discovered his false dealing, owned that he had cherished a grudge against me, from the evening of that meeting at Mr. Shore's, on account of my public rebuke to himself; that Booker had taunted him with the story several times, and, meeting him in the road on the afternoon of Christmas day, offered him a chance of paying off the score by annoying and mortifying me. The job was an easy one, and if carried through well he was to receive ten dollars. He had only to give me this letter and declare that he had had it from Mr. Robert Lay; that he had met him at such and such a place on the road, and been commissioned to deliver the envelope into my hands. The rascally hypocrite did his work well. "Oh!" he groaned, arising and striding through the room, "how dull—how madly stupid I have been!"

Helen sat like a statue.

"Dearest!" she ventured to say, after a while, "where, then, is Robert? What has become of him?"

He stopped—letting his clinched fist fall heavily upon the table. "Before Heaven I speak what I believe to be the truth, when I declare that Colonel Floyd *murdered* him—either with his own hands, or by means of his servant Booker!"

In his overwhelming excitement he had not made due allowance for his wife's weaker nerves; had not appreciated the fact that she had had but one little hour in which to receive and comprehend the dread conviction that had been growing in his mind for three days.

As the word "murdered" left his tongue, she sprang to her feet with a wild, horrified stare, and when the sentence was finished, gave a cry, and fell back fainting.

CHAPTER XV.

It was not long after sunrise the next morning when Aleck Lay dismounted at the Greenfield gate. Returning slightly, and with an absent air, the surprised salutations of the few servants who were about the stables and yard, he went quickly up the walk to the house door, unlocked it, entered, and shut it behind him. The confined air in the halls struck coldly to his heart; the shadows lurking in corners, the feeble light glimmering through the barred shutters, had something ghostly about them. Unconsciously, he trod softly in ascending the stairs;—more lightly and slowly as he reached his brother's vacant chamber. It was very dark, and, to his imagination, colder than the rest of the house. It required an effort of courage to pass the threshold, and he had to grope his way across the room when he wished to draw a curtain and throw wide a blind. Every thing was in perfect order. Aunt Ruth had spent half a day there, during the first week of Robert's absence; had arranged clothing and furniture; swept and dusted, before, in obedience to Aleck's directions, she had shut up the chamber and turned the key on the outside. She had performed her self-imposed duty with many tears, but the housewifery eyes were not therefore dimmed, nor had the neat, swift fingers lost their cunning. Aleck's present expedition was undertaken at his wife's suggestion, and Aunt Ruth's motherly care for her absent boy, joined to her spinsterly particularity, was the main cause.

When Helen was fully acquainted with the nature and extent of her husband's dreads, and had regained some measure of her usual firmness and penetration, he found her acute intelligence and correct memory invaluable assistants in forwarding his researches. She had recapitulated Sally's account of the dishonorable conduct of Colonel Floyd on the night of the rendezvous at the spring;—his attempts to induce Robert, and then herself, to consent to a marriage contract; his chagrin and rage at his failure, which, after overhearing the conversation under the oak, he must have known was irremediable. The maid had never dared to confide the truth of her discovery to her mistress until they were safely installed at Maple Hill, and, when she did impart it, had joined to the tale such confused details of Lily's attempted elopement, and the scene between master and man on the back porch, while she cowered under the steps, as awakened Helen's amazed curiosity, but not her fears. Now these were recalled, and Sally subjected to a thorough examination. Upon sifting her evidence, little that was new could be elicited, and she was stout in her conviction that Colonel Floyd and Booker were out "hunting runaways" when his ward was married.

Aleck, reverting to his impression that the note brought by Gabriel to Robert, on the morning of their parting, was not directed by Helen, but Lily, and coupling it with Robert's declaration that he had an appointment at ten o'clock, was sure that this assignation was, in some manner, the plan by which he was lured into danger and destruction.

"If I only had that note, I feel assured that I should hold the key to the whole mystery," he said, wistfully. "How I wish that I had not obeyed the mistaken delicacy that forbade my questioning him as to its contents!"

"Do you remember what he did with it?" asked Helen.

"I cannot say with certainty—but my idea is that he thrust it into his vest pocket so soon as he finished reading it."

"Aunt Ruth told me not long since," said Helen, thoughtfully, "that the hardest trial she had had, in all the sorrow connected with Robert's departure, was sitting down in his deserted room and mending a vest he had thrown aside just before going out, Christmas morning. She met him on the stairs directly after breakfast, and observing that the vest had lost a button, and was frayed about the collar and pockets, advised him to change it before he went to the court-house. It was not until she visited his chamber, several days afterwards, to put away his things, preparatory to locking it up, that she knew how well he had obeyed her injunction. The vest lay on the bureau, where he had tossed it upon taking it off. She was exceedingly touched by this proof of his regard for her wishes. It may be that the Providence who has so strangely guided your investigations thus far, may lead you to further discoveries by means of this seemingly insignificant incident. Say nothing to Aunt Ruth about it. The trouble will fall upon her soon enough. Wait for certainty."

To find this cast-off garment, then, was Aleck's object in revisiting an apartment where every thing he beheld aroused poignant grief and vain, bitter remorse. The drawers at which he began his explorations were carefully packed by Aunt Ruth's tidy hands, and his, although less skilful, handled each article with reverent tenderness. A great change had come over his thoughts of Robert. In place of the flush of shame and anger he had been used to feel warm his brow, at thought of his disgraceful flight, and the unmanly conduct that preceded it; his supposed infidelity and duplicity; the old tide of fostering fondness for his young, handsome brother joined with anguish at his loss, and deep repentance for the rank injustice he had done that gentle, noble spirit, in thought and speech, and swelled his heart almost to bursting. There was no time to be wasted in unavailing lamentations, or he must have bowed before the torrent of feeling and memory that flowed at sight of many familiar, and now sacred relics. The homeliest article of apparel—Robert's hunting suit, the heavy, muddy boots he had worn upon their last tramp through the low grounds—a stained and shapeless straw hat, discarded as past worthy when the fishing season was over, and left, forgotten and useless, hanging upon a peg in the closet; these had become most precious in his sight.

One master emotion drove him onward in the work to which he believed destiny had appointed him; forced him forward over the graves of early and dear association and later loves; forbade the burning, bloodshot eyes the indulgence of a tear—the aching heart the relief of a sigh. Justice—justice, swift and awful, upon the head of his brother's destroyer! He was not malignant or vindictive by nature, but he experienced a savage thrill of exultation in the thought that the bloodhound Detection was ready to spring at the murderer's throat,—ready, and straining at the leash, which he—the rightful avenger of blood—held.

"At last!"

He had feared lest he might not recognize the garment he sought; yet he knew it at a glance, as it was revealed by an opening drawer of the wardrobe. It lay uppermost, smoothly folded, the wrong side out, but he recollected the glossy black silk, and its tiny embroidered rose-bud, in the portion of the fabric composing the collar. He snatched it up, then stood for a moment, powerless to end his anxiety by further examination. He had to summon physical nerve with moral resolution before he thrust his fingers in trembling desperation into the pocket. They touched a paper, dragged it forth—an envelope directed to "Mr. Robert Lay,

Greenfield," and bearing in one corner the words—" by Gabriel." He was obliged to sit down to read it, he was so utterly weak. The ink was very pale, the pen-strokes delicate. An exclamation of extreme impatience escaped him at the trifling delay caused by the necessity of approaching a window before he could decipher the few lines upon which depended so much.

"Robert"—he read—"I am very, very sad to-day, and there is no one excepting yourself to whom I can speak of my great trouble. It would do me good, be an unspeakable comfort, if I could have one, just one more talk with you before there is put between us a barrier that must last for a lifetime. Believe me, I am not jealous of Helen's superior claims. I pray hourly for your happiness and hers; yet I cannot help feeling lonely now that I am about to lose my brother—my best—I had almost said, my only friend! If you have a half hour to spare this morning, will you not meet me at ten o'clock under the spruce pine? the pic-nic ground, you remember! It is not so far from the road to the court-house that you will lose much time in complying with this, as it may seem to you, bold request. I will explain my reasons for making it when we meet. Until then, trust me so far as to believe them good and sufficient. What I have to say concerns you no less than myself. Do not disappoint me! I shall wait for you until twelve o'clock. Your fond sister, LILY."

Five minutes later, Aleck stood upon the piazza and shouted to a negro in the stable-yard—

"Ben! saddle Hero, and bring him around directly! directly! do you hear?"

"Hero, did you say, Mars' Aleck?" said the man, coming nearer.

"Hero! and hurry! are you deaf?"

The groom shook his head as he disappeared in the stable, implying that he could say much more on the subject if he cared to risk further parley with his impatient superior.

While he waited, Aleck walked the porch-floor fast and furiously; gnawed his lip, as was his trick in moments of intense excitement; drew his breath in hot pants, like a wild animal thirsting for prey. Hero was led around to the door, a splendid creature, full-blooded and thoroughly trained, stepping high and daintily.

How poor Robert loved that horse! The brother's look was not less fierce in the recollection, but the pat upon the arched neck, the word of salutation—"Hero—old fellow!" that accompanied the hand caress, were signals of the inward thought.

"He's dreadful skittish now-a-days, Mars' Aleck!" cautioned the hostler, respectfully. "Not a man on this place dars to back him. Pears like he's been bewitched sence he was fetched home from Rock's tarvern! He flung Art'ur three times on de way from dar—as you heerd, may-be. Sumthin or somebody's sp'ilt him for good an' all—I'm afeard!"

"He won't throw me! Whoa!"

A spring seated Aleck in the saddle,—the horse bounded forward, and steed and rider swept down the lane with the rush of a whirlwind.

"Thar's a par of 'em!" commented Ben, recovering his breath. "How Mars' Aleck's eyes did snap! Wonder what's crossed him now? I'd rather meet de debbil on de darkest night dat ever shone dan to stan in his way when his blood is up!"

It so happened that the illustrious Gabriel was at that very moment sauntering along the middle of the high road, in the direction of Belleview, snuffing in copious draughts of the pleasant air, and enjoying mightily the increasing warmth of the sun's rays upon his back. His mother, the baker of Belleview, had had "poor luck" with her last jug of yeast, and designing, on this day, to repair the misfortune, had, as he discontentedly phrased it, "rousted" her hopeful son from his bed at an unconscionably early hour, and despatched him to a neighboring plantation, to borrow from a sister in the profession a small quantity to "raise" the fresh supply. This was the meaning of the small tin-pail—in southern parlance, "bucket"—that dangled from Gabriel's hand, and was occasionally whirled dexterously about his head without a drop of its contents being spilled; for the errand-boy was an adept in all arts of prestidigitation that came within the range of his observation and practice.

As he walked he sang, kicking up the loose dirt in the road with his toes; stopping, now and then, in his march, never in his song, to shy a stone at a bird, or a bushy evergreen where bird or hare might be hiding.

"In old Kentuck, in de middle of a brake,
Dar lives a nigger, an' dey call him Jake:
Aroun' de wood his axe am ringin',
An' dis de song dat he am singin':—
    Oh, whar did you come from?
    Knock a nigger down!
    Oh, whar did you come from?
    Knock a nigger down!

"Hi! what dat?"

Ballad and feet were arrested that he might hearken. From afar off came to his ears the long, rapid gallop of a strained or fiery horse, beating loudly upon the softened ground; ringing sharply against the stones.

"Somebody in a hurry soon in de mornin'!" and evidently considering this a ridiculous instance of non-improvement of the rights purchased by early rising, he laughed, and went on in the roundelay:—

"Oh, come, my lub, an' go wid me!
We're gwine for to leave dis back country;
Hoss an' a cart for to tote you roun',
Walk up hill an'—

"Lor! ef 'taint Mars' Aleck!"

There was a level and straight stretch of road before him, and just entering this vista he descried a horseman bearing rapidly down towards him. Aleck Lay had never spoken unkindly to the boy; on the contrary, the graceless imp had received from both brothers pleasant jests, friendly notice, and donations which were innumerable by his arithmetical powers. There was no conceivable reason why he should fear to encounter either of them, if his conscience were void of offence as was their conduct—yet he stood stock still for an instant, eyes starting from their sockets, staring at the advancing terror;—then, seized, as braver men—ay, and brave armies have been since—by an unreasoning panic, he darted to the road-side fence, scrambled over it, and scampered across the field beyond, fast as his legs could carry and fear could drive him.

"Hallo—there! Gabriel! I want to speak to you!" called Aleck, who by this time was near enough to identify the flying figure.

Gabriel ran on the faster, looking over his shoulder to see whether he were followed; and, irritated at his contumacy, Aleck put Hero at the fence, cleared it, and galloped over the fallow ground upon the fugitive's track. A race so unequal could not last long.

"Stop! you scoundrel! or I will ride you down!" came so distinctly to the boy's ear that he again glanced back, to calculate his chances for gaining the next and a higher fence.

Not a dozen yards in his rear was his pursuer; his orbs of fire seemed to scorch his sight, even in that brief glimpse; before he could run ten steps further, the horse, whose streaming mane, glaring eyeballs, and open mouth, gave him the aspect of a demon, would be upon him. He yelled with affright, and dropped prone upon the earth.

"You young villain!" Aleck leaned from his saddle, and grasping the boy by the collar, dragged him to his feet. "You audacious rascal! what do you mean by running away from me when I order you to stop?"

"Lor' a massy, Mars' Aleck! is it you? I 'clar 'fore gracious I thought 'was an evil! I 'most skeered out of my senses!" stuttered the victim, affecting the uttermost astonishment.

His captor was in no humor to be amused.

"If I served you right, I would flog you soundly!" he pursued, giving him an admonitory shake, under which Gabriel staggered more than was at all necessary. "You knew me perfectly well before you started to run. If you want to save your bones, tell me the exact truth in answer to the questions I am about to ask you."

"Yes, sar!" Gabriel surveyed the heavy hunting-whip in the rider's hand with an air of serious reflection.

"You brought a letter to Mr. Robert Lay, on Christmas morning. Who sent it?"

"How was I to know, Mars' Aleck?" whimpered the hypocrite, the picture of aggrieved innocence. "I didn't see it wrote."

"Who gave it to you?" Aleck tightened his hold on the collar and raised his whip. "I'm not to be trifled with, boy!"

Gabriel studied the lowering visage above him,

"If you won't tell on me, sir! Dey said dey would kill me ef I let on a word, an' what dey says, dey will do, Mars' Aleck!"

"So will I! you may be sure of that! What did you do with the letter Miss Helen sent by you, which you promised so faithfully to carry safely?"

"Wasn't dat de same I gave to Mars' Robert?" letting his under jaw drop, and looking as like a fool as he could.

"I shall have to do it, I see!"

Aleck jumped from his horse and clutched the liar's arm, his mien so full of wrathful determination that the last spark of Gabriel's audacity expired.

"Ef you jes won't, sir, I will tell you all—every single thing!" he begged, quaking with fear. "Marster, he nabbed me in de stable, while I was gettin' de horse ready, an says he, 'Gi' me de letter!' and fore I knowed whar I was, Mars' Aleck, he had it in his hand, an says he to daddy, who had come in arter him—'Keep him here till I come back!' and he went to de house. Byme-by, here he come, wid anudder letter, or maybe de same—I can't read, you member, Mars' Aleck—an tells me to ride like fury over to Greenfield an 'liver it, an ef I ever breathed a word of what he said or done he'd make mince-meat of me; and daddy says, 'Ef you open yer ugly mouth 'bout dis I'll mash it in for you;'—an what was a poor feller to do, Mars' Aleck? Miss Helen, she can tell you how bad I felt when she talked to me so kind dat day, an I didn't dar', for my life, to let her know how I had 'ceived her. I'm sure I allers set a deal of store by Miss Helen."

"And that is all you have to say?" interrupted Aleck. "To whom did you give the note Mr. Robert Lay sent back by your hand?"

"To daddy," the boy confessed, shame-facedly. "He was waitin' for me at de fur gate, an I dar'sn't say 'no' to him when he speaks his mind. He gi' me orders as how I was to tell Miss Helen dat Mars' Robert hadn't wrote nothin', but jes said 'All's right,' an I stuck to de story, as Miss Helen knows."

"That is all now, is it?" interposed Aleck, as before.

"Every thing, sir! I clar fore gracious I don't know nothin' besides, and I never told a lie in my born days, only 'cept that once—"

His auditor had other work before him than staying to remind the pattern of juvenile veracity of the array of fibs he had endeavored to palm off upon him five minutes previous to this solemn asseveration. It was not certain that he heard any part of it beyond the first section, for, before it was finished, he was scouring the field, at full speed, towards the highway. Gabriel stood motionless and agape until he saw Hero leap the fence and the centaur-like figure vanish, with meteor swiftness, at a curve in the road.

Then he remarked, with philosophical coolness—

"Dat ar' horse is done some fox-huntin' in his day, I reckon!" and bethought himself of his pail of yeast.

Not a drop remained in the fallen vessel;—worse than that! Hero had put his iron foot upon it and crushed it—to borrow Gabriel's simile—"flat as a pan-cake," cover and all! Here was a predicament! Explanation of some kind was unavoidable, and a flogging equally inevitable. The only question that remained for his fertile genius to work upon during the melancholy stroll homewards, was whether the aforesaid flagellation would be lighter if he made a partial confession of the facts in the case, or if he plied his maternal parent with an entirely original version of the accident.

To these perplexing lucubrations we are compelled to leave him, that we may follow the proceedings of a more interesting personage.

CHAPTER XVI.

About noon of the same day, a party of four horsemen halted in the public route to the Court House, at the entrance—if entrance it could be called—to a disused cart-road which led into the Belleview woods. There were still "draw bars," that is, rails, that could be slipped back through their openings in their supporting posts—marking the spot where vehicles—wood-carts and farm-wagons—were once wont to pass in, but they were now moss-grown and decayed, and sumach and huckleberry bushes grew thickly on the other side. None of the band hesitated, however, to follow their leader when he tore the rotten rails from their rests, and, remounting, rode boldly past the sign-board—a new and staring one, that forbade trespassing "under the severest penalty of the law." One pointed this out silently to another as they entered the gap, and the exchange of looks was pregnant with meaning.

"That was put up the first week in January," said a third. "A queer time to warn off poachers. Especially when there is no game worth shooting in these woods at any season!" said his companion.

The fourth man said nothing—only pushed on deeper into the forest. He knew well the position of the "Spruce-pine" and the "old picnic ground." The tree, the solitary specimen of the kind in the vicinity, stood on the verge of a little glade, a natural break in the wood, turfy, and not too densely shaded, where, years ago, the young people for miles around had held a sylvan fête—a bounteous dinner, and a dance on the grass that lasted until dark. Robert had danced with Lily Calvert more frequently than with any other girl there, and Helen was oftenest his brother's partner. How strangely the vision of the holiday scene arose before the latter now, bent, as he was, upon a mission so fearfully at variance with the events of that midsummer day!

He was diverted from his saddened musings by the extraordinary conduct of his horse. He had ridden Hero that morning at Helen's desire. She fancied that she would be able to decide, upon seeing him now, whether he were the animal Booker rode upon that momentous Christmas day; and although, after hearing Gabriel's story, Aleck had not deemed it necessary to afford her an opportunity to apply this test to her memory, he had not cared, or indeed thought, to exchange the steed for his own riding-horse. He had gone by the most direct road to the Court House, laid his story before a magistrate, obtained a search-warrant, and authority to arrest the suspected man; collected a few friends in whose zeal and discretion he could confide—the magistrate asking permission to be one of the number—and having despatched a line to Maple Hill, to allay the solicitude his wife might feel at his prolonged absence, had set out for the spot designated in Lily's note. They had quitted the faint wheel-ruts that marked the windings of the old road several minutes before, and were making their way, still piloted by Aleck, in the direction of the spruce-tree, when Hero stopped short, threw up his head, and uttered a shrill neigh—a sound so expressive of terror, so like a human utterance of fear or anguish, that it thrilled every heart.

"Is this the place?" asked one of the party, in an awed whisper, riding up close to Aleck's side.

"No! it is fully a hundred yards off! On, sir!" he urged the animal, and mad with impatience, forgetting that it was Robert's horse, and entitled to all gentleness of treatment at his hands, he struck him sharply with the whip. Hero reared once, then stood like a rock, his fore-feet planted deep in the damp, woody soil, ears pointed forward, eyes dilate, and nostrils quivering widely—the picture of mortal fear.

"There is something in this, Lay!" said the magistrate—a grave, judicious man, whom no one had ever accused of excitability of imagination or a too ready credulity. "Gentlemen, if you please, we will examine this ground before going further!"

Every man was upon his feet in a moment. The undergrowth was thick thereabouts, and they literally crawled upon their hands and knees in their anxiety to make the search thorough. Stones were upturned; leaves swept away, that the bare earth might testify of any recent disturbance; broken twigs and boughs inspected; but the keenest eyes discerned nothing unusual, nothing that varied from the ordinary aspect of a winter forest.

Leaving their horses, they went on foot to the natural clearing marked by the evergreen spruce, and there the examination was, if possible, more narrowly vigilant, and with a like result. There was absolutely naught to indicate that any deed of violence had ever marred the peaceful quiet of the pretty glade. The sun shone brightly upon the young turf, already sprouting under the genial skies; and warm breezes of the past week; there were birds twittering in the naked branches above their heads; and as they drew together in the centre of the grass-plot, for conference upon the next best step to be taken, a hare, the most timid of forest-bred creatures, scudded by on her way to her not distant form.

"We must make the arrest without additional evidence,

gentlemen!" decided Mr. Reverdy, the magistrate. "Colonel Floyd's possession of the watch and bonds must be accounted for, and the matter of the supposed forgery cleared up, before we can lawfully or conscientiously abandon the task we have undertaken."

"It will be a bad business for us all if he gets clear, after we have brought so serious a charge," demurred one of the quartette—a nervous, cautious man, and a near neighbor of the Floyds. "The colonel is a troublesome customer to manage, when his blood is up. I shouldn't relish being at enmity with him, if he is to go at large. He never forgives an affront."

"Then, Mr. Dickson, you had better not accompany us!" rejoined Mr. Reverdy, in calm contempt. "For my own part, I shall probe this affair to the bottom, at any and every cost to myself. If no one else will go with us, Mr. Lay and myself will serve the warrant. Shall we return to our horses?"

Murmuring something to the effect that he had been "misunderstood," and that he was as "little afraid as any other man," Mr. Dickson walked back with the rest.

"Lay! this is certainly very singular!" said the foremost of them, going up to Hero and laying his hand upon his neck:

The poor beast was covered with sweat, and shook in every joint. He responded to the friendly touch by another frightened neigh,—wild and piercing as the former; and when Aleck took him by the head to lead him on again, struck his hoofs deep into the earth and pulled back with all his might. They all gathered about him, in wonderment and inquiry. Aleck was the first to remark that the creature paid no attention to their movements; that his eyes were fixed upon a cluster of saplings not four feet off. This they had examined more than once in their fruitless quest, but the change in his features now directed the attention of the others to the place.

"There are no pine-trees near! Those are hickory saplings! Why should the ground under them be covered with pine-needles!"

The exclamation acted like an electric shock. All sprang forward to the work of clearing away the thick brown covering. It was several inches in depth, and looked as if swine had been bedded there during the cold weather—an illusion that had completely imposed upon the search-party, until they observed that the leaves could not have fallen from the trees above; and the improbability that they had been brought from a distance for such a purpose, when the herd could as well have been littered under the pines themselves, presented itself to every mind. A hoe, spade, and pickaxe were hastily produced from a bag which was lashed to the front of Hero's saddle, and while three used these to rake off the matted needles, the fourth scraped it aside with his bare hands.

It was removed in less time than it has taken to describe the process, and there remained exposed a considerable area of lighter color than the black, rich soil around it, as if the earth had been carefully spread over a wide space, to avoid the appearance of elevation in any one spot. Near the middle of this was plainly visible a sunken spot, long and narrow, and perfectly regular in outline. Not a word was uttered, of command or remark, as each of the three men bent to his work, and dug as if his own life or death depended upon his diligence.

Of the three! The spade had fallen from the nerveless hand of the fourth, and his next neighbor, he who had labored with his fingers only, caught it ere it touched the ground, and struck it boldly into the soil. Sick with horror, Aleck leaned against a tree, and watched the rapidly deepening chasm at his feet;—noted the signs of a former excavation, in the leaves and sticks mingled with the earth they cast up. Would they have to dig far down?—and if so, would his strength and reason endure this racking suspense until they reached it?

The pit was already two feet deep, and the dirt lay compact as ever, settled by the snows and rains of two long winter months. Three feet! they worked well! Four!—they must be nearing it.

Ha! how carelessly that man plunged the pick-axe up to the helve! Had he no thought of what he might strike—into what substance the keen, cruel point might sink at any moment! Again he swung the implement in the air—and Aleck seized his arm convulsively when he would have brought it down.

"For heaven's sake, Dickson! be careful! you cannot be far from it now!" he cried, harshly.

None of the excited laborers had realized their exact position before; but they eyed the dimensions of the pit now with careful, wondering attention, and the man who wielded the pick stepped one side and laid down the dangerous instrument. The others kept on with their task, but delved warily, more slowly—scraping instead of digging. The tedious process, necessary as he felt it to be—their expression of watchfulness as each spadeful was removed—were more horrible than all that had gone before.

"This is dying by inches!" he whispered to Dickson, who stood at his side; and he put up his hand to wipe away the cold beads that, dripping from his forehead, were literally blinding him.

"My God!"

The low cry broke from one of the workmen, and at the same instant Dickson clutched Aleck's shoulder, dragged him some paces before he could recover from his surprise at the movement.

"You must not see this, Lay! indeed you must not!" remonstrated the neighbor, withstanding, with friendly violence, Aleck's struggles to escape from his hold. "Sit here!" He pushed him down upon the trunk of a fallen tree—"Sit here, until I go and see whether it is best for you to be there!"

Misled by the apparent obedience of his charge, he ran back to the grave.

A grave, in truth, it was, and within it a figure, from whose features gentle hands were that moment withdrawing the only shield between it and the earth—a coarse, gray blanket spread over the body, after the manner of a pall. Unchanged, save by the pallor of death, he slept there peacefully, as if loving, and not bloody hands had laid him down to his long rest; as if a costly coffin had sheltered his mortal frame from the contaminating touch of his mother earth, and costly marble sought to immortalize his name and memory.

A hollow groan caused the beholders to look up, and Aleck Lay's white face was seen leaning forward beside Mr. Dickson's, turned for one second to the blue, smiling heavens, and his arms were tossed aloft, none doubted, in agonized invocation of Divine vengeance upon the murderer; then, he spoke in accents more stern than sad—

"Lift him out! Mr. Dickson, your house is nearest; will you ride over and send some conveyance in which the body can be carried to Maple Hill? Frank! you will stay here until he returns, then gallop ahead, and prepare my wife for what she must see—that is, if I am not at home myself by that time. I will exchange horses with you; I think that mine will follow *him*. Mr. Reverdy, if you are ready, we will go direct to Belleview."

They left the corpse upon a bed, hurriedly made of dry leaves—a cloak wrapped about it and concealing it, save where one curl of fair hair, escaping from the folds, caught the reflection of the afternoon sun—Frank Travis, a cousin of the Lays, and Robert's bosom friend, and the faithful Hero, its only guards.

NOTE.—It may interest the reader to know that nearly every incident relative to Robert Lay's murder had its counterpart in a case which came within range of the author's personal observation. The most important variations in the history, as here narrated, are the needful changes of dates, names, and locality. No portion of the story is more authentic than the phenomenon of Hero's behavior when in the vicinage of the hidden grave, and the discovery of the body as a direct sequence of the horse's remarkable conduct.

CHAPTER XVII.

COLONEL FLOYD'S horse and buggy were at the door that morning at an unusually early hour. He had business to transact with a man who lived ten or twelve miles off, and he grumbled loudly at his wife's negligence, and cursed the cook's laziness in not having breakfast precisely at half-past seven, according to the mandate he had issued over night.

"Lily, my love, you are eating nothing!" said Mrs. Floyd, solicitously, as she witnessed her niece's want of application to the tempting repast.

"I am doing very well, thank you, mamma!" and the girl made a feint of using her knife and fork.

"Colonel! I wish you would call at Dr. Bryan's as you are passing through the village, and ask him to drop in to see her," pursued the aunt.

"What's the matter with you?" snarled the master of the household, addressing Lily.

"Nothing, sir. I feel quite well—the warm weather makes me a little languid—that is all!" she answered.

But the slight agitation occasioned by his harsh, abrupt query, brought a tremor to her lips and tears into the large eyes, now sadly sunken and unnaturally bright.

Her uncle scrutinized her sneeringly.

"Which means that you are lovesick, and have the vapors! Vastly pretty and interesting these look to younger men, but I don't believe that Dr. Bryan will admire them any more than I do. I sha'n't be home to dinner,

Mrs. Floyd," and having made these affectionate adieux, he stalked out.

"Nine o'clock! What is that confoundedly slow fellow lagging about now, I wonder?" he uttered, stamping upon the front steps. "Dick!" he hailed a boy in the kitchen door. "Tell Booker I am waiting for him. Make haste, you rascal! Do you hear?"

"Yes, sar!"

The colonel waited, nevertheless, for a quarter of an hour more, when the dilatory factotum emerged from his dwelling, at one side of the yard, and came towards his irate master.

"Come, Booker!" called the latter, in a milder tone than he would have employed towards any other person guilty of the heinous offence of delaying a departure he designed should have been immediate upon the termination of his morning meal.

Booker drove him everywhere, now-a-days. Since his apoplectic attack in December, Colonel Floyd seemed distrustful of his continued physical vigor or mental soundness. Booker had accompanied him during a week's absence in January—a journey whose direction and intent were not revealed to his own wife—which, Aleck had accidentally discovered, extended as far as Baltimore. The negro was not remiss in the improvement of the privileges accruing to him from his superior's partiality or conscious weakness. He lorded it with a high, hard hand over his subjects—nominal and real—upon the estate, beginning, some were bold enough to whisper, at the haughty proprietor of the manor.

"It is half-past nine, Booker! and we have a long jaunt before us."

"Yes, sir; but I should like to have a word with you first," replied the man, coolly, motioning his master further away from the porch to a position upon the lawn, where nothing they said could be overheard by the inmates of the house.

Colonel Floyd followed, submissive as a child.

"If you take my advice, sir, you will get ready for a very long jaunt," said the confidant, meaningly. "If I ain't mightily mistaken, there's mischief in the wind—and a deal of it!"

"Mischief! of what kind?"

"The worst that could come 'pon you, sir; I'd better not mention it, even though there's nobody near enough to hear. Jeff Martin was here betimes this mornin', to say as how Mr. Aleck Lay stopped at his house yesterday, on his way back from Baltimore, and scared Jeff's wife—he was from home himself—into confessin' that I had left a strange horse thar, Christmas day. The woman wouldn't allow to Jeff that she had told any thing, but one of the children was listenin', and let on to his father what a fine gentleman she had had for a visitor. Jeff gave her a proper lesson how to hold her tongue hereafter, you may be sure, but that didn't undo what was done."

"Well?"

Colonel Floyd—his complexion purple-gray—was biting his nails, and grinding his heel into the turf, in a frenzy of anxiety.

Booker's tone and look were dull to stolidity.

"That's one item, sir. Another that I've just picked up is, that Mr. Aleck Lay overtook that boy of mine, Gabriel, on the road, about an hour, or may-be an hour and a half ago, rid him down, and flogged him within an inch of his life, till the young fool was obliged to tell him that the letter he carried to Greenfield before breakfast, Christmas morning, wasn't the same Mr. Lay's wife that is now—Miss Helen that was—had given him. The boy swears this was all that he got out of him, and considerin' that I've been thrashin' him for half an hour, off and on, to find out the truth, it may be as he says. Now, sir, I think you'll 'gree with me when I say that, in my 'pinion, Mr. Lay has struck a dangerous scent—one that'll most likely bring him this way before night, and you'd better not be found too easy. Eight miles' ride will take you to the ferry, and by going six miles on the other side of the river, you will strike the railroad. I've got no more advice to give, 'cept that you'd better have a few clothes and a plenty of money along. It's lucky you're not short of cash just now—and oh! before I forget it, colonel—you'd as well leave me a hundred or so, for family expenses, while you're gone."

The unsurpassed effrontery of this address in the mouth of a menial—the fellow's bold, insolent visage, and disregard of all the forms of respect he had hitherto affected to observe in his master's presence, passed unobserved by his horror-stricken auditor. Filled with one overwhelming conviction; to wit, that his sin had found him out, and that his one chance of safety lay in precipitate flight—a disordered recollection of his conversation with Aleck Lay upon the preceding day, combining with Booker's revelations, to heighten his dismay, he ran up to his room, his so-called servitor at his heels; with his assistance, packed a valise with clothing; took from his secretary bank-notes and gold to a large amount—how obtained, the cashier of the ——— bank, Baltimore, could have told—secreted these about his person; in blind, obedient haste, placed in Booker's hands the sum he required, and they were back again upon the piazza, in the buggy, and driving off ere any member of the family discovered that they had not set out at the hour originally appointed.

"Colonel!" screamed Mrs. Floyd, hastening out from the dining-room.

Booker reined up, and the meek spouse bustled down the steps to the side of the vehicle.

"My love, Lily would like to go to the court-house this forenoon, just for the ride, you know, and I think the air and exercise will do her good. Can she have the carriage and Simon?"

"She and you can go to perdition, if you like!" foamed her husband. "Stand back! Drive on, Booker!"

The whip was not spared during the earlier stages of the journey, nor was there much conversation between the travellers so long as they were in their own proper neighborhood, regarded by them as peculiarly perilous. They were within sight of the river, when Colonel Floyd inquired:

"What do you intend doing, Booker?"

"I shall go back home, sir," with a flourish of the lash about the horse's ears.

"Won't that be unsafe?"

"For me, do you mean, sir?"

"Certainly. You may be taken up as an accomplice. Had you not better stay with me?"

"No, *sir!*" returned the man, impudently. "That would be the unsafest course for us both! Why, it would double the chances of being caught! 'Twould be the easiest thing in creation to track a gentleman travellin' with a body-servant. I shall go home, as I said, may-be hide for a day or two, until I find out what is really in the wind, and if I must clear out, I sha'n't run in the same direction you've done. If I'm took, that's the worst thing that can happen, you know, sir. There's no proof, sech as inconvenient papers and the like, against *me*."

Colonel Floyd writhed in his seat.

"You will not turn informer, Booker? That would be a bad day for you, my man!"

The negro half laughed at the impotent menace; the ludicrous pretence of the power of revenge from one so completely in his power. The sneer made that moment the most humiliating—save one—of Colonel Floyd's existence, yet he could not resent the insult.

"As to the matter of that, Colonel Floyd, we won't argue who would be worst hurt by what I could tell. But make yourself easy, sir. My evidence could not hang you—"

"Hush!"

The other started at the word, and looked around to be sure no one was within hearing distance.

"Could not injure you very badly, I mean, sir—I am a colored slave—you a free white man"—with a scornful emphasis. "They wouldn't swear me in a court of justice, sir."

It was pitch dark when Booker re-entered the outer gate of the Belleview plantation. He had contrived his journey so as to arrive at home under the shadow of night. The sky was cloudy; the air misty. Better opportunity of concealing his approach could not have been desired; and congratulating himself upon these, he drove carefully down the middle of the road, eyes and ears on the *qui vive* for any suspicious appearance or noise. There were lights in the windows of the dining-room, and Mrs. Floyd's chamber, and from the open kitchen-door issued a stream of reddish light, darkened occasionally by a moving figure within. A slave in name alone, he had long cherished ambitious dreams unknown by others, divined least of all by him whom he styled "master." By dint of peculation and undisguised extortion, he had amassed a larger sum than was possessed by any other bondman in the country; treasured it secretly against such time as he should see the way clear for the prosecution of his darling scheme—viz: the acquisition of his freedom, without expending one cent of his money in its purchase. Now, he said exultingly to himself, was the propitious season! His master a fugitive under the ban of the law, the hue and cry of the neighborhood directed after him—himself the owner, or what, in his ethics, amounted to the same thing—the possessor of an additional sum, sufficient to carry him to Canada, if he wished to go so far—what remained to be done but to secure his hoard, and such valuables as he could lay his hands upon, and flee under the cover of the favoring darkness?

"Whoa—there!" said a deep voice at his very ear, and betwixt him and the kitchen door he saw the dark outline of a horseman;—before he could realize the fact of the apparition, he felt the reins snatched from him on the other side; heard the trampling of hoofs and men's feet in every direction, while murmurs of inquiry and consultation were defined into a simultaneous exclamation as a lantern was unceremoniously flashed into his face.

"We've caught one of them, at all events."

He had not expected the indulgence of sleep that night, but neither had he anticipated lodgings in the county jail.

It was not often that Lily was allowed the privilege of a ride without the attendance of her aunt or one of her cousins, but this morning she had avowed frankly to Mrs. Floyd her desire to visit Helen Lay, and asked for the carriage and driver, that she might carry her plan into execution in her uncle's absence.

"He would not consent to it, mamma, and you disapprove of it, I know, but I must see Helen! I feel sometimes as if I must die unless I learn something which she only can tell me. I am not so strong as I used to be, and things worry—oppress me more than they did when I was well."

Mrs. Floyd's heart melted.

"My dear child! I would do any thing in my power to

make you happy—but I really thought that you and Helen had had some quarrel about the time she was married, and not been on good terms since."

"I behaved foolishly, and, I believe, was altogether in the wrong," answered Lily, sadly. "Helen used to be very kind to me. I think she cared for me then. Nobody loves me very long!"

This pathetic petition it was that emboldened Mrs. Floyd to stay her husband's departure for the space of a whole minute and a quarter, and Lily decided to avail herself of the uncivil permission that responded to the request.

Pitying affection was Helen's predominant feeling for the erring, cruelly deceived child, yet she had rather, on this particular day, have seen a basilisk creep into her sunny parlor than Lily's wasted figure glide up to the window where she and Aunt Ruth sat at work;—the younger lady pensive and abstracted, yet trying to appear as usual; the elder mild and sedate, quite content with the world since she had witnessed the affectionate parting of her adopted children after their early breakfast, and learned that it was Helen's headache that made her so pale and her eyes heavy—not inward disquiet—or disappointed love.

"Yes!" ejaculated the dear old creature, dropping her spectacles upon the floor, Lily's entrance having occurred at the moment when she was resetting them for some superlatively fine stitching upon a collar for her nephew.

Lily understood the "particle" as well as Aleck or Robert could have done. "It *is* I, Aunt Ruth—not my ghost!"

"Lily!" said Helen, rising to embrace her, "dear child! how long it is since we have seen you!"

"I know it, Nelly, but it has not been easy for me to get here until now. I have longed for you lately."

Helen seated her in a lounging-chair, removed her mufflings, and smoothed the pale gold hair, gazing on the altered lineaments of the lately happy, thoughtless girl, with an unspoken heart-ache.

Aunt Ruth picked up the key-basket and trotted out.

"Helen," said Lily, catching both her hands, and speaking with feverish energy—"now that we are by ourselves, tell me—have you heard any news of him—of Robert?"

Helen shook her head mournfully.

"Have you nò idea where he is? What does your husband think has become of him?"

"He has a variety of surmises, Lily dear. It would do no good to repeat them—they are all so uncertain, as yet. We are both much distressed at his continued absence. It seems unaccountable, and he was not apt to do unreasonable things," rejoined Helen, commanding her looks and language to the best of her power.

"Why do you say 'was?' He is as good now as he ever was. I have faith in him, although all the world may blame him—faith to believe that he would do nothing dishonorable or unkind. Yet his silence is breaking my heart—breaking my heart!"

She bowed her face in her hands with a sobbing, plaintive cry that sounded indeed like very heart-break.

Helen took her in her arms as she would have done a child.

"Dear Lily! my sweet little sister! there is some cause for the silence that we cannot now understand—but it will be explained in time. I have all confidence in Robert's excellence and honor—and so has Aleck."

"Then you don't blame him?" Lily smiled faintly through her tears.

"We do not consider that he was in fault in any particular. The trouble was, according to our belief, that he trusted unwisely and was betrayed—"

"Not by me!" cried Lily, in alarm. "My great sin was

loving him too well and envying you because of that love. I did wrong you often in thought, Helen! There were seasons when I was tempted to do it; indeed, of many little acts of spite I was guilty; but I never committed any overt deed against your peace until the day you were married. Then I received his letter—and, dizzy with the hopes it opened up to me, I forgot honor, truth, every thing except him and the blessed assurance that he loved me. I would have gone to him, but my uncle overtook me on the way."

"I know!" said Helen, gently, for the girl's bright eyes and rapid incoherence of speech made her uneasy. "You need not enter upon a vindication of yourself, dear. Let bygones be bygones. If I have any thing to forgive, it is forgiven, provided you forget the heart-burnings and misunderstandings of that unhappy time. Let us keep up hopeful hearts for the future, and if sorrow should come, help one another to bear it."

"Only a glass of milk punch, dear!" cooed Aunt Ruth at Lily's right ear, "with an egg beaten up in it to make it nourishing! You ought to drink one every morning of your life at this season. These warm days are debilitating."

She set down a salver, containing, besides the glass of punch, a plate of light cakes, and a saucer of calves'-foot jelly with cream poured over it. "To make it more strengthening," she represented.

"Ah! Aunt Ruth! you were always a sad child-spoiler!" said Lily, with a flash of her old archness. She sipped the creamy foam mantling the cordial. "It is the genuine old receipt, isn't it? Do you remember how often you came over to Belleview to make it for me, when I was recovering from the measles? and how, after I had that tedious spell of fever, you carried me off by main force to Greenfield, and kept me there for a week, cosseting me with all manner of good things? I couldn't have been more than eight years old then, and was such a wee thing that Robert used to draw me about in his go-cart, as if I were a baby. Aunty, it would have been a happy thing for me if I had died of that fever—don't you think so?"

Aunt Ruth looked thunderstruck at this, according to her principles, impious observation.

"Why, my love," she commenced, when Helen spoke up cheerily.

"Nonsense, little one! you will change your mind when you have finished your luncheon. You need something to make your blood rich and warm, and then you will feel no proneness to misanthropy."

"It is very nice to be here!" murmured Lily, gratefully, obeying the injunction to refresh herself with the delicacies provided.

"And here you shall stay for one while!" said Aunt Ruth, energetically. "After you have drunk the punch, you must come with me to my room, and lie down until dinner-time."

"Oh! I dare not keep the horses so long!" objected Lily. "Uncle is to be away until night, it is true, but he would be angry if he heard that Simon had lost a whole day's work."

"If that is the trouble, we will send him home, and Helen or I will ride over with you this afternoon in our carriage," persisted Miss Ruth, never doubting Helen's cordial acquiescence in the arrangement, and bent upon affording "the poor baby," as she pityingly termed Lily,—a holiday—and trying the effect of an abundance of "nourishing" food upon the wan face and attenuated frame.

Lily was evidently strongly tempted. "Would it do, Helen?" she asked.

"You are the proper judge of that, dear," said Helen, very kindly.

She dreaded lest any display of her opposition to the plan should be attributed by Aunt Ruth or Lily to an indisposition to entertain her cousin in her own house—yet trembled at the thought of the tidings which the next hour might bring.

Lily took in the manner, more than the matter of the reply, and deliberated a moment.

"I will stay," she said. "It may be an age before I have another such chance of happiness."

"Yes!" said Aunt Ruth, triumphantly, without in the remotest degree assenting to the sentiment of the last clause of her pet-child's remark. "Now when you have given Simon his orders, you shall go and see what a beautiful room Aleck and Helen have given me. There is a nice, soft lounge, where you shall lie, and I will tuck you up snugly for a fine nap. The punch will make you drowsy, pretty soon. That's the good of it."

"A clear case of involuntary intoxication!" laughed Lily. "Then I suppose I had better use my limbs while I have any control over them—hadn't I?" and she went to confer with Simon.

The lounge justified Aunt Ruth's recommendation, and so did the punch. For awhile, Lily lay enveloped in the soft shawls Miss Ruth had tucked about her shoulders, and watching the placid, motherly countenance, whose eyes, ever and anon, strayed from her work to herself, in tender solicitude. There was a clear little fire upon the hearth, and by Aunt Ruth's footstool, a gray cat, sleek and sleepy; the clock ticked as if it too were drowsy. Lily wondered whether this were owing to some peculiar knack which Aunt Ruth had in winding it, and, amused at the conceit, sank into a slumber.

She seemed to have slept but a few minutes when she awoke, and saw that she was alone in the chamber. The clock said that her "fine nap" had lasted two hours.

"Aunt Ruth has gone to see about dinner, I suppose!"

she thought. "I am glad she didn't stay here on my account. Her lounge must be stuffed with poppies. I only wish I had one like it at home!"

She sighed at the recollection of the many sleepless nights that had been her portion for weeks past; drew back a curtain that she might have more light for her toilette; brushed her hair; replaced her collar, and was ready to rejoin her friends. There was an empty chair just outside the door—and, lying upon the seat, an unfinished piece of knitting-work—a coarse blue worsted stocking.

"Isn't that like Aunt Ruth? She stationed one of her maids as a sentinel to prevent my slumbers from being disturbed, and the poor girl grew weary with waiting for me to release her. No wonder!"

She went down a flight of stairs and through a side-passage, without encountering a single person. In her ignorance of the topography of the house, she had taken a private way, one seldom used except by the servants in carrying wood, water, etc., to the several rooms. Then she reached a porch—enclosed on three sides by the wings and central building, and on the fourth by Venetian blinds; and amused at her mistake, resolved to go on until she found some inhabited region, unclosed the door at the other end of this recess, and found herself in a small, dark entry, another door just ahead of her.

This series of *contre-temps* Aunt Ruth and Helen had done every thing that seemed necessary to prevent. The maid posted at the chamber door had strict orders to remain there until Miss Calvert awoke, and then to conduct her to Mrs. Lay's own room, there to await that lady's coming. But the girl, who had her share, and possibly more, of Eve's foible, had been seduced into a short absence. To do her justice, it was very brief, for while Lily was wandering in the by-ways of the rambling old house, her janitor, ignorant of the prisoner's flight, was sitting in the chair without Miss Ruth's apartment, knitting and listening dutifully for any sound from within. The parlor and main hall were peopled with gentlemen who would inevitably have arrested Lily's progress, but by her blunder—perhaps we should say through the design of an inscrutable and higher Will than that of short-sighted mortals—she had avoided all these hindrances, and now stood at the outer entrance of the library, Mr. Lay's especial study.

Still smiling at her adventure, Lily laid her hand upon the lock, and went in. Her motion was very fairy-like and noiseless, and her approach was unheard by the occupants of the room. A solemn group was collected there. Aleck Lay, his features settled into stern anguish, stood with one arm upholding the drooping form of his wife, who wept upon his shoulder, at the back of a sofa which was wheeled into the middle of the apartment. In front of it knelt Aunt Ruth, hands clasped as if in prayer, her furrowed cheeks bathed in tears, and eyes steadfastly bent upon the visage of him who was stretched upon the couch. A black cloak—the same that had been thrown over him when first disinterred, hid the earth-stained garments—only the face and bright hair were exposed, and these, Lily's second step forward revealed to her horrified vision.

CHAPTER XVIII.

Another Christmas Eve, frosty and starry, was upon the earth—and through the fading light shed from the lately crimsoned West, Aleck Lay rode slowly up the winding avenue leading to his home. Greenfield was his now, also, but he preferred a continued residence in the house to which he had brought his bride, one year before. There were associations connected with the paternal mansion, that both he and Helen felt would rest, a perpetual moveless shadow, upon the brightness of their hearth-stone. Very rosy and cheerful looked the radiance from this now, through the windows of the old place, and as the smile of cheer and welcome caught his musing eye, he quickened his horse's gait.

"All well, Cæsar?" he asked of the man who held the rein, as he dismounted.

"All well, sir!"

Aleck glanced into the dining-room in passing, and spoke a kind word of greeting to the plump figure attired in black, which, knitting-work in hand, was overlooking the movements of the butler, while he laid the snowy damask table-cloth for supper.

"Helen is in her room, I suppose?" he added.

"Yes!" and to her chamber he proceeded accordingly.

She had heard his step in the hall, and met him at the door with a smile and kiss of right wifely affection. But the smile was chastened by sadness or thought—a slight cloud that did not disappear even when she stood with him by a cradle at the corner of the hearth, and saw him stoop to leave a kiss upon the sleeping face of his first-born.

"How are you feeling to-night?" he asked, fondly, after they were seated, her hand in his.

"I am very well. Aunt Ruth says I may eat my Christmas dinner with the rest of you, to-morrow. I am quite strong again now, and shall be more cheerful when I can go about the house as usual,—especially when I can breathe the outer air."

"I am glad you are to take your old place to-morrow. It will brighten greatly the gloom that must always recur upon the sad anniversary—sad—inexpressibly mournful in the recollection of one event—while it commemorates to me another—that has proved the best blessing, the richest happiness of my life. Joy and woe have flowed closely together, yet in divided streams, in our married life, darling!"

"I have been thinking of it as I sat here alone in the twilight, and reviewed the scenes of last Christmas," said Helen, a tear starting in her eye. "Then, my anxiety to hear the report of your visit of this afternoon has been painful. Was the interview a trying one to you?"

"Are you well enough to speak of these things, love? Had we not better postpone the discussion to another day?"

"Not on my account! As I have said, the anxiety and uncertainty do me more harm than a full knowledge of the truth could. How did the wretched man appear?"

"Like what you have called him—wretched—miserable beyond comparison!"

"And penitent?" interrogated Helen.

"Not in the least! Not that he does not express remorse for the deed, but it is palpably sorrow for the awful consequences to himself, not hatred of the crime, or compassion for the grief it has brought upon others. I went to the jail at his summons, prepared to grant the forgiveness which I supposed he, as a dying man, wished to entreat from the dearest earthly relatives of his victim. Instead of humble confession, I was forced to listen to a labored extenuation of his act, and an appeal to my sympathy in behalf of himself,—'a man in the prime of his years—the scion of a long line of honored ancestors, condemned to perish ignominiously,' as he said, 'like a common convict!'"

"Incredible! I wonder you had patience to hear him to the end!"

"It was only by bearing in mind that in three days more he would be beyond the reach of human approbation or censure, that I compelled myself to remain in his loathed presence. He was very free in his communications. The disappointment of his preposterous hope that a petition for his pardon would be presented to the governor, has apparently taken from him all desire for concealment—so far as the actions of his Past are concerned. I imagined that he experienced some relief in the horrible recital,—I am positive that the attempt to excuse his motives for the committal of these atrocities brought consolation—so deplorably depraved is his conscience. That his forgery of Robert's name was not his first essay in that species of crime, he avowed with infinite coolness. From his youth the facility with which he could imitate any manuscript presented to him, had been a mighty temptation to him, 'the impulse to employ the unfortunate talent for some practical purpose,'—I quote his exact words—'had been well-nigh irresistible.' His pecuniary difficulties had proved the incentive to this 'error,' in every instance,—and he rambled off into an insupportable lamentation over the mortifications and hardships to which these had subjected him, until their accumulation and pressure drove him almost to insanity. Your fortune was imprudently risked in speculations that, 'promising in their commencement, eventuated unsuccessfully.' That meant, I knew, that the sacred trust had been squandered at the card-table, and I told him this, with no show of passion or indignation—only to recall him to the facts of the matter. Without pretending to deny this statement, he went on to speak of his embarrassment in view of your marriage; his hope that he could prevail upon Robert to execute a contract that, by appointing your former guardian the trustee of your property, would allow him an opportunity to retrieve your losses before the deficiency was detected; at any rate, prevent the institution of a legal process for the recovery of the missing amount. Foiled in this—and as he 'accidentally discovered'—unquestionably referring to the conversation he basely manœuvred to overhear, that night, at the spring—baffled then, as he learned through the instrumentality of your influence over Robert, he devised sundry other expedients for averting disgrace and ruin. Among these, was his endeavor to surprise you into signing the papers he presented to you on Christmas Eve, and the manufacture and exhibition to you of the letter which was, after the murder, transmitted to Lily—in order to delude her into the idea that her supposed lover had left his home for her sake, and, through her attempt to fulfil the appointment she believed he had made for her, to mislead others from the real track. Finding that you were bent upon keeping your promise to Robert, and disdained even to examine the proofs of your betrothed's perfidy which he professed to have obtained, he resolved, as he would have had me credit, upon a final application to Robert himself—a statement of the real condition of his affairs, and an appeal to his generosity.

"To this end he suppressed your letter to Greenfield, substituted a note purporting to be from Lily, asking for an interview at ten o'clock—couched in language he was assured Robert could not read unmoved. Leaving his horse in

Booker's care, at some distance from the spot designated as the place of meeting, Colonel Floyd was proceeding on foot towards the spruce pine, when he descried Robert mounted upon Hero, slowly making his way through the underbrush, a little way ahead of him. 'Like a flash of lightning,' he said, 'the thought seized me how easily I could rid myself of the difficulties that hampered me—avoid the humbling revelation, and abject petition, whose anticipation galled my proud soul into madness. My gun was in my hand,'—I stopped him there—I could not hear how my only brother was killed like a dog—ay, and buried like one! God forgive me! but I could have murdered him as he told the tale!"

He covered his face with his hands.

"God forgive *him!*" said Helen, by-and-by, in a voice broken by weeping. "If ever man stood in need of the mercy which is infinite, he does!"

"I may be able to say 'amen!' some day," replied Aleck, resuming his former tone and demeanor. "I cannot yet! still less could I entertain a forgiving thought, while I saw his unmoved countenance; heard his garbled representations. I felt as certain then, that he had deliberately laid in ambush and fired upon his prey, as I did after I proved this to his face, thrust the lying plea of manslaughter down the villain's throat!"

"Dearest husband, remember he is, as you said just now, a dying man. He will soon stand before his Judge and ours!" interposed the wife, softly and sweetly. "In a very short time, human justice will have its full course."

"My angel monitor!" Aleck raised her hand to his lips—"I have never needed you more, my precious one, than during the hour I spent in that cell. Think how hard it was for me to learn that the vile, odious letter to myself, that, for a season, seduced me into the conviction that one of the noblest beings Heaven ever created, was a weak, perjured hypocrite, unworthy of my love as of yours; that this diabolical composition was framed and committed to paper within an hour after the murder was done! He actually penned it, sitting at Mr. Willis's private desk, Mr. Willis being in the outer office, while he, Floyd, was pretending to await the coming of him whose life he had taken!"

"Oh! horrible!" cried Helen, shuddering. "Was his conscience then altogether dead?"

"His ruling consideration then was to avert suspicion; to account to the community for the disappearance of one whose absence must, before many hours elapsed, excite universal surprise. To effect this purpose, he could imitate, with a true and cunning hand, the style and writing of our poor brother, append his name to the letter, and devise a plan by which it should reach me, without implicating the author in the remotest degree.*

"His account of the concealment of the body in the bushes, and Booker's being sent off with Hero to the free negro's house, as well as the large bribe paid to the latter to undertake the secret service required of him, without asking any questions, tallied with that given by Booker himself, and by Jeff Martin, at Booker's trial. He alluded, likewise, to the circumstance of the seemingly miraculous preservation of the corpse for so long a time, which was owing, he supposed, to its having been nearly or quite frozen when it was interred. But to these details I could not listen, nor shall you."

"You said that you convicted him of premeditation in what he did?" said Helen, inquiringly.

"Yes! I happened to mention Booker's confession. His face darkened instantly.

"'The cowardly knave!' he said. 'But for his treachery, I should not be where I now am. He, and he only, could

* Fact.

have put the officers upon my track; for no one else knew my route or destination.'

"You are mistaken, Colonel Floyd, I rejoined. If the negro had had it in his power to give us the intelligence we required, we need not have consumed months in the search. A few days would have sufficed to find you out in your hiding-place, and a glance would have penetrated your disguise. Do your instrument, criminal as he was—justice! It was not until he was condemned to death as an accessory in the murder, and had taken his resolution of cheating the gallows by self-destruction, that he said any thing with regard to your share in the deed. Then, I allow, he spoke freely, and, I believe, truthfully. He was cognizant of several things that you have not admitted—as, for instance, the letters sent to the post-office in Washington and Vicksburg, for remailing to my address.

"'It would be sheer folly for me to deny that his information was correct in that particular,' he remarked, without a sign of shame. 'It was a needful stratagem, Mr. Lay. The first wrong step involved the necessity of the rest.'

"And what do you say, I proceeded, to another part of your man's evidence, wherein he stoutly affirmed that although he knew that you meditated some iniquitous measure, he was not aware that it was so great a crime as murder, until you called him to take the horse, after you had killed the rider?

"'It was a lie—an infamous lie!' he exclaimed, thrown off his guard by the question. 'The scoundrel knew what my design was from the moment I summoned him to accompany me to the woods. Why, if he had received no orders to that effect, did he leave my horse and hasten to join me, so soon as he heard my gun?'

"The report of the gun was then a preconcerted signal? I inquired.

"'It was!'

"Recollecting himself, he stammered, and would have added something else, but I gave him no time.

"Then, sir, I said, rising, your servant went into eternity as you would wish to do, with a lie upon his tongue! You have declared to me, in the most solemn manner, that the intention of shedding innocent blood never crossed your mind until the second before the fatal shot was fired. What then means this talk of a previous purpose, and instructions to your accomplice? I believed, when my agents sought you in every town and city in the Union; when I urged them incessantly to greater diligence by promises of greater rewards; when I gave in my testimony at your trial; when I heard the verdict of the jurors; when I came here to listen to your dying confession, I have believed always, without a second's wavering, that you murdered foully, in cold blood, with malice and purpose aforethought, a man guiltless of wrong against you or any other mortal, and I go away more firmly persuaded than ever that my conclusion was just. I can stay here no longer. It would be worse than useless, for each falsehood makes heavier the load of your sin.

"'One question more—but one instant!' he begged, catching hold of me, as I would have left the cell.

"I could not help tearing myself from his hold.

"I will hear what you have to say, I said, if it does not relate to the subject of which we have been speaking.

"'It does not!' he assured me. 'I wish to inquire after my niece, who has been, since last spring, domesticated in your family—Miss Calvert. How is she?'

"Her bodily health is good, I answered. In mind she will probably never be better than she is now—a mere child!

"'The physicians regard her case as hopeless, then, do they?'

"I replied in the affirmative.

"'It might have been expected!' he said, with no more show of feeling than he had manifested heretofore. 'The circumstances of her birth were peculiar, and without doubt predisposed her to this malady. She is harmless, is she not?'

"She is, perfectly, I answered.

"'But idiotic—hey?'

"Indignant at this cool questioning, I said that it was rather a partial failure of certain powers of mind, a loss of memory upon many points and a weakening of the higher intellectual faculties; repeating, in effect, my former declaration that she was now a child, with occasional lapses into a gentle melancholy, more painful to us than it appeared to be to her.

"I cannot but consider her state a blessing instead of an affliction, I concluded, when we remember the events that robbed her of reason.

"'Ah! she was predisposed to it!' he reiterated. 'I always dreaded some such calamity to her. Is it your intention, may I ask, Mr. Lay, to continue to take care of her—or will you send her to an asylum?'

"Neither my wife nor myself will ever consent to part with her, unless her health should require a change, I said. As to an asylum—we are assured by the best medical authorities upon these points, that no beneficial effects to her could arise from her residence in one.

"Desperately hardened as I knew him to be, I was not prepared for his next observation—

"'You may not be aware, Mr. Lay, that my niece has no property of her own—that she will be a great expense to you?'

"That does not alter my resolution, sir! I replied haughtily.

"'You are very generous! I thought it but just to yourself that you should be notified of the fact of her poverty. My sister, Mrs. Calvert, left some little money and a few slaves in my care, but I regret to say, that my own failure has swallowed up the modest provision for her daughter's livelihood. I was the trustee of my sister's small fortune—an appointment that gave her husband much discontent,—and, I may say to you, Mr. Lay, was productive of more than one quarrel between us. Our last was a serious one, and to him very disastrous!'

"He checked himself with the same expression he had worn upon perceiving that he had contradicted himself, a while before—put his hand to his head and tried to smile. Such a ghastly grimace as it was!

"'I think that my mind wanders slightly sometimes, Mr. Lay. You will excuse any incoherence or strangeness in my language or behavior. It has been long since I had occasion to refer to these family affairs, and the mention naturally agitates me. After all, what was done so many years since, in the heat of passion, and under extreme provocation—we were both fiery tempered—what was done then cannot be mended now, and had better rest in oblivion.'"

"He must be deranged!" said Helen, wonderingly.

"You would have thought so, had you seen him at that instant," replied her husband. "In another, he was himself again; desired me to give his love to Lily and his respects to you. 'Say to Lily,' he called me back to say—'that I always intended to provide for her myself—if only as some atonement—but no! perhaps you had better not repeat the message. She might not understand it.' And thus we parted."

"May I come in?" A silvery voice at the door ended the pause that succeeded Aleck's strange, sad story.

"Come in, dear!" said Helen, brightening up, and a diminutive figure in white crept forward on tiptoe.

Her beautiful hair had been shorn during the dangerous spell of brain-fever that had attacked her ten months before, and now clustered in short, golden curls about her colorless face. Her eyes were timid and soft, like those of a shy child, and her smile infantine in simplicity and sweetness of expression. She had taken an unconquerable fancy to wear white constantly ever since her illness, and her kindly guardians indulged her whim. To-night she had dressed herself in muslin, and binding her curls was a wreath of holly-leaves and berries. A knot of the same was in her bosom.

"Good evening, Aleck!" she said, putting her hand confidingly in his, outstretched with an air of brotherly fondness he could not have shown her a year ago. "I am glad that you are home again. Did you remember that it was Christmas Eve?"

"Remember!" thought he, with an inward groan. He smiled pleasantly at the querist. "Is that the reason you have made yourself so fine to-night, Lily?"

"Yes! Sally got the holly for me, for I thought I had heard that people wore it on Christmas Eve. It looks pretty, doesn't it?"

"Very!" replied Helen, cheerfully.

Lily surveyed herself in the mirror with unaffected and guileless complacency.

"And to-morrow night, Sally is to get me some orange-buds. I made her promise, if you had no objection, Aleck. There are plenty in the green-house."

"Why should I object?" asked Aleck. "The flowers belong to you and Nelly here, not to me."

"Yes, but I had a notion that you did not like orange-blossoms; or was it you, Nelly?"

"Neither of us, I think," she responded. "It was all a 'notion,' little one."

"It makes me very happy to hear you say so, for, do you

know, I wouldn't miss wearing them on Christmas night on any account," sinking her voice to a mysterious whisper. "Who was it, Nelly, that told me that it would be a terrible thing not to wear orange-blossoms on Christmas?"

"Another notion!" Aleck hastened to dispel the cloud of perplexity he saw gathering upon her brow. "What have you in your hand, Lily?"

"Oh!" she laughed out gleefully, "it is a pair of new socks for baby. I knit them myself, on purpose to hang in the chimney-corner to-night. See!"

They were united by a bow of blue ribbon, and she suspended them upon a hook at the left of the fire-place, directly above the cradle.

Helen laughed. "I will venture to say that no younger gentleman in the length and breadth of the land will hang up his stockings this Christmas Eve. Why, Lily, he is but a month and two days old!"

"He understands all I say to him!" retorted Lily, triumplamtly. "Look! he is awake! Don't you see that he laughs at me!"

The little arms tossed down the covering that bound them, and the babe actually smiled in the face bowed over his.

"He knows me best!" She patted the tiny face. "Lily's baby! Lily's pet!" And while father and mother looked on with smiling lips and moistened eyes, there came another name—breathed in accents of such magical sweetness that one might have thought the child-woman had learned it from angel teachers.

"LILY'S ROBERT!"

THE END.

MARION HARLAND'S WORKS.

Uniform editions of the works of this favorite authoress are now ready.

ALONE. 1 volume. 12mo. Price $1.50.

HIDDEN PATH. 1 volume. 12mo. Price $1.50.

MOSS SIDE. 1 volume. 12mo. Price $1.50.

NEMESIS. 1 volume. 12mo. Price $1.50.

MIRIAM. 1 volume. 12mo. Price $1.50.

HUSKS. 1 volume. 12mo. Price $1 50.

Notices of "Nemesis."

"It is a story of surpassing excellence—its scene laid in the sunny South, about half a century ago; its characters limned with a master's hand; its sketches graphic and thrilling, and its conclusion very effective. Such a work is beyond criticism, and needs no praise."—*Troy American.*

"In all the characteristics of a powerful novel it will compare favorably with the best productions of a season that has produced some of the most successful books that have appeared for a long time."—*Courier and Enquirer.*

"'Nemesis' is, by far, the best American novel published for very many years.—*Philadelphia Press.*

"It is worthy of note that the former works of this authoress have been republished in England, France, and Germany—indeed, no other American female writer has the honor of a republication in the Leipzig issues of Alphonse Durr, which embraces Bryant, Longfellow, Hawthorne, and Prescott."—*N. Y. Home Journal.*

"Marion Harland, by intrinsic power of character, drawing and descriptive facility, holds the public with increasing fascination."—*Washington Statesman.*

www.ingramcontent.com/pod-product-compliance
Lightning Source LLC
LaVergne TN
LVHW021309110826
845150LV00003B/530

* 9 7 8 1 4 2 5 5 5 8 5 8 1 *